Raves for Stephen Birmingham's bestseller

The Auerbach Will

"Colorful, riveting, bubbling like champagne."
—Philadelphia Inquirer

"Delicious secrets—scandals, blackmail, affairs, adultery . . . the gossipy, Uptown/Downtown milieu Birmingham knows so well."
—Kirkus Reviews

"Has the magic word 'bestseller' written all over it . . . Yet what matters about this novel is not so much the absorbing story as the way it is told. Birmingham's narrative drive never falters and his characters are utterly convincing."
—John Barkham Reviews

"Stephen Birmingham has spent his life—built a career—writing about the rich, and he is almost perfect at what he does."
—Los Angeles Times

Books by Stephen Birmingham

"THE REST OF US"
THE AUERBACH WILL
THE GRANDES DAMES
DUCHESS
CALIFORNIA RICH
LIFE AT THE DAKOTA
JACQUELINE BOUVIER KENNEDY ONASSIS
THE GOLDEN DREAM
CERTAIN PEOPLE
REAL LACE
THE RIGHT PLACES
THE LATE JOHN MARQUAND
THE GRANDEES
HEART TROUBLES
THE RIGHT PEOPLE
"OUR CROWD"
FAST START, FAST FINISH
THOSE HARPER WOMEN
THE TOWERS OF LOVE
BARBARA GREER
YOUNG MR. KEEFE

STEPHEN BIRMINGHAM

THOSE HARPER WOMEN

BERKLEY BOOKS, NEW YORK

This Berkley book contains the complete
text of the original hardcover edition.
It has been completely reset in a typeface
designed for easy reading, and was printed
from new film.

THOSE HARPER WOMEN

A Berkley Book / published by arrangement with
McGraw-Hill Book Company

PRINTING HISTORY
McGraw-Hill edition published 1964
Berkley edition / January 1985

For information address: McGraw-Hill Book Company,
1221 Avenue of the Americas, New York, New York 10020.

ISBN: 0-425-07384-X

A BERKLEY BOOK ® TM 757,375
Berkley Books are published by The Berkley Publishing Group,
200 Madison Avenue, New York, New York 10016.

PRINTED IN THE UNITED STATES OF AMERICA

Once again,
TO NAN

One

"OH, he made pots and *pots* of money," Edith is saying, leading the young man into the library where her father's picture hangs. "Some say he was worth a hundred million dollars—before Prohibition came along and ruined the rum market. Compared to what he had, what the Harpers have today is chicken feed, Mr. Winslow—*chicken feed!*" She moves around the room turning on one after another of the lamps with their tasseled pull chains. "This is such a *dark* room. I planted that palm tree from a coconut, and now look what it's done to my sunshine!" She turns on a final lamp. "Well," she says, "there he is! Can you see him in this gloom?"

Mr. Winslow steps in front of the portrait and looks up at it. "Wow," he says softly and then, as if thinking aloud, "Tall. Almost Gothic. But eyes like an evangelist's. And why did I expect him to be wearing a pith helmet, not evening clothes? You must have had your hands full with him, Mrs. Blakewell."

"Oh, but I expect he had his hands full with me, Mr. Winslow," Edith Blakewell says.

"Does your brother Harold take after him?"

"Take after Papa? Dear heavens no. There's no resemblance. Papa was the athletic type. Harold can barely tie his own shoes. And Harold has my mother's coloring. Oh, but in a business sense I suppose they have a lot in common. Papa taught Harold everything he knows."

Mr. Winslow nods and writes this down. He has become, Edith notices, a bit overheated. Perspiration has formed a long dark welt down the back of his blue jacket, and his shirt collar is limp. Poor man, he has not dressed for the tropics.

Turning to her, he says, "Were these his books?"

"No, they are mine. The bindings are not exceptional, but it would be true to say that I have read every book in this library. Living alone, you see, I have time on my hands."

Mr. Winslow picks up his drink and takes a swallow of it and, because his pencil and pad have been slipped back into his pocket, Edith supposes that he does not consider this last remark worth quoting. Ah, well. Outside the windows, a breeze in the garden sends the heavy palm fronds scratching across the glass and, in the silence that follows, she tries to think of something interesting or entertaining to say. Above them hangs the John Singer Sargent portrait of Edith Harper Blakewell's father, Meredith Harper; it has even been supplied, on a small bronze plaque, with his dates: *Aug. 1860—Jun. 1923*. The picture looms over the two of them now just as he loomed over everybody when he was living. It is a large portrait, nearly seven feet high, in a heavily carved gilt frame (he must weigh as much dead as he did alive, Edith thinks), and it leans away from the wall. Some day, Edith imagines, the cord will break from the picture's weight, and the thing will come crashing down. It will probably be her poor fortune to be standing underneath it when it falls, and poetic justice will be done: she will be crushed to death beneath her father's portrait. Smiling up at the Sargent, Edith says, "Hello, Papa. How are you today? You see, Mr. Winslow, I talk to him. He's like a pet, but he's better than a parrot because he doesn't talk back. You can see that, as Leona would put it, I am as nutty as a fruitcake!"

He smiles at her now, and she sees that he has a good smile. He has a good face too—not handsome, but with a strong chin, nice eyes, and his dark hair has good cowlick configuration which, Edith's mother always told her, was an important thing to look for in a man. ("A *whorled* cowlick is a sign of muddle-headedness, dear, and of course a double cowlick means that he will live under two flags, like your father.") The cowlick and the chin were the main points. The chin should not be cleft, for that was a sure sign of weakness—weakness for women, for drink, or for worse—and the deeper the cleft the greater the weakness. And of course the nose; if it was on the small side, it meant that a man was apt to be proportionately small elsewhere. Almost shyly, Edith Blakewell looks at Mr. Winslow's nose, and decides that it is satisfactory. Lord knows, he is not at all what Edith expected from Leona's description of him—"A very sharp young journalist, Granny." Mr. Winslow seems to be, of all things, a gentleman.

Absorbed in her study of him, Edith is suddenly unnerved to see that he in return is looking at her with an intent, expectant stare. "Well," she says quickly, "am I being any help to you? If it's background material on the island you'd like, nobody can give it to you better than me. I've lived here for over sixty years. I'm a walking fossil, you might say. What sort of story *is* it you want, anyway?"

"To be quite honest with you, Mrs. Blakewell, I'm still not sure."

"If it's lurid details you'd like, there are plenty of those. But permit me to safeguard my *own* family skeletons, kind sir!" She laughs.

He has moved to one of the windows and looks out. "I see you have a swimming pool," he says.

"Yes. And if you put it in your article, please be sure to mention that it is a *salt*-water pool. It cost me a lot of money to have that salt-water system put in—it's piped all the way up from the sea—and I'm very proud of it. Water is short in St. Thomas, and I am on the water-conservation committee. We are very much against those people who waste eighty thousand gallons of fresh water to fill a swimming pool, the way some of my neighbors do—the new neighbors. Did you know that during the dry season now we sometimes have to *import* drinking water from Puerto Rico? It's true."

"Mmm."

"And if you want spice for your article, you may say that I always swim in that pool in the raw—half a mile, daily." He looks at her over the rim of his glass, imagining, perhaps,

Edith's plump, squarish body splashing about the pool like a large white seal. She winks at him. "No pictures of that, please," she says.

He moves to a tableful of photographs. "And these?"

"Oh, family, family. Nieces, nephews, grandnieces and -nephews."

"This one?"

"My husband."

"Killed in the first war, wasn't he? And this?"

"Leona when she was a little girl. Even then, you see, she was a beautiful child. . . ."

It was Leona's idea, of course, that this young man come to see her. Edith was opposed to it; but Leona had begged her. "He's doing a story about the family, Granny," she had said. "You know we are rather historic. You can tell him all your wonderful stories about the old days on the island——" And so, because Leona when she asked a favor was hard to deny, Edith had consented to have Mr. Winslow come. Later, she had overheard Leona talking to him on the phone. "She's sweet, you'll love her," Leona said. "You may find her a bit—well, *peppery*. But remember that she's seventy-eight years old." (Leona, in her efforts to have the man regard her grandmother charitably, had added four good years to Edith Blakewell's age.)

"Do you find me peppery, Mr. Winslow?" she asks him now.

"Hmm?" he says, frowning slightly.

"And despite what Leona told you, I am only seventy-four, not seventy-eight. I'm sure you'll want that straight, for your article. You see, I eavesdropped on every word Leona said to you about me."

"Seventy-four," he repeats, jotting it down, "and your brother Harold is—"

"He's twelve years younger. He's sixty-two, and Arthur is the baby. Isn't that funny? I still think of Arthur as the baby. A sixty-year-old baby!"

"I gather Arthur Harper's pretty small potatoes."

"Small potatoes? What do you mean?"

"I mean Harold Harper's the kingpin in the company. Isn't Arthur just his mouthpiece?"

"Oh, I think Arthur has a lot to say, Mr. Winslow! Don't

put it in your story that Arthur's small potatoes. That wouldn't be kind to poor Arthur."

With a faint smile he says, "No, I guess it wouldn't."

"You are going to write a *nice* story about the Harpers, aren't you?" Edith Blakewell says. "And of course you want it to be accurate." When he doesn't answer for a moment, she says, "Don't you?"

Gazing into his glass he says, "I'll tell you a little secret about my trade, Mrs. Blakewell. Whenever you try to be accurate about people, they never think you're being nice. And vice versa."

"You mean it's your job to ask *me* the questions, not the other way around. Come, let me show you this little room." She leads him out of the library into the small sitting room, where some of her favorite paintings hang in their lighted recessed frames. "My favorite room," she says. "'Won't you come into my parlor?' said the spider to the fly." She points to the pictures. "That is a Bellows, and this is an Inness, and those two are Turners. The one over the fireplace is a Vuillard—"

He is squinting at one of the paintings. "That's by my friend Sibbie Sanderson, a local artist here," she says. "Do you like it?"

"Tell me a little more about your father," he says.

"About Papa? Well, he was a very athletic man, as I told you, and—"

"I meant something about how he conducted his business."

"Well, let's see. Oh, there's his famous tennis story."

"Did it have something to do with the sugar business, Mrs. Blakewell?"

"Yes. You see, there was this man named Mr. Frère, whose sugar plantation Papa dearly wanted to get his hands on. He used to say, 'The Battle of Waterloo was won on the playing fields of Eton, but I won the Frère estate on an *en tout cas* tennis court.'"

"Just a sec," he says, setting down his drink and picking up his pad again. "I want to get this down."

"Mr. Frère thought Papa's offer was too low," she says, "so Papa challenged him to a set of tennis. Papa won, of course—he always won. And when the set was over, Papa said, 'Frère, you're supposed to jump over the net and shake the victor's hand.' And Mr. Frère said, 'Mr. Harper, I'm afraid I'm too old to jump a net.' And then Papa, of course, jumped the net himself, and shook Mr. Frère's hand, and said, 'You see, Frère, you're too *old*. You're finished, you're through. Everybody else knows it. Why don't you admit it?' I believe the deal was closed that afternoon—at Papa's price."

Mr. Winslow is scribbling, scribbling.

"It shocks you, I suppose. But that's the way things were done in those days. Oh, there are so many stories, Mr. Winslow, about Papa. He was an excellent horseman too. He taught me to ride, and he taught me to jump. He taught me to jump—the hard way." Edith Blakewell laughs abruptly. "When I was a girl I was terrified of jumping, but each time as we would approach the fence he would pull his horse next to mine, so close our legs and our stirrups touched, and he would reach out and grab my horse's bridle, and—" But suddenly she stops. She has not thought of all these things in years, and is not sure she wants to think of them now.

"And he pulled your horse over the jump? Quite a trick."

"But these aren't the sort of stories you want for your magazine," Edith says.

"No, but they're kind of interesting. Go on."

"Well," Edith says, "my father was a—a very complex man. And—well, I guess he was a bit of a despot. But they were *all* despots then. There were no taxes in those days, and very little government. We were a Danish colony, but Denmark didn't pay much attention to what went on. 'Each man is his own policeman here,' Papa used to say. It was perfectly within the law to shoot a native, if you caught him starting a fire."

"Did your father shoot any natives?"

She hesitates. ("I let his black blood put out the fire," she remembers, but no, no, she must not tell Mr. Winslow about that.) "I don't know. But things like that were done; they happened. You've never seen cane burn, Mr. Winslow. You can't imagine—whole hillsides going up like tinder, and the noise of a sugar fire—deafening. And the terrible smell in the air. You know what burnt sugar smells like. Imagine that choking smell in the air for days. The natives started fires, you see, because burnt cane can still be harvested, but it has to be harvested quickly—in three days it begins to ferment and the whole crop is lost. The natives wouldn't work the burnt cane unless they were paid double the wage. It was a very rough-and-tumble period, Mr. Winslow, and most of us are glad it's passed."

"Yes . . . yes," he says, writing furiously.

Encouraged, she goes on. "There were opportunities then, for men like Papa—to make money. But there's a saying here that wherever you find sugar you will also find flies. It's true. The flies swarmed—big flies, little flies—after Papa's money."

"And these—these business techniques you speak of. You say he taught them to your brother Harold?"

"No, no. The things I've been talking about—if you put such things in your story, you must remember what the West Indies were like at the turn of the century. It was every man for himself. No, he taught Harold things like—oh, investments. Harper Industries is very spread out nowadays. We're in more than sugar now. All we have left here is the one distillery, where we make our rum. Of course it's not very good rum. It never was. Cheap rum. Have you tried our rum? I have some in the house, if you'd like a sip. You won't like it."

"No thanks," he says. "But to get back to your brother Harold—"

"Harold's business methods are more—*sophisticated.*"

"What do you mean by that?"

"Well——" She has just noticed the odd way Mr. Winslow has of steering everything back to Harold; Harold seems to be the topic of the day and yet, alas, Harold is the topic Edith knows the least about. She hesitates, trying to think of ways to explain that to Mr. Winslow. What if she said "Harold and I are estranged," for instance, or "Harold and I do not get on"? But neither of these statements would be true; how could two people who hardly knew each other be said to not get on? How could two strangers be estranged? Finally she says, "I can't discuss Harold's business, Mr. Winslow. He's in New York, and I am here."

"Everybody in Wall Street is calling your brother a genius."

"I guess Harold knows his onions where money's concerned."

"You know how Harper stock has been climbing on the Exchange—"

"No. I never read stock reports, Mr. Winslow."

"You don't know that your stock has doubled in the last six months?"

"Gracious! Is that good or bad?"

He smiles at her. "Most people would think it was pretty good."

"The business has always bored me to tears. As long as my checks come in once a month I don't ask questions."

Writing in his notebook now, he is shaking his head slowly back and forth. "Now just a minute!" she says a little sharply. "If you're writing down that Edith Harper Blakewell is a financial nincompoop, please don't. I'm not. It's just that I've been lucky enough to have two brothers to take care of my money for me. Harold is president of the company and trustee of Papa's estate, and he manages things for us. It takes the weight off my shoulders. That's all."

"Then you know nothing about this Luxitron affair?"

"Lux—? What's that?"

"The electronics company your brother is trying to gain control of."

"Oh, well," Edith says with a wave of her hand. "Papa was forever gobbling up companies. And now Harold's doing it? Well, well."

"Some things have changed, though, since your father's day."

"To me it seems more of a case of *plus ça change, plus c'est la même chose*. Can I freshen your drink, Mr. Winslow?"

"No thanks."

"And I'll wager if Harold wants this whatchamacallit company, he'll get it—provided he follows Papa's rules." There is another long pause.

"I gather, then, that you neither approve nor—disapprove. Of any of his activities," he says at last.

"Why should I? I keep out of all that."

"I know you're a long way from New York, but—Mrs. Blakewell, has it ever occurred to you that your brother might bear watching?"

She looks at him with surprise. "Watching? What for?"

"I mean, for your own personal financial sake. You say he controls all your money. What if—"

"He controls *some* things, Mr. Winslow, not all. Are you trying to imply——"

"Wouldn't you be affected if his bubble burst?"

"Are you trying to suggest Harold's in some kind of *trouble?*"

"Playing his kind of game is like walking a tightrope."

"What *is* he—a balloon vendor or a tightrope-walker? You're confusing me, Mr. Winslow, with all these questions about Harold. I thought this story was to be about *all* the Harpers."

"I guess I'm trying to put my finger on the Harpers' Midas touch."

"Well," she says, "you saw old King Midas himself hanging in there in the library. *He* had the touch. Harold's just a caretaker!"

Smiling, he says, "May I quote you on that?"

"Certainly not."

"Still, I'm getting the impression you're not terribly close to your brother."

"There was that difference in our ages. But she here—" She breaks off to study his face again. Despite the good chin, nose, and cowlick, is there (she suddenly asks herself) something a little shifty about Mr. Winslow? With a chill, she realizes that, through artful dodging, he has not yet given her so much as a glimmer of what his "story" is to be about. He seems to want speculation about Harold, and not only about Harold's present activities but his future chances. And why should a man come all the way from New York to St. Thomas to talk to a woman about her brother who lives in New York? Quickly, she races back in her mind through all the things she has told him. Has she made another of her famous mistakes—simply because Leona said that this Mr. Winslow was a friend of hers? Edith decides there is only one tactic to employ. "Have you known my granddaughter long?" she asks him.

"I've known Leona for—oh, four years, I'd say."

"Well," Edith says, weighing her words carefully, "I'd consider it a very low trick—and you a very low human being indeed—if you've used Leona's friendship to gain access to *my* house, to talk about *my* brother, and about *his* personal financial affairs, which I know nothing about, just to get gossip which you can put—"

"Hey!" he cries. "Hey, please! Look, I—" He takes a final swallow of his drink and puts the glass down. Turning to her, he says, "Mrs. Blakewell, I'm sorry. That wasn't what I intended. Forgive me."

"I can *be* peppery, you see, when I want to be!"

"I honestly thought that you, as a Harper, and as a major Harper stockholder—"

"A Harper! Why must I always be thought of as a Harper? I am Edith Blakewell."

"—might have an opinion on this latest Harper activity. Cross my heart, that's all I was getting at, Mrs. Blakewell." Then, in a different voice, he says, "And I'll tell you another little secret of my trade—it's tough to try to be objective about the family of someone I'm awfully fond of. You see?" He holds up two fingers in a V. "A dilemma. Here are its horns. On one side, a job to write a clinical analysis of the Harper fortune—using scalpel where necessary. On the other, a lovely girl. Between the horns hangs young Edward Winslow. Now I'd better say good-by."

"Now wait," Edith says, reaching out to touch his arm. "Don't run off. I got *too* peppery, didn't I? Now it's my turn to apologize."

From the town below, the Customs House clock strikes the half hour. "Pay no attention to that clock that just struck," Edith says. "It's always at least twenty minutes off. Come. Sit down." He smiles at her.

"Please let me sweeten your drink," she says.

Edith had planned, since he was a friend of Leona's (though not knowing he was a beau), to make a little party of his visit. She had been going to offer him tea, and she had asked Nellie, her housekeeper, to fix toast, and to open a jar of her English green gooseberry jam, and to make one of her special ladyfinger cakes. But, when he arrived, Edith had offered him a drink, and he had accepted one. Now, remembering all Nellie's preparations, Edith adds, "Or there is also tea."

"Another drink, I guess. Very short."

She takes his glass to the cellaret and pours a little whisky in it. Stirring it with Perrier water, she says, in a quiet voice, "Three husbands . . . three divorces. Now what? What's going to happen to her? Since she's been here I haven't had a clue." She returns with his drink. "Mr. Winslow, I want you to know that I'm not unconcerned."

"Well," he says slowly, "Neither am I." He lifts his glass. "And I also like her grandmother," he says. "Which doesn't help me off my horns."

* * *

Upstairs in her room at her grandmother's house, Leona Harper Ware Breed Paine Para-Diaz, *née* Ware, who has been enjoined by her ex-husband's relatives not to employ the title *La Condesa de Para-Diaz* (not that she'd ever consider using the silly title anyway), but to use, instead, the "American" form for a divorced woman, Mrs. Ware Para-Diaz (not that she'd bother with that nonsense, either), sits at her dressing table and picks up—for what must surely be the fiftieth time that afternoon—the letter she has been writing, and reads it through again.

Dearest Mother—

It's been over three weeks now since I sent off my last letter to you . . . and I haven't heard from you, so I guess I must have sent it to the wrong hotel. I got your itinerary from Perry's secretary in N.Y., but I guess she must have had it wrong. Anyway, this time I am writing you c/o Morgan et Cie so let's hope I have better luck! Hey, how are you two, anyway!!? As you must have guessed from the postmark, I am at Granny's, who is just the same. Flew down last week, and my other letter was partly to tell you I was going. But it was also to ask you a tremendously big favor, Mother. You see, Mother, the thing is

And this is as far as the letter goes. Each time she has come to the words *the thing is* she has stopped, and of course the trouble is that it took her so many pages before, in the other letter, to say what the thing was, that somehow she does not have the spirit to go through all those pages of explanation again. Once more, she puts the letter down, thinking: Perhaps I should wait one more day. Perhaps I'll hear from her tomorrow. Tomorrow is Thursday. I'll wait and see what happens Thursday. Hotels hold mail, or forward it.

From the town below she hears the striking of the Customs House clock and, downstairs, she can hear the rise and fall of voices. Eddie Winslow is still talking to Granny but, through the shuttered summer doors of the old house, she can make out no words. She has been tempted to open her bedroom door, just a crack, and eavesdrop on them, but she has resisted this. (Even though, she knows, Granny eavesdrops on her from time to time—standing very quietly at the top of the stairs while she was down in the hall below, talking to Eddie on the telephone.) She has considered going downstairs to join the two of them, but has decided against that too. She would rather let Eddie see Granny pure, to see, hopefully, the things about Granny which Leona sees. She has decided that she must not interrupt them. "Just don't let her cow you," she had warned him. "And don't be put off by her appearance, or the clothes she wears. She's an anachronism, but she knows it. She's an *honest* anachronism."

She picks up the unfinished letter, folds it at the center, puts it into the top drawer of the dressing table, and closes the drawer. Then, her chin cupped in her hand, she confronts her image in the oval mirror, and the reflection that comes back is mottled, leprous. Moisture and mildew have invaded the silver backing of the glass, and it is no longer possible to get a clear view of herself between the grayish patches. But, making allowances for the mirror, she decides that for twenty-seven (twenty-seven years, five months, and thirteen days, my dear) there are not too many signs of wear and tear. Not too many little lines. Isn't it funny that nothing shows on the outside, but nothing ever does show. She used to think that having sex showed in a woman's face, but it never did show. Nothing showed. She looks away from the mirrow now and reaches for a cigarette, and, striking the match, holding the match to the cigarette, Leona's hand trembles. She steadies the shaking hand with the other, but still it is a moment before she can get the cigarette going. Granny has noticed the hands, and Leona has tried to explain them away. "You know I'm a coffee addict, Granny," she said. "And I go right on drinking it even though it gives me the shakes." She is not sure whether Granny believed her. Holding her hands straight out in front of her now she orders them to stop, but they do not obey, and how queer it is to have all at once two parts of your body that you cannot control, which seem to be running on little motors of their own. She cries *"Oh!"* as the lighted cigarette falls from her hand and rolls across the top of the dressing table, *"Oh!"* as she scrambles for it with her fingers. And, when she finally has the cigarette again, she sees that it has left a little bubble in the mahogany top. She rubs furiously at the bubble with her fingertip, which only dents the bubble, and then she quickly covers the burn with the ashtray, hoping Granny will not notice it—Granny has already scolded her about smoking too much—

and stabs out the cigarette in the ashtray. Oh! Desperate! But no, she tells herself, no, she cannot be desperate; admit that you are desperate and you might as well give up entirely. To the despairer belongs defeat: that is a stern little rule of life. And how can she be desperate when she has so many plans? Oh, yes. Ambitious plans. Wonderful plans. Plans that are *already* beginning to work out. Thinking of the plans, her thoughts fly up in a wordless prayer. She jumps up quickly from the stool, smoothing the front of her skirt with her hands. "Leona Ware strode defiantly across the room."

She kicks off her shoes and lies down on her bed, on the white quilted coverlet, on her back, her arms straight at her sides. Outside, a warm breeze billows the white window curtains, and the green ipomoea vines on the wall outside the windows cast gray, marbly shadows on the white ceiling. Why does lying like this, on her back, on top of the coverlet, in the exact center of her big old bed, always make her feel young, and virginal, and small? "The search for beginnings is important," Dr. Hardman had said to her, and this, of course, is why she came back here—because this was where it all began, here, in this room, under these high ceilings; here, in this huge old-fashioned bed with a carved pineapple topping its tall headboard, surrounded by heavy furniture, chairs, and dressing table, the windows hung with long white (turning a bit yellow now) organdy curtains, Belgian, embroidered with fleurs-de-lis, their holes artfully mended with a spiderweb stitch; this room, behind the thick stone walls of this house, walls covered with vines that occasionally poked their way into the house, across the window sills. "You're a hard man, Hardman," Leona had quipped to him. He had returned her a look of stone. She had just been telling him about her odd habit of thinking about everything she said and did as though she were reading about herself: "Leona Ware paused thoughtfully in the doorway." "Leona Ware riposted artfully . . ." "With a cheerful smile, Leona Ware interjected . . ." And so on. She had thought it might amuse him, might make him like her a little better than he seemed to. But he had suddenly interrupted, saying, "Why do you suppose you've had all these marriages, Mrs. Paine?" "But I've only had *two!*" she had cried, which was the correct number at the time. And then, "I think it's because I'm a very moral woman, Doctor Hardman. I don't sleep with men. I make them marry me first. It's the New England blood in me. Did you know I'm one eighth Boston?" The only thing he ever said to her that made any sense at all was the business about beginnings. And so she came back here to try to retrace her steps. It was like a game. You went back to *Go*. Then, trying to keep your wits about you, you tried to play it better the second time.

Leona closes her eyes. She makes of herself a long, heavy sack full of sand and, at one corner of the sack, there is a tiny hole and, very slowly, the sand trickles out, trickles out. Then, in another corner, another leak appears, and more sand pours out, slowly. All at once, unbidden, Edouardo appears and seems to hover over her closed eyes. "Oh, go away," she whispers aloud. "Haven't you done enough?" You are banished, she reminds him. You are gone, finished, over, dead, out of my life and dropped from the face of the earth. She likes to think of Edouardo Para-Diaz as in outer space—circling the moon, perhaps, in endless orbit. Or landed there. Ah, Edouardo, she thinks, how do you like the moon? How do you like the Sea of Tranquility, or that other sea you would surely love—the Sea of Sighs? Any cold, beautiful place will do for you. And what are the things Leona Para-Diaz loves? I love the touch of soft things, the feel of cotton cloth, the feel of my hair between my fingers, the soft, smooth place at the back of a man's neck; and this place, the unannounced seasons, and the sea; all islands; and this house, and the tree-of-heaven in the garden, and the veranda where she used to have tea with Granny when she was a child, and the heavy, curving mahogany banisters on the stairs, and Granny's great Chippendale desk full of clutter that Leona was never allowed to touch, and the damp, salt-sweet smell of the rooms, and Granny's smell, and the smell of linen sheets that have been hung to dry in the sun. Is that list enough? And beautiful things: a celebration of lilies opening in a lilypond beyond their house on the coast of Spain. "How beautiful the lilies are!" Edouardo said. And she had wanted to say to him, Yes, and you are beautiful too—beautiful as a lily yourself, you beautiful man. Two identical-feeling tears form at the outer corners of her closed eyes and run down the sides of her face, into her hair, just above her ears. Oh, but this isn't the way, she tells herself. No, this isn't the way at all.

The words form in her mind again:

You see, Mother, the thing is

"Her first husband was a rip," Edith is saying, "and that didn't last long. Her second was a decent sort, but apparently he didn't suit her either. The third of course, the Spaniard, was an absolute bad hat, a rotter, a thorough Skeesicks."

"I met her between number two and number three," Eddie Winslow says. And he chuckles softly.

"Why are you laughing?"

"I like the way you tick each one of them off, Mrs. Blakewell."

"Now this last one," Edith says, lowering her voice, "*he* was romantically inclined, it turns out, toward members of his own sex—if you can believe such a thing!"

"Well, I guess I can believe it."

"Of course she made me promise, when she came here, that we would not discuss it. I can understand why she prefers not to talk about it. But now it seems as though she won't discuss *anything* with me!"

"As a matter of fact, I sort of promised her I wouldn't discuss her with you," he says.

"Yes. Well, you see? That's how she's become. Secretive. But I do care about her. And why—" She has started to say, Why do I come upon her at times, and look at her, and see a look of absolute tragedy on her face? But she decides not to say this, and says, instead, "I want her to find the right person."

He nods and puts down his glass. "I'd really better be going," he says.

"Leona's upstairs resting. She'll want to see you. Won't you stay?"

"Don't disturb her. I'll be seeing her later on," he says, rising and pocketing his notebook.

Standing up, Edith says, "I'm afraid I haven't been much help to you. Of course anything you want to know about the company you can get directly from Harold."

"The fact is, Mr. Harper has refused to see me."

"Refused? Why should he refuse? I'll tell him to see you."

"Would you?" he says eagerly.

"Well," she hesitates, "I can't actually *tell* him to see you. If he chooses not to—it's a man's world, and the two boys do run the business. Still, I can try. You see, Mr. Winslow," she says, "the thing is that where the business is concerned *I'm* the one who's small potatoes."

Following her out of the sitting room, he says, "This is a beautiful house, Mrs. Blakewell."

"My father built it for my husband and me as a wedding present. But it's too big for one old woman. It needs a man in it." She smiles at him. "Where are you staying on the island?"

"The Virgin Isle."

"Poor man. You must be miserable. Do you know how many gallons of water it takes to flush a toilet?"

"I admit it's something I've never thought much about, Mrs. Blakewell."

"Five gallons! While the rest of us hoard our fresh water, and use salt water in our toilets, the Virgin Isle Hotel flushes away thousands of gallons of fresh water daily in its Mrs. Joneses. It's a disgrace."

Crossing the drawing room she sees Nellie crouched in a corner, about to plug in her vacuum cleaner, and she gestures to Nellie to delay, please, her vacuuming until the guest has left. Nellie is a good girl, and has been with Edith many years, but one must keep reminding all these girls of certain things, again and again. "If you have time," she says to Mr. Winslow, "you really should go over and take a look at what's left of my father's old house at Sans Souci. It burned in nineteen thirty-five, but the foundations will give you an idea of the size of *that* place. No one knows what caused the fire. My mother used to claim that the Roosevelt administration burned it down. She said that Mr. Roosevelt's agents burned it to spite her because she was trying to sell it to the Navy. If you go, you will notice three enormous urns standing on what used to be the terrace. In the old days they were filled with plants and shrubs, and there were four urns. But suddenly, one morning, a few years after the fire, there were only three. Someone must have walked off with one of those urns, though they must have weighed tons apiece. Why would anyone want an iron urn? It's always interested me."

"Yes," he says, "well—"

They are at the front door now, and moving out onto the

long veranda that stretches the length of Edith Blakewell's house. "If you are writing a story about us," she says, "you mustn't believe the stories you hear about the Harpers. Gossip travels differently on an island than it does on a land mass, remember that. It travels in circles because it has no place else to go. And there are some people here, a few, who still resent my family. You'll hear that I am practically the Charlotte Corday of the West Indies, and—" smiling at him, touching his arm "—that I absolutely devour handsome young men like you. Pay it no heed."

"Yes. Well, thanks very much, Mrs. Blakewell."

Callers are so few; she would like to detain him. Standing on the veranda, she says, "Do you like my garden, Mr. Winslow?"

"It's a nice garden. You've got a nice view of the sea too."

"I never look at the sea," she says with an impatient gesture. "The sea is just something that takes people away from here. I look at the shore. It is the shores of life that have meaning and importance to me. The shores are where penetration begins, where humanity begins. An island is *all* shore, all edge, all lip. The sea rushes against it, but the lip fights back. Have you ever thought of that, Mr. Winslow?"

Running his finger under the band of his collar (poor thing, he looks so hot), he says, "Yes, I guess you're right."

"None of the others ever saw it that way—Mama or Papa, or my brothers, or my husband, or my daughter. Leona—perhaps. But mostly it is my thought." And then she says absently, addressing the garden, really, more than Mr. Winslow, "And then of course there was the Frenchman."

"Who is the Frenchman?"

"A Frenchman who once worked for my father. One of the flies. One of the swarm."

If it is background material Mr. Winslow wants, there it is, a beginning. Perhaps it is not the story he came to get, but it is a story nonetheless and perhaps, without knowing it, Edith is offering it to him out of sympathy for him, tossing the Frenchman to him as one would toss a ball to a bored and panting puppy on a sweltering afternoon. The place seems proper, the garden, and the time, and, inside her, a voice says, "Quick! Go pick up my Frenchman. If you don't, I'll not give you another chance." They would, of course, have to go back into the house and begin all over again, and Leona would have to join them, and hear the story too. But he says, "Well, I'm only concerned in this story with members of the family—" shifting his weight from one foot to the other.

They move to the top of the veranda steps.

"I've just thought of something," Edith says, "something my daughter Diana, Leona's mother, once said. About Papa's houses. The house at Sans Souci burned, and the house at Morristown is now a Roman Catholic convent, and the Paris house is owned by a French *duchesse*. And Diana said, 'Fire, God, and Royalty have taken over Grandpa's houses. If he knew, I imagine he'd approve.' Diana can be witty. You may use it in your story, if you'd like."

"Well, thanks. Maybe I will." He starts down the wide stone steps.

"Good-by," she calls from the top of the steps. "Goodby. . . ." She watches him through the garden and out the gate, and in a moment she hears his car start up.

The garden is dry and withered-looking. She has let it go badly. There is so much that needs doing to it. Behind her, in the house, she hears a summer door open, then close, and the low whine of Nellie's vacuum cleaner in the drawing room. (What a queer hour to vacuum. Five o'clock.) And, endlessly and invisibly, the evening birds chatter in the jungle foliage beyond the garden.

Suddenly the past, with its stories, seems a journey that stretches behind her like a corridor, a corridor as long and narrow and crowded as her veranda. Her veranda is filled with porch swings and wicker furniture and hanging wire baskets of old ferns whose fronds reach to the floor, and collections of seashells from Lord knows how many long-ago shell-hunts of Leona's when she was small. And, like the veranda, the journey doesn't seem to stop at the steps, but to run on down them to the walk, and wind through the garden to the gate, and out the gate into the street and down the long hill in a luckless joyride. She was four years old when Katharine Lee Bates wrote "America the Beautiful." She is exactly the same age as the Eiffel Tower. The journey is a long and bumpy distance. Once, when Leona was seven years old (while Diana and Leona's father were trying to solve their insoluble domestic problems), Leona sat on the veranda painting a water-color picture of the outline of Signal Hill and the cloudless sky above it. She showed her grandmother the picture.

"But look, Leona," Edith said, pointing to it. "You've left a big white space between where the green of the hill ends and the blue of the sky begins. Look at that horizon again. The blue and the green come together."

But Leona shook her head. "No, Granny," she said, "I've been up to the top of that hill, and they don't come together."

Sometimes this is the way Edith Blakewell feels—like a strip of white space between the future and the past. A strip of white space disguised in green lace and emeralds. Slowly she turns and walks back into the house, and into the library. She begins turning out the lamps.

"Hello, Papa. What do you think of me now?" It is an unnecessary question; she knows exactly what he would think.

After her father died, when she and Harold and Arthur and their respective wives had gone through the house at Sans Souci, dividing up the furniture, deciding what should be sold and what should be kept and who wanted what, the only thing Edith had asked for was the Sargent.

"Nothing else, pet?" Barbara Harper, Harold's skinny wife, had said. "But why would you want that? Everybody knows how you hated your father, pet."

"Perhaps if I can hang his portrait in my house, I can get used to him," Edith had said. They had had to cut Papa's frame in sections, and roll his canvas, to get him out the front door of his house, and into hers.

On her way up the stairs Edith meets Leona coming down—hurrying, very pretty in a dress that looks like flowers blowing in the wind.

"Where are you going, Leona?"

"To a cocktail party, Granny. Some people named Chisholm. Do you know them? No, I guess you don't. How was the interview?"

"I don't know how much help I was to him. He asked a lot of questions about your Uncle Harold. Is Harold up to something, Leona?"

Leona laughs and runs down the rest of the stairs. "He's *always* up to something, isn't he, Granny?"

"He isn't in some sort of—difficulties, is he, dear? Your Mr. Winslow seemed to imply—"

Leona looks quickly up at her grandmother on the stairs. Then she dumps her purse on the lowboy in front of the hall mirror, and many little tubes and sticks and pencils come rattling out. She pushes them around, picks up a lipstick, uncaps it, and begins applying color to her lips. "Well," she says to the mirror, "just leave Eddie Winslow to me, Granny. I know how to handle him."

"He seemed like a nice young man."

"Eddie? Yes, he's a good egg." She recaps the lipstick and, leaning close to the glass, pulls one lower eyelid down and looks at the eye.

Edith comes one step down the stairs. "Leona," she says, "can we talk a minute?"

Leona looks up at her imploringly. "*Now*, Granny? Gosh, I'm late already. Later, huh?"

With her hairbrush, Leona yanks one lock of her dark hair straight up and, with the comb in her other hand, quickly rats the hair. It makes an electric sound, and Leona makes a sour face at the result.

"Is someone picking you up?" Edith asks.

"I called a taxi, Granny."

"Oh! Why don't you let John drive you? He's right here."

Laughing, scooping all the cosmetics off the lowboy into her purse, Leona says, "*I* was taught that it was rude for a houseguest to use her hostess' chauffeur."

"Well, tell the taxi to put it on my bill."

"Oh, Granny! See you later." She starts toward the door.

"Will you be home for dinner?" Edith calls.

Leona calls back an answer that is either yes or no, and is gone.

"Don't be too late!" Edith calls after her, and immediately regrets it. After all, one doesn't tell a grown woman not to be late.

Outside, Leona runs across the veranda and down the stone steps into the walk. Halfway down the walk, she hears her grandmother's voice, and stops. "What?" she calls. She hesitates a moment, wondering whether to go back to see what Granny wants. Poor Granny—she has such a surfeit of love, such a residue, that sometimes it seems to pour out around

Leona's feet, wherever she walks, like a thick glue, tripping her up. "Good night, Granny!" she calls, and then continues on through the twilight garden to the gate where her taxi waits.

"Good evening, Miss Harper!"

"Good evening." The driver touches his cap and opens the door for her. As they start down Government Hill, she opens her purse and, with jumping hands, fishes for a cigarette.

Edith Blakewell moves up the stairs. The house is quiet. Nellie's vacuuming is finished. In the distance, the Customs House clock begins to strike the hour, as usual a little off, and, as he sometimes does when Edith is alone, her husband joins her in the upstairs hall and accompanies her the little distance to her room.

"This house echoes, Edie," he says.

"A new house always echoes, Charles. It will stop once we've lived in it a while."

The clock dies on the seventh stroke, and Charles with it, and Edith Harper Blakewell lets herself into her room, feeling all at once that it has been an unsatisfactory day. Everything about the day seems unfinished, unresolved, full of unanswered questions, and now, apparently, she must dine alone. Then she remembers that it is Wednesday, Alan Osborn's day to call, and that he will be arriving at any minute. So the day may not be a total loss after all.

Two

MEREDITH Harper, Edith's father, had a grand design for all of them, based on the phenomenon of generations. They were to be links of a chain, human beings in a relay race through time. Each of them was to run a little distance, his arm outstretched, carrying the torch to the next one who was waiting to seize it and run on with it. Whenever Edith sees a full moon in a muzzy tropic sky, a moon silvering the sea with an endless avenue of light, she is reminded somehow of that vision of her father's, and the fire they were supposed to carry. Her father was no fool. "I assume you detest me," he once said, "but at least you'll never forget me." Leona ought to understand these things, Edith thinks, because so much of what Leona is can only be explained by her great-grandfather, and what he was, and what he made of all of them. But Edith has been a poor torchbearer. Her torch should by rights have been handed to her daughter, Diana (Goddess of the Hunt!). But somehow, along the line, one of them stumbled and dropped the torch, and it went out, and it is hard to kindle it again for Leona who does not know it ever existed and, in the meantime, is running fast in another direction.

One of the troubles is that Edith has no more idea of the norm of youth in Leona's generation than she had of her own. Or of Diana's, for that matter. (Did Diana represent that norm? Or did her first husband, Jack Ware—Leona's father? Or Diana's second husband, Perry Gardiner? Perhaps; Edith doesn't know.) Sometimes, when Leona is at the beach, Edith sits on the veranda and tries to pick her out with her father's binoculars—an excellent pair, prewar Bausch & Lomb, a gift, in fact, of Kaiser Wilhelm himself to Meredith Harper, a memento of the days when he thought Germany should win the war. Edith prowls the beach with the glasses, and she sees the young men: crew-cut, wearing their wispy Lastex loincloths, hopping across the bay like kingfishers on water skis. Then she finds Leona. And she sees one of the young men wander over to her, and begin to talk to her. Others gather, and their faces are laughing, and all at once a pair of the crew-cuts seizes Leona, one by the armpits and one by the ankles, and they begin to run with her down the beach toward the water. But then, plans changed, the young men set Leona down, and the group disperses, and Edith sees Leona seat herself opposite a blond young Titan who is sitting on his heels, holding a native steel drum between his bare knees. Leona's hands clap rhythm. Edith tries to picture these young men clothed, and cannot. She tries to ascribe to them parents, addresses, occupations, and cannot. They are originless people. Passing through, passing through. She has no idea of what they long to achieve or of what they have cast aside—no more than she has of what they are saying, or singing, to Leona. Watching them, their mystery deepens, and their inaccessibility becomes more complete. At every turn of Edith's life, youth has evaded her.

Being the donor of a wing to the St. Thomas hospital entitles Edith Blakewell to a few privileges. For instance, the hospital's head physician calls on Edith at her house once a week. Alan Osborn is a short little bantam rooster of a man, but a good doctor, very proud of his circumflex mustache, of his full head of hair, and famous for his supply of spicy island news. He is a few years younger than Edith, but she has known him for many years. Many of her friends and certain of her relatives express horror at the thought of her being treated by a doctor who is a bachelor. ("You surely don't let him examine you *internally!*" Barbara Harper said.) But every Wednesday evening, like clockwork, he comes to her house.

And so, after Leona's departure, Edith busies herself getting ready for him, taking off her dress and putting on her nightgown and robe. At a quarter past seven, there is a tap on her bedroom door and Nellie ushers Alan in. Edith gives him a little wave. "Well, well," he says in his chirp-chirp of a voice, "how're we today?"

"Alan," she says, "some day I wish you would stop addressing me in the first person plural. Despite appearances, there is only one of me."

"Hmm," he says, opening his bag. "Shall we assume the position?"

Edith assumes the position on the bed, and he begins the ritual of poking and patting and prying at her with his little instruments, humming under his breath as he moves from one part of her to another. "This will be no more than reasonably uncomfortable," he says, making a delicate invasion of her anatomy. And then, "No pain?"

"Not much."

"How are the pills holding out?"

"I take one whenever I think of it."

He pokes and pats and pries some more. "Well," he says finally, "I'd say we were holding our own."

"Holding our own?" she laughs. "What does that mean?" But then, suddenly, his exploring fingers touch her in a place where it does hurt, and she cries out.

"A little tender there? Sorry, dear."

"You pinched me," she says, biting her lip.

"In a few days I want you to come down to the office," he says. "I want to take some more pictures. I'll have Susan set up an appointment for you. Meanwhile, please keep taking the capsules."

"Your pictures are so unflattering," Edith says. She pushes herself up on her elbows in bed and arranges her nightclothes. It still hurts, and deeply, where he touched her and, sitting up, she loses her breath for a moment, and gasps. She says, "Dear Alan—I always feel when we sit here alone in my bedroom that we should be lovers." Then a curious and unexplained thing happens because she suddenly reaches out to him and puts her hands on his shoulders, and begins to cry.

"There, there," the little doctor says, patting the back of Edith's neck. "It *is* a temptation, isn't it? There, there."

"Why didn't we, Alan, when we had a chance?"

"We knew each other too well, my dear. We shared too many little secrets."

The tears are over as quickly as they began, and Edith puts her feet heavily over the side of the bed. "Sorry," she says. "I don't know what's the matter with me. Come—let's have our brandy."

They punctuate each visit this way. Edith gets up, goes to the decanter on the dresser, and fills two glasses. Handing him his, she says, "Here's mud in your eye."

He smiles at her. "And here's mud in yours, my love."

They sit on opposite corners of the big bed and Alan touches her hand.

"Any more thoughts about your house?" he asks her after a minute.

She shakes her head.

"I'm sure you know about the tax advantages you'd have, or rather your estate would have, if you deeded the house to the hospital. You'd have lifetime tenancy, of course—"

"Which you'd all be praying would be a matter of months!"

"If the house itself had to go eventually, you know how valuable to us it would be to have the pool. For water therapy, polio patients—"

"I've heard all those arguments before. That hospital's got my skin, and now they want my guts! Tell them Leona's come back for a while, and I can't make any decisions now." Thoughtfully, he twirls the brandy in his glass. "I've been thinking I might do over the east end of the house as an apartment for her," Edith says. "For her to have permanently—or whenever she wants to use it. You see, as things stand now, this house and everything goes to Leona under my will—everything but some odds and ends. Whenever she's been in trouble—like now, after this divorce—she's come home here, to me. Ever since she was a little girl, Alan, it's been so. I think some day she may want this house for her own."

He looks at her steadily. "Just don't try to trap her, Edie," he says.

"Trap her? How could I trap her?"

"With this house. With the kind of life you've had here."

Edith Blakewell is silent.

"It's taken you all these years to be even tolerated here," he says. "It will take her just as long."

"'Edie, Edie, fat and greedy, how does your garden grow?' Remember that, Alan? That's what you're talking about, isn't it?"

"You may think this island has forgotten your father. They haven't forgotten. Everywhere she goes, they say, 'There's Leona Ware. Her great-grandfather was Meredith Harper.'"

He takes a final swallow from his brandy glass and puts it down. He removes his large watch from his vest pocket, snaps open the case, purses his lips, and snaps it closed again and returns it to the pocket. Steepling his fingers in his best professional manner, he says, "I must be on my way. Susan will call you about an appointment for the pictures." Then he reaches out and gently tweaks Edith's nose. "Good night, my sweet." He rises and picks up his bag.

Edith follows him to the door. "I just want her to be happy, Alan," she says. "She's had so much, but still she isn't happy."

He stands in the open doorway. "The only trouble with Leona is she's just like her grandmother. A little spitfire." He takes her hand and squeezes it. "One of these days we'll become lovers, wait and see."

"But first I'll have to give my house to your hospital. Correct? Come here a minute," she says. He steps forward. "Want to hear something dirty in Danish?" she asks him.

He tips his little head forward eagerly. "Yes? What is it?"

She whispers the naughty words to him.

"Very interesting. What's it mean?"

"Fire up your behind!" she says, and laughs loudly. "Now listen, Alan. There's a dark-haired young man named Edward Winslow staying at the Virgin Isle. Do some snooping for me. Find out all you can about him, what his background is, what his qualifications are—you know what I mean."

"His qualifications as a suitor for Leona, dear? Or for you?" He pats her bottom.

"Shoo!" she says. "You're a nasty old man with a nasty mind. Now run along." Still laughing, she closes the door on him.

She continues laughing noisily to herself, moving slowly

about the room, undressing again, getting ready for dinner. She takes her blue crepe off its hanger, struggles into it, leaving the zipper undone for Nellie to do up when she comes downstairs. But she is not really in a humorous frame of mind and when she sits down at her dressing table she spills face powder all over the glass top. It floats up in a cloud in front of the mirror and in its reflection she looks as though she were being dissolved—*pouf!*—by a conjurer's trick, and powder settles all over the backs of her hairbrushes, over silver picture frames, into an open jar of cold cream, and across the front of her dress. She tries to brush the powder away, but the powder clings and smears, and she thinks for a moment that she is about to cry again, and it is not like Edith to cry without reason. She starts to stand up, but there is a deep and painful stitch in her left side, and so she sits where she is. Bitter and old, withered and dry. She wants to ring for Nellie, but the electric bell is on the other side of her room. Trapped, beyond calling for help in a houseful of servants, her situation strikes her as absurd. She is thinking of what Alan said. Why hadn't she asked Alan to dine with her? He always made a great fuss about it being time to leave, checking that enormous turnip of a watch, clicking his tongue, but Edith knows that he never has any place to go, except back to his little rooms in Krystal Gade and his mystery magazines. His dinner is a sandwich and tea with Ellery Queen. Lovers indeed! Though once, in an older, more naïve, almost-forgotten time, someone (yes, it was Alan) at a masquerade ball (how romantic it sounds!) lifted his mask and kissed her behind a stiff little palm tree in a dark garden. It was another Alan and another Edith then, but she remembers the look on his face, poor thing: terror! From having kissed Meredith Harper's daughter. Outside, through the open windows, the sun is setting, the garden is taking its dim colors of evening, and is being peopled with its night sounds—the voices of dead populations in the old trees. "Edie, Edie, fat and greedy—"

"There is a certain value in anonymity, Edith," she hears her mother say. "But whether we like it or not we will always be Harpers."

* * *

Seeing him at last across the cocktail party, Leona murmurs "Excuse me" to the people she has been talking to, and makes her way toward him through the considerable crowd on the terrace. She waves to him over heads, but he does not see her and stands, drink in hand, alone, on the steps, looking oddly lost and bewildered. Dear old Eddie, why does he always look—wherever he is—as though he didn't belong there, as though he had found himself an unwilling tourist in a foreign-speaking city where he did not even know how to ask the way to the nearest hotel? "Hey!" she calls to him. "Here I am!" But he does not see her until she is practically in front of him, waving her fingers in his face. "Hey, remember me?" she says. He grins and seizes her elbow. "Who the hell *are* these people, anyway?" he asks her.

"The cream of the Winter Colony." Then she whispers, "But dolts. Dolts and bores. Quick—let's escape. Let's hide from this party." She takes his hand and they run down the steps.

"Where'll we hide?"

"Behind the arras—anywhere where we can talk."

"Find an arras. I'm with you."

As they run along the edge of the terrace someone calls, "Leona?" And Leona whispers to Eddie Winslow, "Don't answer! Hide!" And she runs with him down a gravel walk between banks of sea-grapes and out onto a strip of dark beach. The light from Scorpion Rock sweeps across their faces and Leona says, "Now quick—give me a cigarette and tell me what you thought of her!" He hands her a cigarette and holds a match to it. Then he lights one of his own.

"I think she's terrific," he says, waving out the match.

"Wasn't I right, Eddie? *There's* your story!"

He kneels and pats the sand. "Dry," he says. "Can we sit down?"

Leona kicks off her shoes and kneels beside him on the beach which is still warm from the sun.

"Your grandmother told me she swims half a mile every day in her pool—in the nude."

Leona laughs. "Well, that's *color* for you! What else?"

"But the main thing was, she honestly doesn't seem to know a damn thing about your great-uncle."

"I told you that. But don't you *see*, Eddie? *Granny's* your story—not him. Everybody knows Uncle Harold's a stinker!

Where's the news in that? But Granny—how many like her are there left? She's a vanishing breed, Eddie—the end of an era. She's a—a kind of symbol of what the old West Indies used to be. All the other planters made their money and got out—like Uncle Harold. Of all the old sugar families there's not a one left—only Granny. Did she tell you any of her stories?"

"A few."

"She can remember when the foremen in the cane fields used to stand over the natives and whip them with the flat sides of machetes to make them work faster. And if anybody said 'Oh, how awful!' do you know what their excuse was here? 'Those blacks are Jamaicans and Dominicans, not Saint Thomians'—which made it all right. And the great old Danish families. The men all had native mistresses, and their great-grandchildren are walking around St. Thomas today—Negroes, and Granny can tell you just who they are. And about the parties and sit-down dinners for three hundred, with a redcoated footman behind each chair. Talk about Paris or Vienna—things were every bit as gay and as elegant here, and Granny remembers all that. And the women in their jewels, and their dresses from Worth and Molyneux, and the men in their cutaways and ribbons and sashes and medals—but Granny says that when you danced with a gentleman even at the most formal ball you could always feel his shoulder-holster under his coat!"

"That's all very good, Leona, but—"

"And the way she continues to live now, Eddie. That's why I wanted you to see her house. It's really the last of the big old places. Do you know that my room is still called the nursery? And that Thursdays are still the days when Granny *receives?* Every Thursday afternoon her chauffeur goes around and delivers calling cards to a handful of other old ladies, and the other old ladies drop their cards at Granny's—one of her maids brings the cards in to her on a silver tray. And her teas—they're *beautiful*, Eddie, the way she *presides* over teas, sitting there in her drawing room like a queen on a throne! Who else has silver that gets polished every single day of the week? And her dining-room table. Her girls rub it with the palms of their hands—it's polished with the oils from their skin. 'It's the only way to polish good wood,' Granny says. Oh, I know you probably think it's shocking that all those people do nothing but wait on one old woman. But it has such *dignity*, such perfection, such *integrity* about it. Sure it's old-fashioned, and maybe it's stuffy and silly, but I sometimes think there are things from the old order—the old kind of graciousness—that *should* be preserved. I sometimes think Granny's whole way of life should be government-subsidized!" She pauses. "Don't you?"

When he makes no immediate answer, she laughs and says, "Well, end of sales pitch!"

"You know, it's funny," he says in a quiet voice. "But it sounded to me like a pitch for the kind of life you'd like to live."

Leona considers this. "Well," she says thoughtfully, "maybe you're right, Eddie. Maybe it's some of that—dignity—that I need. Just a bit of it. It should be a part of me, I suppose, since I'm her granddaughter and grew up in her house. But it hasn't been. And maybe that's why I came back here—to take another look."

"Would you like to run a household like hers?"

She smiles at him, though his face is invisible in the darkness. "Of course not. But the things about her that have integrity. That's what I'd like to have."

"Poor little rich girl. After sowing her wild oats with three husbands on two continents, she's ready to settle down as a lady of grace and leisure—"

"Stop it! You know what I want. It's got nothing to do with that."

"Your art-gallery idea, you mean?"

"Yes. And it's not just an idea, either. I'm going to have it, and I'm in the process of lining up my backers right now."

"Can I see you as the hard-boiled proprietress of an art gallery?" he says. "I don't know, but I'm trying."

"And you can help me too," she says. "When you do this story on Granny you can mention my gallery. See how hard-boiled I can be? I know the value of having a friend who's with the press."

"Look here," he says, "will you get it through your beautiful head that I'm not doing a story about your grandmother? Who the hell cares?"

"Who the hell cares about some Wall Street tycoon, either!"

"Now wait a minute," he says roughly. "A lot of people

might care, including maybe the Securities and Exchange Commission! There's suddenly something awfully fishy-looking about this character named Harold Harper."

"You're out of your mind," she says. "Uncle Harold's so honest and upright it's boring!"

"How well do you know this guy? What are these deals of his—these companies he's angling to take over? Is he maybe pumping up the price of his own stock, and bilking millions of dollars out of innocent investors? Where the hell's his money coming from?"

"He's a rich man! He's always been rich."

"Sure, but *that* rich? This is big stuff he's after now, and I'd like to find out if he's just a simple-minded Social Register smoothie or a fast-talking garden-variety swindler. If you ask me, there's something rotten in the Harper empire, girl, and his name is—"

"I thought you were a friend!" she says. "How can you talk to me that way about a member of my family!" And she is grateful for the darkness of the beach because he cannot see her face. She is afraid she is going to cry, and she doesn't want him to see her cry.

"Well, that's thc story *I'm* after, girl! That's why I was sent down here to case this joint—not to have tea with some old lady whose crappy silver gets polished every day, and who lives like Louis the Fourteenth! If I were that old lady I'd take all that silver and bury it in the garden!"

Leona jumps to her feet. "I don't care what you write!"

But he reaches up quickly and takes her hand. "But *I* care," he says.

"Please let go."

"I care, because I think I'm falling in love with you."

"What?"

"You heard what I said."

"Oh, no—"

He kneels silently in front of her, gripping her hand in his, and his eyes glitter briefly in the sweep of light. He's joking, she thinks instantly; or he's drunk. How can he have said a think like that after those other brutal things? How can he use the word *love* in the same breath with words like *swindler*, and *crappy?* "Eddie?" she says. She thinks: *Are you really Eddie?* The dim shape in front of her becomes the shape of a stranger who, in the dark, has been substituted for Eddie Winslow—her dear, comfortable old friend; reliable Eddie, the available extra man for parties, the man whom she could always call when she was in New York alone, and be sure of a gentle, undemanding date for dinner or the movies. He once told her he liked her because she was a good listener. He used to say that he should have been a poet, but had been born in the wrong century, and so he had to be satisfied with a job he hated. He'd never go anywhere, he said, and he blamed his family. He came from somewhere, nowhere, in Massachusetts—*Nowhere, Mass.* he called it—and his parents were poorer than Job's chickens. They'd given Eddie nothing but a coach ticket to New York, where he'd put himself through journalism school slinging hash at a Columbia fraternity house. Once, walking home from a movie, he had put his arm around her shoulders. And yet now, all at once, Eddie—or some new incarnation of him—is here, on his knees, holding her hand, pressing her knuckles so hard against his mouth that she can feel his teeth, talking about love, and for a terrible moment she is afraid she may laugh out loud. His eyes are murderously bright. "Oh, please stand up," she whispers.

"I can only say these things because it's dark," he says, rising and facing her. "And I'd like to revise what I just said. I don't *think*. I know I'm falling in love with you."

"Then why can't you be nice?" she says in a voice that sounds childish and querulous.

"I love you, Leona."

"Did I do this? she pleads. "I didn't mean to. I only wanted——" Wanted what? Wanted to help you, she thinks. But that sounds patronizing.

"I've loved you for a long time. When you told me you were marrying the Spaniard I wanted to die. I want to marry you, Leona."

"Oh, but I can't love anybody yet—I want to start my gallery!" she says wildly. "Do you want to invest in it?"

"You know I don't have any money."

"I was only joking! Oh, Eddie—I *do* like you. But why did you have to—to suddenly *upset* everything?"

He releases her hand, and she steps backward, catching her balance. She pushes shaking fingers through her hair. "Forgive me, Eddie!" she says a little hysterically. "But everything was so wonderfully simple! Now I'm all mixed up. I don't know what to think. I can't—"

"Never mind," he says in an icy voice.

"I'm sorry!"

"Skip it!"

"Ssh!" she says. "Someone's coming!"

Between the sea-grape hedges, the arcing light from the lighthouse picks out the figure of a man coming toward them along the gravel path.

"Here's a guy who can finance your gallery," Eddie says, close to her ear. "He could do it with one of his leftover oil wells. Maybe he's the sort of man you're after."

"Oh, please!"

"Hello, Purdy!" Eddie calls.

"Winslow!" the man calls. He is on the short side, broad-shouldered and heavy-set, and he carries a drink in one hand. "Hey, why aren't you up at the party? We're having a hell of a time. There's a girl up there who—oh, excuse me," he says, seeing Leona. "I thought you were alone."

Eddie says, "Leona, I'd like you to meet Mister Arch Purdy. Arch, may I present Leona Para-Diaz? Pardon me," he says without a trace of sarcasm. "I meant to say *La Condesa* de Para-Diaz."

"Well, how do you do?"

Standing very stiffly, Leona says "Hello." He shakes her hand.

"Well, Winslow," the man says, "what kind of dirt are you digging up these days?" Leona shivers.

"Look," Eddie says, "we poor working men have to get back to our jobs. You two party people stay around and get acquainted, okay? So long, Arch. I'll see you around, Leona." He starts back across the beach.

"Eddie," Leona calls weakly. But the only answer is the sound of his retreating footsteps in the gravel.

"Did I interrupt something?" the man next to her asks.

She shakes her head. Leona stands there, unable to think of a single thing to say, stupidly conscious only of the fact that her shoes are off and lying somewhere on the sand beside her. "Excuse me," she says at last. "My shoes . . ." The man supports her with one hand as she struggles back into them.

"I noticed you back there at the party," the man says. "I

thought, there's a cool girl who knows exactly what she's doing. Tell me: Are you as cool as you look?"

Laughing lightly, Leona adjusts her sweater around her shoulders.

"Let's you and me go have a tall, cool drink."

"As a matter of fact, I could use a drink," she says.

Leona has sometimes teased her grandmother about the formality with which Edith chooses to dine alone. So be it, Edith thinks. It is too easy for a woman, living alone, to let down the side little by little and end up eating her suppers over the kitchen sink. Edith prefers to have her table set, at a regular hour (eight o'clock), with her pistol-handled knives, her three-pronged forks and her coin-silver spoons, with a Directoire place-plate, a hand-edged damask napkin in a silver ring, a glass of good wine in a Tiffany goblet, and lighted candles on the table and in the wall sconces. It is what Edith chooses, and Nellie has been well trained to observe her choice. Edith's finger bowl arrives at the proper moment on a plate, with the dessert spoon and fork on either side. She separates the spoon and the fork, sets them beside her plate with a little click, and removes the finger bowl with its doily, placing it, as she was taught by her old French governess to do, at "eleven o'clock," never using it, merely checking to see that it contains a floating petal. She enjoys thinking that someone like Mrs. Grundy is watching her every move, and that if she should die while she is at dinner someone will say, "She died using perfect table manners."

And so, this evening at dessert time, just as Edith is setting aside the finger bowl, she is considerably annoyed to have her routine interrupted by Nellie, who suddenly runs in from the kitchen to cry out the news that Edith is wanted on the telephone, Long Distance from New York. "Who is it?" Edith asks, but of course Nellie has no idea. (Nellie sometimes speaks of "the island of the United States.") Edith hesitates, familiar with the way Long Distance calls at this hour of night have of bringing unpleasant tidings. Then, somewhat reluctantly, she goes out into the hall to the telephone.

Through the forest-fire cracklings of the long-distance wire, the operator is demanding to know if Edith Blakewell is Edith

Blakewell. "Yes, yes," she says, and then she hears a sharp voice on the other end of the line say "Edith? It's Harold."

"Hello, Harold."

"I hear Leona's with you. You'll never give up on her, will you?"

"What do you mean by that?"

"Why don't you junk her? She's a lost cause."

"I'm certainly not going to junk her, as you so charmingly put it. She is *not* a lost cause."

"Listen," he says, "Diana called last week from Paris, said she'd had some sort of letter from Leona, full of drivel, and asked me what I thought she should do about it. I told her to tell Leona to go to hell. Diana said frankly after this last divorce she doesn't give a rat's ass what Leona does."

"Somehow," Edith says carefully, "that doesn't sound like my daughter Diana talking. It sounds more like Harold Harper."

Now there is a very characteristic Harold pause at the other end of the line, a pause Edith has learned over the years to answer with a matching pause of her own. It was a pause he used, even as a little boy, to make you think that, while he said nothing, his mind was running up a considerable score against you, and that while he sat frowning lips pursed, you were really not his twelve-years-older sister, but his much-younger, much more foolish one. And yet, she remembers, if you went on talking to him while he sat like this, he would let you continue until you had said too much, or committed yourself too deeply. To plague him, now, Edith jiggles the bar of the telephone up and down, and says, "Operator? I've been disconnected. Operator?"

"I'm still *here*. Listen, the reason I called was to tell you not to talk to any reporters who come snooping around asking questions about me. You can pass those instructions on to your friend Leona too."

She could lie to him about Mr. Winslow's visit. But Harold would probably find out about it anyway, sooner or later. So she says, "I see." And then, "Harold, what's going on? What are you up to?"

"Is that any of your damned business?"

"No," she says. "I merely asked."

"But from that very transparent question I gather that you've *already* talked to someone. Christ! What a stupid woman you are, Edith."

She says nothing.

"Spill it," he says. "Who did you talk to? What did you say?"

"A man came," she says wearily. "We talked about the old days. About Papa."

"What did you tell him about the old man?"

"I showed him the Sargent. I told him the tennis story."

"Christ! How do you think that will look in print? Did he ask you anything about me?"

"Yes, and I told him I didn't know anything about anything."

"Well, *that* was the truth, wasn't it! What else?"

"Harold—what's wrong? Please tell me what it is."

"Shut up, nothing's wrong. But you know—or at least I thought you knew—that it was the old man's policy never to talk to the press. Now listen here, Edith. If this guy comes around to you again—or if anybody else comes around—you are not to see anybody. Do you understand that? Just stick to your charity work, and I'll take care of things here, and everything will be all right." There is another pause, and she hears him laughing softly. "After all, sister mine, I should think that *you,* of all people, would be aware of the—ah—unfortunate effects of personal publicity. Am I right, sister mine?"

Edith hangs up the receiver. She stands there by the telephone, momentarily without a sense of direction. She cannot remember where she was before the telephone call, or where she is headed next. All she knows is that, quite obviously, she has made another mistake. Then she remembers dinner, and returns to the dining room.

An interruption such as this deflects Nellie from her routine also. Like everyone else, servants function best when they can follow patterns. Nellie has served Edith's dessert, a *mousse au chocolat,* but in Edith's absence from the table it has become unjellified. But Edith has no appetite for the dessert now anyway. She rings for Nellie. "You may clear," she says. In the distance, the telephone rings again. "Don't answer that, Nellie," she says. "Let it ring."

"Are you really a countess?"

Leona laughs. He has brought her another drink from the bar and, in his blunt, abrupt way, this man is beginning to amuse her. Though heavily built and stubby-fingered, he is not bad-looking. It is a face that seems to have many little muscles working in it, and he has an odd way of wrinkling his nose when he asks a question. "Nearly everybody who marries a Spaniard is a countess these days," she says. "Just plain *señoras* are hard to find. Yes, my ex-husband is a count—or so he says."

"I guess Europe is full of phony counts."

"You're terribly right." She sips her ice-cold cocktail. It is not a bad antidote, a cocktail, to despair and confusion; not the best antidote, perhaps, but not the worst either.

"So you and I have a lot in common, Countess."

She smiles at him. "How is that? What makes you think so?"

"We've both, as the saying goes, shaken our spouses."

"Oh," she says. "Well, yes."

"Have you been divorced from the Count long?"

"Four months." She can play this game as well as he. "And you?"

"Two years," he says. "It was one of those things. She was a mercenary bitch. She really socked me for alimony, too. Do you know how much it costs to keep her in the style to which I got her accustomed? A thousand dollars a week. She said 'I'll never get married again just so you'll be paying me this for the rest of your life.'"

"Well! Were there children?"

"No kids. Too busy for kids. I was making money in the oil business, and I was afraid kids would tie me down. Sometimes I wish I had had kids, though. You have kids?"

She shakes her head.

"Never wanted any?"

"I'm not sure," she says. "I think I did."

"What do you mean you *think* you did?"

She runs a finger around the rim of her glass, hesitating. They seem to have gotten on awfully intimate terms in a very short space of time. "Well, it was Gordon, my second husband, who wanted children more than anybody," she says. "And it was when I was married to him that I came closest to considering it seriously. But—I guess I was scared. I'd been divorced already you see, once—and perhaps I was afraid it would happen again. And it did. And that's an honest answer, Mr. Purdy."

"Say, you've been divorced and *divorced,* haven't you?"

She holds up three fingers.

"No kidding? Not bad for a little girl."

"It's funny. As a child, I was never accident-prone." She smiles at him briefly over her glass. "It's not much of a solution. Marriage."

He aims his finger at her, an imaginary gun. "You're right," he says. "You never wanted kids with the first guy?"

"Oh, Jimmy was—we were both so young. That's a familiar excuse, I know, but it's true. Jimmy was just a nice, screwy kid from Princeton, and we ran off together. He came up to me at a dance, and cut in on the boy I was with, and said, 'I've been watching you. I'm going to run away with you tonight and marry you.' 'Oh, *are* you?' I said. 'What confidence!' And we had a drink at the bar, and twelve hours later we were man and wife."

"Just like that."

"Just like that . . . and for weeks we ran all over the United States in his little car. We had this crazy idea that we were being followed, that the police were after us, or our families, or the FBI, and that there was a nation-wide search for us, and that if they ever caught us, we might be arrested because we were under age. We went from motel to motel, using false names—it was mad. But the awful thing was that we found out later than nobody was looking for us at all. Nobody cared where we were except a few newspaper reporters."

He nods.

"Still, there was an almost-baby of Jimmy's and mine once—not much of a one, but a little almost-baby, in a hospital—who never—"

"Miscarriage?"

She nods, blinks, and takes another swallow of her drink. "Nobody knows this, not even Jimmy. It was after the divorce. Why am I telling all this to you?"

"Maybe," he says smiling, "because I'm such an honest, decent fellow."

"Maybe."

"Did you ever take alimony from any of your husbands?"

"No. I never wanted anything from them."

"Well, in my book, for that you deserve the Nobel Prize."

"Thanks."

"Did you ever love any of them?"

"Hey, no fair!" she says. "Did you love your wife?"

"Sorry," he says. "It was a no-fair question."

They are silent for a moment as the noise of the cocktail party rises around them.

"Pearls on sunburned skin," he says. "I love the way pearls look on a woman's sunburned skin."

She touches the pearls.

"You have wonderful eyes."

Her smile is noncommittal. Back in her boarding-school days, this man would have been known as a fast worker.

"Say," he says, "what do you say we duck out of this party and get some dinner? Okay?"

She hesitates. There is, she supposes, no reason why not.

"Let's go to the Club Contant, have a couple more drinks, then dinner."

"Well, all right," she says.

As they cross the terrace together, his hand moves as though to circle her waist but, with a slight movement of her body, she avoids him.

"Where are you staying?" he asks her.

"At my grandmother's. She lives here."

"With your *grandmother?* Doesn't that cramp your style a little?"

"Not really."

Going down the walk to his car, he says, "You know, when I first met you there on the beach with Ed Winslow—I couldn't figure it. You and Winslow. He doesn't seem your type."

"Eddie is—a very dear friend."

"When you shook hands, I didn't think you liked me. But now I think maybe you do like me. I think maybe we can be buddies, don't you?"

"Well," she says, "why not?"

Holding the car door open for her, he says, "Hi, buddy."

Leona slides into the front seat. Smiling at him, she says, "Hi."

Beside her in the dark car he says, "One more question. Were your folks divorced too, by any chance?"

"Why, yes. What made you ask that?"

"Just psychic. Mine were too. Did it make a difference with you?"

"Of course it did."

"At least after the divorce the fighting stopped," he says.

Leona nods. "I was very little when Mother and Daddy got theirs," she says. "That was when they began sending me here, to Granny's—to get a little sunshine, they told me, but I knew better. I was only five or six. I loved those trips on the plane, though, and coming to see Granny. But one day when I was here, my great-grandmother came to call—Granny's mother. She was a terribly funny-looking old woman, all painted up like a doll. She must have been eighty and she had a terrible stammer. She used to scare me to death, the way she talked. I overheard her talking to Granny once, saying 'Edith, you know that Diana'—Diana's my mother—'is just *mooching* on you, parking Leona here all the time. She's turning Leona into a regular little *moocher*. You should not allow it, Edith.' Granny didn't say anything, so I assumed that she agreed, and that that was what I was—a little moocher. I used to go around thinking that I was a little moocher. It was a long time before I knew what a moocher was, but I used to think of it as a funny little hairy animal, with a snout—"

She laughs, but this story seems to make him remote from her. He looks straight ahead for a moment, and then shrugs. "Well, I guess we all have experiences like that when we're kids, buddy," he says. He starts the car.

After Charles Blakewell left to go to the war, Edith's father called one of those little family meetings he called in any crisis. They had assembled—Edith, Harold, Arthur, and her mother and father—in his big study in the old house at Sans Souci. Edith was twenty-nine then, Harold was seventeen, and Arthur was sixteen. But they gathered as they always did—like solemn-faced children to listen to what Meredith Harper had to say. "Now that Edith's husband has departed," he began. Edith remembers looking around the room at the others. Harold was smoking a French cigarette, and he gave her a sly look out of the corner of his eye, then raised his pale eyes heavenward. Sad-looking Arthur gazed at the toes of his shoes. Edith's mother twisted the rings on her fingers.

"Now that Edith's husband has departed, and she is alone with her small child, I shall expect you boys to be of whatever assistance you can to your sister," he said. "Though she is older, she is a woman."

The boys nodded.

"We have heard that there have been some unpleasant stories circulating about your sister," he said. "I shall not mention them again. During the time Mr. Blakewell is—absent—I suspect the gossips will find increased opportunities to exercise their malicious tongues. I expect all of you to do absolutely nothing about this—neither to repeat the stories to anyone else nor to deny them if you hear them. In other words, ignore them. People like ourselves, who enjoy a position of respect and power in a community, are the natural targets of rumor. We are objects of envy, and envy breeds malice. We cannot allow ourselves to suffer from this fact. We cannot even allow ourselves to care about it. We must conduct ourselves in such a way that no one can accuse us of caring. This way, rumors about us will collapse of their own weight. We are above rumor. It doesn't exist for us. Do you understand?"

The others nodded again. Edith sat very still and closed her eyes.

"Edith," he said, "you are independent now. You might take a little trip. There are plenty of places you could go, war or no war. The Morristown house is staffed and furnished. You could go there, or—"

"I want to stay here."

"It seems an odd choice," he said.

"I have my house here."

"I can't force you to go anywhere, of course."

"I'm going to stay here, Papa. Till Charles comes back." Of course she did not expect him to come back. And he had not come back.

Remembering this scene now, which Harold's call has brought to mind, Edith sits at her large desk in her quiet house, searching through the drawers and cubbyholes trying to find her will. It is exasperating and thoroughly incomprehensible how—in a desk where everything, for years, has been so perfectly organized that the things she wanted were always at her fingertips—this one document should have now decided to vanish, and somehow this too seems Harold's fault. She knows exactly what it looks like—a thick, many-paged affair, paper-clipped with a great many little notes and memoranda to herself, and notes attached to other notes with common pins: reminders of the disposition of certain pieces of jewelry, a ring to this one and a necklace to that, and special bequests to certain servants whom she had overlooked when the will was drawn. She has been working on it lately, going over it in careful detail before taking up the small additional matters with her lawyer and having codicils added.

The will is also liberally sprinkled with Harold Harper's name; it appears in paragraph after paragraph, like a small, ugly worm. It is essential that it be there, Mr. Morris, her lawyer, told her; though Harold is not a beneficiary, he is her trustee. Well, Edith has at last decided that his name shall not be there. If she should predecease her brother, which is a possibility, she is not going to have Harold taking charge of Leona the way he has been in charge of Edith all her life—certainly not after his remark this evening that everyone had given up on Leona. No, she will insist upon it: Harold's name must be removed, deleted, expunged.

Now the will unearths itself from under a pile of letters (What was it doing *there?*) and Edith unfolds it carefully and reads:

THE LAST WILL AND TESTAMENT

> Of Edith Bruce Harper Blakewell, resident of the City of Charlotte Amalie, of Saint Thomas, Virgin Islands (Territory of the United States of America) having as a place of business Number One William Street, New York City, New York, c/o Harold Bruce Harper, made and published this twelfth day of August, in the year of Our Lord One Thousand Nine Hundred and Fifty-Seven. In the Name of God, Amen. I, Edith Bruce Harper Blakewell. . . .

The position of Harold's name, between her name and God's, strikes her tonight as sinister. She is tempted, in fact, to take a pen and cross him out here and now. "Just stick to your charity work," she can hear him saying, "and everything will be all right."

But one does not say "everything will be all right" unless

there is a distinct possibility that everything will be all wrong. The house around her, as she considers this, grows even quieter. "Very well, Harold," she says in a soft voice, "what is going on? Your business is my business too, young man."

She refolds the will carefully and places it in its proper spot in her desk. Then she picks up her pen and a sheet of her stationery and quickly writes:

Leona—

If it's not too *late when you come in, will you* please *knock on my door and wake me? I* must *talk to you!*

E.B.H.B.

She folds the note and goes upstairs, and places the note on Leona's pillow where she will be sure to see it.

Three

AT nine o'clock, Nellie brings Edith her glass of hot milk. Edith picks up her book, sipping the milk, and tries to read, but after reading a dozen pages realizes that she has no idea what any of it is about, and puts the book down. She is listening for Leona to come in, and her head is a jumble of thoughts. She is remembering what Alan Osborn said, that being a Harper meant something, and she is thinking of all the things that being a Harper means, and through it all she cannot seem to rid herself of Harold's voice, recalling all the old unpleasantnesses of years ago, all the old stories.

There was Diana's wedding, a winter wedding in 1934, at St. James's in New York. It was supposed to be the wedding of the year, or so someone said. They came out of the church into Madison Avenue, and the street was crowded with people, and there were newspaper photographers with exploding flashbulbs. Diana was smiling. Edith looked blank at the cameras. Then she smiled. A woman broke through the police cordon and spat at Diana. Diana went on smiling. That evening the headlines said BRIDE AT $100,000 WEDDING LAUGHS AT HARD TIMES, and the story continued:

> "Let them eat cake—wedding cake," seemed to be the motto of beautiful Diana Harper Blakewell at her marriage today to society playboy John Hamilton ("Jack") Ware. While hundreds of guests waited to greet the happy couple in a glittering receiving line, hundreds of thousands of Americans across the country waited in bread lines. The bride, a granddaughter of the late Meredith D. Harper, West Indian sugar baron, is the daughter of Mrs. Charles M. Blakewell and the late Mr. Blakewell. The groom is the son of Mr. and Mrs. Lucius G. Ware of New York, Fairfield, and Palm Beach. The bride's mother, who has maintained homes in Morristown, N.J., and Paris, currently resides in St. Thomas, V.I.
>
> For the reception, reliably reported to have cost in the neighborhood of $100,000, the Morristown Club was transformed into a replica of the Petit Trianon. The only thing that could have dampened the poor little rich girl's spirits today was the fact that the sun did not shine. Wedding guests included. . . .

No, Edith remembers, the sun did not shine; it snowed buckets.

There are many snowy scenes, some happy, some not. She remembers best the snows of Staten Island, where she was born, and where she spent the first eight years of her life. She remembers the sundial in the yard outside her window, and watching it rise, like a cake, in a fresh snowfall. Meredith Harper was in the wholesale hardware business in Staten Island before he made his money in these more prosperous islands. In her bedroom Edith Blakewell keeps a picture (only a reproduction, not the original) called *Tracks in Winter*, by Francis Speight. It is not a pretty picture, but Edith is fond of it. It shows railroad tracks running parallel, and footprints in the snow that have shuffled across the tracks toward a gaunt looking house. A great deal of ugly smoke rises from a pair of smokestacks on the horizon. No people are in the picture. Though there is no resemblance, when she looks into it Edith can see

Tottenville when she was a girl, before everything that there is now came to be. Leona thinks little of the picture. "It looks like bad nineteen-thirties realism," she said. "It's dull and old hat, Granny."

Leona seems to prefer the moderns, the spatter people. Edith told her that this was a famous painting and that the original hangs in an excellent New York collection, but Leona was unimpressed.

"It's Depression art," she said to Edith. "And what in the world do *you* know about the Depression, Granny? You came sailing through."

"Sailing. But with my jib backed to windward." But it was not the Depression Edith was talking about. Pointing to the picture again, she said, "Your background, Leona."

"Then you should be proud that great-grandfather Harper made enough to take us away from that sort of place."

"It was sheer luck. Seventy years ago my father accepted a handful of leases on a couple of unknown Danish islands in settlement of a debt. He had no idea the leases were for cane fields and rum distilleries."

("Darling Edith!" she remembers her mother saying to her one snowy morning, coming into her room and lifting her out of her sheets and hugging her. "Your Papa has become rich! *Rich!*")

"But Granny, he had factories all over the place."

"Eventually, yes. It's easy to buy up factories once you've cornered the West Indian rum market."

("My husband got his *start* in spirits," Dolly Harper would explain carefully, years later. "But his real interests were in bringing certain industrial techniques, which he had studied in Europe, to the United States." There was always, to Edith's mother, something undignified about the liquor business.)

"You always rather run him down, don't you?" Leona said. "I should think you'd be kind of grateful for all his money."

"Grateful?" Edith cried, despairing. "Why? Are *you?*"

Being a Harper was what Meredith Harper made of it. "I want you to be a princess!" he would say to her, and he would lift her by her armpits high into the air. She was still a little girl, and he was becoming an industrialist. She was his princess, and he was her king. "Touch the ceiling!" he would say. "Reach way, way up—try to touch it. Remember that to be a princess you must always be trying to touch the ceiling. If you can touch it, then the ceiling's too low, and you must order them to build you a taller castle with higher rooms." And, when he had built this house for Edith and her husband and had taken them to see it on the afternoon of their wedding day and handed them the key, he had said, "I had the ceilings built high. Are they high enough, Edith?" smiling at her over their old joke, his eyes shining with tears.

People often ask her for impressions of her father. "How would you sum him up—in a word?" someone will say. There are so many words, some delicate and pretty, some stained and embarrassing. "Majestic," she often says. "He liked kings." But another thing about him was that he wept well. His ability to cry at will must certainly have been a business asset, for tears created an instant illusion of honesty about him. Edith remembers one old friend, one of the few who had known him as a youth, describing the weeping phenomenon. "He used to deliver ice, you know, in the neighborhood before he bought the hardware business," this woman said. "He brought it to our house three times a week, on a cart behind his bicycle. He must have been sixteen or so, and very handsome—those enormous black eyes—and terribly polite, and he worked so hard. He was so ambitious, and he was such a gentleman—we knew he'd go far, even then. But I remember one afternoon when he came to collect for the ice, and I was short of money and asked him if he could possibly wait until next week. He said yes, of course, but those great black eyes looked so sad—I thought he was going to cry. So I rushed right into the house and got the money for him—and even tipped him a little extra."

Everyone speaks of those manners. "Your father was so polite," Edith's mother once said to her. "When he asked me to marry him, my parents were against it, of course. But your father was so insistent, and begged me in the sweetest way—I didn't have the heart to turn him down." (A few years later, however, Edith was to hear a somewhat different version of his proposal scene.)

He never mentioned parents. They were a closed subject. Where did the manners come from? Biographies of him have always given his place of birth as New York City, and perhaps, after all, he was born there. But Edith has long suspected that he was Canadian, and may have entered the United States illegally. Once, during one of their quarrels, she heard her mother say to him, "Why don't you go back to *Canada*, where you came from!" And she remembers the terrible look her father gave her. She thought he was going to strike her mother. Later, after he died, they would sometimes discuss him. "Where do you suppose he came from, really?" someone would ask. "He just materialized," someone would say—materialized, with his handsome face, his manners, and a sense of his destiny, Edith supposes.

At nine or ten Edith would spend whole afternoons in front of her mirror, mourning over her brownish-blondish no-color hair, wondering why it grew all different lengths and wouldn't curl. She made up her mind that she was ugly, and decided that only some tragedy would make her memorable. If only half of her face should become hideously scarred—then she would have to wear a black veil over the ravaged half, and no one would mind that the half that showed was plain. This was in the days when her father was building all the houses—the house at Sans Souci, and the house in Paris, and the one in Morristown. The schedule was devised; they would divide their year between the three places. (And contrary to what that newspaper said, Edith never maintained houses anywhere but in St. Thomas; she only lived in them. Nor did Diana's Depression wedding cost more than a quarter of the $100,000 figure "reliably reported.") Wherever they went there was a smell of wet plaster and paint, of sawdust and new wood. Edith would decorate her ears with the curled shavings from the carpenters' planes—a princess with pine ringlets.

At Sans Souci, the room behind his study was Meredith Harper's office, and Edith and her father used to meet there to go over her accounts. For her twelfth birthday she had been given a bank account. Regular deposits went into it, and she was authorized to draw checks. Her father lectured her about the importance of managing money, about interest rates, and how to keep a checkbook balanced. Nothing mattered more, he said, than understanding money. There was an element of secrecy about their meetings because her mother was not supposed to know about the checking account. Dolly Harper had no such luxuries. "She wouldn't know how to handle it if she had one," her father said—not having been trained in the intricacies of finance at an early age.

Edith would tap on the door and be admitted to the office, and would sit there quietly while he opened his large ledgers and went over the bookkeeping entries of the week. He would explain how many tons of sugar had been harvested, how many had been sold, how many barrels of rum had left the distillery, and what the shipping and labor costs had been. He explained the intricacies of the Danish export tax on sugar and the various import duties of northern ports. Then he would show her comparative balances for other sugar harvests of other years. "I see no reason why a woman shouldn't be able to run the sugar business," he said. "The only thing you need to be is hard—hard and strong, and never listen to the complaints the natives make. Is it impossible that a woman should run this business someday?" he said looking at her intently. "Why shouldn't it be possible?"

Then he would turn to her bank statement, matching the canceled checks with the stubs—but this was awkward because there were almost never any canceled checks. He would stare, perplexed, at the unfolded statement, poring over the nonexistent entries, and then say, "Well, you've certainly been a thrifty princess. I suppose that's good."

She wanted him to love her, and she wanted him to pity her. She spent no money because she wanted him to know how little in the world there was that interested her beyond this. Oh, she had wanted to buy a cow. She had wanted a cow more than anything, but she was sure that if she told him about the cow he would laugh at her, and so she never told him, and never had a cow.

"No trinkets that have caught your eye in the shops?"

She shook her head.

"Well, perhaps when we get to Paris. . . ."

Once, during one of their meetings, a native houseboy came in with a letter for her father. He was a new boy in the house, which meant that he had just been elevated from work in the yard. The boys all liked housework, her father said, because the work was clean, there was less to do, there were more opportunities to steal, and there were more corners for them to fall asleep in unobserved. The boy's gray jacket, Edith remembers, was a fusillade of proud brass buttons, and his black face gleamed with the importance of delivering a messsage to Meredith Harper. Her father clapped his hands over the open set of company books—though surely this boy was no different from any of the others and could not read or write.

"How many times have you been told to knock before coming in here?" her father demanded. The boy gaped. "Now go out and try it again." The boy tiptoed out, and closed the door behind him. Then he knocked.

"Come in."

The boy opened the door again.

"That was better," her father said. "Now take off that uniform and report back to the yard." You paid them the equivalent of three dollars a month in St. Thomas in those days, and you expected strict obedience. The greatest danger with native servants was that they would become too familiar. "They'll learn," her father said.

He returned to the problem of her bank statement. "Well—" he said, and Edith is certain now that he did not pity her for having nothing she wanted to spend her money on. Probably he only thought her dull. Finally he folded the statement, put it in the strongbox with the others, and locked the box. The safe was in a closet. He put the locked strongbox in the safe, then locked the safe, then locked the closet.

He would give her a sad little smile, "Well, run along now, princess," he would say. "See what your mother's up to."

The house at Sans Souci was large and sprawling, and what her mother was usually up to was cleaning it. Edith remembers her hands—thin and long-fingered and strong, forever reaching out, straightening and tugging at things, at each bedspread and dresser scarf, each sofa cushion and table runner. It was the era of the Turkish corner and the era of cut glass and the era of tiny pillows gritty with beads, and her mother's hands would fuss at, and pat, and plump up, and rearrange the multitude of beaded and embroidered and tasseled cushions of the Turkish corner. Her hands would pat and tug at Edith too, when she appeared—at hairbows, skirts, shirtwaists, hair. She had a habit of referring to Edith as a thing: "You're an untidy thing." "You're a spoiled thing." "You're a dirty thing—run and wash."

Cleanliness obsessed her. She followed her servants around the house, repeating their work after them. Her silver gleamed because much of it was polished twice a day—once by the girls, once by her. One day Meredith Harper found his wife down on her hands and knees, waxing the ballroom floor. "Dolly!" Edith's father shouted. "Get up off your knees! I won't have my wife on her knees."

Though Dolly Harper may have understood the value of anonymity, she was rocketed into a kind of celebrity when she became a rich man's wife. Still, she took comfort in the fact that she was a Bruce from Boston—an old New England family. "Remember," she once said to Edith, "that for all the talk of Meredith Harper and his money, you are also a Bruce. The name Bruce is more important than the name Harper, which is why you are called Edith Bruce. When I married your father, I was considered to have married beneath me," she said. "They were afraid he couldn't provide." She had trouble sleeping and, when she did sleep, she often had nightmares. Late at night, she would slip into Edith's room and Edith would wake to find her mother lying across her with her arms around her, holding Edith so tightly that she could feel the thin bands of muscle in her long arms. They would lie like that for what seemed hours, like two spoons nested in a drawer. "What did you dream about, Mama?" Edith would ask her. The dream was always the same. "I dreamt that your Papa went away and left us all alone," she would say.

And Edith remembers one night in the Morristown house when she was twelve. The air was chilly, but the house was new, and all her bedroom windows were opened wide to carry out the paint smell. Her head ached and she couldn't sleep, and downstairs in the drawing room she could hear her mother and father quarreling. She got out of bed and went down the hall to the top of the stairs.

Her mother was sitting in one of the French chairs with a copy of the *Delineator* spread open in her lap. "There's absolutely nothing here that I like," she said, and snapped the book closed.

Meredith Harper walked across the room to her. "How can you sit and look at dresses when we're discussing a thing like this?" he said.

"Meredith, please," she said in a tired voice. "I've said all I can."

He stood over her, staring down at her. It was the year Sargent painted him. Tall, straight, in his black velvet smoking jacket with braided cuffs, his eyes glittered. "You still refuse? Very well," he said.

"Please," she said again, her hand across her eyes. "I can't."

"It's not that you can't, is it? It's that you won't. But very well."

"I can't take the risk."

"I take risks every day, to give you the things you've got. But very well, Dolly. Very well."

"Stop saying 'very well,'" she said. "Can't you understand? It nearly killed me having Edith, you know that. Doctor Mallory said that I mustn't have another—ever."

"You listen to what some country doctor said years ago? When now you can afford to have the best medical attention in the country? But *very well,* Dolly. The subject is closed."

She reached up and touched his hand. "Forgive me," she said. "He made me promise him."

He smiled at her then. "And what about your promises to me when we were married, Dolly?"

Her hand withdrew. "You haven't exactly suffered in the meantime, have you, Meredith?" she said.

The room was very still for a moment. Then he said, "You're quite right, Dolly. I haven't suffered."

"Have I ever criticized you for that? Haven't I tried to understand—even when there were things that seemed to me impossible to understand?"

He turned away from her, walked across the room, and sat down in a chair, crossing his legs. "Why don't you look through some other magazines, Dolly? You might find a dress that would amuse you."

"Why do you want this so much?"

"I want a son."

"We have our family! We have Edith!"

"I need a son. What good is Edith? What good is a fool daughter ever going to be to me? I need a son. Or two sons. Or three."

"*Why?* So you can found a dynasty?"

"I need sons to carry on."

"And you'd risk my life to get them!"

"No," he said carefully. "I wouldn't. There is another solution, Dolly, to this problem. I could find, my dear—rather easily—another wife."

She stood up and went to the small commode where the sherry decanter stood on a footed tray. She lifted the decanter, her hand trembling very lightly, and filled a glass. Then she stood holding the glass in front of her with both hands like a small chalice, shoulders hunched, head bent over the glass, taking little sips. She said something then that Edith could not hear, and apparently her father had not heard it either, for she heard him say sharply, "What?"

"A threat," she said. "Isn't it?" She sipped her wine.

"Not really. I'm just being honest with you, Dolly."

She laughed, but there was an edge of fear in the laugh. "You mean a divorce? How could you? What would people say? Your position. Your reputation. Your precious name. Your pride. The scandal."

"But Dolly, it would be your scandal—not mine. It's you who've made our marriage what it is."

"Wait," she said. "Have you forgotten? We agreed long ago—"

"No, it would be your own private little scandal, Dolly." And he smiled. "I'd have to see to that. And will."

Reaching for the decanter she filled her glass again. Then she filled another glass. "Come, let's have some wine and talk. Forgive me, my nerves are bad. Do you remember, in the old days, years ago—"

He stood up. "The subject is closed."

"We used to say never let the sun set on a quarrel. Remember?" With a laugh that was almost gay, she stepped toward him. "I've been in an irritable mood, this is all my fault. Come, we'll drink to—"

"I don't care for any wine, Dolly."

The glasses shook in her hands, and wine spilled across her fingers. She set the glasses down. "Meredith—" she whispered.

"I'm going to my room. Excuse me."

She blocked his path. "Meredith, listed—you know how much I love you. It never had anything to do with not loving you. It was what Mallory said—"

"Please get out of my way."

She cocked her head coyly on one side, facing him. "Meredi-i-th!" she said. "Ah, don't you look so cross!" She reached up and touched his mouth. "Do I taste like wine? Darling, listen—"

"Stop this, Dolly."

"Listen—perhaps with a *good* doctor—perhaps you're right. Come sit with me for just a minute."

"No."

Her arms went around his middle. "I love you so. Oh, remember . . . remember." He tried to pull away but she held him. "Wait," she said. "The big copper beech tree in that field outside Malden, when we—"

"Let . . . me . . . go . . . please." Carefully, he disengaged her hands from about his waist.

She sank to the floor at his feet and seized his legs. "Don't you know I'd do anything for you?" she said. "Papa? You're my precious Papa. I'll try—I'm saying that I'll try. Oh love . . . let me try."

"How naked you make yourself, Dolly."

"Wait," she moaned. Her hands curled around his thighs and her cheek was pressed against his dark trouser leg. "Please—no more cruel things. Wait. I'll try!" He was moving across the floor, pulling her with him.

"Go back to your magazines," Edith heard him say.

Her voice rose to a scream as his feet moved to untangle themselves from the weight of her. "Meredith—wait! Dear God, I love you so—let me try! I'll try so hard! Love—can't you let me try?"

Edith turned and ran back down the hall to her room and buried her face in the satin comforter to drown her mother's screams. She lay shivering, not crying, and even today, the smell of fresh paint makes her think of her mother screaming. Then Edith believes she did cry herself—but rather abstractedly, as only a twelve-year-old can cry, for nothing in particular as well as for everything, for the things she had understood and for the things she had not, for a part of himself that one of the colored boys in the yard had showed her, for the whole race of adults.

Later she realized that the house was quiet, though she had not heard either of them come up. She got up and went to the top of the stairs once more, and when she looked, they were dancing—dancing! They moved slowly and silently about the floor, between tables and chairs and lamps and pieces of bronze statuary (shiny and new, all the new things of that new house) in each other's arms. There was no music, but they danced as though they heard music, and now each of them held a wine glass in one hand, and her mother was smiling. Periodically they paused and took sips. Once her mother put her head back and laughed—an unfamiliar, throaty laugh. "I need more wine!" she said, holding out her glass.

Her father stepped to the commode, filled her glass, and they returned to their dance. Her mother's arms went up, around his neck, and she bent backward, and they curved together, making one silhouette. An expression of absolute absorption was on Dolly Harper's face.

When Edith woke the next morning, she found an explosion of bright blood in her bed, and her first thought was that someone had come into her room in the night and stabbed her in her sleep.

Some fourteen years later, before Diana was born, she suddenly remembered that night in Morristown again. Her pains had begun, and Charles was with her, and she gripped his hand in her own. "I'm frightened, Charles," she said. "What if it should kill me? What if I should die?"

"You won't die, Edie. It will be all right, Edie," he said. "It will take more than having a baby to kill you, Edie."

She had thought it an odd remark for him to make, and she had looked at him. But his eyes were merry, and she knew he had not intended it to hurt her but to cheer her. "Are you sure?" she asked.

"Quite sure," he said. "Remember you're a fighter, and be brave."

And, of course, it was all right.

Sometimes Edith has imaginary conversations with Diana. It is not true, as Leona—who does not get on with her mother—once said, that Diana has icewater in her veins. It is certainly not true in the conversations Edith has with her. She lets Diana talk to her.

"What is wrong, Mother" [Diana says] "with having a daughter who looks well in clothes? What is wrong with that? I am proud of my figure, my hips are good, and my legs are slim and long and do not possess a single vein. I know what my good points are, but I'm not as vain as many women because I also know my bad. I have never been a beauty. I have been called striking, because I happen to be tall, and because I have nice hair (oh, yes, I dye it now; I'm forty-nine years old, nearly fifty; what is wrong if I dye my hair?)—and striking because I work rather hard at it because I know that striking is about all I can look. I spend money on my clothes, yes. But then I *have* money. And I don't spend as much as many women do. Take the Duchess of Windsor. Does she actually buy her clothes, or do the couturiers give them to her free? I happen to know that the Duchess of Windsor *pays* for her clothes and, to say the least, she spends more than I. I make a good dress do for years. Take my oatmeal suit.... Why do you look at me like that? You're giving me your policewoman look again; you look exactly like a matron in a girls' reformatory, or one of those stiff little *gendarmes* that stand outside the Meurice, glaring at every automobile that comes along the Rue de Rivoli. What is wrong?

"What is wrong with saying that I get bored with the Meurice? It can be a very boring place, and when it is I want to get out of it, and do. Traveling is a hobby of mine, and one should not let oneself get bored with one's hobbies. Palm Beach can be boring. Rome is the most boring city in the world. There are boring places and there are boring people and there are boring horses and boring cars and boring houses and boring hotels. I know you are angry with me for divorcing Jack, but he was a bore. I know you liked him, Mother—I liked him too. He had many endearing qualities and still has. I wish him well, I wish him luck. I wish him a beautiful woman in his bed at night, but I am forty-nine years old, nearly fifty, and one doesn't have forever. And Mother, even you must admit he was an awful doormat. You could walk all over him and he didn't mind. And he'd believe everything you told him. No woman wants a man who believes everything she says. You could tell him that a large flock of Himalayan goats had just flown, in perfect formation, over the Everglades Club, bombarding the lawn with their droppings as they went, and he'd say, 'Gee whiz. No kidding?' I really think that if Leona sometimes displays a certain lack of brains it's Jack Ware's genes that did it. You know Leona never did well in schools. *I* always did well in schools. Not that I'm an intellectual, but I'm smart, I'm clever, I talk well, I think well, and I look well, considering my age—forty-nine, nearly fifty. I don't show my age. I have passed the climacteric, and no one ever knew I was going through it. I have never consulted a psychiatrist, nor an astrologist, nor a faith healer, nor a spiritualist to try to talk to Daddy. I think I have been very good about Daddy, considering—considering I can't remember him, never knew him except as a photograph, never missed him, since one can't miss a photograph. I think I am a realist. I think I know what life is about, and that is why I married Perry because Perry knows what life is about—what *my* life is about anyway, and what his life is about. I never slept with Perry while I was married to Jack, though many people are convinced I did. In fact, I never slept with anybody while I was married to Jack. Perry is very good to me, Mother, and he lets me sleep late in the mornings, which I just adore—not being bounced out of bed at dawn by some hairy-chested type and made to go sit in a damn duck blind, or to watch the field-dog trials, or to park my fanny on a shooting stick while a bunch of men shoot grouse. I don't cheat at cards. I don't beat my horses, I don't get drunk, my dogs love me, why don't you? What is wrong if I like good clothes? Would it help matters if I wore smocks, and went around looking like a bindle stiff, and let my figure go, and my hair get gray? Mother, why do you look at me that way—like a mother superior, like the president of the P.T.A., like a lady dogcatcher, like the chairwoman of the League of Decency, like Queen Victoria, like a goddamn lady Emperor Augustus? I'm forty-nine years old! Mother—Mother, what is *wrong?*"

Since these conversations are imaginary, Edith is not required to answer any of Diana's questions.

Four

THE years after Edith's brothers were born (Harold in 1901 and Arthur some fourteen months later) were an uneasy period on the island. There were labor troubles—uprisings in the canefields, fires, shootings, and robberies in the distilleries. The planters exacted stern reprisals and, in turn, the natives had their own methods of revenge; a planter, Edith remembers, was kidnaped and found, three days later, his body dismembered by machetes, on the rocks below William Head. As a result, Meredith Harper's children were carefully watched and guarded within the gates of Sans Souci. Meanwhile, life for the island's rich continued in its pose: dignified, mannered, and elegant and splendid, a pose borrowed from the great capitals of Europe. At night, doors and window-shutters were closed and barred against what crept outside and, at a formal ball, the barking of a dog sent tail-coated gentlemen rushing into the garden with drawn pistols while, inside the great candlelit and mirrored rooms, the women cowered in a knot, whispering of *la ceinture de mystère* which circled them in the dark hill villages. These were the years when Dolly Harper worked hardest to establish herself with the Danish colonial society of St. Thomas. But island society had crystallized itself at least a century before her arrival and, though they accepted her invitations, few of the older planters' wives ever asked her back. ("Danish women have no manners," she would say. "Or else they *choose* to hurt me. Which is it?")

Edith devised her own lonely games—"Going to Siam," with the terrace, and its row of four enormous urns full of hibiscus and geraniums as Siam, and driving about in her own little donkey cart with a blue-and-white-striped parasol on top and Cyrus, the young native boy assigned to be her bodyguard, at the reins. She was fond of Cyrus; they were in league. Sometimes, he would take her outside the gate in the cart, and into the streets of Charlotte Amalie. And sometimes, pretending to doze, he would let her escape from his watch, and she would walk.

More often she would run—run across the dry brown grass at the road's edge, through a gap in the oleander hedge, and up into the hills covered with weeds and black rocks, where grasshoppers flew like bits of scattered gravel in her path, and tiny gray chameleons spurted across the stones; run until she reached the highest places where the rocks were sharp and loose, and where she would stop for breath. Though all this land was still, technically, a part of Sans Souci, and she had not really left home at all, it always seemed to her remoter than the moon. Below she could see the dust-red threads of roads winding through angular valleys between the motionless heads of palm trees and clumps of wilted vegetation and, beyond that, the still-blue sea. But there was always a burning wind in the hills, and the sky would be brilliant, and, looking up at it, the sun seemed particularly large and close and intensely personal, as though it were aimed just at Edith Harper and not shining over half the world as well. Once, coming over the brow of a steep ridge, she had been startled to see her mother and her father standing below her, hardly fifty feet away. What they were doing there on this forsaken hill, so far from the house, she couldn't imagine, and she quickly knelt behind a flat rock to hide; for a moment she was certain they were looking for her.

"I followed you!" she heard her mother's shrill voice say.

"This is where you meet her, isn't it! Just tell me who she is."

"You're ill, Dolly. Get back to the house."

"Just tell me this—is she a white woman or a black!"

Edith saw her father raise his walking stick in a threatening gesture. Her mother screamed, turned, and stumbled back down the hill, her skirts blowing in the wind. Edith's father stood there very stiffly.

All at once Edith jumped up and went running down to him.

"What are you doing here?" he demanded.

Looking up at him she said, "Papa? Do you love Mama?"

"What are you talking about?"

She was crying now. "Papa!" she said, trying to cling to his sleeve as she had seen her mother do, "Papa, please—tell me that you love Mama! Papa—please? Please——" He jerked his arm roughly away and stepped back.

He turned on his heel and started away.

Remembering it now as she lies in her bed with her book, unread, spread open on her knees, Edith thinks that it is an altogether strange way for a girl of fourteen to behave, and she has no idea what came over her. And yet she remembers it so clearly: him walking, almost running, away from her, taking huge, stiff-legged strides across that brown hillside, his stick flashing, and herself pursuing him, sobbing and repeating that already-answered question: "Papa, please! Tell me that you love Mama!"

Her daughter Diana, Edith sometimes thinks, has inherited some of her grandfather's formidable traits. They have skipped a generation, as those things sometimes do, and have landed, in somewhat diluted form, on Diana. It is not that one's children disappoint one. It is just that they startle one. Suddenly, there they are, completed beings.

Diana keeps a large apartment in New York, which she shares with her present husband, and she has the Palm Beach place which she designed (she says) on the back of a paper cocktail napkin. The architect took that paper napkin and built Meadowcroft as it stands today. To open the house, she planned to throw a large party but, on the afternoon of the party, there was still no grass on the lawn. Diana got on the telephone and, by five o'clock, the lawn was so perfectly sodded that not a seam showed.

As her grandfather had, Diana has a high-handed, aristocratic manner. High-handed, that is, but not tightfisted. (And Leona is wrong, Edith thinks, when she calls her mother a snob.) There was the time, for instance, when Edith was visiting Diana in Palm Beach while the pool house at Meadowcroft was being built. Though it upset Diana to see the workmen sitting around the pool at lunchtime, eating their sandwiches from their lunchboxes ("Wouldn't you think they could go somewhere else to feed?" she kept repeating), she nonetheless gave each of those workmen an expensive wrist watch when the job was finished.

But perhaps the greatest trouble with Diana, for Edith, is that Diana has always been so difficult to pin down. Again, this is like Papa. "Mother's on AC and you're on DC, Granny," Leona once said, which was putting it pretty well. Edith remembers the time, after Diana and Jack Ware were first separated, when Diana delivered little Leona to St. Thomas, and Edith had made a last-ditch attempt to talk to Diana and to stave off, if possible, the divorce. Edith had thought that, perhaps, if she could tell Diana a little bit about her own marriage (she was even going to tell Diana about the Frenchman who had caused her such problems years ago) Diana might see that, in a sense, her case was similar. She had gone up to Diana's room where Diana sat in bed, writing letters. Diana's hair was in a net and curlers, her face shined with cold cream, and her chin was in a strap. Seeing her daughter this way, supported by a scaffolding of cosmetics, made her seem to Edith even thinner, paler, and more woundable. She began to talk to her. After a moment, she noticed that Diana had picked up her pen again and was scribbling something on the corner of a sheet of paper. "What are you writing, dear?" she asked her.

"Just a note, Mother, to remind myself to be sure and write the butler in Palm Beach. There are fourteen breakfast trays that *must* be sent back to Milano for relacquering." Then "What were you saying, Mother? About this Frenchman?" And then, *"Mother!* Your're giving me your Emperor Augustus look again! *Now* what have I done?"

But Leona, Edith thinks, is different from all the Harpers. She is a mutation, a creature none of them could possibly have contributed to, who seems to have sprung to life from a kind of fire. She is certainly the most beautiful child in the family.

She is out of Degas, though she hates to have Edith say so. They are so rare, beauties like these. They appear out of nowhere, like soft explosions of stars, and they walk through the world untouched, cheering everyone. Edith closes her eyes. Across her vision the Degas girls dance, and each of them smiles at her with Leona's face.

When she was seventeen Leona ran away from Miss Masters' School where Diana had sent her. She took a train to Grand Central, crossed the street to the airlines building, carrying her coat and her blue airplane suitcase with the white leather binding, went up the escalator and said to the clerk at the counter, "I'd like a one-way ticket to St. Thomas, please."

"When would you like to go?" the clerk said.

"On the earliest plane."

"There's a flight at four o'clock."

"That will be perfect," she said. "The only thing is, I haven't any money. I shall have to fly collect."

"Well, that's very interesting," he said. "I'm afraid you won't be able to fly at all."

"Oh, but I have to," Leona said. "I'm running away."

"That's very interesting too," he said, and he started to reach for the telephone.

"Please," she said, "don't call the police or anything like that. I'm not running away from *home*. I'm running away from a terrible girls' school where the girls all wear white raincoats over their bloomers on the way to gym. My mother is in Florida, but I don't want to go there. I want to go to St. Thomas where my grandmother lives."

"Everything you say is very interesting," the young man said.

"My grandmother is very rich, and she's very well known in St. Thomas. She'll pay for the ticket, I know, as soon as I get there. So, if you'll just put *Collect* on the ticket, it will be paid for at the other end."

"Now look here—" he began.

"Or," she said, "once I'm on my way, you could telephone my grandmother in St. Thomas—collect, of course—and verify everything. And while you have her on the phone you could ask her to meet me at the airport."

"Or," he said, "you could telephone your grandmother yourself—collect—and tell her what your plan is, and ask her to wire you the money. How about that, sweetheart?"

"Oh, but that wouldn't work at all, would it?" she said. "If my grandmother knew what I was doing, she'd stop me, and I wouldn't be able to go at all."

"Well, I suppose you've got a point there," he said.

"And I don't think you should call me sweetheart," she said.

"And I don't think *you* should be trying to wangle free plane rides by making eyes at me," he said.

"I wasn't making eyes. And I'm not trying to get a free ticket. I told you—it will be paid for as soon as I arrive in Charlotte Amalie."

He leaned across the counter and studied her. "Look," he said, "are you kidding me or something? Are you for real?"

"I'm for real. And please," she said, "can't you help me?"

He looked at her for a long time. "Look, there's nothing I can do. But I can let you talk to the traffic manager if you'd like." And he opened his little gate and took her to the traffic manager's desk.

"What's your grandmother's name?" he asked her.

"Mrs. Charles Blakewell."

"Blakewell? Isn't that some relation to the Harper family down there?"

"My great-grandfather was Meredith Harper."

Late that afternoon there was a telephone call from the St. Thomas airport. "This is a little unusual, Mrs. Blakewell," the man said, "but your granddaughter Miss Ware is here, and she seems to have arrived on an unpaid ticket. You might say she came collect."

Meeting Leona with her car, Edith had been quite provoked, thinking of all the telephone calls that now had to be made, to Leona's mother, to the school, to her father, to everyone else who might be wondering where she was. "And don't forget. I expect to be reimbursed for this, Leona," she said. "And not by your mother or father, but by you."

They sat in the back seat in silence while Edith's chauffeur drove. Leona began rummaging in her purse. Leona took out a piece of paper, folded it carefully so that only the lower edge showed, and said, "Granny, will you sign this please?"

"What is it?"

"Just something I want you to sign. Sign it here—at the bottom."

"I never affix my signature to anything unless I know what it is."

"Well . . . read it then," and she unfolded it.

It was written in Leona's round, progressive-school printing.

RUN AWAY LICENSE

I, the undersigned, do hereby grant and permit my granddaughter, Leona Harper Ware, to run away from where ever she may be at the moment when the conditions (in the place where she is at the aforesaid moment) become so intolerable and hateful that they become a threat to her sanity and reason.

(signed) ______________, Grandmother

Edith had taken the document and looked at it for a minute or two. Then, taking a pen, and bracing the paper against her knee as the car bounced along, wrote, "With the specific proviso that whenever said granddaughter runs away she runs to me," and signed it.

Leona took the paper. "Thank you, Granny," she said.

"And the price of the ticket you may consider my birthday present."

She had squeezed Edith's hand and, looking straight ahead, her eyes opened and closed rapidly.

"Don't ever tell your mother I did this," Edith said.

When they got to the house Edith said, "Here are two keys. One is for my gate, and one is for my front door. Keep them with the license, Leona."

Barely two years later, after Leona's divorce from Jimmy Breed, when Leona arrived with her suitcases in St. Thomas again, she had looked so dispirited that any thought Edith had had of reproving her had vanished. She simply put her arms around the child and said, "Well, you stuck to the terms of our contract, didn't you, dear? You came home to me." And she was touched to see that Leona still carried the two keys on a velvet ribbon.

Thinking of this now, Edith realizes with a start that she has allowed a perfectly awful thing to happen. This is one of the worst things she has ever done. For today—or rather yesterday, since it is now past midnight—was the birthday of Poo, Diana's very small son by Perry. Poo is four. No, five years old. Poo is what Diana calls "my menopause baby," and also says was "the result of too much brandy one night in Burgenstoch." Poo, though his true Christian name is Harper, is called Poo because *Poo* was his first word, addressed to one of the poodles. One hopes that name will not adhere to him through life. But even more awful than forgetting Poo's birthday, or being uncertain of his present age, is that Edith cannot for the life of her think of what to send him. She usually sends him an outfit, but she can never, at any given time, be sure of his size. And, worst of all, it has been months since she heard from Diana, and she really has no idea at the moment where Poo, or Diana, or Perry, or any of them are. She thinks to herself, then says it aloud to the empty room, "You're a terrible grandmother . . . a terrible grandmother."

"Say, you're a real *nervous* girl, aren't you?" he says. "Look how your hand shakes lighting that cigarette."

Leona blows out the match and makes a wry face at him. "Are you always so *personal,* Mr. Purdy?" she asks him. "Is this always your approach to women you've just met? The direct question?"

Grinning at her he says, "Only with some women, I guess. Women with nervous hands." He reaches out with his index finger and touches her wrist. "Calm down," he says. She withdraws the wrist.

"Perhaps your questions make me nervous," she says. "Besides, doesn't a gentleman usually offer to light a lady's cigarette?"

"Oh-oh," he says, still grinning. "Huffy."

No, she thinks, not huffy. Just all at once trapped-feeling, and wondering why am I here. Oh, but you know why, she tells herself. It's because you're a girl who likes attention, and knows how to get it, and along came a man, and here you are. Even Doctor Hardman hadn't been able to discover that simple, dreary little truth. "Leona Ware tilted her chin coquettishly, and the man became putty in her hands." With a rueful smile she glances at Mr. Purdy, Mr. Putty, who is still smiling at her, and then she looks down at her nearly empty drink, a drink she didn't need, and she twirls her swizzle stick in its remains. The bar at the Club Contant is beginning to fill with after-dinner drinkers, and the air is moist and heavy with smoke, and a native steel band has just started to play.

"I know what you're thinking," she hears him say over the music. "You're asking yourself: What's a nice girl like me doing out with this mutt?"

"Oh, Arch!" she laughs. "Really!"

"Well, the answer to that question is that I happened to come along and rescue you from a very awkward situation with Ed Winslow. Am I right?"

"Well, partly."

"You see? I'm a smart boy. I did well at school. And I've gotten you to call me Arch." He signals the waiter for another round of drinks. "Now tell me one more thing," he says. "What is it that you want?"

"*Not* another drink. Honestly."

"But the night's so young," he says. "And you're so beautiful. What is it you want—besides your art gallery?"

Looking at him she says, "Actually, the art gallery is the *only* thing I want at the moment. I want that very much. And besides—"

"Besides what?"

"And besides, I'm *going* to have it!" She exhales a sharp stream of smoke and cuts through the smoke with her hand. "And until my gallery opens, nothing—literally *nothing* else is going to involve me in any way. Did I tell you I'd selected a location, on—"

"On Fifty-Ninth, just east of Madison, a floor-through in a brownstone."

"Oh. Well, then you know how serious I am."

"A good address is always important," he drawls. "When'd you get bitten by the art bug, anyway?"

"At—at Bennington," she says defiantly.

"Uh-huh. Two months at Bennington and you'd learned all about art there was to know."

"I was there a whole term!" she says, and then feels her cheeks redden, seeing his eyes mock her. "Why are you giving me such a hard time?" she demands. "I've always been—"

"Just one thing puzzles me," he says easily, "and that is: What's a girl who's all fired up to start an art gallery in New

York doing spending a few weeks of sun and fun in the Virgin Islands?"

"I'm only here for a few *days!* Besides—"

"Besides what?"

"Besides, my building won't be available until May, and besides that—"

"And besides that, what?"

"And besides, none of this is any of your damn business!" She feels her eyes beginning to fill with tears, and she blinks them back. "I just don't understand you!" she says. "You told me you thought the gallery was a good idea, you said it was a wonderful idea—and now you're—"

"Sure, I think it's a good idea," he says. "A good idea for somebody. Like a girl who's got plenty of money, and wants to work off her frustrations."

The waiter arrives at that moment and sets down a trayful of drinks on their table—otherwise she would push the table aside and get up and leave him. His hand is on her wrist again. "Rum's your favorite drink, I see," he says. "Miss Harper."

"Oh, that's such a tired and stupid joke! Everybody's called me Miss Harper here for years. Where did you pick it up?"

"I told you, I'm smart. I have a retentive mind. And I notice details."

"Well, would you take care of one detail for me? Would you ask for the check and take me home? Or shall I call a taxi? And *please* let go of my arm. You're hurting—"

"Listen," he says in a new, more gentle voice. "I only meant—"

"*I* heard what you said."

"I only meant that to open an art gallery like the one you're talking about takes money. And obviously you're a girl with money."

"Oh, I'm so sick of being called a rum heiress! Because I'm not! I'm not any kind of heiress."

"Then what'll happen if you lose your shirt?"

"I won't!"

"Or will it be somebody else's shirt? Have you got an angel? I might be interested in being your angel. Or, let's say you could make me be interested—"

"Then you can come and buy some of my pictures. Which, for you, I'll make very expensive!"

"You get mad," he says, "in the most delightful way."

"And you're the most—impossible man I've ever met!" She jumps to her feet, pushing aside the table, and then, all at once, she thinks she is going to fall, and she steadies herself, bracing her hands hard against the tabletop, gripping the edge while the room goes in and out of focus before her eyes. "Oh," she says, "Oh, I think I—"

Instantly he is standing beside her, supporting her arm with his hand. "Are you all right? Are you a little tight, buddy?"

"No," she says. But she knows she is, yes.

"Sit down a minute."

She feels herself sinking back into the plastic cushions of the banquette. Bending forward, she hugs her elbows against her sides and presses her fingertips against her forehead, which has suddenly begun to throb.

"Take a deep breath," he says.

"Not tight," she says, trying to suppress a surprising and totally involuntary urge to giggle. "I can say *She sells seashells by the seashore*. I can say *Try tying twigs to tree twine*. I can say *Toy boat, toy boat, toy boat, toy boat*. . . ." And then she says, "My mother."

"What about your mother?"

"She's my—my angel. Didn't you ask me who my angel was? My darling mother is putting up all the money for my gallery, my mother, the rum heiress. Oh—"

"I don't get it. What is this—Hate Mommy Day? What's the matter with this grandmother of yours? How come you don't let her?"

"Ha!" Leona says. "No. I don't want *Granny* to lose her shirt! No, let Mother lose her shirt—" and she suddenly waves her hand. "She can *afford* to!"

"Oh-oh. It *is* Hate Mommy Day."

"No, but I don't even know where she *is!* Where *is* she? Oh, look—I am tight. That's the sign. Whenever I begin to talk about my mother. Next comes—crash bang. Something spectacular. Take me home."

"You know you hardly even touched your dinner? We'll get you some coffee, and then—"

"Please!"

"Listen, buddy," he says. "You're here, I'm here. Where have we got to go? Is there really anyplace? Is there a single blessed place on God's green earth where you and I have got to go?"

"Home," she says. Then, hopelessly, horribly, the tears do come.

Beside her he says, "You've been hurt; I've been hurt. But that doesn't mean we have to hurt each other, does it, buddy? Go ahead. Cry a little, nobody's watching you. Then we'll go out and get a breath of fresh air."

"Toy boat," she repeats. "Toy boat."

Edith's bedside clock says half past two, and she knows that she cannot any longer reasonably sit up waiting for Leona. Leona, at this point, coming in and seeing the light on, would know that Edith has been sitting up waiting for her, and this might annoy Leona. She places her book on the table beside her bed, and snaps off the light. In the darkness now, the headlights of cars on the hill trace across her windowpanes, false comets, and she waits for one of the cars to be the one delivering Leona.

Now a long pain begins and settles on her body, stretching familiarly like an old and practiced lover. Then, abruptly tightening, it snaps Edith's body together, knees to chin, under the bedclothes. The pills are there, the carafe of water, but she refuses to take them. Why is she so stupid about pain? Why does she prefer to endure it, suffer through it, rather than take one little Demerol which will, in the course of a few minutes, make the pain go away? There is surely something perverse in this—masochistic Leona would probably call it. Masochistic and without meaning because it exists beyond all other human experience, a battle of self with self, Edith versus Edith, and it does not matter which side wins. Though it brings tears to her eyes she remains, curled like a small fist in the pain's grip, with a terrible kind of joy. Then she begins an experiment: forcing herself upward, away from the pain, separating herself from her body and moving upward, out of the bed, out of the house, up into cool air and into a landscape of mountains and snow and, above the snowcaps, into a sky where the pain, earthbound below her, grows smaller and smaller until, in the farthest distance, it is a small, wriggling object, a dot, as small as the pill she has not taken.

Then, perhaps, Edith sleeps. For she is all at once skating—

skating arm in arm with Diana across a high, shimmering lake. The wind makes them laugh and they twirl like children on their skates. Then smoothly Harold glides toward them and takes Diana away on his arm. "I'm in charge, Edith," he says. "You're not in charge!" she cries, and her eyes fly open in the dark bedroom, and she knows that she will not sleep again.

"And so, then, for a few weeks, I sat in New York doing the telephone bit," Leona is saying, her bare arm trailing out the open window of the car, in the wind, as the car climbs slowly up into the dark hills. "'Hello! How are *you?* I'm fine. Don't you know who this *is?* It's me, Leona—yes, it's *me!* Well, I'm fine. . . . Yes, I'm divorced, you heard right. Happy? Oh Lord, but I'm happy. Well . . . we really ought to see more of each other, it's been so long. Yes, we must get together, Will, Harry, Oscar, Mike, whatever your name is—we really must. Oh, yes, I'll be here for a while—I guess! Well . . . why don't you call me one of these days? Yes, I'm in the book. No, I'm not unlisted any more. *Yes*. I'm *listed*. Yes . . . well, it's been nice talking to you. Good-by.' You hang up. Then you pick up the phone again and call another old number, another old friend, and try again. 'Hello! How are *you . . . ?*' It's known as the telephone bit, as trying to get yourself back in circulation, and it's not a great deal of fun."

Beside her he says, "You're a nice-looking girl. Hell, you're actually beautiful. I should think a lot of guys—"

"There was always Eddie Winslow, my old reliable. Tonight he—"

"Tonight he what?"

"Never mind. I'm talking too much. Anyway, it was then, after doing the telephone bit for a while, that I suddenly thought—dear God, there's got to be something *else*. And then I thought, yes, something else like an art gallery. Something to *do*."

His hand falls on her knee, just lightly enough so that it could be accidental. "I see," he says.

"And so, after about three weeks of going to every gallery in town and living on a diet of tiger's milk and peanut-butter sandwiches, I decided to come down here, to Granny's, and finish making all my plans."

"And fate threw us together."

"Yes," she says. And then, pointing, "That's the house—ahead on your right. That big stone gate."

He stops the car in front of the gate, switches off the headlights, and turns to her across the darkness. "You feel better now?"

"Oh, much."

"You see? Old Doc Purdy's home cure really works."

She laughs, her hand on the handle of the door. "Thanks," she says. "And I'm sorry you had to use it."

"It was my pleasure. You just had a little too much of great-granddaddy's rum on an empty stomach. You see, I'm not such an s.o.b. after all."

"No, I guess you're not."

"Where are you going now?"

"Inside, up the stairs, and into my little bed."

"Going to ask me in?"

"I can't, Arch. Granny's home." She opens the car door and slides out across the leather seat.

"Hey—wait a sec."

Closing the door, she leans in through the open window. "What?"

"Haven't you forgotten something?" He opens the door on his side, gets out, and walks around the car toward her.

Leona checks for her bag and gloves. "What is it?"

He starts up the walk toward the gate.

"You can't come in. Honestly. It's awfully late, and Granny's—"

"I'd just like to take a look at this place."

She hesitates. In the darkness she cannot see his face. "Well—you can come into the garden, but just for a minute. But not in the house."

She unlocks the gate with a key on a velvet ribbon.

"This is quite a place," he says.

"It's one of the last of the big old places. And when Granny goes—"

He moves after her through the dark garden where, lying on the dry grass, someone has left a set of lawn bowls. "Ouch!" he says, as his foot strikes one of the bowls.

"Ssh! Granny's sleeping."

"You really care about this old lady, don't you?"

"Once, years ago, she did something awfully kind for me. That's enough, isn't it?"

"Yes," he says. "That's always enough." His arm circles her waist, and he pulls her to him.

Arching her back against the pressure of his hand she faces him across the darkness and shakes her head very rapidly back and forth. "No," she says. "Please, no. There's nothing for you here. There's nothing for anybody. I'm sorry. Please—"

But he continues to hold her and then, his other hand cupping the back of her head, he pulls, rather roughly, her face to his and presses his mouth against hers.

Mutely, while he kisses her, she goes on shaking her head, back and forth, keeping her body rigidly stiff and her lips unyielding. And, for some queer reason, she is now thinking for the second time today of Edouardo Para-Diaz. She had banished him to the moon, but he would not stay put. What was his one kind thing? She tries to remember. Her mind fills with the doorways of the villa at Alcalá de Chisvert, and he enters through the Moorish archway, a figure slim and emphatic in his white shirt and tight black trousers. He stands there, and all the other details immediately supply themselves: the purple Mediterranean air, the juniper-scented wind, mimosa and talisman roses in a gold bowl on the piano by the door, the sour-plum tree outside the window, the rustle of waves on the beach. Neither of them is aware any longer of the man who is kissing Leona. Edouardo stands there, smirking at her, but he will not speak.

Edith has heard voices in the garden, and gotten out of bed and gone to a window. What she sees, in a very unsatisfactory glimmer of moonlight that comes through the trees, is Leona in her pale flowered dress, and a thick-set man in a blue blazer and white canvas trousers. The man is unfamiliar to her; it is certainly not Mr. Winslow. They move about the garden, where the lawn bowls have been left out, scattered in all directions on the grass. Edith hears Leona whisper something, and the man puts his arm around her, pulling her to him. Edith does not want to watch, but does watch, and the man kisses her while Leona stands very still, her arms at her sides, her head tipped backward.

Now a few more words pass between them, and the man releases Leona. She begins walking up and down and back and forth, slowly across the grass, between the scattered lawn bowls.

She seems totally intent on this odd task, weaving a path in and out among the bowls. She moves gracefully and silently, without pausing. The mood between them has changed.

"What're you doing, buddy?" Edith hears him ask her.

"It's a game. Don't you know this game? It's called go in and out the windows. You go in, and you go out. See? In . . . and out. And you mustn't touch—"

"You know," the man says, "you're a cool girl. But just don't let yourself turn into an iceberg. Watch out for that."

But she does not acknowledge hearing this remark, and continues her slow, zigzagging path. The breeze smells of dew, and the night smells of nicotiana and jasmine, and in the middle of all that dark and scented tropic quiet, Edith thinks of the streets of large cities in the icy cold, of newspapers and crumpled Kleenex blowing through the canyons between old buildings, of the steamed windows and smoky lights of restaurants with the smell of beer emanating from their doorways, of empty apartments in the reflected glare of street lamps. Oh, what will become of her? she thinks. She sees the man turn quickly and walk out of the garden. She hears the gate close behind him, and his car start and drive away. Leona is alone.

Then, as Edith watches, Leona does a strange thing. She suddenly falls to her knees on the lawn and, bending over, her dark hair tumbling across her face, she digs the fingers of both hands hard into the dry grass. Clutching and pulling at the grass she rips up two handfuls, then lets them fall. Then her fingers claw and tear at the grass again, pulling it up by the roots, clenching it in two more small hysterical fistfuls, then scattering the grass, with a sob, again.

Edith puts her hands on the sill and calls softly out to her. "Leona—come to bed now."

Leona sits dead still, then lifts her head. Her hair falls back and her pale face looks up at Edith. "Why are you spying on me?" she cries. "Why can't you leave me alone? Why can't everybody leave me alone?"

Five

Edith Blakewell returns to her bed in the dark room, a convicted spy. But you have always been a spy, she reminds herself: always. The electric clock, its hands respectfully bowed at half past three, purrs on her bedside table and emits a faint, sulphurous glow. Looking at the clock, Edith is suddenly presented with an astonishing thought—astonishing because it is cheap and unworthy and yet, like all unpleasant things, there is something fascinating about it. She toys with this nasty, charming notion. Suppose she told Leona she is dying?

Could she, she wonders, bring herself to employ a trick like that? And yet, if she did, wouldn't Leona at least be willing to talk to her a little, open up to her a little? Wouldn't Leona come to her, take her in her arms, and say, and be— And be what?

"And become my property again." Is that the answer? No. "And come to your senses, young lady, and start acting your age."

Spying was the word Leona used. Years ago, with her father's old field glasses slung over her shoulder, Edith would go for long walks up Signal Hill, on the pretext of bird-watching but sometimes to meddle, vicariously, in the affairs of her household. She would perch herself on a flat rock on the hill-side, and survey the house down there among the coconut palms and the sea-grapes: Nellie, at the kitchen door—past sixty, poor thing, but still with the faith of a girl in her charms—flirting with a grocery boy, often letting him kiss her passionately and touch her intimately, sometimes asking him in. Or she would watch Cyrus, an old man now and now one of her gardeners, put down his trowel and stretch out on his back under a tree, scratching his stomach with a slow, disinterested hand. Or, for a change of scene, she would train the glasses on her bedroom windows to watch her laundress tiptoe in, open the cedar closet, and take Edith's stone marten cape off its hanger and put it on, dancing and posing with it barefoot in front of the pier glass.

She did not always spy. Sometimes she would simply watch the sea, and the huge clumsy pelicans rising from the water and curving through the sky like boomerangs, and the ducks rocking on the waves in the lagoons, and the pigeons, at dusk, rising from their feeding-places in the woods to their nests in the mangrove trees. And once, turning her glasses from the birds to survey the harbor, she had suddenly seen the Frenchman, Louis Bertin. He was sitting on the pier of the old West India Company coaling wharf, smoking one of his small cigars. She could see Louis in every detail; the thin nose, the hooded gray eyes. Then a curious thing happened. He raised his head, shaded his eyes with one hand, and looked directly at Edith. With a gasp, she lowered the glasses. He was now invisible; she could barely make out the outlines of the coaling sheds. But when she raised the glasses again his eyes still met hers, and their look had been so exact, so appraising, that she couldn't believe that he was not watching her, though it could not have been possible. At the time, the experience unsettled her. It was as though there was no such thing as privacy, no places where snoops such as she could hide.

But about two months before Leona arrived Edith had a fall. The fall frightened her more than anything Alan Osborn has told her about what is going on inside her, and the fall did not happen, thank goodness, or a hillside but in her own house.

A perfectly ordinary and familiar little Oriental runner that extends from her bedroom to her bathroom door suddenly and without warning betrayed her, and moved. That was it. The rug moved. She lay for a number of minutes on the floor where she had fallen, certain that her hip was broken, and seeing with dreadful clarity the brittleness of the bones that held her poor body together. Then, when she decided that the hip was perhaps not broken, she got to her feet and managed to get to a chair where she sat, feeling ill. She never mentioned the fall to Alan or to anyone else, even though, in the weeks after it, the most she could do was move painfully from chair to chair, and the stairs presented a twice-daily Everest, down in the morning, up at night. Now, whenever she approaches the treacherous rug, she stares at it. She has not moved it, or removed it, since the fall, but she and the rug now eye each other with mutual suspicion and distrust. From an old friend it has become a capricious enemy. Since the fall, there have been no more spying walks with the field glasses.

I spy, she thinks to herself in the dark bedroom, only on what pertains to me, Leona. Furthermore, from spying I always find out something.

There is, she realizes now, a ritual quality to these thoughts of hers; she has been reciting them to try to figure out exactly what she feels about Leona now, after seeing her down there, on her knees, gouging up the lawn with her fingernails. Edith finds herself mentally walking a very thin line between pity for Leona and indignation. An extremely thin line separates sympathy from exasperation, sorrow from anger. Edith is certainly sorry that Leona had a bad time of it with her last husband, and she is sure that getting a divorce has its harrowing side. But plenty of other people get divorces and manage to survive; movie stars get divorces the way other people get colds. For Leona to be upset is one thing; for her to give in to emotional self-indulgence is quite another. We Harpers, Edith reminds herself, do not succumb to moods and melancholy like that because our roots reach down into hard, dry West Indies soil, and our hides have been toughened by the endless sunshine, which is why we—we Harper women, especially—are long-lived. Yes, she has a good mind to tell Leona this. We Harper women, allowing for exceptions, are not softies. We do not dissolve to jelly at a crisis. Our flesh may ache, but it doesn't tremble. We do not let down the side, even when we are all alone. We endure the pain rather than swallow the pill. "The tropics do strange things to some people," she remembers her father saying. "But not to the strong. Only to the weak."

Now Edith hears Leona coming up the stairs, and moving along the upstairs hall. "Leona!" she calls. But there is no answer. She hears Leona's door open, then close with a click. "Leona!" she calls again. "I want to speak to you." Perhaps Leona hasn't heard her. Well, then she will find the note and be in in a minute. She gives Leona a minute by the glowing clock to find the note, read it, and come in. Then two minutes; then three. Is it possible, she then asks herself, that Leona is simply going to *ignore* the note? *"Leona!"*

"Please leave me alone," Leona whispers to her empty bedroom. She picks up the note on her pillow, quickly reads it, and crumples it up into a tight, fierce ball. *E.B.H.B.* What does that first *B* stand for, she wonders? Borgia, perhaps. She tosses the crumpled note on the bed and goes to her dressing table and lights a cigarette.

"Leona!"

"Please," she repeats softly to the mirror. "Not now." She puts the cigarette down in a tiny ashtray. Then she returns to the bed, smooths out the note, and reads it again. She goes back to the dressing table, picks up her cigarette, and stands there for several minutes, deciding.

Hearing Leona's tap on the door, Edith sits straight up in bed, and says "Come in!"

Opening the door, Leona says, "Hi, Granny."

"Now see here, Leona," Edith says to the dark silhouette in the doorway. "I was not *spying* on you! If I hear strange voices in my garden at three-thirty in the morning, don't I have a right to get up and see what's going on? If I see a strange man in my garden at this hour, don't I have the right to wonder what he's doing there and who he is? Who is he? May I say I didn't like his looks? Do you realize I've been waiting up half the night to talk to you? And what makes *you* think you can come in, and bring strangers in, at all hours of the night? I do not run a hotel, Leona. Come in here and close the door. I want to talk to you."

"Granny, I—"

"And what were you *doing* down there, on your knees like a washerwoman pulling up my grass?"

Leona's hand rests on the door frame. "I dropped an earring," she says. "I was looking for it."

"I *see!* And who was that man? What was he doing here?"

There is another pause. "He's a friend of mine. He's interested in old houses," Leona says finally. "I was showing him the garden."

"I *see!*" Edith says again. Interested in old houses, she thinks, and also in young ladies. "Baloney!" she says, reaching up and snapping on the lamp beside her bed. "Now come in. There's something I want to tell you."

Leona closes the bedroom door and leans against it. "I'm sorry, Granny. Oh, please don't be mad at me. I've had so many people mad at me tonight," and she laughs a little helpless laugh.

"This is not a laughing matter, Leona," Edith says. "I'm very upset." She slaps the bed sharply, twice. "Sit down. And, as my mother used to say, 'Being sorry doesn't help.'"

Carrying her cigarette, Leona crosses the room and sits down on the edge of Edith's bed. "Use this," Edith says, lifting her empty milk glass and extracting the saucer from under it. "I don't have any ashtrays in here."

"I didn't mean to yell at you, Granny. But you startled me."

"Never mind that," Edith says. "Your Uncle Harold called tonight."

"Oh," Leona says.

"Yes. I wonder if you have any idea what he called about?"

Leona shakes her head.

"It was about your young friend Winslow. Whom you had me see."

"Oh," Leona says, with an odd little sidelong smile. "So we come full circle."

"You seem to think there's something *amusing* about this!" Edith says, her voice rising, "Well, if *you'd* been given the rough edge of Harold's tongue the way I was, you wouldn't smile. I should not have seen that young man, Leona! You should not have *asked* me to see him. That man had no right—"

"Granny, please, I—"

"Let me finish! I want you to go to Mr. Winslow tomorrow,

and tell him that he is to write *nothing*—not even a word—about any of the Harpers. Tell him I have changed my mind about everything I said. Do you understand that, Leona? Do you?"

Leona sits very still, her shoulders hunched, on the edge of the bed, and Edith wonders if perhaps she has been too harsh with her. Now that Edith's eyes are becoming accustomed to the light she studies Leona's face, which looks flushed and smudged, the features somehow blurred, and Leona's eyes look tired. Leona's cigarette has gone out now and, in the silence that follows, Edith watches as Leona tries to get it going again. The match wavers out, and Leona tosses it into the waste-basket—a careless habit she has—and she strikes a second match, and Edith has an odd thought that this may be her most enduring picture of Leona: not young, not laughing, not glowing out of Degas, but frowning, hunched, occupied with a cigarette. Then she remembers that, after all, it *is* late, Leona probably *is* tired, and certainly wherever she has been she has had a cocktail or two. Normally, Edith thinks a cocktail improves Leona—as one tends to improve most people. But tonight Leona looks almost unwell. She has the cigarette lighted now, and she inhales deeply.

Edith pushes the saucer a little closer to her across the bed and says in a gentler voice, "It was no fun, dear, being spoken to the way your great-uncle spoke to me tonight. But unfortunately he's right. We do not want publicity. There are plenty of things Mr. Winslow could say about us that wouldn't look well in print. My father wasn't exactly a saint, you know. And what about your mother and Perry? Or yourself? What if he chose to say something about your divorces?"

"Granny," Leona says, "that isn't the story he's after."

"Which brings me to my next question. What *is* he after?"

"It's a story about—Uncle Harold, I guess."

"Is Harold in some sort of *difficulties*, Leona?"

"Granny, I don't *know*. Honestly I don't. Eddie seems to think so—that's what he wants to find out!"

Edith takes a deep breath. "Financial difficulties, Leona?"

"That's what Eddie seems to think."

"That's impossible!" Edith says. "Your Mr. Winslow could be sued for saying things like that! How could Harold be in any financial difficulties? He couldn't!" And then: "Could he?"

"Granny, Eddie told me all sorts of crazy things—about the business—about—"

"Then we've got to stop him! Tell me what he said. If there's something funny going on with Harold and the business I have a right to know."

"Oh," Leona cries, "who *cares* about Uncle Harold! I'm so *sick* of talking about him. To hell with Uncle Harold!"

"Harold is *Harold*," Edith says sharply, leaning forward and gripping Leona's arm. "He's my brother! He's a powerful man. He controls—"

"I *know*. He controls all the *money!* And where would this family be without the lousy money!"

"Lousy money?" Edith cries, shaking Leona's arm. "Do you realize that Harold's the trustee for my share of my father's estate? And my custodian for practically everything else I *own?* I'm an old woman, Leona—I don't intend to die in the poorhouse! And do you realize that when I die everything comes to *you?* What's mine is going to be yours someday. You can say to hell with Uncle Harold when I'm dead, but not before!"

"Granny, please . . . stop!"

"And what about your mother's lousy money? And Arthur's? And Arthur's and Harold's children? The business is the family, and the family is the business—that's what my father used to say, and it's still true, my dear young girl—"

"Oh, stop!"

"And you!" Edith says. "What lousy money do *you* live on, pray? The same lousy money that the rest of us do! And Harold's in charge of it. Somehow I can't see *you* enjoying the poorhouse, Leona!"

"Who said anything about the *poorhouse*, for God's sake, Granny?"

"I can't see you as a member of the working classes, either! Have you ever earned an honest nickel in your life, my dear?"

"Oh, stop!" Leona cries, trying to pull away from Edith's grip.

And suddenly Leona screams, and Edith, seeing what has happened, answers Leona's scream with a shriek of her own, for Leona's lighted cigarette has flown from her fingers and dropped on Edith's bed. "Oh, for heaven's sake!" Edith cries as they both lunge for the cigarette together, chasing the small smoldering cylinder that rolls like a mad live thing back and forth across the sheets. "We're all going to go up in *flames,* Leona!" Edith sobs. But at last Leona reaches the cigarette, and brushes furiously at the bedclothes, wildly scattering the ashes, and then, all at once, they are in each other's arms, locked in a violent embrace, weeping and moaning together. "Dear God, we must have wakened every servant in the house, Leona," Edith says, patting her shoulder, and then, in a whisper, "It's just that there mustn't be any scandal! There must not be any stories." Then there is silence.

Edith's knees, under the bedclothes, make a mountain, and Leona's head rests heavily against this slope. "I did this," Leona says in a choking, muffled voice into the blanket. "I got you into all this, Granny."

Edith strokes Leona's dark head. "Well, so you did," she says. "But I wouldn't worry about it, dear. I'm sure it's not as serious as we're making it. Harold himself said everything would be all right."

"I have a knack for messing things up, don't I?" Leona says. "It's practically the only knack I have."

"There, there," Edith says, stroking, stroking Leona's soft hair. "We both got a little—overstimulated."

For several minutes there is no sound in the room except the low hum of the electric clock; its hour hand has dipped toward four. Quietly, Edith says, "You say that these are not exactly things that Mr. Winslow *knows* about Harold, but things he would like to find out."

Against her knees, Leona nods.

"There was a man who ran a newspaper here in St. Thomas once," Edith says. "He wanted to write a story about Papa. It was a story Papa thought would be embarrassing to him. Papa gave the man some money. The story was not printed."

When Leona makes no immediate reply to this, Edith says, "What are Mr. Winslow's personal financial circumstances, do you know?"

Leona sighs. "Ah, Granny. . . ."

"I just wondered, dear," she says, stroking Leona's hair.

Leona lies very still. She still holds the lighted cigarette in one hand, and, as Edith watches, a long, looping ash forms. Leona's hand, Edith sees, still quivers slightly as though her body, even in repose like this, knew no peace. Smoke curls upward into the quiet air. Edith forces herself to watch with equanimity as the long ash falls. Then, suddenly wondering whether Leona has fallen asleep, she reaches out and very gingerly takes the cigarette from between her fingers and stubs it out in the saucer.

Leona stirs slightly. "Thanks, Granny," she says.

"I thought you were asleep. Do you care for him, Leona?"

"Care for whom?"

"Mr. Winslow."

Again, there is no answer right away. Then she says, "He's just a good friend."

"He cares for you, though. He as much as told me so."

Into the blanket, Leona says, "Yes, I know. He told me tonight he loved me."

"Then," Edith says gently, stroking Leona's hair, "you must tell him to leave us alone."

Leona sits up now and looks straight at Edith, her eyes wide and thoughtful. Edith smiles. "If he's fond of you, that shouldn't be hard to do," she says. "He'll do it as a simple favor."

"No," Leona says. "It won't be hard."

"Well, then," Edith says.

"No, it won't be hard," Leona begins slowly. "Because he loves me, and I don't love him. I've never loved anybody."

"I beg your pardon?"

"When you asked me that—did I care about him?—I suddenly thought, have I ever cared about anybody?"

"Oh, Leona—"

"And it's true. I've never cared about anybody, Granny! Not anybody! Did you love your husband, Granny?"

"Well of course. Very much!"

"And anybody else? Ever?"

Edith laughs. "Well, there were a couple of others. One or two. But—"

"But not me. I didn't love the men I married—I just married them. All of them. I let them make love to me, and I *loved* their making love to me, but I didn't love them. Granny, why can't I *love* someone?"

"But you *will*, my dear," Edith says, a trifle uneasily, turning her eyes from Leona's intense look. "You're young, you're beautiful—"

"I'm *tired* of being beautiful! Why do people keep saying that, as though it made everything else all right? Is that all I am—beautiful?"

"Of course not, dear. But meanwhile—"

"But meanwhile, why can't I love someone? I'm afraid I never will because I'm afraid I don't know how. Do you know what I feel like sometimes?" she asks in a distant-seeming voice. "I feel as though I were frozen. The man I was with tonight—he saw it right away: *ice!* I'm like a centerpiece, Granny—one of those pieces of frozen ice sculpture in the middle of a party. Only the party's over—there's no one there but me, frozen in the center of the room."

Edith says, "Sometimes I think if you'd had a child. A child, you know, can hold a marriage together. Sometimes."

"If I had a child, would that help me now?" Tears are hanging in her eyes again. "Oh, no. Thank God we didn't have a child."

Edith considers this. "By *we*, whom do you mean?"

"Jimmy and me. It doesn't matter which, does it? But if only somebody could teach me—if only you could teach me, Granny—how to love—"

"But my dear," Edith says, "how can I ever teach you that?"

Leona stares at her hands. "No," she says at last, "I guess nobody can. I'm a mess, Granny. No, I'm not even that. I don't know what I am." She stands up quickly and starts across the room.

"There's so much I'd like to talk to you about, Leona. About your plans, and—"

"Plans," Leona says. "Oh, yes, I've got plans."

"But—"

"I know. It's late." She opens the door. "Good night, Granny."

"Now wait!" Edith says. Leona's hand on the half-opened door seems suddenly symbolic, prophetic. This is the door, yes, that Edith has been waiting for Leona to open all along; Leona has opened herself, just a crack, perhaps, to Edith and now the door is about to close again, maybe forever. "Wait," she says urgently, holding out her hand. "Don't go off like this, don't leave me with *this* thought to dream about—that you can't love anybody! I mean, real love is—it only happens once or twice in a lifetime, I think, and even then—"

"Then no wonder the rest of the time people can't even talk to each other. Right?" She smiles. "Good night, Granny. It *is* late."

"Look," Edith says, half-rising. "What difference does *late* make? We're both night owls, aren't we? Why don't you run in, put on your pajamas and robe, and come back in here. We'll have a brandy, a nightcap, how's that? And have a good talk right now. Would you like that?"

Leona seems uncertain. Then she says, "All right."

"Good!" Edith says, suddenly excited. "Then hurry!"

Edith gets quickly out of bed and puts on her own robe. She fetches the brandy and the glasses from the dresser and sets them out, unstoppers the brandy, fills both glasses and, still holding the decanter in one hand, gives herself a giddy sip. Love? Well, there was precious little of that wasted in *this* family, she thinks. So where shall she begin with love? With the Frenchman? No, she thinks, pushing her feet into her slippers, the beginning goes back farther than that, back to Mama and Papa, and Harold and Arthur, and Cyrus in the cart, back to those early days when she was a girl growing up in St. Thomas—back to before Charles, to when Edith was younger than Leona is now, but when Edith was just about the same age as Leona when she was first married. And Andreas. Would Andreas do? Perhaps. Seeing him dimly, she asks him: Will you do? Come closer, anyway—closer, where I can get a good look at you. There were so many beginnings, so many branches to reach into and pick from, in that tree of years—for love.

Standing in the middle of her bedroom, she thinks: Diana! It's a pity you can't be here to listen to what I'm going to say!

It is a moment or two before she notices that there are no sounds from the direction of Leona's room. She goes quietly out into the hall and looks. Leona's door is open, and the light is on, and Leona is lying, still in her dress, across the top of her bed. The end of another cigarette is burning in a little ashtray placed on the floor by the bed.

Edith puts the cigarette out, and puts the ashtray on the table. Leona's breathing is in the soft, gulping rhythm of heavy sleep. Leona is too heavy for Edith to lift up, and undress, and put into bed, but Edith pulls the comforter up around Leona's shoulders and tucks it in at the sides. She is afraid to kiss her good night, afraid of disturbing her. She turns out both lamps, and goes to the door. "Good night, dear," she whispers, and goes out the door, closing it quietly behind her.

Six

"GOOD afternoon, Miss Edith Harper. How are you today?"

"Very well, thank you."

"And your daddy? He still make money?" Laughing, the old man would put his hands on the strings of his guitar and sing, "Oh, I wish I could make music like that man make his money. . . ." Edith would laugh and wave to him. The old man was always there, sitting in the same doorway, his battered guitar across his knees. She never knew his name.

Edith's mother would have been horrified to know that in the year 1907 her eighteen-year-old daughter had taken to wandering through the town, speaking to dark-skinned native men as she went. To Dolly Harper, all the St. Thomas Negroes were dirty, diseased, depraved. "Why are they dirty, Mama?" Edith remembers asking her once.

"We don't *know* they're dirty," her mother said. "It's just that, with that nigger skin, we can't tell."

Why did she do it, Edith wonders now? Why did she take

those walks and make those curious, nameless acquaintances? Starved for company, she supposes, and yet there remains something a bit irrational about her behavior that year, like the time she had stolen all the bottles of French perfume off her mother's dressing table and emptied one bottle after another over herself as she lay on her bed, turning the air around her into a thick, sweet syrup, and ruining the dress she wore. Why? And each day, when her mother would take her second glass of wine from the lunch table and go upstairs to her room to rest, Edith would escape the house—free until six o'clock, when it was time to tap on her mother's door and wake her for dinner. She would go down the hill into Charlotte Amalie, walking slowly along the steep and narrow streets, past the old houses that leaned against each other like so many tipsy old friends, the afternoon sun turning their peeling stucco walls to gold, past archways and shuttered windows, little grilled balconies crowded with flowerpots, and sleeping cats on windowsills. She would try to imagine herself a part of this strange city. Naked children playing in the dusty streets would look up at her as she passed, holding out thin gray hands for coins, and, here and there, a familiar face would nod to her and say "Good afternoon, Miss Edith Harper. How are you today?"

It was on one of these walks that she met Andreas. He was standing in the street talking to a group of young men and, as she passed, he turned and spoke to her. "You're Edith Harper, aren't you? Do you remember me? Andreas Larsen?"

"Yes."

She remembered him from years before, from the donkey-cart rides with Cyrus and the boys. His father was a Dane, a planter. But lately, she had heard, his father had sold his fields and gone into the insurance business. Andreas had been a towheaded youth when they had waved to him from the cart but now, at twenty-two, he was tall and slender, his shock of fair hair was bleached almost white from the sun, and his face and arms were the color of brandy.

"I often see you, walking by," he said.

"Yes. I take walks."

Smiling, he said, "May I walk with you, Miss Harper?"

"Yes," she said, "if you'd like."

By the end of that walk, foolish and romantic though it sounded to say it, she had fallen in love.

* * *

It was strange that, in over eleven years of living—for a part of each year, at least—on an island, it should have taken someone like Andreas to introduce her to the sea. Up to then, she had always associated the sea with the livid waters of the harbor that lapped under the wharves where the coal ships loaded and the lighters sat—still, smutchy waters full of off-scourings and teredo worms—the harbor that was always her first view of St. Thomas arriving, each autumn, on the old Quebec Line steamer from New York. She knew there were beaches, but her mother had warned her that the beaches were dangerous, that the worst sort of natives were encountered there, and that heaven only knew what tropical monsters swam offshore. So she had only seen the beaches from a distance.

She is sure Magens Bay is not the same today. She has not been there in years. She has not chosen to go there and watch boys and girls cavorting in their bikini suits, preferring to remember it when it seemed like Eden, a sloping beach that emerged from the cottonwoods, where the sand was always scattered with shells, leading down to the surprise of the water which seemed to run through every shade and variation of color, from the palest yellow to a delicate green, to sapphire, to purple. They shared Magens Bay, in those days, only now and then with a net fisherman or two, or a boat on the horizon. Otherwise, they owned it all, the water and the shore, the island of Brass Cay, far out in the Bay's mouth, and the rocks of Picara Point. Andreas taught her how to swim there. She remembers them lying side by side on their stomachs in the sand.

"What are you thinking about now?" Andreas asked her.

"What I always think about when I'm here. That I shouldn't be."

"Why shouldn't you?"

"I should be home, with Mama. It's where Papa wants me to be."

"She takes naps in the afternoons."

"Yes. But if I told Papa that, he'd probably tell me to sit with her while she takes her nap."

"Why would he want you to do that?"

"Because she's *ill,* Andreas—that's why."

"A person who's ill should have a nurse."

"It's hard to find a person he can trust."

"Ah," he said. "He wants you to nurse her because he trusts you. And because he trusts you, you can meet me here."

She laughed guiltily. "Yes."

"What do you do with your mother when she's awake?"

"Sometimes I read to her. Or we play cards. Rubicon Piquet. Écarté. Games like that. Then we have lunch."

"Then she takes her nap. What's wrong with her, anyway?"

"It's—nerves," she had said.

What was wrong with her mother was no longer any mystery to her, but it was a secret. It was never to be mentioned, never discussed, even though it had grown steadily worse since Arthur had been born. There had been more of the sudden tantrums followed by longer silences, more of the long, drugged sleeps. "It is *la saison furieuse* of a woman's life!" Mademoiselle Laric, the boys' governess, had exclaimed dramatically, rolling her eyes, and clutching her breast. And, when Edith had asked her what *la saison furieuse* was, Mademoiselle had explained it, and followed this explanation with an enthusiastic, and highly Gallicized, description of sex. ("At last he comes pouncing upon you, *ma chere*, his teeth biting into the flesh of your lips, his loins afire! With a thrust he possesses you . . ." and on, and on, with furious gestures of her hands—a surprisingly vivid account for a maiden lady.) Then there was the problem of the little glasses of wine which were now never very far from Dolly Harper's reach. The wine, she said, was the only thing that could 'relax' her, or make her sleep. The word *alcoholic* was not in use in those days. There was only the uglier word *drunkard*, which no one had been cruel enough to use about Edith's mother either. And so her mother's drinking, like *la saison furieuse*, had become something one accepted mutely, without comment, a secret guarded closely within the family. She was ill. It was nerves.

"Why do you ask me so many questions about my family, Andreas?" she asked him.

"Because I know I'll never meet them."

"You'll meet them. Some day."

"Why not now? Why not today?"

They had talked this way before. Perhaps someday an answer would offer itself. Meanwhile, wasn't it enough that they loved each other? "If only there was someplace we could go," she said. "I hate this island."

"Hate St. Thomas? Why?"

"I miss winter! It's been eleven years since I've seen snow, and besides, this island hates me. You know that, Andreas. They laugh at the Harpers. But they really hate us. Do you know that when I was walking in the town the other day, a group of little Danish children came running up to me and stood in a circle around me, and sang a song about me? 'Edie, Edie, skinny and greedy, how does your garden grow? With your daddy's rum and your silly old mum, and dollar bills all in a row.'"

Andreas laughed. "Next time they sing that song to you, here's what you should say to them." He leaned over and whispered Danish words in her ear. "Say that, and watch their faces, Edie."

"What does it mean?"

He laughed again. "I'll tell you when you're older!"

"And even that old man, the old man who's always sitting in that doorway in Christian Street with his guitar, and who sings *his* little song about making music the way my father makes money—he laughs, and smiles, but he hates us too. They all do."

His face was serious now. "This is the price of being a rich man's daughter," he said.

"But your father's rich! They don't sing songs about him!"

"Not as rich and powerful as your father, Edie. And besides—" He paused, scowling, pushing little wet mounds of sand together between his hands. "My father doesn't own people," he said. "They say slavery hasn't existed here for sixty years, but your father has slaves. He owns people, human lives. . . ."

"Who does he own?" It had been a totally new thought to her.

"Otto Frère. His latest purchase."

"Papa won that plantation in a tennis match!"

"He *bought* it. Cheap. Have you seen Otto Frère lately, Edie? Take a look at him. You'll see what a man who's sold his life looks like."

She was silent then. "Well, you see, that's why they hate us," she said.

He reached out and took her hand. His hand was warm and rough with sand. "Do you hate this island now, Edie?" he said. "This afternoon?"

She had smiled and told him no, she didn't hate it that afternoon.

He raised himself on one elbow and leaned across her. "I've shown you the sun, haven't I, Edie—the sun and the sea. Look at you now." Slowly, he drew a straight line across her forehead with his fingertip. "You're turning my color. You're beautiful."

She lay there, very still, feeling the pressure of his finger and the sun on her skin. (Once, when she was little, Leona had stared at a cracked and browning photograph and said, "Granny? Were you beautiful?" "I believe," she had answered carefully, "that I was considered beautiful. By some." By him. That afternoon at Magens Bay.)

"I wouldn't like you in the cold country," he said. "All pale and pinched-looking, with your nose dripping."

"Do you like me, Andreas?"

He bent and kissed her, his lips cracked and salty from the sea air. "I love you," he said.

"Perhaps—this summer, when I'm in Paris, and you're in Copenhagen—"

He had jumped up then and stood over her, tall and broad-shouldered, his arms folded across his chest, looking exactly like a Viking chief. "I'm not going to Copenhagen. I told my father this morning."

"What did he say?" She knew that his father wanted to send him to the University.

"What would he say? He knows I make my own decisions."

"Are you going to stay *here?"*

"This is my island, Edie," he said. "My future is here." He began pacing up and down, smashing his fist into his palm taking long, swift strides and kicking up arcs of sand. "What a future this place has," he said. "Look at it—" He spread his arms. "Have you ever seen anything so beautiful? Can you *see* it, Edie? What this place will be like some day? Rich—with people coming here from all over the world to see how beautiful it is? There are fortunes to be made here, Edie."

"Papa says this island is good for nothing but sugar."

"Sugar? Your father may not know it, but sugar is in trouble here. For a hundred years they've planted nothing but cane, and the earth is dying. I'm not talking about sugar. I'm talking about hotels! Yes, and rich houses. These hills with nothing on them but *ceibas*—some day they'll have pavilions on them, and cafés, and shops—and there'll be sailboats in the bay. I know this, Edie, I can see it coming."

His blue eyes would seem to grow bluer as he spoke.

"And irrigation. With irrigation, the canefields could yield three times what they do now. Even the sugar men know this. But nobody *does* anything." He dropped on his knees beside her in the sand. "Listen," he said. "Just for a minute stop and think what would happen if we could find some simple way to store up rainwater. Tanks under the hills perhaps." He quickly built a hill of sand and punched a crater in its top with his finger. "Water storage." He drew curving pathways down the side of the sandhill. "Irrigation ditches. But now—" destroying the hill with the back of his hand "—every extra drop of rainwater runs into the sea. But what if there were some way to take the salt out of the seawater? Why not? Is that so crazy? 'No, no, it wouldn't work,' the planters say. 'Take away the tax on sugar,' they say. 'Then we'll make more money. While the sugar lasts.' Well, we'll see . . ."

She was dazzled by all the things he saw. And remembering these words now, more than fifty years later, Edith sees that his vision, like all visions, was flawed. Yes, the ragtag and bobtail from all over the world have come, and to house them there are many inferior hotels. For pavilions and cafés there are night clubs and bars, and a few inadequate catch basins have been built to collect the spring and autumn rains. And a bit of cane still struggles up, between times, from the dry earth.

"Listen," he used to say, "they say that this place is dying. But it's *Denmark* that's dying—Copenhagen! The United States wants to buy these islands, but Copenhagen keeps refusing. They want to hold on, hold on—while we sit and rot."

"Doesn't the King care about the islands?" she asked innocently.

"The *King?*" he said in a mocking voice. "Christian the Tenth, King of the Vandals and the Goths, Duke of Slesvig, Holstein, Stornmarn, Ditmarsh, Lauenborg, and Oldenborg? *That* King?"

"Is that what he's King of?" she asked, laughing. "But it's your own country you're talking against, Andreas."

He sneered. "My country. Denmark is being run by the Germans. No, this is my country, here. And I'm not going to let it lie here and be robbed by foreign exploiters, men who suck their money out of human lives, parasites, men like—" Suddenly he broke off.

"Men like whom, Andreas?" she had asked him quietly.

For a moment his face was dark. Then he smiled. "Pardon my political speeches," he said.

"Men like my father is what you meant. You hate us too."

"Come on. Let's swim." He jumped up and pulled her up with him.

It is morning. Nellie has just tiptoed into her bedroom and opened the curtains and the wooden shutters. The sun streams in. "Good morning, Nellie," Edith mutters, pretending to be still half-asleep though, for the last half-hour or so she has been wide awake and thinking about Andreas.

"Let Miss Leona sleep late, Nellie," she says. "She's tired."

"Yes, Miss Edith."

Nellie tiptoes out again. Edith thinks about that swim that afternoon fifty—oh, Lord, nearer *sixty*—years ago. She remembers that they undressed, as they always had, in the manner of European bathers, with their backs to each other. He walked to the water first, and then she had slowly turned her head to look at him. He never knew. It was the first time she had seen him, or any other man, naked, and she remembers being stunned by the sudden taut beauty of him. As the first wave spooned about his ankles, the muscles of his calves quivered and his buttocks tightened. He hesitated, then waded deeper, the waves rising like cuffs around his brown legs. He took two quick steps, then dove, his body splitting a wave as it broke. She saw him next only as a stained blond head above the water, still with his back to her, and an arm raised, beckoning her in after him. She ran into the water and swam after him.

"I'll race you to Brass Cay!" he said when she reached him.

"All right," she had said, laughing, sure that he was joking, since Brass Cay was more than four miles out. They began swimming outward, Edith using the easy natural stroke that he had been teaching her, Andreas swimming beside her.

"Faster!" he shouted. "Faster!"

She swam faster, but he was outdistancing her. "Come on!" he heard him call her. "We haven't got all day."

Then she could no longer see him, and she called—"Andreas?"

She stopped swimming, treading water, trying to find his head in the waves. "Andreas?"

She had no idea how far out she was. The beach had vanished behind the heavy swells, and the shoreline was only a dark smudge of hills that appeared to be miles way and then sank entirely behind a wave, and reappeared in a different place as she turned in the water, trying to rest, treading water. Her arms and shoulders ached. Her waving feet explored the water and found nothing. She took deep gasps of breath. "Andreas!" She suddenly knew that he had swum on to Brass Cay and left her foundering there. Hours later, he would swim back—but not to find her. He hated her father, he hated her. And so, of course, this was what he had planned. How could she have been so stupid? This was his trick; he had tricked her. In a fury, she told herself: I must simply rest, simply get my breath. She put her head back, looking up at the sun, opened her mouth wide for air. A wave struck her face and water poured into her mouth. She reached up as though the sun were something tangible and solid that she could catch hold of. Gripping the edges of the sun, another wave hit her, and she thought: I am drowning. Very well. And it was curious, the peace that this simple knowledge gave her, a kind of drowsy joy. Thinking of nothing any more, she let go the sun, and spread her arms wide and let herself sink beneath the surface, into the green depths, where the water that filled her lungs was warm and sweet, watching the green grow darker. Then she felt his hands seize her under the armpits and pull her to the surface. She struggled with him. "Murderer!" She screamed, trying to twist from his grip, flailing at him with her fists and feet. "Murderer! Let me go!"

"Don't move, Edie!" he was shouting at her. "Don't move!"

His arm swung around her neck like a vise, and briefly her head went under the water again.

When at last he had her, coughing and gasping, stretched out on the sand, and she looked up at him, his face was very pale and there were tears in his eyes. And she remembers thinking, now he has seen me, just as I have seen him, and because he made no move to cover her nakedness she thought: perhaps I please him too.

"My God, Edie—I shouldn't have left you!" he said. "I almost lost you."

"Andreas," she said, "are there barracuda in the bay?"

"Barracuda? If all the barracuda in the sea attacked you, Edie, I'd fight them off for you."

In her vision his face swam. She stretched her arms forward and rested her hands on his knees. "It wasn't your fault, Andreas," she said. "I got tired. Oh, I'm so weak. Don't hate me for being so weak, Andreas. I'm sorry. What did I say to you? Forgive me..."

"I know. Don't talk." He lay down beside her then, on the sands, the lengths of their naked bodies touching, his arm across her back. He lay without moving. Once she felt his fingers press into her side, then relax.

In the stillness, she could hear his breathing, and she waited. In the secret pages of her diary she had written, just the day before, "I love Andreas Peder Larsen. I love him with all my heart and with all my soul and with all my body. I want him and need him and want to give myself to him wholly and have him take my body with his love—" using all the words she had heard and read and wanted to discover. Now, she thought, what was going to happen—what had been bound to happen all those past weeks—will happen. She was ready for him, waiting for him. She would not have resisted him now; she would have welcomed him, and she wanted all her thoughts to be telling him that this was so. But, though they lay there very still for a long time, he did not make love to her. At last, he stood up and silently dressed himself.

"Are you awake, Edie?" he whispered.

"Yes. Awake."

He turned his back. She rose and put on her dress. They walked home from Magens Bay in silence. She only knew that he had not made love to her, though she had been willing. And, at the time, she was too young to understand why, and was to frightened of her own willingness, and too uncertain of him, to ask him why.

"But I was only eighteen!" she says now to her empty bedroom. "Only eighteen!"

Edith does not expect Leona down for breakfast at the regular hour, and, after breakfast, Mr. Barbus arrives to tell Edith, all over again, what is wrong with her garden, and why he is the only man who can set it to rights. Mr. Barbus is one of the locals in St. Thomas—though he is not as local as Edith Blakewell—and his title, painted on the shingle of his shop just outside town, is NURSERYMAN & LANDSCAPE DESIGNER & LAWN DOCTOR. Perhaps he is all these things. In any case, every month or so, J. Everett Barbus appears at her front door to describe shrubs, plants, paving stones, organic fertilizers, manures, and mulches.

"Now you can tell this soil of yours is starved, Mrs. B," he says, poking his toe into a spot of lawn beneath Edith's bedroom windows where, it might appear, someone has pulled up a few small tufts of grass. "Just look at the grainy, chalky color of that dirt. Now, for four hundred dollars I'd dig this whole yard up—and that's bottom prices I quote you, Mrs. B, family prices you might say—and lay in a layer of good, well-rotted cow manure, foot, foot-and-a-half deep. Then—"

"Mr. Barbus, I can't make any decisions about this house now. My granddaughter Leona's here, and before I can decide what to do about this place I've got to find out what *her* plans are."

"Thinking of leaving the place to her, are you? Sure wish somebody'd die and leave a place like this to me, Mrs. B. Why, I'd tear this old ark down and put up a nice motel. You could fit a nice sixty-unit job on this lot, with place left over for parking. Build it right around that swimming pool of yours, Mrs. B, and I bet it'd pull in twenty, twenty-five thousand simoleons a year. But to get back to this-here starved soil. Come over here a minute, where you're trying to grow roses in this-here bed. *Roses!* Why, Mrs. B, did you ever see a hungrier, more malnutritioned rose?"

They continue across the garden. "They say when your husband was alive, this garden was the real showplace of the island. Now ain't it a shame how you've let it go? Just think, Mrs. B, what your poor husband would say if he came back and saw the way it looks now!"

"But Mr. Barbus," Edith says firmly. "That is not the point. I do not expect my husband back."

Leona is having a hectic dream, and she struggles to pull herself up out of it. It is a meeting of all her husbands. Someone has summoned them all, and the subject under consideration is, of course, Leona—what to do about her. Jimmy Breed arrives late, as usual, all smiles and enthusiasm. Taking his seat at the conference table, he scarcely seems to notice that she is there. Edouardo is sulking. Someone has told him that all Latins must be permitted long, unreasoning sulks—that this is part of his temperament and heritage—and today his sulk is impenetrable. Gordon Paine has taken charge of the proceedings. With his logical lawyer's mind, he is all efficiency, all business, rubbing his palms together as he reads the agenda and the minutes of the last meeting. ("Oh, you've had these meetings *before!*" she exclaims, trying to be funny, but the words have not come out.) If anyone is to be appealed to, it is Gordon. She knows this. She tries to rise to defend herself, but she is made of iron, and cannot move from her seat. The men all stand up to welcome Doctor Hardman, who has just come in. Looking at her, Doctor Hardman says, "This woman tells nothing but lies." "White lies!" Leona says. "Beige lies," he insists. "Ecru lies." She opens her eyes.

The room is dark, but through the heavy curtains she can see that it is sunny outside, broad day. She asks herself: Do I have a hangover? The answer is both yes and no, and disappoints her a little. Considering how much she had to drink last night, the hangover really should be more severe than it is. All she has is a dull headache and a dry region in her throat.

She gets out of bed, goes into the bathroom, and runs cold water in the bowl. She swallows two tumblerfuls of water and, with the second tumbler, two aspirin tablets and a vitamin-B-complex capsule. Then she scrubs her face fiercely with a wash cloth and cold water, and looks in the mirror at the result, which is considerable damage to her waterproof mascara—which, apparently, she forgot to remove last night before she went to bed. Only then does she notice also that, obviously, she has slept in all her clothes. This discovery steps up the beat of her hangover considerably, and for a moment or two she leans against the washbowl, thinking Dear God, what is *happening* to me? Then she flips on the water in the shower and begins to unbutton her dress.

The shower is a benediction, a purification. She runs it alternately hot and cold, standing directly underneath the spray with the water rattling deafeningly on her plastic shower cap, and she begins to feel a little better. Bit by bit, details of the evening before come back to her. What time was it? Three or four o'clock, surely, and she remembers that he needled her about her art gallery, and about her brief career at Bennington. Well, perhaps he had a point there, about Bennington; Jimmy had kidnaped her from Bennington. And then, later—oh, she remembers, oh, *dear*—having a maudlin conversation with Granny, sitting on the bed, talking about love. *Love*. This was exactly, precisely, absolutely, the one sort of conversation she had promised herself *not* to have with Granny. And now in some stupid, sentimental moment, she has done it. Probably she cried. A crying drunk. And now, of course, Granny will be involved. Granny will give her no peace, no peace at all, until she has spread open Leona's soul. She shuts off the shower, and steps out, dripping. "Why does she *do* this to me?" she asks herself. Why does she want to get so close that she can see and touch all those deep and secret places which, all her life, Leona has so carefully guarded from any other human being's view? Why does she want to *know* me? she asks, banging her forehead with her balled fists. Then, without thinking, she answers her own question. It is simple. "Because she loves me."

She takes a large towel from the rack, wraps herself in it, and goes back into the bedroom. She starts to open one of the pairs of curtains, and then sees, through the crack, her grandmother outside in the garden. She is with a funny-looking little man in a rumpled blue suit and a stained fedora; they walk about, pointing at shrubs, and planting beds. And Leona, watching them, thinks with a swift pang: How terribly slowly, these days, the old lady *moves*. . . . She lets the curtain fall.

Turning back into the room, Leona notices, for the first time, the colored postcard lying on the floor where one of Granny's maids has slipped it under the bedroom door. Leona stares at the postcard for a moment, then slowly crosses the room, kneels, and picks it up. Wrapped in the towel, she studies the face of the card. It is a cartoon card, and its humor is of a sort that would appeal to only one person Leona knows. It is a drawing of the Eiffel Tower, and from the top of the Eiffel Tower a merry little man has jumped or fallen. As he sails downward, his hat in his hand, he cries *"C'est la vie!"* Leona looks at the picture for a long time before turning the card over to read the message, thinking, *C'est la vie*.

* * *

An hour has passed; Mr. Barbus has gone, and Edith is alone in the garden thinking, as she ties back a trailing ipomoea vine to the wall with a piece of green wire, about last night and how, at last, Leona is willing to talk to her. Last night, of course, with Leona obviously exhausted, was not a good time. Today will be their day. The vine refuses to be tied, and springs back, and Edith gives up on it. She sits down on the stone bench. She thinks: If only Leona could see me as I really am.

This notion reminds Edith of a thing that happened, about three years ago, when she flew to Palm Beach for one of her rare visits with Diana. Waiting in the lobby of the West Palm Beach airport for Diana (who was late) to pick her up, sitting there with her suitcases, she noticed a woman who sat facing her across the room. Looking at the woman, she experienced one of those sudden sensations of disliking someone intensely at first sight. Everything about the woman repelled her. She was dressed in a dust-colored dress, decidedly wrinkled and frumpy, and there was something about the set of the shoulders and the tilt of the chin that was arrogant and cruel. The way the feet were planted—solidly, wide apart, on the floor, in heavy dark shoes, the legs encased in gray stockings—suggested an enormous self-satisfaction. A handbag was plunked in the woman's lap. She clutched it as though it contained the crown jewels, and her whole air of pomposity was so absurd that Edith almost laughed, until it dawned on her that the opposite wall was a mirror, and that she was looking at herself. The two of her sat there, gazing at each other in dismay, like a pair of squat bookends across an empty shelf.

Diana, when she had finally shown up, had not helped matters, either. When they were in the car together, Diana said, "Mother, you really must do something about your *hair*."

All this, of course, was the result of those years after Charles died, when Edith became a secret candy addict, a voracious eater of chocolates, gluttonishly gobbling up pound after pound of creams and nougats—hard centers or soft, it made no difference—those beautifully wrapped Maison Glass boxes ripped open with greed. . . . Perhaps, she thinks, those wonderful candy orgies were responsible for what is wrong inside her now, with that mischievous organ whose name she cannot bear to think about, since thinking about it brings back the pain.

In the car that day, Diana had gone on about which hotels in which cities had, in her opinion, the best hairdressing salons. Then she had turned to Edith and said, "I know, Mother, that it's like pulling teeth to get you even as far away from your house as Palm Beach. But I'd really like to take you to Rome with me sometime, and let Simonetta spruce you up."

Now Edith sees Leona walk out onto the veranda and stand at the top of the steps wearing a white Shantung robe cut like a coolie's, tied loosely at the waist with a red sash. She stands there, one hand holding a cigarette, the other a cup of steaming coffee. The sleeve of the robe hangs down, and the sun catches the astonishingly white skin on the underside of her arm. Her hand, holding the coffee cup, trembles.

"Good morning, dear," Edith calls. "Did Nellie get you breakfast?"

Leona nods, and comes slowly down the steps. "I had a grapefruit."

"Is that all?"

Leona sits down at the round garden table with a little sigh, and the plastic-covered cushion of the chair exhales a small matching sigh of its own. She smiles at Edith, but it is a small smile, and it looks as though it hurts every muscle of her face. They sit in silence then while Leona drinks her coffee with little sucks and gasps.

Edith waits until Leona sets down her coffee cup. Then she stands and, looking up at the windows of the house, her hands on her hips, she says, "Leona, I've been thinking. How do you feel about this place? Do you like it?"

"I've always loved this house."

"Would you like to own it some day? After I'm gone?"

"Oh, Granny—"

"I'm quite serious. It's got to go to *some*body. The hospital wants it for an annex. Mr. Barbus wants it for a motel."

"Who is Mr. Barbus?"

"A manure man. Tell me honestly how you feel. The property has some value, if you don't want the house to live in. Mr. Barbus estimates that, as a motel, it could earn twenty or twenty-five thousand simoleons a year."

"Oh, Granny! I don't want to talk about what's going to happen after you're *gone*." She smiles again, and her smile is better this time. "Besides you're never going to *be* gone. You're indestructible."

"I wish you were right, Leona, but—"

"Now *please*. I mean it. Don't. I'm—depressed enough today."

"Depressed?" Edith sits down again, this time at the table opposite Leona. "Well, don't be," she says. And then, after a moment, "That was so—*nice*, last night. Our little talk. I only wished—"

"Granny," Leona says, "I've got to apologize for that. I must have sounded like an idiot. To be honest with you, I'd had too much to drink. I'm sorry." She smiles again. "Too much of Great-Granddaddy's rum."

"What? Oh, Leona—I thought you knew better than to drink that firewater! It's for peasants. How do you feel today?"

Leona reaches out and squeezes Edith's hand. "I was joking," she says. "But I was N.E.S., as Jimmy used to say. *Not Entirely Sober*."

"Well, you seemed perfectly fine to me. In fact, it was very cozy." After a moment she says, "But I think Uncle Harold's call upset us both a bit."

"Actually," Leona says, "I don't remember exactly what I said."

"Well," Edith says, beginning carefully, "*one* thing you said, which interested me, was that you didn't really love any of the men you married. You merely married them."

Leona's face is a blank. "Well, I guess that's true," she says finally.

Edith sighs. "Yes, I suppose that's the trouble. It seems to be what Americans do. Americans marry. Europeans have love affairs. Amours."

Suddenly Leona laughs. "Yes, I guess that's why I've had three husbands." With one hand she executes a brisk salute. "I did it for my country, suh! But what about *you*, Granny? You were only married once."

"In your generation, Leona, Americans seem so much more *American* than they were in mine."

"Or in Mother's?"

"It's progressive, dear," Edith says, beginning to enjoy this conversation, even though it has taken a somewhat silly turn. "I was married once, your mother was married twice, you've been married three times and, I trust—at twenty-seven—"

"Twenty-six."

"At twenty-*seven*, Leona—I know how old you are—I think it's safe to predict that some day you will have been married four times. It gets more so and more so, you see."

Leona is smiling still. Lifting her coffee cup, she says, "It must be wonderful to be old. Old and wise and *through* everything."

Edith detects a note of sarcasm in this; perhaps not. Anyway, she decides to ignore it. "It's holy hell being old," she says briskly, "as you'll find out one day when it's happened to you."

They sit silently now. Meditatively, Leona sips her coffee.

"Which—" Edith begins "—which of them did you *like* the best?"

Leona seems to have trouble deciding. "Oh, I guess Gordon."

"Have you thought you might try seeing him again?"

"You know, I saw him the last day I was in New York, before I came here. I ran into him on the street. He was on his way to play squash at the Racquet Club. We stood there, Granny, grinning at each other like two monkeys, trying to think of something to say. 'I'm on my way to play some squash,' he said. 'I'm on my way to St. Thomas,' I said. We said goodby. Isn't that funny? We'd been married four years, and we had absolutely nothing to say to each other. After Jimmy, I wanted somebody solid, I guess. Gordon's solid all right, but he's also an awful prig. I didn't know that when I married him, but he turned out to be a prig." Smiling she says, "I bought a prig in a poke."

"Did I tell you Jimmy came by to see me—about six months ago? He called me up and came for lunch and a swim."

"How was he?"

"Fine. The poor boy is losing his hair, though, which is a shame. He seems too young." Crossing her fingers under the table, Edith adds, "Still, he seemed more *mature* when he was here. A bit more—calmed down."

"Oh, Granny, there must be something else!" And Leona looks quickly up into the green leaves of the tree-of-heaven that shades the table, as though that something else may be hidden somewhere in its branches.

Edith purposely does not bring up, in the silence that follows, the name of Leona's last husband. Edouardo Para-Diaz's mother, she remembers, was a thief, in addition to having produced a highly unusual son. He and Leona were married in Sevilla, and the "Condesa" asked to borrow Leona's diamond earclips to wear to the wedding. *"Si, con mucho felicidad, mi condesa,"* Leona said, and lent them to her. She never got them back. They were after Leona's money, the whole pack-lot of them, Edith is sure. And it wouldn't be surprising to Edith to learn that it cost Leona more than the earclips to get rid of the Spaniards. After it was over, Leona took up her residence in Florida. (To Edith, in a note once, Diana said, "She's lucky that I have the Palm Beach house. It's handy for divorces.")

"And you never loved any of them," Edith says at last.

"Can't we change this subject, Granny? Please?"

Edith leans forward. "But you said, last night, that you didn't think you had the *ability* to love anyone."

"Well," Leona says sharply, "if I did, where would I have got it from? Could I have inherited it, do you suppose? From *Mother?"*

"Now don't be so hard on your mother, Leona. She—"

"Listen!" Leona says. "Do you know what she *wrote* to me today? On a *postcard*—a stupid comic postcard—not even airmail? She said, 'It's fun at the Ritz. Just forget all your troubles, sweetie, and come over here and have some fun.' She didn't even bother to sign it!"

"What prompted this message?"

"Just a little, simple—request for a favor, that's all! Just a favor I asked of her, Granny! And that was her answer—it's fun at the Ritz! Oh, Granny!" Suddenly she closes her eyes tight shut and pounds the heels of her palms on the edge of the table. "Just a favor! Oh, damn!" Her eyelids blink rapidly, and she bites her lower lip hard. "Sorry," she says. "Blew up, I guess." Edith watches her as she fumbles in her pack for a cigarette.

"Which Ritz is she at?" Edith asks finally.

"Paris. She's there for the collections." Blowing out cigarette smoke, she says, "Maybe I'll do that—fly over and have fun at the Ritz."

"Oh, don't leave me yet!"

"I'm joking. She has Poo with her."

"Poo for the collections? How ridiculous."

Edith stands up and walks to Leona's chair. Standing behind her, she places one hand on Leona's shoulder. Quietly, she says, "Can you tell me, dear, what the favor was?"

"Just a *simple* one!" Then she shakes her head. "No, it was a big one, I guess. A project of mine. Something I want to do. Anyway—*c'est la vie!*"

"Can you tell me about it?"

"Not yet, Granny; honest I can't. It's still too much—up in the air. More so today than ever."

"Leona," Edith says, "someday I'd like to take you to Magens Bay—to the beach there. I want to see that beach again, suddenly, and besides I want to show it to you. There's something I want to tell you. Would you like to go today, dear? Right now? John could drive us."

Leona shakes her head again. "Not today, Granny. I have a mission to perform today. Remember?" Leona looks up at at Edith over her shoulder. "Have you forgotten? I've got to see Eddie Winsow and ask him to call off his hounds."

"Oh, yes," Edith says. "That's true." She had, she realizes, completely forgotten. "Well, then, soon. We'll go to Magens Bay soon."

Leona stands up. "I'd better get dressed." She starts toward the house.

"Mr. Winslow could wait till tomorrow," Edith says.

"Better get him quick, Granny, before he buzzes back to New York."

"Yes," Edith says. "I suppose——"

Watching Leona as she runs up the steps to the veranda, she calls, "Will you be having dinner with me tonight, dear?"

"Sure," Leona says. "At least I think so."

"Good," Edith says thoughtfully, standing alone in the garden.

Running up the stairs to her room, Leona glances at her watch. It is nearly noon. She has no clear idea where to look for Eddie. He will certainly be out of his hotel now. Perhaps one of the beaches would be a good place to start. Yes, he is probably at the beach now, having lunch. She slips off her coolie robe, thinking, yes, I'm a girl who, given a job to do, does it; it's one of the things you taught me, Granny. She will look for him first at Morningstar. And this Magens Bay that Granny was talking about, she wonders—where is that?

Seven

THEY had met often again at Magens Bay that winter of 1907—whenever they could without Edith's mother noticing it. And, one afternoon, Edith remembers finally saying to him, "I want to stay here with you, Andreas." She had made her mouth form the words she had planned to say, "Stay here—and marry you."

She had been afraid he would laugh at her for saying it, but he hadn't laughed. He looked at her for a moment, and then looked away.

"I want to marry you," she repeated.

"Edie—"

"Then will you?" Suddenly she knew she didn't want to hear his answer at all.

"You're leaving for Paris in five weeks."

"I don't want to go to Paris. I want to stay here, with you."

His voice was thoughtful. "But you're going to Paris, on the fifteenth of May. Then, from there, you'll go back to your place in New Jersey for two months, the way you always do. And then you'll come back here in the fall, and I'll be here."

"Please don't joke about it, Andreas. I don't have to do all those things, do I?"

"Have you asked anyone about this?"

"No."

"Because you're afraid to ask, aren't you? What are you afraid of?"

"No one," she insisted, "but—"

"It's your father, isn't it?"

"Yes," she admitted.

He said nothing.

"But I will! I'll ask him. I won't even ask him. I'll tell him—simply tell him that I'm going to marry you."

"Will you really do that?"

"Andreas—do you think he'd ever let me?"

"You see," he said, scowling darkly at the horizon, "you know he wouldn't. You're as free now as you'll ever be, which isn't free at all."

"Still, I'll do it—if you want me to."

He was silent for a while. "I can't tell you that I *want* you to do it," he said finally. "Because you've got good reasons to be afraid of asking him. If you do it, it will be up to you."

"Then I'll do it—as soon as he comes home. Meanwhile, I'll tell my mother."

He had smiled at her then, holding her fingers in his hand, separating and lifting them one by one.

"Do you love me, Andreas?"

He nodded. "Yes."

Talking to her mother was harder, that winter, than it had ever been before. Even awake she seemed asleep now. More and more of their card games were played in an endless quiet and, when Edith spoke to her, her mother would either change the subject, or interrupt, or appear not to have heard her at all.

"It's your trick, Mama," Edith would say.

"Oh . . . is it?" The cards would flutter and spill from her hand.

She even seemed to have lost interest in talking about the servants and whether they stole or not, which had always been a favorite topic. Finding her perfume gone the day after Edith had inundated herself with it, Dolly Harper had merely muttered, "It's gone . . . they've taken it." She never seemed to notice now who waited on her. There was one girl, Alicia, who brought Edith's mother flowers from the garden every day—a beautiful, mahogany-skinned girl with opal eyes who came with armloads of roses and lilies and bougainvillea. Her mother never asked Alicia to bring her flowers, and Edith doesn't remember her ever thanking the girl for them. But she does know that her mother noticed the flowers because of a thing that happened.

They had been playing cards one evening, after dinner, and her mother got her headache and said that she was ready to go upstairs. She got up and crossed the room to put the cards in the drawer of the lowboy where they were kept and, as she tugged at the drawer, a lamp on the lowboy fell over and crashed to the floor. It was a kerosene lamp (there was no electricity in St. Thomas in those days) and was unlighted, but Edith ran quickly to pick it up before oil spilled on the rug. The cut-glass globe was broken and lay in pieces on the floor, and Edith picked up the bits of glass and put them in a wastebasket. Then she went upstairs with her mother.

Late the next morning they were seated again at the card table, and her mother said suddenly, "That girl . . . that flower girl."

"Alicia?"

"Yes."

"What about her, Mama?"

"She broke a beautiful crystal lamp when she was dusting. It was a treasure of a lamp, it came from Paris. And she had the nerve to stand in front of me and deny it! Oh, they're impossible, these niggers. And I had all the evidence too—right in the wastebasket where she'd thrown the pieces."

"But Mama," Edith said, astonished, "don't you remember? You broke that lamp yourself last night when you were putting the cards away."

"I did not!"

"But Mama—you *did.*"

She blinked, and her face reddened. "Oh," she said.

"Go tell Alicia you're sorry—hurry."

"I'm afraid it's too late," she said slowly. "I dismissed her."

"How could you do a thing like that, Mama? Even if she *had* done it, it would have been just an accident. And it was only a lamp!"

"Well," she said even more slowly. "I'm afraid there is

nothing to be done about it now. She has gone." She sat there with her cards gripped in her hands, fanning them out, then pressing them together again. Her knuckles were white and her mouth was askew. Two tears squeezed out of her eyes and ran down her cheeks. Suddenly she jumped up. "I'm going to find her!" she said, and she ran through the room and out into the hall, pulled open the front door and ran down the steps into the drive. Edith called after her; one of the other girls could find her, she said. But she wouldn't stop. She ran down the drive and into the road.

Edith waited. Her mother was gone for hours, it began to grow dark, and she knew that she would have to send someone out to look for her or else go out herself. Then there were sounds outside the house, and Edith went to the door. Dolly Bruce Harper was coming up the steps and Andreas was supporting her. She leaned on him heavily, and her silk dress was covered with dust and torn at the hems, her hair was unpinned, and her face was dirty and streaked with tears. Andreas said, "I found her like this—running through the streets."

Her head lay against Andreas' shoulder and she moaned, "I can't . . . can't find her. I've looked everywhere, but nobody knows her. What's her name? I can't remember her name!"

Edith put her arms around her mother and, together, she and Andreas helped her into the house and up the stairs.

In the middle of the stairs, Dolly Harper shrieked, "She used to bring me flowers! She was my flower girl! Beautiful flowers!"

They went on to her room, and Andreas lifted her up onto the bed.

"Who is this young man?" she asked in a dreamy voice.

"This is Andreas Larsen, Mama."

"Pink roses. And lilies—"

"I'll get you a glass of wine, Mama." She went to the carafe on the dresser.

Andreas was bending over Dolly Harper's face, and suddenly he straightened up. "Is that what you give her?" he asked sharply. "Wine?"

"It helps her sleep," Edith said, filling a glass.

He turned quickly, with a sad look on his face, and walked toward the door. "I'll wait for you outside," he said.

When she met him, a few minutes later, in the shadows

outside the gate, she said, "I told Mama about us!"

He held her shoulders. "What did she say?"

She laughed a little wildly. "Why, she didn't even seem to *care!* She just smiled and nodded. Isn't that wonderful?"

His face was hidden from her in the shadows, and she couldn't see his eyes. "Come on," he said. "Let's walk a little."

"Aren't you happy, Andreas? Isn't this a good sign?"

"I think it means—absolutely nothing," he said.

He was right, she knew. They walked in silence for a little way.

"You have a sunburn, Edith," her father said. He had arrived home unannounced, late that afternoon. "It is not becoming." He tweaked her nose playfully. "I don't want a red-nosed little princess."

"Papa—" she began.

"If you arrive in Europe looking like a lobster you'll be laughed out of every drawing room in Paris. There is also such a thing as sun poisoning."

"Yes, Papa."

"If you have occasion to leave the house, you should wear a hat or carry a parasol." He continued to hold the tip of her nose pinched between his fingers. "It's hardly ladylike to be sunburned."

"Yes, Papa."

"Yes-Papa-yes-Papa-yes-Papa," he mimicked. "I have a dutiful little princess, anyway. Now tell me how you got this lobster face."

"I've been out walking, Papa."

"Walking with your mother?"

"When she's resting or not feeling well I sometimes walk—"

"You mean you walk *alone?* You leave her alone?"

"Sometimes she doesn't seem to want me with her, Papa."

He pushed her face aside with his hand, and all at once his voice was harsh. "Whether she wants you with her or not, whether she is well or unwell, you are to keep your mother company. Where is she now?"

"In her room, Papa," Edith said.

* * *

"He's home tonight," she whispered to Andreas when she met him. "But he was cross with me. It's useless to ask him anything when he's in a mood like that."

He stood very silently in the moonless night, a tall shape. "Edie," he said at last, "when are you going to believe me? It's going to be useless to ask him at *any* time."

"Couldn't I just try?" she begged him. "Then, if he said no—"

"Asking isn't going to get you anywhere, you know that. No, there's only one way to do it."

"Without asking," she said.

In the darkness, he nodded.

"But he might say yes!"

He shook his head. "No," he said. "Edie—there are so many reasons why I will not be—acceptable to him."

"Why won't you be?"

He shrugged. "For one thing, my family. Not good enough for Harpers."

"But your father is one of the most important men in St. Thomas!"

"It isn't a question of importance," he said. "It's something else. I have the tarbrush."

She had never heard the expression before. "What do you mean, Andreas?"

"I have black blood. On my mother's side. She is half black."

"Oh!" For a moment her head reeled and she stepped away from him. "That's not true!" she cried. "It's a lie! You just mean you don't want to marry me!"

"Of course it's true."

"True! How could it be? If it's true, why didn't you tell me?"

He turned his back to her. "Why should I have told you?" he shouted angrily. "Why should I have to apologize to *you* that I am a quarter Saint Thomian? Why should I have to apologize to *anyone*—much less you, a *Harper!* I'm proud of it! I have island blood, and I'm proud. I will not get down on my knees to *you* and apologize for anything!"

"Andreas," she said, "I didn't mean apologize! But—couldn't you at least have told me?"

"Why? Why should I?" Then his voice changed. "This

changes everything, doesn't it, with you?"

Suddenly she ran to him across the dark road. "No," she said urgently. "It doesn't change a thing. I don't care. I'm going to marry you anyway! We'll run away. Andreas, I don't care!"

"It will be the end of your life—the end of everything you've known."

"I can't bear my life! I love you."

"Promise me that?"

"I promise you."

"We'll have to run away," he said in a dead voice. "I'll have to see if I can get a boat, and some money. Perhaps to Tortola. Go home now and get some sleep. I'll see that I can do."

Early the next morning, her father came into her bedroom. "You've been seeing the Larsen boy" were his first words. How he had found out she did not know.

"No, Papa."

He stepped quickly toward the bed where she lay and struck her hard across the mouth. "Don't lie to me!" he said.

"Yes, Papa! I have."

"Juel Larsen's son. Did he spoil you? Did he try to give you one of his filthy nigger babies? Did he—"

What happened after that is now a little jumbled in her memory; the details are blurred for everything that happened after that happened very quickly. She remembers screaming at her father, "No—but we're getting married, Papa! And you can't stop us, Papa! Isn't it wonderful that you can't stop us, Papa? Because you can't. Nobody can. Because nothing you say or do can stop us, and isn't that nice, Papa dear? Isn't that lovely, Papa dear?" She remembers that the experience of speaking to him like this exhilarated her, and that she went on and on, lying there crouched on her bed, screaming at him, waiting for him to strike her again, begging him, "Hit me, Papa! Hit me again, Papa dear! Because even that won't stop me! Hit me, Papa." But he didn't. He merely stood looking down at her for a moment or two, smiled, turned, and walked out of the room.

She got out of bed and dressed hurriedly. She scribbled a

little note and gave it to one of the maids to deliver to Andreas, telling her to wait for a reply. When the girl came back with the answer, it said simply, "Come to my father's house after ten tonight. Perhaps he can help us."

She remembers that leaving Sans Souci that night was an odd sensation, very odd. Because no one did try to stop her. Her father had been out of the house most of the day and had not come back. She went down the stairs unhindered and unquestioned, feeling lightheaded. The rooms were empty, and she noticed for the first time how large they were—how large without point of purpose for being large. Her father had designed this house himself, an edifice suitable to his proportions and to the scale of his dream. Empty, the rooms seemed like painted friezes—huge backdrops with bits and pieces of gold-painted paper pasted against them to resemble furniture. The rooms were stage settings for dramas that would never take place, in which no human action would ever occur, and with this new vision she saw her father's dream as his delusion.

She went down the drive and out into the road. Being free was now almost an anticlimax because none of the scenes she had expected had materialized. She had foreseen restraining hands, imprecations, accusations, entreaties. Instead, she walked quietly along the dark road down Government Hill, and had gone some distance toward the Larsens' house before she began to realize that something might have happened.

The Larsens' butler looked alarmed when he opened the door and saw her. But he let her inside the lighted hallway, and asked her to wait there. Presently, Andreas' tall and beautiful mother, whom she had never seen before, started down the stairs. Halfway down she stopped. She looked very frightened. "What are you doing here?" she said.

"Where is Andreas?"

"Get out of here—please. You can't come here. Get out—quickly."

"What's happened?" Edith said. "Where is he?"

"Please!" the woman said. "Get out of here. Just go. *Go!* You stupid girl, you can't come here, you're not wanted here—get out."

"Where is he?" Edith repeated. "Just tell me where he is."

She remembers the tall woman standing there in a long black dress, gripping the carved banister, screaming for the butler.

"Billy! Billy! If this girl won't go, you'll have to throw her out! Just get her out of here! I can't endure it!" she sobbed. She turned and ran back up the stairs, and Edith remembers the butler, Billy, smiling apologetically, bowing, making little pushing, shooing motions with his hands, advancing toward her, saying, "Please . . . you go now, Miss Edith Harper? Yes. Please, Miss Edith Harper . . . you go now? Yes?"

The next morning they had all gone. The Larsens' house was closed, its shutters drawn and locked. Andreas' father's office was also closed. The whole family had vanished. There had been typhus in the household, someone told her, and they had all had to leave the island. But of course this wasn't true. Somehow, her father had removed them all.

The family would leave for Europe earlier than usual, her father informed them curtly at a family meeting. They were to be ready to leave for San Juan in two days, and they would sail from there to Cherbourg.

On the boat Edith sat in a deck chair beside her mother, who looked particularly ill and tired under the steamer rugs. "It was the only way," she said at last. "Your papa did the right thing. Try to understand."

Edith said nothing.

"He was only after your money—only that."

"That isn't true."

"Of course it's true. It will always be true. You are Meredith Harper's only daughter."

"What do you mean it will always be true?"

"Edith, I should have told you before. Unless a girl is beautiful—"

"Which I am not."

"Unless a girl has—exceptional endowments, a man does not want to marry a plain girl. If the girl is rich, however, the money will—compensate. Do you understand? This can be both a blessing and a handicap, my dear. The blessing is that you will certainly someday find a nice husband—and not be one of these poor souls who never marry. The handicap is that you are the natural prey of fortune hunters. I didn't make these rules of human nature. They just exist! No matter what else a man likes about you, the money will always be his first consideration. Once you accept this about yourself, my dear, you can be happy." She covered Edith's bare hand with her gloved one. "And remember—time heals all wounds."

Edith was out of the deck chair and running to the rail of the ship. Her mother came after her, and for several minutes they struggled there in violent silence, their feet sliding together on the polished deck, making absolutely no sounds until Dolly Harper began to scream, "Steward! Steward! Steward!"

This is how Edith remembers that April crossing that year, when her nineteenth birthday was just a month away.

On the beach at Morningstar, Leona sits in the sun, oiled and polished, scanning faces. A blond young man waves to her. "Hiya, Leona baby!"

"Hi. Have you seen Eddie Winslow?"

"Nope. He should be along, though."

She lies back on her towel, her face upward, arms at her sides, eyelids closed and trembling against the sun's red glare. It is important, in the sun, to keep one's face composed and unsquinting because there are such things as wrinkles. And twenty-seven is not young, no matter what anybody says. No, it is darned near middle-age. What *is*, technically, middle age anyway, she asks herself? Well, if threescore years and ten is the normal human lifespan, then middle age is precisely thirty-five. Thirty-five for her is just seven and a half short years away. They will pass as swiftly as the last seven and a half have—and the last seven and a half have scooted past her on roller skates. *Over* her. A whole roller derby of days has passed over her, and those hard little wheels have hurt. No use trying to move middle age, as some women did, to forty, and then, with another discreet nudge, to forty-five. It would be on her before she knew it, her life half over. And yet, she thinks, figuring this way means that her grandmother's life ought to be wholly over which, of course, it isn't. And so, perhaps. . . .

Someone's foot jogs her bare toe, and she opens her eyes and looks up. He stands, a foreshortened shadow, over her. "Ah," she says, sitting up, "I was waiting for you."

"Hello."

"Come," she says, spreading out her towel, "sit down."

Squatting tailor-fashion on the towel beside her, he gives her a bitter smile.

"Eddie, I'm sorry about last night. Are you still mad at me?"

"No," he says. "I never was, as a matter of fact." Cupping his hands over his eyes he looks out at the glittering water of the bay.

She touches his bare knee. "It was all so sudden, as we say."

"Yeah," he says. "I guess it was."

"You really should give a girl a little time to gather her wits after you say things like that."

"Sure. Sure."

Gently, she says, "Eddie—dear Eddie. I am awfully fond of you, you know that."

"Sure. You think I'm perfectly swell."

"Listen, Eddie, don't you understand? After my last divorce I promised myself that I simply wouldn't rush into anything again. Next time, I've got to be terribly sure. That's all."

She smiles at him, but his dark, good-looking face is still scowling at the sea. "Just give me a little time, Eddie, to think about all the things you said."

He nods.

"And don't go running off on me. I had a low blow today about my gallery. It's going to be more important to me than ever to have a friend with the press."

"Sure. I'm always here. Good old reliable Eddie."

"Don't say that!" she says quickly, because these are the words, of course, with which she has always thought of him. "And don't think that what you said didn't make me terribly pleased and flattered and—yes, honored, Eddie. Because it did."

They sit in silence for several minutes. Then Leona says, "I had a rather quaint evening after you left. Who is this Arch Purdy, anyway?"

"A smart customer. I did a story on him once. Got to know him pretty well."

Leona shakes a cigarette from her pack and lights it. "An odd man, I thought. I'm not sure I liked him much. He was full of questions—all about my marriages, and things like that."

"Well, if you're worth ten million dollars you can afford to be odd," he says. "Just the way you can afford to get divorces."

"That was a mean crack. And quite untrue, by the way. But

I'll overlook it. At least he bought me dinner—after you abandoned me."

He says nothing to this.

"Eddie," she says, "I talked to Granny last night about your story. She's changed her mind. She doesn't want to be quoted on anything."

"Oh?" he says, turning to look at her. "Oh, is that so?"

"Yes. I want you to forget the whole story, Eddie. The family's always been that way about publicity. I should have known."

He continues to stare at her. "What are you asking me to do?"

"Cancel the whole thing. Forget about the Harpers. Granny's really awfully upset, and the whole family's getting into a tiz. I'm going to be right in the middle if they don't like what you write, and the Harpers can be pretty nasty when somebody does something they disapprove of. So please, for me. Write about something else." When he says nothing, she says, "Look, the real, honest-to-gosh truth about the Harpers is that they're just ordinary dull, stuffy, grubby businessmen. There's nothing colorful about them at all."

"I see," he says quietly. "I see."

"Will you, Eddie? For me?"

"The magazine's paid my way down here, they're paying for my hotel."

"Well, perhaps we could—"

"Let the *Harpers* pick up those tabs?" he says sharply. "Is that what you're saying?" He jumps to his feet and stands over her. "Is it?"

"Eddie," she says, "you said you loved me. Won't you do this as a favor for me?" She reaches out for him. "Please? For me?"

But he turns abruptly and starts away from her across the beach.

"Eddie!" she calls.

But he had abandoned her again.

Edith's brother Arthur, always her favorite of the two, has a pronounced limp from a wound he received in the Italian Campaign, during the Fifth Army attempt to cross the Rapido River. (Right after Pearl Harbor, at the age of thirty-nine, Arthur enlisted in the Army as a private; when he came out he was Major Arthur Harper, wearing the Silver Star.) When he first came back from overseas, the limp was not particularly noticeable. But, in the years since, as he has grown older and somewhat heavier, walking has become more painful to him. And this is too bad because, once, just as Leona dreams now, Arthur dreamed of there being something else, something besides being a Harper. (*Something else . . . something else. . . .* It seems to Edith to be a recurring echo from Harper voices.) For Leona, there is still a chance that she may find what that something else is. Arthur, when he thought he found it, let it go. Three or four years ago, when Arthur came to St. Thomas for a visit (he came alone because his wife, Hannele, dislikes the tropics), he and Edith talked about it.

"You know, Edie," he said, "the Army saved my life."

"I know," she had said, thinking he was referring to the hospital weeks when they pieced his leg together.

"I don't mean what they did in the hospital," he said. "They saved my life in another way." They were sitting on Edith's veranda having a drink, watching the sun set. "I guess it taught me something in terms of people, and in terms of what life is about. You see, you and I—"

"What about you and me, Arthur?"

"Well, there was Papa. Then there was poor Mama. And—"

"You mean Papa ran us all the way he ran his plantations and his mills," she said. "And you found out that there were some people who didn't let themselves be run that way."

But he changed the subject. "I love Hannele," he said. "We're really very happy. We get along fine. We're as happy, I guess, as any other couple. It's a good marriage. But—"

"But *what?*"

"You mustn't ever tell her, Edie," he said. "But after I was patched up, you know, and waiting in the hospital, and they'd offered me a discharge—well, I didn't have to take it. I had a chance to re-enlist—in an administrative capacity, and, well—suddenly, the Army *meant* something. Nothing else meant anything. And I decided all at once that re-enlist was what I was going to do. I was going to stay in the Army—for good. I was going to say the hell with everything else!" He looked at his sister, his eyes bright.

"Really, Arthur?"

"Yes. I had it all figured out. I knew Hannele would never understand. Can you see Hannele as a career Army officer's wife? Having tea at the Wives' Club?" He chuckled softly. "No, I knew she'd never go along with it. It would mean leaving Hannele and the children."

"Which of course you'd never do."

"No!" he said. "That's not the point. I could have done it, I would have done it. And do you know something?" He hunched forward in the wicker chair, his face eager and intent and assured, and she had a sudden glimpse of how he must have looked in command of his battalion. "Do you know? Call me a bastard if you will, but once I'd made up my mind that I was going to do it I don't think I ever felt so happy in my life. Why, it was as though half my life had been submerged someplace, and I'd suddenly come up for air!" Slowly, the wicker creaked as he sank back into his chair again. He took a swallow of his drink.

"And yet you changed your mind," she said.

"Yes. Of course. I couldn't do it. I had to come back. I couldn't chuck everything and begin a whole new life."

"No," she said.

"But it wasn't because of Hannele and the children." He looked at her. "It was because of me. What I am. *I couldn't do it, Edie!*"

"I understand," she said, "but I still don't see why you say the Army saved your life."

"It taught me that another possibility existed. Just knowing that—helps."

She nodded.

"Funny, isn't it," he said, "the way things tie you down? You stick to the pattern that was cut out for you. Harper Industries, Incorporated. Harold Harper, President. Arthur Harper, Secretary-Treasurer. That was the way the old man planned it. Harold was to be whiz kid. I was to be the assistant whiz kid—the pattern. But of course you managed to escape it, Edie."

"Oh, Arthur," she said. "You know better than that. I didn't escape anything. The pattern was for me to be exactly what I am."

He stared into his glass. "Well, perhaps you're right," he said. "What an incredible guy the old man must have been. I was always too scared of him ever to get to know him. I suppose you knew him better than anybody. From hardware to sugar to steel mills. What do you suppose his secret was?"

"Faith in himself," she said. "All the gall in the world, and a child's faith in himself. The only thing he never realized was that that faith could be broken, just like a child's faith can be broken, with a snap of the fingers."

"Yes."

"He believed he could be a king. Do you remember nineteen ten?—no, you'd have been too little. That was the year he was invited to Berlin to meet Kaiser Wilhelm. He came home from that visit, and he kept saying 'Kings know my name—just think, kings know my name!'—like a little child."

"You're awfully charitable about him, Edie—considering."

"I keep his portrait, don't forget," she said. "I've grown accustomed to him."

Sitting there on the veranda that evening, she had felt a warm flood of affection for Arthur. They were two old gray people now, and all the signs of brotherness and sisterness had blurred with the years, and yet there was still a tight and tender bond between them. Poor little Arthur, the baby they had never bothered to tell anything—thirteen and a half years younger than she, the youngest of them all—he had always had to account for himself to an elder. First to Papa, now to Harold. Nobody had ever quite trusted his judgment or believed anything he had to say. Sitting there opposite him she was grateful for the few times she had been able to defend him. She watched him as he stood up and walked across the veranda, with that heavily uneven gait, to freshen his drink. There was the time, for instance, right after he came home from the Army when a woman in Italy had written the family a letter accusing Arthur of being the father of her bastard child. Arthur had denied the charge and, of course, Harold hadn't believed him. But Edith had believed him, and had persuaded Harold that the woman only wanted money. So finally the letter was ignored, the woman never wrote again, and that was the end of it; there was no scandal.

He came back, carrying his drink, and sat down again. He cupped his glass in his hands. "You see," he said quietly, "if I had re-enlisted back there, Hannele would have known why. That was the real trouble. She would have known I was running away from her and the children. I didn't have the—the reasons Charles had when he went off to war."

"*Charles'* reasons?"

"Yes. In his case, it was something inside him, something personal—pride, duty to his country. Charles went into the war because he believed in what America was fighting for. Good reasons. But I just wanted to get away, by nineteen forty-four, and there was another woman."

Edith closed her eyes briefly.

"I don't know whether you remember, Edie. There was an Italian girl who wrote—later—"

"Yes," she said. "Indeed I do."

"Well—" he said. He took a sip of his drink. It was growing dark. The wind had changed, and a cool breeze was blowing off the shore, rustling the fronds of the ferns in their hanging baskets on the veranda. It was a clear night; the lights of St. Thomas were coming on below.

"Arthur," she began, "in Charles' case—" (She had been about to say "In Charles' case, he wanted to get away from me." But she had not said it, not so much because it would have been a betrayal of herself, but of Charles as well, and of Arthur's dream about them both.)

Arthur was saying, "Yes, my case was different. Her name was Estella. She was—"

But he left that sentence unfinished too, which was just as well. He sat there, a little drunk, the lights from inside the house falling on his gray hair, on the tips of his polished shoes. Somewhere between the comical appearance of what we are, Edith thought, and the sublime shape of what we dreamed of being is where the truth about our character lies.

"Damn lucky the old man was dead by the time that happened," Arthur said. "Can you imagine the hell he'd have raised? Remember that Danish boy you wanted to marry—before Charles?"

"Andreas Larsen."

"I don't remember much about it; I was pretty small. The old man threw him off the island, didn't he?"

"Andreas came back. Did you know that? He came back—years later."

* * *

"But you must remember," Andreas said to her slowly, "that those were very demoralized times on this island."

He returned to St. Thomas in the spring of 1950, and it was several months after Edith learned that he was back before she actually saw him again. She truly thought he might have forgotten her. But he hadn't, and one afternoon he came to call. She saw him walk into the garden, the sun flashing on his white hair. She saw him without shock or surprise or feeling, and recognized him. He was still Andreas, only grown old.

"But I still don't understand how he did it, Andreas," she said.

"I don't like to speak ill of your father," he said carefully. In fact, this was really the only new and different thing she noticed about him: a certain slow and cautious way of speaking.

"Oh, gracious!" she said. "Don't expect me to care if you do! *De mortuis,* indeed! Let the old tyrant have it."

"And it's important to remember," he said, "that besides being a demoralized period, life on this island was not like life in other countries."

She nodded. "Nor has it ever been, nor is it now."

"It wasn't that there was no such thing as justice. But justice was always outweighed by power." He spread his palms open. "And your father was more powerful than mine. It was as simple as that."

"But *how?* How did he do it?"

"It was a threat."

"What kind of threat would make you all leave like that? Your father wasn't a cowardly man. Nor were you, as I remember."

"He left with pride, Edie. We all left with pride."

"Tell me about it."

"Your father came to my father's office that afternoon," he said. "Your father made my father a very simple proposition. My father had just started his insurance brokerage business, if you recall. He had several good clients—planters whose crops he was insuring. They were friends of his. Your father said that I was to get off the island. If I didn't go, he said, he had people who would see to it that my father's clients' fields were burned, and my father would be ruined."

She said, "Oh, no."

"It was winter, and the cane was ripe."

"He couldn't have got away with it," she said. "Someone would have stopped him."

"But that wasn't the point, Edie. Yes, someone *might* have stopped him, but that wasn't what concerned my father. He assumed, you see, that he was dealing with a madman."

"A madman—"

"We discussed it then—my mother, my father, and I. We tried to weigh the possibilities. I was for staying and fighting it out. There might be a way to stop your father—possibly. But there were other considerations. It wasn't our own lives and futures we would be risking. It was the lives and futures of my father's clients. These people counted on him to protect them. What if even one field was burned? Your father had been known to get away with worse than that. Could my father take a chance? He went up to his room for a while, to decide what we'd do. Whatever we did, he said, we'd do together. He was up there for about an hour. When he came down, he said, 'I have decided that we would not wish to live any longer in a place where such things can happen.' I confess to you, Edie, that when I heard him say those words I agreed with him. I was very proud of him."

She nodded. The day seemed to have become uncomfortably close. She sat there, thinking, and the heavy air swarmed with sounds. A fly batted against a window screen somewhere; a butterfly with dusty wings lighted on a lily in the garden, delicately invaded its corolla, and the lily nodded while Andreas and Edith faced each other on garden chairs. "Well," she said at last. "I've often wondered if you blamed me, Andreas."

"Why should I blame you, Edie?"

"Just for being Papa's daughter, I suppose."

"No," he shook his head slowly. "If I blamed anyone I'd blame myself—for falling in love with you the way I did." He smiled at her.

"What an extraordinary thing to say."

His eyes traveled away from her. "You have a beautiful garden, Edie," he said. "A beautiful house."

"It—suffices."

"And your mother? How is she?"

"Pretty well. She lives very quietly now. She's built a new house up on the road to Ma Folie. The old house burned, you know."

"She must be getting on."

"Eighty-five." (Her mother was to die the following summer).

"I have a wonderful wife—Sigrid," he said. "You'll meet her. And we have two grown sons. The elder isn't married yet—no time for it, he says. Not until he makes a million *kroner!* But the younger boy is married, and his wife is going to give me my first grandchild in June."

"How wonderful." A copy of *Town & Country* lay on the garden table, and Edith picked it up. "I just ran across a picture of my daughter in this magazine," she said, flipping the pages. "Ah, here it is—that's Diana, the one in the long gloves. I don't know who those other people are."

"Handsome."

"I have a little granddaughter—Leona. Let me show you a picture of her." She fetched it for him.

"Very pretty," he said, smiling, holding the picture.

"Fourteen—already very vain, I'm afraid."

"She looks like you."

"Oh, Andreas!" she laughed. "No."

"But she does."

"And this is Charles, who was killed in the first war."

"A very handsome man."

"Yes." He returned the pictures. "And what else have you done all these years?" she asked.

"Well, my mother and father stayed on in Copenhagen," he said. "They're both buried there. In nineteen thirty-nine, when the pact with Germany was signed, some Danes thought Hitler would keep his promises, but I did not. I took Sigrid and the boys to England—two months before the Nazis invaded us. I went into business there—insurance still. When the war was over, the boys went back to Denmark, but Sigrid and I stayed on in London. You see, Edie, despite everything I've always been very fond of islands." He rose a little stiffly from his chair to go.

"Everything except English weather," he said. "When you get to be my age, you begin to want a little sunshine. So we decided to come back."

They stood at the edge of the garden, suddenly a little hesitant and awkward. It was as though they had taken separate paths, and met at the end of a peninsula, and all the ground behind them had washed away.

He smiled at her again. "Those snows you used to say you

missed so much. I've seen a lot of snow since last we met."

She was terribly touched and moved. "Come back and see me again some afternoon, Andreas," she said, "and bring your wife. We'll have tea and talk." And he smiled at her in a way that told her that, of course, he would not come back. They shook hands.

Later, she heard that his insurance business was becoming very prosperous in St. Thomas, which pleased her.

After lunch the telephone rings, and it is Alan Osborn to tell Edith about her appointment for the X rays. "Monday afternoon at three o'clock for our little posing session, dear," he says.

"Fine, Alan. I'll be there." Then there is a long pause at the other end of the line, as though he expects her to have something more to say.

Finally, he says, "Well, aren't you going to ask me if I did my little errand?"

"What little errand?"

"To find out about your Mr. Winslow." He clears his throat. "Edward George Winslow, Journalist. Age thirty. Graduated Columbia School of Journalism nineteen fifty-four. Specializes in financial reporting. Impecunious parents. Ambitious—"

"Oh, Alan," she says. "Never mind, never mind! I know all this, and besides—"

"Oh," he says, and he sounds disappointed that Edith does not want a complete dossier on Mr. Winslow any longer.

"No, Alan, it really doesn't matter any more," she says in a soothing voice. "Mr. Winslow is now completely out of the picture."

Eight

"THANK you for the lift, Arch," Leona says, her hand on the handle of his car door.

"Don't mention it, buddy. I'm always glad to help a lady in distress." He looks at her curiously. "And you know something?" he says. "I think you *are* a lady in distress, in a funny way. But what are you distressed about?"

"Distressed?" Leona says, forcing a laugh. "Why should I be distressed? I could easily have called a taxi from the beach, but you came along and offered me a ride. That's all."

"I'm not talking about that. I'm talking about you—something about you I can't quite figure out."

"No girl likes to think she's been completely figured out."

"Look," he says. "I'm a sucker for punishment. Will you have dinner with me again tonight?"

"I can't, Arch. I promised Granny I'd have dinner with her tonight."

"Then maybe I could pick you up after dinner."

She shakes her head. "I haven't spent a single evening with her since I've been here. I'm sorry . . ." Leona looks up at the house and sees, at one of the tall French windows, recessed behind its ornamental grillwork balcony, the figure of her grandmother. She looks away quickly, hoping that Arch has not seen Granny watching them. But he has seen her.

"Is that her?" he asks.

"Yes."

"Well, look," he says, "if you change your mind later on, and feel like going out, I'm not doing anything. You know where I am. Give me a call." The tiny muscles of his face are gathered in a grin.

They have both looked up at Edith, and have looked away, which means that they have not seen her standing there. For if Leona had seen her, she would certainly have smiled and waved. Edith has recognized him, the old-house enthusiast from the night before, and thinks that he looks less appetizing by daylight than he looked by night. His neck, she thinks, is too short and, as everybody knows, men with short necks tend to assume the characteristics of Napoleon. And as for the formation of his cowlick, it almost looks—with that very short, brush-cut hair of his—as though he has no cowlick at all, a bad sign. His open car looks expensive. Perhaps it is the automobile which amuses Leona about him. But, quite obviously—a fact which may not have dawned upon Leona—the car is rented; touring gentlemen do not, as a rule, ship their automobiles to St. Thomas. The man leans unpleasantly close to Leona, saying something to her, and Leona nods. Poor Leona. She wants to get out of the car, and he will not let her; she has her hand on the handle of the door. Edith feels that she should warn Leona about this man, exactly as she used to warn her, when she was a little girl, to put on her arctics in the rainy season. At last, Leona manages to make her escape. She steps out of the car and waves to him. She walks slowly into the garden, up the steps, and into the house.

"Is that you, Leona?" Edith calls.

Leona pauses in the hall for a moment. Then she says, "Hi, Granny," and starts up the stairs. "What time is it, d'you know?"

"Twenty past five, dear."

"Oh—I'll have time for a swim before dinner then."

"Fine," Edith calls. "I'll join you at the pool."

* * *

When Edith arrives at the pool, Leona is already there, lying on an inflatable air mattress, wearing a face mask and snorkel, propelling herself about the surface of the water. She looks up once, seeing Edith coming down the path, and waves. Then her head bobs under the water again.

"Well, how was your day?" Edith asks.

Leona's breath spits and gurgles through the snorkel tube. It is difficult to talk to a submerged granddaughter.

At last Leona rolls off the mattress and swims to the pool's edge, pulls herself out of the water, and removes the mask.

"Well," Edith says, leaning toward her, "did you speak to Mr. Winslow, dear?"

Leona nods.

"And did he—did he agree not to write anything about us?"

Leona says nothing for a moment; then she nods.

"You mean everything is going to be all right?"

"Yes," Leona says. She sits very still at the pool's edge, her arms hugging her knees. The sun has left the pool now. A cool breeze stirs the heavy tops of palm trees, and Leona shivers.

"Oh, good!" Edith says, sitting back. "You see? I told you that you could persuade him. Oh, I'm awfully relieved, Leona—really I am. Thank you so much, darling."

Once more Leona nods. Her eyes travel away from Edith, across the pool, to the chattering leaves of the palm grove.

"And now," Edith says, "have you given any more thought to our talk this morning?"

"This morning?" Leona says absently. "What did we talk about this morning?"

"Well, among other things, about Gordon. Don't you remember?"

"What did we say about Gordon?"

"You said that, of the three, you liked Gordon best."

"Oh, yes."

"Because, you see, *I've* always been fond of Gordon too. He's an awfully nice man—a very sensible and mature human being. And he hasn't remarried," Edith says.

Leona's smile is small and bitter. "None of them has," she says. "Do you suppose I soured them all on marriage, Granny?"

"Of course not! They still love you, that's all."

"Well, it's a pretty thought."

"Now tell me, Leona. What went wrong with you and Gordon?"

"Wrong? Oh, Granny—" She pauses, looking at Edith briefly. "It's so hard to say. Gordon is—well, you know the type, don't you? Voted Most Likely To Succeed at Dartmouth. Editor in *Chief* of the Yearbook! As a boy, Gordon was famous in his neighborhood for all the things he could make out of his Lincoln logs. Then he graduated to an erection set—"

"Erec*tor* set, I believe."

"And he was treasurer of Beta Theta Pi. He could have been *President* of Beta Theta Pi, but he *declined* the nomination in a noble gesture—on the basis that some other man was better *qualified*. Gordon's remembered at Dartmouth for that!" She jumps to her feet now and begins marching stiffly up and down along the edge of the pool, her hands clasping her elbows. "The Eye of Wooglin was upon him, he said, telling him not to accept the nomination. Dear Lord, I think the Eye of Wooglin is *still* upon him, Granny!"

"What in the world are you talking about?"

"And then, later, his senior year, after so much mental anguish—so much *Angst* that you wouldn't believe there could *be* so much *Angst*—he decided that fraternities were undemocratic. That's Gordon Cogswell Paine for you in a nutshell!"

Leona lights a cigarette and waves the match out, and Edith sits there wondering why she bothered bringing up the subject. "I'm glad you're having dinner with me tonight, Leona," she says finally. "I've asked Sibbie Sanderson to join us. You remember my friend Sibbie, don't you?"

"Yes. The one with the sandals." Then Edith hears Leona say in a different voice, "But still— Still, he was very kind to me once. Gordon."

Edith sits forward again in her canvas chair, feeling that she has suddenly scored something of triumph. "There!" she says. "You see? That's exactly what I meant. He's so much nicer than any of the others. So much better for you than that man you were with last night—"

"Now *wait* a minute, Granny—"

"I noticed he brought you home this afternoon."

"Granny, that man means nothing to me at all!"

"Or your Mr. Winslow. Now, I have an idea, Leona. Tell me what you think of it. I'm thinking of writing Gordon a letter—asking him to come here and visit us for a few weeks. The invitation would come better from me than from you, I think. What do *you* think?"

Leona stands quite rigidly for a moment. Then she says, "Playing Cupid, Granny?"

"Well," Edith says with a small, uneasy laugh, "isn't that what grandmothers are supposed to do?"

Leona steps to the edge of the pool once more, and Edith watches as she curls her toes over the lip of the coping, looking thoughtful. "Well, I suppose it's all right," she says, and performs a neat little dive into the water, making almost no splash.

"Wonderful. Then I'll do it."

Leona comes to the surface, takes two quick strokes across the pool, catches hold of the coping, and looks up at Edith. "Whom you invite to this house is your business, Granny!" she says sharply. "After all, it *is* your house, not mine! But I must ask you not to interfere in my affairs! Or feel that anybody you invite has anything to do with *me!* Because if that's the case—"

"Now wait a minute, Leona—I only meant—"

Leona pulls herself quickly out of the water and stands dripping in front of her grandmother. "Oh!" she cries. "If you really want to know what I think of your idea, I think it's just—terrible! And what do you *mean* this is the way grandmothers are supposed to behave? Is there an Ilg and Gesell *Guide to Grandmothering?"*

"Leona—"

"Really! If you're not careful, you'll turn into Mary Worth—just like that! You're already displaying a number of very disagreeable Mary Worth tendencies!" She tugs at the strap of her bathing cap and pulls it off, shaking the dampness from her hair. "Don't you have enough to keep you busy taking care of your own affairs? Without meddling in mine?"

"Leona, *please*. I was only trying. . . ."

"Don't try! Just don't. Don't try to arrange peoples' lives, Granny. You're not qualified! As a marriage counselor, you stink! Why, you don't even have amateur standing. You presume to try to doctor up some old dead marriage of mine, but your own was hardly a prizewinner, was it? Was it? It was a phony-baloney from the start. Everyone knows the whole thing was completely prearranged!" And she turns on her heel, and runs away, barefoot up the path, leaving Edith seated by the pool.

After a moment or two Edith stands up, picks up Leona's beach clogs, bathing cap, sunglasses, and cigarettes, makes a sort of vagabond's tote-bag for these articles out of Leona's damp towel, and walks back into the garden, under the wilted bougainvillea vines, the acacias struggling for life in their starved soil. How can a garden hope to survive without the ministrations of manures, or the caress of mulches, or the attention of someone who cares about it? Well, Mr. Barbus, she thinks, there is nothing for you to do. This house will go to the hospital, and the starved soil with it. The house will be torn down, and the garden will be bulldozed under, and the sooner it can all happen, I suppose, the better.

Pausing there, thinking about it, she hears the sudden clatter of a stick pulled sharply across the grillwork of her gate, and the children's voices:

> Edie, Edie, fat and greedy,
> How does your garden grow?
> With your husband dead
> And your lover in bed
> And dollar bills all in a row!

Edith Blakewell smiles. It has been a long time since she has heard that little verse. The song passes on, she supposes, from one generation to the next, and once in a while a group of them, drunk with twilight, dares to chant it outside her gate—then runs off into the shadows, expecting the old lady to come charging out of her house after them with her cane.

Edith goes up the steps and into the house, and picks up the evening mail that lies, neatly arranged by Nellie, on the long table in the hall. There is a letter from Edith's insurance agent, a postcard from a New York department store urging her to hurry-hurry-hurry to a fifth-floor better-dress salon to take advantage of many bargains, and a small brown package for Leona. *Leona Diaz* it says—a name Edith simply cannot accustom herself to. Leona Diaz! It sounds like the name of some fandango dancer. Oh, wasn't it nicer when Leona had those clean, neat, American names—Leona Paine, Leona Breed, Leona Ware?

Edith puts the package down. Nellie is behind her, saying something.

"What is it, Nellie?"

"Miss Sanderson's here, Miss Edith."

Edith turns toward the drawing room, preparing herself for Sibbie's bellowed greeting.

If she had heard the song the children sang, Leona, alone in her room, would not have known what to make of it. But the only sound in her ears is the roar of the electric hair-dryer she holds in her hand, letting its jets of warm air blow all over her head and face and neck and bare shoulders.

She has just had an interesting thought. It is a new thought, a new plan of action. Now that her mother has turned her down (not even turned her down but, more typically Mother, has simply laughed at Leona's request), suppose she asked Arch Purdy if he would be interested in financing her gallery? If he is as rich as Eddie Winslow says he is, the amount Leona needs certainly wouldn't be any hardship to him. And besides, he even suggested it, didn't he? Kiddingly, perhaps, but still he did mention becoming her angel. She has never thought of approaching a man and asking him for money—especially a man she knows so slightly as Arch Purdy. And yet he is a businessman. If she were to approach him on a straightforward, businesslike basis. . . .

"Arch," she says to the mirror, "I'd like to prove to you how serious I am about the gallery. How determined I am to make it a success. If you will lend me—" Is *lend* the right word? "If you will buy stock in my company . . . If you will help me with the financing . . ." It will be strictly a business loan. She will repay him, with interest. Six per cent.

She snaps off the hair-dryer and lights a cigarette. Why not? There is nothing to be lost in simply *asking* him—in putting the proposition to him. Nothing ventured, after all, is nothing gained. Then why not? Besides, she thinks, who else is there to ask at the moment?

There is Granny. But could she ever bring herself to ask Granny for something like that—for *money?* She confronts her face in the mirror, still-damp hair hanging in little wiggling strands, and thinks: I certainly can't ask her for anything at all, not now—not after the things I said to her this afternoon. And how could I say such ugly, cruel things to her?

"Oh, how could you!" she says aloud to her reflection. Then she turns away, making a small fist of her left hand, jamming the knuckles into her mouth, biting the knuckles till they hurt.

"Hello, sweetie!" Sibbie cries, leaping up and giving Edith her bear hug, her grinning face wrinkled and leathery from years in the sun. Edith gives Sibbie's cheek a little peck and murmurs a greeting. She goes to the cellaret and sets out glasses, ice, cocktail shaker. "I like your outfit, Sibbie," Edith says, fixing their drinks.

"Do you? I made it myself," Sibbie says, twirling around in it. She has encompassed her formidable frame, tonight, in a giant dirndl—the kind that always seems to dip down in the back—and a peasant blouse with red ribbons run through the puffed sleeves and across the even puffier bosom. Sibbie Sanderson's dresses have made her a landmark on the island—the dresses, the sandals, the clanking copper bracelets, and the big copper hoops which always suspend from her pierced ears.

Carrying her drink to her, Edith says, "Well, what've you been up to, Sibbie?"

"Oh, busy, sweetie, busy! Painting, painting. I'm working on a big picture now, a really important picture. But I can't seem to get *into* it. The damn thing keeps resisting me, fighting back at me. Where's Leona?"

"I rather doubt Leona will be joining us after all," Edith says. "We had one of our battles royal, I'm afraid."

"Mmm," Sibbie says, "this is a yummy Manhattan, sweetie. You're the best bartender on this island, that's what I tell everybody. What was the tiff with Leona about?"

"She thinks I know absolutely nothing about anything. The point is, I do. I know a little about some things." Edith sips her whisky. "She seems terribly unhappy, Sibbie, and I just can't seem to reach her."

Sibbie's laughter booms across the room, and she gives her knee a whack. "The wisdom of one generation passed on to the next? Oh, come *on,* sweetie! Besides, who's happy? Everybody talks happy-happy-happy, and it doesn't mean a damn thing. I'm miserable ninety-five per cent of the time, and *I'm* happy. Hell, I'd rather be a Harper. Rich."

"I suppose that's the only thing we ever have been," Edith says quietly. "Rich."

"Cheer up. Life's too short."

"That's why I don't want Leona to make any more mistakes."

"How can you stop her? How can anybody stop anybody from making mistakes? Life's a party. Join the fun."

"Life is *not* a party. Sibbie, do you know anything about the history of the St. Croix Indians—before Sir Walter Raleigh came?"

"Huh? What about the St. Croix Indians?"

"They used to sail to Puerto Rico for wood for their canoes. But they were cannibals, Sibbie, and it was more than wood they wanted. They wanted meals. And once, on one of their trips, the Borinquen chief in Puerto Rico demanded seven hostages from the St. Croix, as insurance against future raids. The St. Croix were the most savage and vicious of all the West Indian tribes—"

"What in the world has this got to do with the price of eggs?"

"Let me finish, let me make my point. Do you know what the Borinquen chief did with the seven hostages? Killed them instantly, of course. And when the St. Croix came back and found that their tribesmen had all been murdered, what do you suppose *they* did? Why, they cut the chief and all his family into tiny pieces and ate them all—and then made torches, firebrands, out of their bones, and carried the torches back to the wives of the hostages as proof that their men had been revenged."

"Charming predinner conversation, sweetie. Just charming."

"But don't you *see,* Sibbie? When I was young, I was just like that. Always trying to leave hostages, parts of myself, with other people. But my poor hostages were always being murdered, and I was always charging out red-eyed for my revenge."

"And being left with a pile of bones," Sibbie says. "Sure, I know what you mean. You mean never trust a cannibal."

"The *Harpers* were cannibals. But don't you think—in three generations—some tiny inch of progress has been made? We don't always have to be headhunters, do we, Sibbie? Isn't it time we became civilized? Isn't it time? We'll always be a tribe, I suppose, but can't we be a civilized one at last? Can't I try to explain this to Leona?"

"Isn't Leona civilized? Does she eat people?"

"Three marriages? Sibbie, don't you see? She's following the old pattern, the same pattern as the rest of us—rushing out, full of fury, with blood in her eye, trying to get *even* with life."

"Oh, balls!"

And now there is considerable disconcernment between the two women because, almost exactly coincident with Sibbie's last explosive comment, Leona has appeared in the doorway, all in white, smiling, her hair brushed shiny. "Well, Leona!" Edith says. "You remember Sibbie Sanderson?"

"Of course. Hello, Miss Sanderson." And then, "Don't get up, Granny. I'll fix myself a drink." She goes to the cellaret and drops ice cubes into a glass. "You know," she says, "I could have sworn that when I came through the door I heard someone say, 'Oh, balls.'" She turns and smiles at Edith.

"Your grandmother was debating whether to tell you about her Frenchman," Sibbie says.

This, of course, is hardly the remark Edith was hoping Sibbie would make, nor is it quite true. "We were having a little argument, Sibbie and I," she says, with a glare at Sibbie.

Leona sits down sideways on a sofa opposite them.

"I wasn't sure you'd be joining us, Leona," Edith says.

Leona gives her a private look. "I was looking forward to it, Granny."

"A little package came in the mail for you. Did you find it?"

Sipping her drink, Leona nods. "Yes. Shall I show you what was in it? I'm terribly excited, Granny, because I've been waiting for these for weeks." She puts down her glass and jumps to her feet. Reaching in the pocket of her skirt, she pulls out a number of small black cellophane squares. "Just look, Granny!" she says, handing them to Edith.

"What in the world are these?"

"Hold them up to the light!"

Edith sees that they are transparencies of colored photographs and, as she holds the first one up to the lamplight, sees that it contains a colored design of some sort, small blotches and blobs of different shades. She starts to remove the transparency from its cellophane jacket, but Leona cries, "Oh, don't do that! You'll get greasy fingerprints all over it!"

"My fingers aren't greasy. What are these photographs of, anyway?"

"That's Rovensky," Leona says eagerly. "Martin Rovensky. And now look at this one. Try to imagine it as it is—huge! Ten feet tall and nine feet wide."

"You mean these are *paintings,* Leona?"

"Oh, such paintings, Granny! Rovensky is the most exciting painter working in New York today, *I* think! And he's only beginning to come into his own. He's only twenty-four."

She hands Edith another, of green and blue. "Well!" Edith says.

"Now, there are three painters here," Leona says, sorting out the thirty or forty photographs into three small piles. "Rovensky, Hans Knecht, and Suzy Kirkpatrick. Kirkpatrick I'm not sure about, frankly. She's too—*fluffy,* somehow. A little pretentious? But Rovensky! And *Knecht!* Here's Knecht, Granny—this is a very tiny picture, but, oh God, look what he's got going on inside it!"

Edith looks and sees more or less a spiral of yellow, orange, and white.

"And here's Knecht working big. Knecht works either very big or very small. Isn't that interesting? Tell me what you think of this."

"Leona, this sort of thing just isn't my cup of tea."

"Now here—no, sorry, that's Kirkpatrick. Here's the one I wanted—Rovensky being really explosive. Look at that. Isn't that a wonderful big goddamn burst of *joy?"*

"It means nothing to me. I don't understand it."

She shows Edith a large brown concoction. "And here he is again—in a somber mood."

"At least it won't show the dirt."

"They laughed at the Impressionists too, Granny."

"The Impressionists? Why, there's no comparison, Leona.

The Impressionists created things of beauty—things of loveliness and light. A Renoir, a Monet, a Degas—they painted pictures that shimmered, that lifted the soul. Isn't that what art is, Leona—something that exalts? Not just blobs. It seems strange to me that you, of all people—"

Leona's eyes are thoughtful. "I may look to you like Degas," she says, "but inside I'm a pure abstraction, Granny."

"I can't believe that inside you look like one of your funny-named people. Like Mr. Picasso."

Leona laughs. "Picasso? Oh, Granny!"

"Well, isn't he one of your people?"

"I'll just have to educate you."

Sibbie Sanderson has been so silent through all this that Edith has almost forgotten she is there. She turns to her now and says, "Sibbie, you're a painter. What do you think?"

Slowly Sibbie lifts her lorgnette from where it hangs hidden, suspended on a chain in the cleavage of her breasts, and snaps it open. Adjusting the glasses to her eyes, she examines first one transparency, then another, frowning. Finally she says, "Well, of course." And then, "It's the neo-objectivist thing again, you see. I'm afraid—well, one has seen so much of this stuff before. One almost wishes—"

Leona has sat down, rather abruptly, on the small sofa again. She holds her cocktail glass tightly pressed between her hands, staring at it. "One almost wishes what, Miss Sanderson?" she says in a quiet voice.

"Oh, one *wonders*," Sibbie says, with a disparaging little laugh and wave of her hand, "how long these queer little fads will last."

Leona sits very still. "These three painters," she says, "are important. Vital. Many people feel that they represent the best of the current New York School."

"Of *course!*" Sibbie says, warming to the argument. "A *school*. When one has schools of painting, one has comformity. No individuality. Sameness."

"School is simply a term."

"Well, I'm afraid," Sibbie begins. She lowers her lorgnette and gives Leona a fond smile. "No, my dear."

Leona slowly looks up at Sibbie. "What sort of things do you think an artist should paint, Miss Sanderson?" she asks.

"Beauty!" Sibbie cries. "The sea! The sun in the palm trees! Nature! Life!"

"Life," Leona echoes.

The silence then becomes triangular, each of them at a point of it. It is broken, mercifully, by Nellie announcing dinner.

"Come!" Edith says in her most cheerful voice. "Bring your drinks to table if you'd like," standing up, urging them into the dining room.

At tables as elaborate as Edith Blakewell's, in a dining room as imposing as hers, it is difficult to rescue a dinner party once it has begun to sink. The sinking parallel is almost too exact, Edith thinks, because certainly her party tonight has struck an uncharted iceberg, and is going down with *Titanic* inexorability. As captain, at the head of her table, she has thus far refused to abandon ship, but her two guests have already betaken themselves to separate lifeboats where they seem to have nothing at all to do but watch as the huge mahogany board, glittering with the false gaiety of polished silver, china, glassware, and fresh flowers, continues on its doomed course.

Finally, Edith says to Leona, "Are these paintings you're thinking of buying, dear?"

"No. They're paintings I'm thinking of selling, Granny. I'm going to open an art gallery."

"An art gallery? And deal in paintings like those?"

"Yes. And don't say *paintings like those* so sniffily, Granny. Remember—" and her eyes move briefly to Sibbie, "—that you haven't had your education."

"Well, I think it's a—a very interesting idea."

Softly Leona says, "I have the basis here for my first two one-man shows, Rovensky and Knecht. Suzy Kirkpatrick I think I'm going to turn down." Looking up at Edith she says, "It's going to be a wonderful gallery, Granny! You see, I've got to do *some*thing. I can't just—exist."

"Forgive me if I don't understand the paintings. But I do understand what *you* want." And then, to try to bring Sibbie back into the conversation, Edith says, "And just think—some day you may be showing Sibbie's paintings in your gallery!"

The minute the words are out, Edith knows they were a mistake. There is another heavy silence in which Leona cuts into her pear with her spoon, and the conversational ship sinks a few feet further, listing badly.

Edith says, "Sibbie's had shows in some of the best galleries in the world, haven't you, Sibbie?"

Sibbie now, finished with food, is puckering over a cigarette. "Actually, no." She clears her throat. "I've never believed that galleries were good for the artist, you see. I've never prostituted my art by turning it over to the flesh-peddlers. I believe that if my art is good, it will find its audience naturally."

Leona folds her napkin beside her plate, and the silence now seems both unbearable and unbreakable.

"Sibbie means—" Edith tries to begin, but it is hopeless, and she leaves the sentence unfinished. At least the dinner is over.

Leona pushes back her chair. "I have to make a phone call," she says. "Granny, would you mind if I went out for a little while? There's someone I want to see."

"Of course not, dear," Edith says, almost with relief.

"I won't be late. Good night, Granny. Good night, Miss Sanderson." She moves toward the door. "It's been so nice . . ." Then Edith and Sibbie are left staring at each other across the table and the candles and the wreckage of empty plates.

"It was my fault, sweetie," Sibbie murmurs. "I'm sorry."

Edith rings for Nellie to clear. "It was equally mine."

Sibbie blows out a sharp stream of smoke. "Rovensky!" she says. "Knecht! I just couldn't help it."

"Were any of them any good, do you think?"

"Crap. Absolute and utter crap. If there's one thing I know about, it's art, and I know crap when I see it. The only one who had an ounce of talent was the one she didn't like—the woman. But that was still crap."

"I'm inclined to agree." Edith sighs. "But this, you see, is exactly the way things have been going lately."

"Don't try to understand the younger generation, sweetie. It's enough to do to know your own."

"I don't know my own generation, Sibbie. I just know some people my own age."

In the drawing room again, over the coffee cups and brandy glasses, Sibbie's voice takes on the faintly querulous note it always assumes when she talks about her own career. "All the greatest painters were discovered after they were dead," she says. "Botticelli . . . Titian . . . Leonardo. But I'll be discovered one day, wait and see. My pictures will be valuable some day—except I won't be around to see it happen. Oh, the awful thing about these people, sweetie—these whats-their-names Leona was showing us—the *criminal* thing is the prices they're probably getting for their crap. What do you suppose? One thousand—two thousand—for a single picture? Imagine it! Two thousand dollars for a smear of brown paint—while I, while I. . . . Oh, I just don't know where my money goes. I save and save, make my own clothes, don't spend a cent! And what have I got to show for it? A stack of bills. The electrician, the plumber—that's who I'm painting for these days."

"I want to give you a little check before you go," Edith says.

"Just a loan, sweetie, just a loan. You'll get it all back. I've been keeping track. There's a man in New York right now, very interested in me. Oh, he's *many* times a millionaire, and I've got him nibbling at the hook. He's a great collector. If I mentioned his name, you'd know it right away . . . It's *so* much better to be in a good collection than in someone's funny gallery."

"Let me give you the check right now before I forget."

Edith goes to her desk, takes out fountain pen and checkbook, and writes out a check while Sibbie continues talking. "I expect to hear from him any day now," Sibbie says, "maybe even tomorrow. . . ." Sibbie takes the check and folds it in half without looking at the amount, and puts it in the pocket of her peasant blouse. "Just a loan, just a loan, sweetie. And, as security, I'm going to bring you over my newest picture tomorrow."

"Oh, Sibbie, please don't bother. I've got so many of your pictures already—I just don't have the wall space to hang them."

"It doesn't matter. They'll be worth something some day—after I'm gone. You just hang on to them." She stands up. "This new one may not be my *Arbeit,* but it's good. It says all it needs to say."

"What's the subject this time, Sibbie?"

Sibbie smiles, a little ruefully. "The sea. The sun in the palm trees. Life," she says, and laughs.

They both laugh. And, taking Sibbie's comfortable arm, the two women walk out onto the veranda. It is enough, for Edith, to have this woman as her only woman friend in St. Thomas, and it doesn't matter, doesn't matter at all, that the relationship is based on a continuing series of exchanges, loans of money for loans of pictures. Isn't there in every human relationship a trade involved, something for something else? None of us gives of ourselves freely. Besides, it is their secret.

All the lights of Charlotte Amalie glitter at their feet from the veranda, cascading down the hill in little drops and clusters, ending in a crescent of lights at the harbor's edge. Some are moving, in slow roller-coaster curves, as auto headlights move slowly along the winding roads. Others are fixed stars. There is something about the air here, a texture, that makes the farthest lights seem to wink; on the most distant hills now, the tiny lights wink, wink, wink at them as though some lunatic electrician were flipping hundreds of little switches off and on, on and off, and there is a glittering carnival quality about the night view that makes Edith think that this is what she would prescribe if she were put in charge of the design of heaven.

"Wait Disney couldn't do it better, could he?" Sibbie says. And then, opening her arms wide, with considerable drama, she says, "Your father's island!"

"Oh, *stop* it, Sibbie. You know it wasn't my father's island at all. He was just as much an outcast here as—as he was anywhere else, and as I am now."

"Oh, pish-tush." She kisses Edith lightly on the cheek. "Good night, sweetie. And don't worry about the younger generation."

She turns and goes slowly down the steps into the winking darkness, and Edith watches her out the gate, hearing the retreating sandaled footsteps slap-slap-slapping down the hill. Instantly she has an idea, and makes a mental note to call her lawyer about it in the morning. She will add another codicil to her will, and leave Sibbie her Chrysler.

The lights from the town wink their congratulations to her on the niceness of this thought.

Once a woman tourist, eating a sandwich, walked past Edith Blakewell's house and dropped a crumpled travel folder in the street which Edith spotted, fetched, and read. "The city of Charlotte Amalie," she read with amusement and some surprise (*city* indeed!), "has taken the cosmopolitan atmosphere of Algiers, the gaiety of Paris, and the El Greco coloring of Spain, and rolled them into one. At night, from the fashionable hills above the town, the string of lights around the harbor resembles nothing so much as a string of pearls. . . ."

Nine

PEARLS. Edith's meeting Charles Blakewell began with the pearls. And so, in a sense, did the whole Louis Bertin occurrence. (Because that was what Louis was, really—not a lover but an occurrence.) The pearls, a triple strand with a diamond clasp, had been presented to her by her father, that summer of 1908, on their return trip from Paris, the second day out. Why he should have suddenly decided to give her an expensive necklace, following his behavior toward her during those Paris months after Andreas, was a mystery—unless, as she instantly supposed, he was trying to buy his way back into her good graces.

All through the Paris months there had been her punishment. The first thing he had done was cancel her checking account, removing any chance of her running away. As a little girl, she had been punished by being locked in a closet. Now, in effect, she was locked in the Paris house because she had no money with which to take herself anywhere else. When her father was home, he refused to speak to her. She had tried demanding of him "Where is Andreas? What did you do?" He would not answer. Or, sarcastically, she would say to him, "My sunburn is gone. Where are the drawing rooms of Paris that I was going to be laughed out of?" There was no reply, and there were no drawing rooms for her. It was easily the loneliest, most desperate time of her life, and every avenue of escape seemed closed. Her nineteenth birthday came and passed. And her father's most painful reprisal of all, perhaps, was to take away from her her duties of caring for her mother. An Englishwoman, Miss Mary Miles, had been hired as a nurse and companion for Dolly Harper. (And, to Miss Miles' credit, some headway was made, through constant surveillance, toward controlling the drinking.) There were no more little card games. "What do you want me to *do?*" she had begged of her father. "What reason have I got to exist? Tell me!" And then, "*Do* I exist? Do I exist at all?" But if he knew, at the time, the answers to these questions, he did not tell her.

There were other changes in the Harper household during that summer. Mademoiselle Laric, who had been, in her time, one of Edith's few confidantes, had resigned with the surprising announcement that, at the age of fifty-two, she intended to be married. A sturdy German girl, Fraülein Heidi Schiller, had been engaged as governess and tutor for the boys. And, by the end of July when they were ready to sail for America again, there had been added to this international retinue of employees (based on Meredith Harper's notion that the English made good nurses and the Germans good disciplinarians for small children) a French couple, Louis and Monique Bertin. By the time of that summer crossing, the function of the Bertins was not clear to Edith. She assumed, though, that it was inferior, since they were traveling in second class. She had not set eyes on either of them. When they were referred to at all, it was as "the Frenchman and his wife."

And now, all at once, there was her father standing, looking almost contrite, in the doorway of her stateroom on the *Mauretania*—watching her as she lifted a pearl necklace from a Cartier box.

"I don't want them. I don't want anything from you—now or ever. Take them back."

"They are for your birthday, Edith. From me."

"My birthday was eight weeks ago!"

"The clasp was specially designed. It had to be set."

The pearls were surprisingly hard to break. Tough little knots separated the individual beads. But pulling at the necklace, folding it and refolding it and twisting it in her fists and tugging it apart, she flung the broken necklace on the floor, and pearls rolled about the carpet of the stateroom, this way and that.

Meredith Harper looked at her with curious interest. "Why did you do that?" he asked finally, and knelt, on his hands and knees, and began picking up the pearls.

"Why don't you pay attention to Mama, who needs you, and leave me alone? I like it when you leave me alone." And the sight of him, crawling about on the floor picking up the pieces of the broken necklace, struck her suddenly as so absurd and uncharacteristic of him that she laughed out loud. "You look exactly like a ragpicker, Papa!" she said.

He stood up then, his face full of fury. "I've always taken care of your mother. I married her, didn't I? When she came to me, sniveling and begging and saying that she was four months pregnant with you, didn't I *marry* her? You ought to be thankful to me that you've even got a name!"

Down the corridor, in her own stateroom, Edith's mother was lying on her chaise, having tea with Mary Miles. There was a hospital odor now, a smell of remedies, that traveled with Dolly Harper wherever she went—the smell of the stomachics and antiseptics, syrups and salts that reposed on the table by the chaise in bottles and jars, stoppered and unstoppered. Seeing Edith at the door, Dolly Harper's thin hand flew to her mouth, and the sleeve of her rose-colored gown cascaded down her bare arm. *"What happened?"* she cried. Edith threw herself across her mother's legs and sobbed, "He gave me pearls! I broke them!" And Mary Miles, as though accustomed to having such passionate outbursts take place in her presence, picked up her knitting. Her needles clicked while Edith wept.

Under the deep folds of the gown, Dolly Harper's knees stirred and shifted. "I had a dream," she began in her quivering voice. "That one of the boys fell overboard! I thought that was what you came to tell me!" With one hand she touched Edith's head and neck and shoulders with small, restless ministrations. "Go to your papa. . . . Tell him you're sorry."

"I hate him!"

"Beautiful pearls," Dolly Harper said. "I saw them. He wants to . . . forgive. He was going to take you to dinner tonight. Just you and he."

"He said terrible things! Terrible things!"

"You hurt him. Just remember . . . he can hurt you . . . even more."

"He can never hurt me any more, Mama!"

"Just do—" Dolly Harper began, suddenly choking on her words, "—what he wants!" She put her head back on the pillows of the chaise, her hands falling to her sides, and began to cough—deep, rattling, terrible coughs that shook her whole body and brought tears to her eyes. "No . . . solution," she said between gasps. "Happy again . . . in Morristown. . . ." Quietly, Mary Miles arose and poured red syrup into a spoon. "Here you are, lady," she said. She supported Dolly Harper's shoulders while Dolly struggled to accept the spoon in her gulping mouth. Then, the coughing over, there was silence. Mary Miles threw Edith a critical look and picked up her needles again.

"He's ready," Dolly Harper said at last, "to let bygones be . . . bygones. *Oh!*" Her head went back into the pillows again. She looked up at the ceiling. "Oh, how long must I be expected to suffer?"

"Now, lady!" said Mary Miles.

Edith sat very still, staring at her mother.

"Don't you understand?" her mother said. "Go to him! He'll only punish me if you don't!"

"What do you mean, Mama?"

Dolly Harper's hand reached out and gripped the sleeve of Edith's dress, twisting the cloth hard against her arm. "Do as I say," she said. "Go to him. Tell him you're sorry. Have dinner with him. Pearls can be restrung."

Still Edith said nothing.

"Do it for me! Think of me for once: Not just yourself!" Then her mother leaned close to her, her breath hot in Edith's ear. "Now tell the steward to bring me a glass of sherry!"

But Mary Miles was between them now, her hands pushing them apart. "Now we'll have none of that, lady!" she said. *"I'm* the one who's here to do any little favors for you!" She glared at Edith. "Run along," she said. "You've upset her enough. Run along and speak to your father."

Edith stood up. As she left the room she heard her mother's

voice saying softly to Mary Miles, "Why are you so cruel?" And then, "Where is my life? . . . What's happened?"

That night, going into the ship's grand saloon, her father had taken her arm. "We're getting admiring looks from people at other tables, Edith," he said. "They're saying, 'Who is that attractive couple?' " She said nothing. Violins were playing. At the table, her father ordered champagne. When he asked her to dance with him, she did not refuse. They danced through a wide avenue of potted palms.

On the dance floor a man paused, smiled at her father, and bowed to Edith. "Mr. Julius Keen, the banker," her father whispered in her ear. And, when they were seated at their table again, her father said, "Look—Julius Keen is coming over to speak to us. Best behavior, princess!" The man was crossing the room, and with him was another, younger, white-tied man.

"How are you, Julius?" her father said.

"Excellent. Meredith, may I present my nephew, Charles Blakewell? Charles, this is Meredith Harper."

"How do you do, Mr. Blakewell." They shook hands.

Julius Keen and her father went on talking for several minutes while Edith sat awkwardly wondering why her father did not introduce her. And finally Mr. Keen had said, "Aren't you going to present me to your lovely daughter, Meredith?"

"Daughter?" her father said, looking surprised. "Surely you don't think me old enough to have a daughter this age, Julius. No, this is a young lady friend of mine—*une petite amie,*" and he pinched her arm. Edith blushed violently.

Charles Blakewell was smiling. "May I ask if the young lady would care to dance?"

"Certainly," her father said.

Charles Blakewell turned to Edith. "Would you care to dance?"

On the dance floor, Blakewell laughed and said, "Are you really Meredith Harper's mistress?"

"No! I'm his daughter Edith."

"So I thought." He was twenty-five then, and his hair was dark and curly, his eyes were brown, almost black, and his nose was long and straight and thin.

"Have you been in Europe long, Mr. Blakewell?"

"Six months."

"Traveling with your uncle?"

"And with my mother. My father died last winter."

"I'm very sorry."

"This trip was Uncle Julius' idea. It's done her a lot of good." Then he said, "You, I'm sure, have just closed your house in Paris, and now you are on your way to your house in Morristown, where you spend the rest of the summer."

"How do you know all this?" she asked him.

He was still smiling at her, a little mockingly. "Your father is a famous man. So is his manner of living. They say he's been buying up all the steel mills in France and Germany, and that now he's on his way to buy up anything Mr. Carnegie has for sale."

"Does the steel business interest you, Mr. Blakewell?" she said.

"Not at all."

"Nor does it interest me."

He had seemed to find this remark suddenly very funny because he had laughed and, taking her arm, had said, "Come—there's someone I want you to meet." And he led her, between the dancers, to a table where a thin, white-haired woman sat. "Mother, may I present Miss Edith Harper?" he said. "Miss Harper, this is my mother, Mrs. Blakewell."

The woman looked at Edith very coolly and appraisingly. "Meredith Harper's daughter," she said in an odd, husky voice. "I'd heard he was on the boat."

"Yes—" Edith began, but the woman turned to her son and said, "Charles, it's grown a little chilly. Will you run down to my cabin and get my little seal jacket?" She opened the silk reticule on her lap and handed him a key. "It's on the chair by the window, dear."

Charles had stood very still. "But I asked Miss Harper to dance," he said.

"But Charles, I'm chilly. Do get my seal." Then turning to Edith, the woman said, "I'm sure Miss Harper can find her way back to her table without an escort. Good evening, Miss Harper." She turned her head away.

* * *

Later that night, Edith's mother stepped quickly into Edith's stateroom and closed the door, her finger to her lips. She was still in her long rose-colored gown, and her eyes were glittering. "I just heard!" she whispered. "You danced with young Charles Blakewell!"

"Yes, Mama."

"Oh, Edith! Aren't you excited? Do you know who he *is?* He's related to the Keens! His mother was Nancy Keen!"

"I met his mother," Edith said.

"*Did* you? Oh, Edith! How wonderful!" Then her hands fluttered up to her face. "Oh, if only I could pull myself together a little bit, I could meet her. Cultivate her a little bit. If I could only just get myself pulled together—"

"Oh, Mama," Edith had said. "Mama dear."

"What do you mean 'Mama dear'? Are you implying that I'm not good enough to meet Mrs. Blakewell?"

But just then the door opened, and it was Mary Miles.

"Oh, *there* you are, lady!" Mary Miles said. "I thought I'd lost you. It's bedtime. Come now." And she steered Dolly Harper out of the room.

The next morning there was delivered to Edith's cabin a note which said

> Perhaps you think that what happened was something I intended to have happen. Believe me, it truly was not.
>
> Respectfully,
>
> *C. M. Blakewell*

There did not seem to be any answer required. She did not answer it. She did not see him again until four nights later, the last night out, at the Captain's Dinner, when he came to a large table where she was sitting with a group of other people and said, "You've been avoiding me."

"I haven't. Not really."

"You didn't answer my note. I'm sorry it happened. If I'd argued with her, she would only have made it worse."

"I quite understand."

"Then I gather you're used to that sort of thing."

"What? Used to being insulted by arrogant old women? You're trying to say that you're *sorry* for me being who I am, aren't you? Well, please don't be. Excuse me," and she had turned abruptly to the man on her left, who happened to be the prince of something, an unimportant prince, a ridiculous prince, but her look at him had been so intense that he had offered her a Murad cigarette from a gold-and-enamel case and she had accepted it. He asked her to dance, and she accepted that—waltzing with the prince, holding that outrageous lighted cigarette while everyone stared. ("My God, that's Meredith Harper's daughter—dancing and *smoking!*" she heard someone exclaim; well, it was more like brandishing it than smoking it, as she remembers the Murad now.) The waltz was "Artist's Life." The prince held her too tightly. "I'd like to have a—how you say?—an adventure with you," he whispered through grinning yellow teeth. She had laughed and given him a bold look. He held her even tighter, and she thought: If there were a convenient and discreet place to have this adventure, your highness, I would probably say yes, even with you, with pleasure. I'm ready for an adventure or two.

"And I'm sure she cheats on Perry," Leona is saying. "I have no proof that she does, but I know Mother. And I'm also sure she cheated on Daddy with Perry before the divorce."

"Now wait a minute," he says, "who's Perry?"

"Perry Gardiner, my stepfather, Mother's *present* husband. Why am I sure she cheats on him? Because Mother's a cheater by nature, that's why. She cheats on everybody—on me, on the men in her life. Cheating is the secret of her success. Her one and only talent." (Dear God, I'm on a talkathon, she tells herself—but what can I do when he just sits there, smiling, urging me to go on. "And so Leona Ware continued volubly. . . .")

The bartender winks at her. "Straight rum for you, Miss Harper?"

"Ha ha. No, just another of the same, thanks. And it's Mrs. Para-Diaz now, Tommy."

"Paradise?"

"That's close enough." She turns to Arch. "They'll never learn my name was never Harper." And then, "A cheater. Do you know what she did to Daddy once, way back when they were first married? To this day Daddy doesn't know the truth about what happened, but Mother told me about it—terribly proud of what she did. They were married, you see, right at the height of the Depression, and Daddy's family was very short of money, though they had been rich. She and Daddy had a great big fancy wedding in New York, St. James's of course, which Mother paid for—which was all right because the bride always pays for the wedding. But when it came to the wedding trip, Mother wanted—naturally—to go around the world. If you have a giant wedding and reception you don't top it off with a weekend in the Poconos is Mother's theory. No, you go around the world—*slowly*," and Leona makes a slow circle in the air with her finger. Arch grins at her. "I'm not boring you, am I, Arch?"

"Not a bit," he says. "Look—it's like you've been all bottled up till now. And now somebody's opened up a little valve, and everything that was bottled up is coming out. Go ahead—talk. I like it, and it's good for you."

Leona smiles ruefully at the fresh drink that has been placed in front of her. "*This,* I'm afraid, is what's opened the valve," she says. "But anyway, she knew Daddy'd never let *her* pay for the trip—though she could have paid for it easily enough. So do you know what she did? She went to Granny, and asked Granny to give her the trip as a wedding present. Granny said all right. But, Mother pointed out to Granny, there was a slight hitch. Suppose Daddy was also too proud to take money from his wife's mother? She knew darn well he would be! So she had it all worked out. The money was to come from a *mysterious donor*. The mystery man, it seems, was a man who worked years and years ago for my great-grandfather here in the West Indies. One night this man accidentally fell off the top of one of the watchtowers in the sugar fields—you've seen those towers. They're about ten feet high and if you fell off one you couldn't possibly do more than skin your knee. But this poor man, when *he* fell off, broke every bone in his body and lay there, at death's door, for hours until my great-grandfather discovered him, and picked him up and carried him—piggy-back, I suppose—for miles and miles to a doctor and saved his life. As the years went by, the man became very rich—as though anybody who worked for my great-grandfather ever got rich—but he never forgot old Meredith Harper and the piggy-back ride, that noble deed that long-ago night in the islands. And so, from time to time, that grateful man gives nice big presents to old Meredith Harper's family. Like when someone gets married. A big cashier's check comes from darling Mr. Anonymous. How do you like that, Arch? That's my mother!"

He shakes his head back and forth. "And this is the same mother who's just turned you down on your gallery," he says.

"Yes. On a fifty-*centime* postcard. Well, I was probably wrong to try to turn to the family for financing. That's why I've decided to raise the money from—outside sources." She pauses, stirring her drink with its plastic twirler. "Poor dear, dumb, sweet Daddy fell for it hook, line, and sinker. 'What a wonderful man your grandfather must have been, Diana!' he said to Mother. I guess he said it all the way around the world. And meanwhile, poor Granny was paying for everything and getting none of the credit! That's what my mother's like, you see. Her whole marriage starts out on a cheat and a lie, and she's tickled pink that her husband doesn't know the difference. Mr. Grateful sent along another big check when they bought their first house. 'Isn't Mother clever?' she said to me. 'Yes,' I said, 'a clever cheat.' No, I didn't say that, that's not true—but I thought it, Arch. I couldn't say it to her, but I thought it. And I thought how wrong it was of Granny to go along with such a thing, but then I guess Mother is Granny's daughter, and Daddy was . . . Daddy *is*—Why do I speak of Daddy in the past tense? He *is*. A stupid, wonderful, dumb, nice man. He's . . . I go to see him now and then; not too often any more. He's married again, and has a whole slew of children whose names I get mixed up, and he said to me once—oh, it was long after he was rid of Mother—he said——" Leona hesitates, momentarily thinking she has forgotten the point, lost the thread. "He said, 'I've simply never understood your mother, Leo.' He calls me Leo, the only one who does. It's because I was born in August, under the sign of Leo." (Doctor Hardman's hard voice rolls into her head: "Are you sure it isn't because your father wanted a boy?" And her reply, "Oh, that's too *easy!*")

Arch is still smiling at her, his elbow on the bar. He rubs his chin slowly with his big hand. Then he says, "Will you have another drink? I don't want to shut off that little valve."

"All right." With surprise she sees that the glass in front of her is empty. Wasn't it just full? Didn't whatsisname behind the bar just give her a fresh drink, with the old straight-rum-for-you-Miss-Harper gag? Well, perhaps he didn't. Perhaps it was longer ago than she thinks it was because there's no doubt that the glass in front of her is empty.

"Another round for me and Mrs. Paradise," Arch orders.

"Oh, it's an old, old story, isn't it?" she says quietly. "Hates her mother, loves her father. But oh, she's *some*thing, Arch. You should meet her. No, you shouldn't. Clever—that's the trouble. Too clever. Too good at figuring all the angles, knowing just how much another person will believe, how much he won't."

"Which one are you talking about? Your mother or your grandmother?"

"Oh, Granny's quite different. Except—her life is so remote from mine. She's never wanted anything, never been desperate—" (stop, she tells herself, oh, stop, stop, stop. Your thoughts are running away with your tongue, old girl, running away.) "Thank you, Tommy," she says for the fresh drink. "Let me give you just one more example," she says to Arch, "of Mother. The time Jimmy and I ran away—Mother's reaction. There were the usual headlines in the papers—HEIRESS VANISHES; ELOPING HEIRESS FOUND AT SUN VALLEY. Well, do you know what? Mother *clipped* all those newspaper stories, and put them in a scrapbook! She still has them, and you can catch her *looking* at them! I mean, to Mother those silly newspaper gossip stories were just *wonderful*—the nicest thing I ever did to her was get myself in the newspapers that way! And do you know what the most important word in all those stories was? *Heiress*. The word *heiress*. She loved that. It established her. It confirmed her—her whole purpose in life, as an heiress-owner, an heiress-producer. Isn't that interesting?"

It *was* interesting. And she had truly never thought of it before. That was the good thing about talking, saying things out loud—it made you perceive, all at once, things you had simply never perceived or considered before. Because, of course, this is what Leona has always been to her mother: not her daughter, but her heiress. How simple. How true.

"She didn't like Gordon because Gordon married me properly, in front of a proper little New England justice of the peace, and there was no publicity."

"And what ever happened to Jimmy?" he asks her.

"Jimmy? He happened. It didn't . . ." She is suddenly afraid she is going to cry, and she sets her teeth down lightly on the rim of the glass, and a shiver of cold runs through her teeth. A sure-fire way to stop tears, she says to herself, having just discovered it. "He always asked questions. That was his trouble," she says, referring to Gordon.

"Who did?"

"Gordon. Not Jimmy. Gordon asked questions *about* Jimmy. Wanted to know everything about Jimmy."

"About your sex life with him, you mean?"

"Oh, not so much that. But about that too. Am I getting too tight? Am I talking too much?"

"Go on. Let off all the steam, buddy. I love hearing you talk."

"Do you?" She looks at him doubtfully. "I'm afraid I'm giving away—all my secrets. But oh, he'd ask me such questions as . . . when we were shopping for furniture he'd ask me, 'Did you and Jimmy have twin beds?' And once he said, 'Did you and Jimmy ever take a shower together?' I mean, now really! A shower together! I suppose that's sex. He'd say, 'Did Jimmy wear pajamas?' But it wasn't only things like that. He'd want to know, 'Did Jimmy take cream and sugar in his coffee?' 'Did Jimmy like his steak rare or well done?' And honestly, Arch, it got to be the creepiest feeling—as though Jimmy were still there, somehow, in the room with us, watching us, taking part in everything Gordon and I did. Or even *controlling* what we did. It was as though there was a little voodoo doll of me somewhere, and Jimmy, wherever he was, was sticking little pins in it, making me remember. . . . And meanwhile, poor Jimmy . . . poor Jimmy was nowhere in sight, and he wasn't really sticking pins in me at all. Do you see?"

"Sure," he says. "I see."

"Do you? I'm not sure *I* see." She laughs uncertainly. "But anyway, here we are."

He smiles at her. "Yes, here we are, buddy. Here we both are."

Behind them a voice says, "Hello, you two."

She turns and looks up, and Eddie Winslow's dark face swims above her in the gloomy light of the bar. "Hello, Eddie," she says.

Standing up, Arch says, "Won't you join us, Winslow?"

Eddie hesitates, looking down at Leona. "No," he says finally. "No thanks. I've got to get to bed. See you," he says, nodding to them both. He turns and walks away from them through the crowded bar.

"Eddie . . ." Leona calls weakly after him. He does not turn.

Watching Eddie Winslow's retreating back, Arch Purdy's eyes narrow. "You may not know it, buddy," he says, "but that guy's nuts about you."

She says nothing.

"It's written all over his face. Did you notice it? He gets a real muddy look on his face when he looks at you. He's got it bad. Boy, I've never seen a guy who's got it so bad." Then he smiles at her. "Look, it's still early. What do you say we finish these drinks and go on over to the Virgin Isle? See what's going on over there."

"All right. And meanwhile—you *do* like these pictures."

"I do. I told you I did."

She gathers up the little pile of transparencies that has been sitting, all the while, in front of her on the bar. She gathers them as tenderly and affectionately in her hands as a child gathers a bright bunch of autumn leaves. "And you can see why I'm so—oh, damn! Look what I've done!" One of the little squares has fluttered, leaflike, from her hand and landed in her half-filled glass.

"Here, let me fish it out."

"Oh, how stupid!"

"Look, it's all right." He dries it with his folded handkerchief.

"It's *not* all right! It'll just pucker up. It's ruined." She takes it. "Well, thank God it's Kirkpatrick. But how could I do such a dumb thing?"

"I'd put them in my purse if I were you, buddy."

"Yes. And of course—if you'd like to look at them again sometime—"

"Sure," he says. "Let me get the check, and we'll be on our way."

"I just remembered something Eddie said to me this morning on the beach. He said, 'At least you can afford these divorces.'"

He laughs. "Well, can't you?"

"Oh, Arch!" she wails. "Not you too!"

She stands up now, smoothing the front of her dress, her hand resting on the edge of the bar while he waits for his change. Funny, she thinks, that she had completely forgotten that incredible remark of Eddie's. Don't tell me, she says to herself, that I'm beginning to have blank spots from the mornings after as well as the nights before. Standing there, she knows that she has already had plenty to drink and, at the same time, she knows that before the evening is over she will have a few more. The blank spots. A vision of tomorrow's hangover, much like today's, washes over her, like a flood of filthy water. When you began having the blank spots, it was high time to worry. That was what Jimmy, who was quite a drinker himself, had always said. When he began to have the blank spots, he had cut down on his drinking a bit—yes, he had, and she had admired him for it. *I did,* Jimmy. Jimbo. He had begun to approach each drink with new caution and respect. There was no doubt, no doubt at all, that they moved—were forced to move, whether they liked it or not, with a drinking group. She still did. How could one ever, if one was born Leona Ware, ever hope to move in a nondrinking group? Move to Topeka, Kansas, where ladies had church suppers and worked for the P.T.A.? No, it wouldn't matter. Even in Topeka, Kansas, being born Leona Ware, she would find herself with Topeka, Kansas' drinking group. It would be the same, only smaller. There was no such thing as the grass being greener, anywhere. It was, would be, the same grass wherever she went. She had portable grass. Her own little plot that she set down around her, everywhere.

The dismalness of this realization sinks in, with "Be honest, be honest, face facts" repeating in her head. "How can you talk about your mother's cheating when you cheat too? Not on your husbands, but on yourself; cheat by telling yourself that you have possibilities for changing which you don't have at all." Once, Jimmy had gone on the wagon for a little while, and at the time she had asked him, "Do you really think you'll never take another drink as long as you live?" She had asked it quite seriously, wanting to know. But it was an awfully young and innocent question, and he had laughed at her and said, "Of course not." And she had liked him for that answer. Be honest. Face facts. Well, here is a fact: She has already, again tonight, had too much to drink. Tomorrow, no doubt, all that she is thinking and perceiving now will be a blank spot.

Leaving the bar, she leans on his arm. "Where are we going now?"

"To the Virgin Isle, remember?"

"Oh, yes." And then, with a faint smile, she says, "How can you trust a woman who's had three divorces?"

He laughs. "Well, who said I trusted you?" he says.

"A lady who lives in a shoe, who's had so many husbands she doesn't know what to do. A lady Bluebeard. Or what am I?"

"You're Mrs. Paradise," he says.

Returning to the Morristown house for the months of August and September was never exactly like coming home. It was more like checking into a large hotel. Edith had no regularly assigned room there, since it was a large house—the largest and most ostentatious of all her father's residences. Her room was where she was put. "Now where shall we put you?" her mother would say. The second and third floors were mostly bedrooms; they were similar in decor and furnishings, since all the furniture had been purchased at the same time. It made no difference to Edith which room she had; they were equally impersonal. She would unpack her trunks and suitcases and hatboxes, her French traveling clock, her silver-backed combs and brushes and little mirrors—scatter her itinerant possessions around the room and try to make it feel like her own. But it never really did. It was merely a resting place in which she was a guest entitled to certain privileges, the luxury and hospitality of the house, permission to ring the servants' bells that were nested in the moldings of the doors, and to order her breakfast on a tray. As Edith thinks of it, it was like this in the Paris house too; the atmosphere was the same. Those places were always "the Paris house" and "the Morristown house"; only the house in St. Thomas was really home and contained a room that truly belonged to her.

Since arriving on the *Mauretania* that summer, Edith's mother had been working very hard at "pulling herself together." She had decided, in the process, to try to re-establish herself as a social figure, or at least a woman of importance in that corner of New Jersey—a chore which she had neglected for the past few years. She began to plan a series of large parties. ("Good for her," Mary Miles had pronounced. "It keeps her busy. The devil finds work for idle hands.")

Dolly Harper made an oddly accurate comment about the American social structure of those days when she said, once, to Edith, "In this country there is a distinct society. In Europe, there isn't any, except for royalty. Anybody who has money can be accepted in European society, but in America one must work hard to be taken in." And she had added, "Always remember that you are second-generation rich. This will make it easier for you than it is for me."

Whether her mother ever succeeded in penetrating the fixity of New York, or even Morristown, society is, Edith thinks now, open to doubt. Still, there were then—just as there are now—people who were glad to accept invitations to parties, and the invitations went out. Golf had been sweeping the country for a number of years, and by 1908 it was a popular sport for women. Edith purchased her first golf clubs that summer in Morristown, and started taking lessons. Golf, at least, offered an escape from the afternoons of riding with her father—and the terror of the jumps. But her mother's parties, she soon learned, were being given largely for her benefit, and her attendance at all of them was expected.

"What did you think of the Horsfall boy?" her mother asked her after one of them.

"Which one was he?"

"The blond one, who played crokinole with your father after dinner."

"Oh, he seemed nice enough."

"They say he has the world at his feet. And he's handsome."

"He's a bit of a prig."

"He's a Horsfall."

"That's the trouble."

"Harlan Horsfall comes to my parties. The Horsfalls accept us."

"Yes, but I find him dull."

"It's wrong to have *too* high a standard where men are concerned," she said. "The higher your standard is, the fewer men there are who can possibly meet them. You must not expect perfection."

"I don't expect perfection."

"You're too eligible a girl to go on much longer without seriously thinking of each man you meet as a prospective husband," she said. "And you can afford to be a little choosy. But you can't let too many opportunities pass you by. One doesn't stay eligible forever, alas." Then, after a moment, she said, "Of course you realize now that the other thing would never have worked out. It would have ruined us, all of us, everywhere—in St. Thomas and everywhere. The heart must be ruled by the head in such matters."

Then, a few days later, her mother said, "I am considering inviting Mrs. Blakewell to tea."

"Oh, Mama!" Edith said. "Why do you put yourself up against such things?"

"Against what things?"

"Against the humiliation of having her turn you down flat, in the most snubbing way possible."

"Hmm. Is that what you think will happen?"

"I know it will happen."

"She may need me more than I need her," her mother said with a cryptic look.

"Nonsense. I'll make you a wager that she never even acknowledges."

Her mother considered this. "Very well, what do you wager?"

"My pearl necklace."

"No, I won't wager you that. I'll make you a ladylike wager of one dollar. I'll wager you one dollar that she not only accepts, but accepts rather promptly, and that by the end of our tea she has asked me to call her Nancy."

"Dream on, Mama."

"Because her son, you see, has already accepted my invitation for the weekend."

"What?"

"Charles Blakewell is coming to Morristown to visit us the weekend after next. After that weekend, my invitation will go out to his mother."

"Why did you ask him here?"

"For you, of course. He liked you. He asked you to dance."

"Mama, will you stop trying to run my life?" Edith had walked out of the room and seized, angrily, her bag of golf clubs from the rack in the hall and walked out the door onto the summer lawn.

Her first ball arced straight and high against the sky and sank far beyond the curve of the lawn. The excellence of the shot had exhilarated her and pushed all her hot anger at her mother into the past. Lugging her clubs, she walked down across the grass, which fell in a series of sloping terraces away from the house, in search of the ball.

When she got to the spot, behind a clump of poplars, where she believed the ball had landed and was walking slowly, poking with her club through the taller grass that grew there, she all at once found herself staring down upon—indeed, almost stepping upon—the prone figure of a man lying in the grass, and she screamed.

He rolled over immediately and sat up. Her first impression of him was that he looked very rough and unshaven, wearing a faded blue shirt and denim trousers, and that he must be a tramp or drunk who had wandered onto the place. She dropped her bag of clubs, and began to run.

But he called after her, "Are you Edith?"

She stopped and looked back at him. He was standing now, and smiling. "Are you Edith?" he said again. And there was something in the way he pronounced her name that made her guess that this must be the Frenchman who, with his wife, she had been told, had been given quarters in the gatehouse.

"Are you Papa's Frenchman?" she asked him.

He laughed, stooped and picked up her golf bag, and walked toward her. "I am Louis Bertin," he said.

"How do you do," Edith said, and the formality of her words sounded foolishly hollow there in the tall grass. "Yes, I'm Edith."

"I startled you."

"And I startled you," she said, "—Monsieur."

He yawned. "I was taking a nap. I'm a very lazy man. May I carry this bag for you?"

They started back up across the grass toward the house. He was a small man, scarcely taller than she, but wirily built. He slung her gold bag over his shoulder with ease and hooked an arm through the strap. He was, she guessed, in his middle or late thirties, but his step was springy and youthful, and his face was altogether extraordinary. It was a face that was somehow instantly familiar, and yet totally strange to her—a thin, almost sallow face, with heavy-lidded gray eyes. His cheekbones were high and prominent and he was not, she saw now, ill-shaven, but his cheeks were hollow and dark. It was an ascetic face, a monkish face.

"I was looking for my ball," she said. "But I guess it's gone for good."

"Where did you shoot from?"

"Up there, from the edge of the terrace," she pointed.

"Not a bad shot. You're not a bad golfer."

"I'm sorry my instructor couldn't see it. If I tell her about it, she won't believe it. Are you comfortable in the gatehouse?" she asked him.

He shrugged. "Oh, yes, we are comfortable," he said.

"What sort of work do you do for my father, Monsieur Bertin?"

"I am his tennis opponent."

She had laughed. "Tell me the truth!"

He stopped and looked at her curiously, the hooded eyes almost closing. "I play tennis with him," he said. "That's my job. Your father is a very good tennis player, and so am I. It is important to him to keep up the physical end."

"Have you always been a tennis player?"

"I have always been a tennis player," he said, and laughed as though the answer to her question was so obvious she should not have asked it. Then he said, "Your father is good, but there are things I can teach him. And it keeps the wolf from the door. As I say, I am a lazy man." He gave her a droll look. "But don't tell your father that, Edith."

They walked on toward the house.

"Well, I hope you're happy in this country," she said.

"Oh, yes," he said. "But it's lonely here. At times." At the edge of the terrace, he handed her her bag. "Do you go to school?" he asked her.

"No."

He looked thoughtful. "Your father is an interesting man," he said. "In many ways."

"Well, thank you for carrying my bag. I'm sorry I disturbed your nap."

He took the hand she offered. "Good-by, Edith," he said.

She went into the house, thinking what a pleasantly peculiar man Louis Bertin seemed to be, and how odd it was of her father to employ a tennis player—a personal tennis player—

to help him keep up "the physical end." And yet perhaps it was not so odd. After all, her father was a man, she had been gradually discovering, who modeled himself on the behavior, the attitudes, the manners, the values and examples of other people—other men whose successes he admired. The lives of great men were all he read, the only volumes on his library shelves; biographies of United States Presidents, of kings, of generals, of the great American industrialists, the works of Julius Caesar, of Napoleon, of Nietzsche. From all the champions and would-be champions of the world, living and dead, he had culled bits of advice, traits of behavior, and assembled them into the composite that was himself. She put her golf clubs in the rack and paused in the hall, thinking about it. He was nearly fifty years old now. He needed a strong body to contain all the lives he had digested.

Her small brothers were kneeling on the window seat when she came into the house, and now they came running across the hall to her. "You were talking to the Frenchman!" they cried. "We saw you!"

"Yes, what of it?"

"His wife is a witch! A real witch! Fraülein Schiller says so."

"Did Fraülein Schiller tell you that?"

"Yes!"

"Well, she should be ashamed of herself—and you can tell her I said that. There are no such things as witches, and you know it."

"But every night in the gatehouse an upstairs light stays on! Late. Sometimes it stays on all night long," Harold said.

"What does that mean? Lights in this house stay on all night too. It means the Bertins like a night light."

"It doesn't mean she's a witch and cooking witches' brew?"

"It certainly doesn't. Now run along and stop talking about such things."

And yet, that night, unable to sleep, Edith got out of bed sometime after three and crossed her room to her window from where there was a distant view of the gatehouse. And, to be sure, there was a single yellow light, flame-colored, between the trees.

Lying in her cool bed in St. Thomas now, reconstructing that other night so many miles and years ago, Edith remembers how she had found a position on her bed from which she could watch that tiny yellow light. Something had come over her since that night on the boat when she had danced with the prince and smoked the Murad—a change, or a determination for a change. She wanted to be wicked. She was ready to be wicked and just looking for a chance to prove to everyone just how wicked she could be. All this she had made her mind up to before meeting Louis Bertin. And now, at last, here he was.

Meanwhile, all the changes in the temper of the times had not gone by her unobserved—only unexperienced. The twentieth century was well under way. Though the technical "emancipation" of women was not to come until more than a decade later, many women were already quite emancipated. That foolish prince, in a queer way, had emancipated her. It was the year Alice Lloyd was singing "Stockings on the Line" and "Never Introduce Your Bloke to a Lady Friend," and Blossom Seeley was shouting "Put Your Arms Around Me, Honey!" and Eva Tanguay was bouncing around, showing her legs, and singing "I Don't Care." Everybody was "Doing the Toledo" and having dance marathons, and young men in Morristown were showing that they were on the *qui vive* by calling, "Oh, Lady, Lady!" and "Hot Dawg!" and "You ain't heard nothin' yet!" to each other, and Lillian Russell was a has-been. All these things Edith had heard, and observed, and read about, and was ready to know more about. And Doctor Freud was a figure in her generation too, a fact Leona—who considers him her generation's exclusive property—would have a hard time comprehending.

She had danced with a prince and smoked a Murad, and the prince had said he would like to have an adventure with her. Edith had examined herself. Though she might not be beautiful, she had decided that she was certainly attractive. Besides, there were other qualities that appealed to a man besides a pretty exterior. Wisdom. Companionship of the mind. Humor. Usefulness. Sensitivity. Most of all, she had decided that she was sensitive. Wickedness and sensitivity, it seemed to her, did not need to cancel each other out. She could possess both. Her eyes, whenever she opened them wide before her mirror, hinted at dark pools of feeling underneath, pools of sympathy and understanding and passion. Couldn't a man know that here at last was a woman who could share his innermost thoughts, his hopes and fears? "Somehow, I always knew" he would say to her, "that somewhere in the world there had to be a woman like you, Edith." And there she was, quietly waiting, grown up since Andreas—grateful to him, almost, perhaps ("If you'd been strong you wouldn't have gone!" she had begun to tell him sternly), for having lifted her to this new plateau from which she could view the world both cynically and serenely.

How quickly he had begun calling her Edith. That monkish face was a poetic face, with something dark, a little sullen around the corners of the mouth, a little broody around the hooded eyes, a face that spoke to her of suffering as she lay on her bed and looked out the window at his light; of suffering and longing. Methodically, she erased from her mind all the trivial things he had actually said. ("Do you go to school?") Those words were camouflage for his secret thoughts. Across the dark night she made him be thinking of her, asking himself: Why didn't I dare speak to her of what I really thought? Was it because she seemed so aloof and rare? Was it simply because I work for her father, and live in the gatehouse while she lives in the big house on the hill? Could the impossible ever be possible—that she would care for me?

"Lover," she whispered aloud. "Ah, lover!" And he answered her, and tomorrow, strolling in the poplars or wherever he strolled, perhaps he would meet a man friend, and perhaps her name would come up, as perhaps it often did among men (perhaps he would be the one to bring it up), and perhaps the man friend would look at him quizzically, and Louis Bertin would turn his head away quickly, abashed, perhaps, perhaps, perhaps, by the agony of his desire. She had slept on that thought like a pillow.

Edith Blakewell smiles now, remembering. Wasn't it wonderful to be young? Wonderful and terrible?

The air-conditioned cocktail lounge of the Virgin Isle Hotel is doing a good business, and little low lamps glow from the centers of little low tables. The music is New Yorky, fast and slick. But Arch and Leona have found a table outside, on the open terrace, where only the fringes of the music reach them.

"You've told me a lot about husbands one and two," Arch says, "but not a word about number three."

"Edouardo."

"Yes."

"When I fell in love with Edouardo—" she begins. (Love? Was it love? No. And it is certainly not true, as a friend of hers suggested afterward, that she had wanted to save him—save him from his . . . affliction . . . whatever you wanted to call it. Saving him had not entered her thoughts at all. Many women adjusted themselves to the idea that their husbands slept with other women. Many women too, she supposes, can adjust themselves to the idea that their husbands sleep with other men. Which is harder to adjust to? It doesn't matter, neither is easy.)

"When that happened," she continues, "Gordon insisted on having the Scott Fitzgerald scene. That's what Eddie Winslow called it when I told him about it. It's the scene where the girl and the girl's husband and the girl's new boy friend sit down and talk the situation over. 'I think the three of us should sit down and talk this over, Leona,' Gordon said. 'After all, we're all three mature human beings, not emotional children.' So we sat down to talk it over. It was funny—it *would* have been funny if it hadn't been so bizarre. Poor Gordon doesn't speak any Spanish, you see, and Edouardo—*he* didn't want to have this get-together, of course—he got so nervous he forgot all his English! Gordon would say things like 'I understand, sir, that you have formed a strong attachment to my wife, and that my wife has formed a strong attachment to you, and that the two of you are considering marriage.' And Edouardo would just say *'Que? Que?'* It was—unbelievable. I tried being interpreter for a while. Finally I couldn't stand it any more. I ran out and left them there—those two mature human beings, bumbling along, each one trying to figure out what the other was talking about. Jimmy, at least, bless his heart, would never have insisted on making a scene like that."

"Jimmy, bless his heart," Arch repeats. "Well, that story tells me some more about Jimmy and Gordon, but still not much about Edouardo."

"Perhaps that's intentional," she says quietly. "Perhaps I really don't want to talk about Edouardo."

"Fine," he says, grinning at her. "We'll delete his name from the conversation then." He makes a sweeping gesture with his hand. "He's gone. So long, Mr. Paradise."

Leona laughs. "You're really very funny in a funny way."

He lifts his glass to her and winks. "Thanks. I've always been funny in a funny way, buddy."

"I'm trying to decide. Do I like you calling me buddy all the time?"

"If you don't like it, say so, and I'll quit."

"No," she says, still laughing, "I don't mind it. Don't quit."

"Okay, buddy."

"Arch," she says, leaning forward, "can we be serious for just a minute? You said you liked the painters I have lined up. Do you think you might be interested in putting some money into my gallery? I'm trying to raise fifty thousand dollars, Arch. It would be a good investment. I'd love it if you'd do it, Arch. If not the whole fifty thousand, at least a share of it. You're a businessman, and a smart one too from all I hear. And I can show you all the details, all the plans, the things I've—" She stops, seeing that he is looking at her in a very odd, appraising, even hostile way. "I can demonstrate that it's a very sound business proposition for you," she adds lamely.

He continues to gaze at her in that unfathomable way, not unsmiling and yet not smiling either. He makes a thoughtful steeple of his fingers. "Did I know this was coming?" he asks. "Never mind. First let me ask you a—a *business* question. Why do you want to run an art gallery?"

"For only one reason," she says, looking directly into his eyes. "To make money."

"Good answer. I take it, then, that while the rest of your family is loaded with dough, you yourself are not quite so loaded. Right?"

"That," she says, "is absolutely correct. I also want to do something worthwhile. But that's only a secondary reason."

"I see," he says.

"If you're not interested, please say so and I promise you I won't bring it up again."

"Now wait a minute. I didn't say I wasn't interested. *You* interest me. Now tell me another thing. How badly do you want this gallery?"

"Terribly badly. Des—"

"Desperately. You're a lady in distress, as I said before."

"Desperately badly."

He leans toward her and covers her hand with his. "Look," he says, "fifty thousand is a lot of money, even from a—okay, call me a multimillionaire. I've been called that before. In print—by your friend Winslow, among others. I made a million dollars before I was twenty-five, and I'm proud of that. But fifty thousand dollars is a lot of money."

"I'm trying to recruit *various* investors," Leona says in a voice that was intended to sound matter-of-fact and businesslike, but which she is suddenly afraid sounded childlike and frightened.

"I like you," he says, still looking steadily at her. "I'd like to know you better. Much better. I could advance you the money, sure, just because I like you. But I'm still a businessman. Do you understand? If I let you have the money, I think I'm entitled to ask what's in it for me?"

"Part ownership of an art gallery!"

Smiling, he says, "I mean besides that. I said I like you. One good turn deserves another, doesn't it? You see? The battle lines are now drawn, buddy. I'm putting my cards on the table. I'm setting my terms. I want to go to bed with you. Desperately badly."

She disengages her hand from his grip, and stands up. "I'm sorry," she says. "I misjudged you. I thought you were a nice person. But you're a miserable bastard. Will you take me home, or shall I call a taxi?"

Still seated, still smiling at her, he says, "Call a taxi."

Ten

"THERE must be an end to these walks with the Frenchman, Edith," her mother said. "It will not do."

Edith had discovered the pattern of his afternoons, and would meet him in the middle of his walks. His walks were circular. From the gatehouse he would begin along the edge of the lawn, across the drive, keeping to the edge where the mowers stopped, where the tall field grass began, and the pine trees and poplars that surrounded the house. "Why do you always walk next to the trees, but not under them?" she had asked him.

"Afraid of hailstorms," he had said.

"You're a curious man."

She had also, through a bit of questioning here and there, found out certain things about his wife. Mary Miles, it turned out was an expert on Monique Bertin.

"She's a hussy, that one," Mary had said. "Light on in the house at night? Why it's him waiting up for her, of course! When the light stays on all night, it means she hasn't come home at all. In any civilized country, he'd divorce her. But that's the Roman Catholic of it I suppose, and the French of it as well."

"Where does she go, do you think, when she's out?"

"Well, now I don't know, Edith. But I can guess. Poor chap, I feel sorry for him. He's got his cross to bear."

"Is she pretty, Mary?"

Mary Miles had sniffed. "Pretty? Well, I suppose some might call her pretty. Pretty in a tarty way."

To Edith, Monique Bertin had been only a distant flutter of bright dress once or twice, glimpsed through the trees, and always—as Mary Miles had said—departing. On their walks, Louis Bertin had never specifically mentioned his wife—which, of course, merely confirmed Edith's growing opinion of the woman and their marriage.

Now, to her mother, she said, "Why won't it do, Mama? I enjoy talking to him. He's a gentleman, and he's offered to give me a tennis lesson."

"Really? I hardly think your father will approve of that, Edith, and I'm sure Mr. Bertin realizes it. He's a paid tennis player, and he has been hired only to play tennis with your father."

"What does his wife do?"

"I have no idea."

"Well, I still don't see why I can't talk to him."

"Because he is an employee of your father's. He is a married man. And he is *not* a gentleman. Do you want to get yourself gossiped about? No, you are forbidden to speak to him again."

"Forbidden?"

Her mother had paused. "I am sure your father would be most annoyed if he found out about it," she said. "If he found out, I promise you the consequences would be quite unpleasant."

"I liked you better when you were drunk, Mama."

Dolly Harper sat very stiffly, her hands folded tightly in her lap. "Don't think you can hurt me with a remark like that," she said. "That remark doesn't hurt me. It doesn't hurt me at all."

And Edith had continued to meet him on his walks, but from then on she was more careful, planning the meetings only when she knew her mother was out of the house or napping in her room. It was awful, but she had begun to wish that her mother would have more of her relapses. There had been only one since the "cure" that Mary Miles had begun in Paris. And so great had been Mary Miles' wrath at finding Dolly Harper drunk in her bed, that, literally, Mary Miles seemed to have frightened her out of trying it again. "You want to get yourself a place in society, don't you?" Edith had heard Mary screaming at her. "You want to help your daughter find a nice husband, don't you? What society would ever take a second look at *you* in the state you're in? What man would ever take a wife whose mother gets herself in a state like this? Take a look at yourself in your mirror, lady! Drink that coffee, lady! Sit up straight, lady, and drink that coffee! Lady! Oh, I have half a mind to bring your two little boys in here to look at their mother in the state she's in!"

On her walks with the Frenchman, their talk was oddly impersonal. Edith was never sure, when she met him, whether he was happy to see her or not, though he always smiled with those heavy-lidded eyes and said, "Well, here is Edith. What have you been up to since I saw you last?"

"Trying to figure out what to do with a young man my mother has invited for the weekend."

"Is this a young man you like?"

"I don't care about him one way or the other. But my mother makes such a fool of herself trying to pair me off with people."

He shrugged, either in agreement or disagreement. Once she had tried speaking to him in French, but he had interrupted her rather curtly, and said, "Speak English. Your English is better than your French."

"Are you going with us to St. Thomas?" she had asked him.

"I imagine so. Travel is one of the benefits of this job of mine."

She had started to describe St. Thomas to him, but he had cut her off, saying, "I'll see it when I get there."

"Some day I'm going to run away from home, Louis," she had told him.

But he had not seemed particularly impressed. "We all have to run away from home some day. 'Adventure begins when you run away from home.' Thomas Carlyle."

"You're well-read."

"Not really."

"I might even run away today."

"Today? I doubt you will."

"I might."

They had come to the end of their walk, to the path that led between the posts of the iron fence and, behind the fence, a boxwood hedge, to the gatehouse. It was four o'clock, and the sun slanted through the leaves of the trees overhead. They stood in a green pool of mixed shade and sunlight. A soft breeze stirred the leaves and the grass.

"I've never been inside the gatehouse," she said. "What is it like?"

He leaned back against the iron fence, folded his arms, and smiled.

Remembering the brazenness of that remark, she is astonished that she was ever able to utter it. Certainly these are two different women, the woman remembered and the woman remembering. Yet they are one and the same, though they no longer look alike, and they greet each other, as differing reflections in the dark room and recognize, and accuse each other. . . .

His rooms in the gatehouse had appalled her. She does not know now what she had expected, but it was not what she found. Up a narrow flight of stairs and through a stained-wood door which he opened with a key. They were in a small, dark sitting-room that was clearly a kitchen also. A primus stove stood on a table in one corner and, next to it, a deep wooden sink was draped with dishtowels and filled with dirty crockery. There was a single window, its panes filmed, its shade torn, and from the shade on a wooden hanger hung a woman's shift, freshly laundered but still seeming soiled. The room also contained a very worn-looking sofa and two straight chairs. There was an odor in the air of stove-oil and cooking and dust. He smiled at her and shrugged. "The place needs cleaning," he said.

"Would you like me to come and clean it for you some day?" she had asked, which was hardly the most tactful rejoinder.

He laughed. "You American girls. Always wanting things clean. What do you know about cleaning a house?"

"I used to help my mother clean. I'm not that pampered," she said. And then, stepping to the window, "Oh, and it has a lovely view." Standing there, in his denim trousers and blue shirt, he followed her with his eyes. She stood in silence, looking out. The view was of her house. When she turned back to him, he was still smiling.

"The view," he said, "I never look at it."

Then they were both silent again. The air in the room was penetrating, heavy and still.

"Would you like a cup of tea?" he asked her.

"I thought only Englishmen took tea."

"I'll heat some water."

A fat tortoiseshell cat with pink-rimmed eyes lay on the sofa. As she sat, it stretched its paws, yawned, and kneaded its claws into the sofa cushion. "It's name is Clemenceau," Louis said. "You know—the Tiger of France." Stooping over the table, he was heating water in a saucepan and putting teacups in saucers, whistling under his breath as he set out the dishes.

"Hello, Clemenceau."

The cat washed itself.

He took the water from the stove and filled two cups over a tea-strainer. "Sugar?" he asked her.

"No thank you. Just plain."

"No milk?"

"No."

With a spoon, he ladled two helpings of sugar into his cup. Then he took a pitcher of milk, poured a little into the spoon, and, kneeling on his haunches by the sofa, he offered the spoon of milk to the tortoiseshell cat. When the cat had licked the spoon clean, Louis put the spoon into his cup and stirred his tea. Again the air was heavy and still. The cat purred. And Louis Bertin sat on his haunches in front of her, a questioning look in his deep eyes. Over the teacup, those eyes studied her.

"So," Louis said, "you came to see me." He sipped his tea. "Does your mother know you're here?"

"No."

"Nor your father, of course. How long before someone goes out looking for you?"

"I'm independent," she had said. "I can come and go as I please."

"Can you? And now you've come to the gatehouse. My house."

"Yes."

The cat hopped off the sofa, stood for a moment surveying its surroundings, then jumped up on the wooden sink.

Edith sat there and, simply because he was smiling at her in such an odd way, she felt she had to smile back. But her smile was a stiff and frozen-feeling smile. At least it's a smile, she thought.

"How old are you, Edith?"

"Nearly twenty."

"Nearly twenty," he repeated. "And very grown up. What do you know about men?" In the bottomless silence that followed this question, he rose and sat on the sofa beside her. Finally he said, "Not very much, I guess."

"No . . ." And suddenly, in a burst, she started to tell him about Andreas. She told him the beginning to the end.

"So," he said, "your father sent the boy away. And what do you suppose he'd do to me if he knew you were here, Edith?" he said. "He'd have me arrested. Perhaps even killed. You ought to know these things, because I think you have come up here to find out about men. I'm forty years old, Edith."

"Perhaps," she had said softly. "I'd better go."

"Yes. Perhaps you'd better."

But she didn't go.

"So. You've decided to stay. I don't make you stay."

"No. You don't make me stay."

"We're all alone. We'll be alone here for a long time. Except for Clemenceau." He stood up and picked up the cat, carried it to the window, and set the cat outside, where it crept away across the roof-tiles. "Good-by, Clemenceau," he said, and closed the window. He pulled down the shade. When, in the half-darkness, he sat down beside her again, he put his arm around her. "So," he said, "you've come to find out about men."

Quickly she said to him, "You said you were lonely. I'm lonely too, Louis!"

With five fingers on her chin, he tilted her face toward his. "Yes, Edith," he said. "You don't have to explain." With his other hand he began, very slowly and carefully, unbuttoning the top buttons of her shirtwaist.

"Louis!" she said, putting her arms tight around him and hugging him close to her to blot out everything that was happening to her. "Louis, you know what you're doing . . . but I don't! Remember that I don't know anything at all."

She closed her eyes then. She wanted it to be brief. She thought of pain—"Exquisite pain!" Mademoiselle Laric had said. And to keep from thinking about pain she forced her mind on a precipitous journey through a long unlighted tunnel to other times and places. With her eyes tightly shut she made herself think of green trees and forests, of the curve of Picara Point, and of places she had never seen. Taking her hand in his, he made her touch something fierce and fearsome, but it didn't matter; she made it not matter because she was busy in other hemispheres, other landscapes. And then, rather gradually, the trees and forests seemed to have been replaced by something quite different, but equally foreign, something so extraordinary that she almost said aloud, "How extraordinary!" She heard him say, "You like this, don't you?" But when she tried to moan a reply, his mouth covered hers and she was unable to utter a sound. Then, quite selfishly, she forgot him, and concentrated on the new territory that was closing in around her, gathering, looming. "Isn't this nice?" he whispered.

She cried out once, seizing him. As if from a distant clifftop she heard him murmuring words in French which she couldn't understand.

". . . *revanche*. . . ."

"What?" she heard her own voice gasp. "What?"

And as she clung to him shaking and sobbing she heard him whispering, "Revenge . . . we've got our revenge. Now . . . both of us. We've punished him. Because this . . . this now . . . is what your father does to my wife every night. Now we're punishing him . . . ah, and isn't it nice? Isn't it fun . . .?"

It was a long time before she could open her eyes. Then she opened them wide, and his eyes were a faceless glitter above hers. His head moved upward, away from hers, and he looked down at her, smiling. "Bitch . . . little bitch," he whispered. "You and I are just alike, aren't we? We wanted the same revenge. And wasn't it fun—having our revenge?"

And she was back again, in that hideous room, with the smells of oil and cooking, and the sun poking in dustily through a tear in the windowshade, and the woman's shift suspended crookedly from the hanger, and their two half-filled teacups standing on the table, alone with her father's Frenchman.

"Do you ride, Mr. Blakewell?" she asked him.

"Some. You're a fine horsewoman, I hear."

"I ride," she said.

"Perhaps we'll ride some day then?"

They were walking through the rooms of the Morristown house. He had arrived that morning at the wheel of a Packard touring car, causing quite a stir. All the servants had run out of the house to look at the shiny black machine that was parked under the porte-cochere, so much more spectacular than her father's massive Daimler because it was, in the vernacular of the day, more "up-to-dick."

"This is a fantastic house," Charles Blakewell said. "Everything I've heard about it is true."

"Really?" she said sharply. "What had you heard about it?"

"That it was—exactly what it is," he said. He approached one of the large paintings that hung in the hall—the hall Edith's mother insisted on calling the *orangerie*. "Fragonard," he said.

"In a sense," she said. "It's a Fragonard copy. All the paintings in this house are copies. I'm sure you were smart enough to realize that my father does not own the *real* Raphael *Madonna*. I suppose this is what you mean when you say this house is fantastic, Mr. Blakewell."

He looked at her briefly. "No, that isn't what I meant, Miss Harper," he said. "Will you show me the garden?"

They went out the French doors and across the grass terrace to the garden where a large Italianate fountain, supported by three cavorting bronze nymphs, was in charge of things. It was the hour before lunch, during which, as Edith's mother had put it, "We'll leave the young people to their own devices and let them get acquainted," and Edith could not wait for the hour to be over. "The fountain doesn't work," she said. "It hasn't been connected yet. Everything here, you see, is very new. Have you seen enough?"

"Look," he said quietly, "can't we be friends?"

She said nothing.

"Couldn't we be friends at least for the weekend?"

"I'm wondering why you accepted Mama's invitation," she said.

"Because she made it sound attractive, and I had nothing else to do. And because I'm sorry about what happened that night on the boat. I wanted you to know I was sorry."

"I think you came here just to laugh at me—and the way we live."

He smiled at her. "Well, you're wrong," he said. "Why are you so angry? Angry at everything, aren't you? Angry at this fountain, angry at this house, angry at the fake Fragonard, angry at me, and of course my mother. You're the angriest girl I've ever met."

She stared at him.

"Some day I'd like to find out what's made you so angry. But I'll tell you a secret. Only brave people are angry people."

"I'm not sure how brave I am," she said.

The dark eyes in his good-looking face were humorous. "Of course you're not," he said. "Nobody ever knows when he's being brave."

He had a habit, she noticed, of tossing off short, oblique observations like that. She said nothing for a moment, and then, "Well, it's true. I do hate this fountain. I do hate this house."

"Make a list of all the things you hate," he said. "It's good for you." Smiling at her he said, "Can't we be friends? Can't we just try?"

"All right. Let's try."

"May I call you Edith?"

"Yes."

"And please call me Charles." They moved toward the house.

Remembering those days, Edith often wonders how they ever managed to eat so much—five-course luncheons, with dishes such as terrapin and canvasback duck. Before lunch, her father and Charles were served a Jack Rose cocktail, and then there were wines with the meal. After lunch, it was customary for family and guests to retire to their rooms to rest; one needed a rest after all that food.

Later that afternoon she and Charles met again. "What are you going to do with your life?" she asked him. "Besides be very, very brave?"

"I'm spending most of my time these days trying to straighten out my father's affairs," he said. "For a good lawyer, he left things in kind of a mess. When his things are settled, I'm going to have to decide whether to go into his firm or not."

"I imagine you'd make a good lawyer."

"There's a place for me there if I want it," he said absently. "But I don't know."

And, on Sunday morning, they rode. They took the long path up into the pine hills behind the house. The horses were skittish and wanted to run, but they kept them at a walk. "Do you usually go to church Sunday mornings?" Edith asked him.

"Not since I was in school."

"Mama was afraid you'd disapprove of us for not being churchgoers. I never went to a real school," she said. "Where did you go?"

"I had a proper gentleman's education," he said with a smile. "At St. George's in Newport."

"Mama's dream is to have a house in Newport."

"Tell her not to bother."

"Do you mean she wouldn't be accepted there?"

He was laughing now. "Where do you get all these ideas about being *accepted* and not accepted? Are these your ideas or your mother's?"

"Sometimes I don't know whose ideas I have."

They rode in silence for a while. Then he said, "The kind of justice they tell you exists in church doesn't exist." It was another of his odd, indirect remarks. "I learned that when my father died."

"I gather you were fond of him."

"Yes." They were on an old lumbering road that led between tall stands of white pine scattered with birch. Fallen needles made a thick carpet under their horses' hoofs. The trail led them up a little rise, and then to a level stretch. The morning air had a chill to it. Though it was still August, there was enough of a hint of fall in the air to remind her that they would be leaving for St. Thomas again in four more weeks.

"Let's canter," he said.

"All right."

She dug her heels into her horse's sides. "Feel the wind!" she called to him. And then, holding out her hand, "Oh, look, Charles!" A doe and her fawn stood directly ahead of them, briefly frozen, their heads up in alarm at the sound of the approaching horses, and then, in an instant, they leaped together into the trees and disappeared like a passage of light across water.

The road curved downward, and they slowed their horses to a walk again, and at last the road ended at a split-rail fence.

"This is where our property ends," Edith said.

"I don't believe in property lines," he said. "Let's jump it."

She sat still, looking at the fence; it was not more than three feet high. "I'm terrified of jumping," she said finally.

"Then try it. Try being brave."

She studied the fence. Then she said, "All right. Let's try."

She turned her horse and carefully addressed the jump. Tensed, her knees tight, shoulders forward, head up, she hesitated for a moment. Then she lowered her head, pressed her heels into the gelding's flank, and started for the fence. Holding her breath, she felt herself rise, clear the rail, and land perfectly on the other side. Charles followed her across the fence, and when he turned toward her again she had laughed a little wildly and said, "Charles? Do you know something? That's the first time I've ever jumped without my father watching! Without him forcing me to do it, pulling me over! Do you know—I think I may be brave after all!"

They had both dismounted then. Grinning broadly, he led his horse toward her. "It was beautiful," he said. "You are brave."

"You're good for me!" she laughed.

"It's just because I got you off your father's property," he said. "You're free now." With one finger, he reached up to brush an excited tear from the corner of her eye, and all at once he was embracing her. "Oh!" she cried, and clung to him. He kissed her mouth, fumblingly at first, his lips groping for hers and then, pulling her tightly to him, held her with her head pressing against his shoulder. And instantly she felt herself approaching that unmapped sexual territory. But it was not at all the same as with Louis because the feeling this time was different, more poignant. Apparently the suddenness and intensity of feeling startled him as much as it did her, for he quickly pushed her away from him, held her at arm's length, and looked at her, his face anxious and bewildered. "My God," he whispered, "we've got to be careful, you and I—don't we? We've got to be awfully careful, Edith." And they had looked at each other, flushed, embarrassed, and confused. Finally they had both laughed nervously. He released her. "We'd better be heading back," he said in a quiet voice, and bent to pick up the reins of the two grazing horses from where they had fallen in the grass.

They rode homeward in silence. Edith held her horse back to let Charles' take the lead. Watching his back as she rode behind him under the pine trees, she was glad that he couldn't see her face.

That night, after he had left for New York, Edith was feverish. Mary Miles, fearing influenza, had doctored her with many pills and potions from her large supply. And Edith, listening to Mary's instructions, had wanted badly to ask Mary something about a woman's desires. But how could she ever ask questions like that of someone named Miss Mary Miles?

Two days later, Edith's mother said to her, "Do you remember our little wager, dear? Well, now I'm not sure who's won the dollar, you or I."

"Why, Mama?"

"Before I'd even had a chance to invite *her* to tea, Mrs. Blakewell has invited *us*—you and me! On Friday, at four, at her house on Fifth Avenue! Isn't that exciting? Didn't I tell you she'd see me? Don't you think that dollar rightfully belongs to me?"

On Friday, when they were preparing to leave the house, while the chauffeur and Daimler waited to drive them to the city, Dolly Harper's nerves were in a highly disordered state. She kept plucking at Edith's dress, and at her own, asking questions: "Do I look all right? Is this hat right? Do you think she'll ask me to call her Nancy?"

They went out the door and got into the car. They started down the drive. In the back seat of the car, Dolly Harper kept rubbing Edith's gloved fingers between her own. "If some of those St. Thomas women could see me now!" she crowed.

They passed through the gate, and her mother said, "That was the Frenchman. He waved at us."

"What?" Edith said. And then, "Oh. I didn't notice him." Which was true.

* * *

Edith Blakewell's reverie is interrupted now by the sound of footsteps running up the stairs. She snaps on her bedside light. "Leona, is that you?" she calls.

"Yes!"

"Is something the matter?"

"Nothing! Good night!" Leona's footsteps run down the hall and into her room.

Edith gets out of bed, puts on her slippers and robe, and goes out into the hall, where Leona's door stands open. "Leona . . ."

But Leona is in the bathroom, and the door is closed, and Edith can hear water running. Edith waits, and finally the bathroom door opens and Leona stands in the doorway, looking very strange, her hand on her forehead, her face damp. In her other hand she holds a wet washcloth.

"Oh, Granny . . ."

"What's happened? Are you sick?"

Leona walks slowly to her dressing table and stands in front of it. She sways slightly. Then she rubs her face hard with the washcloth.

"I'll bet you've got the bug the tourists get."

Leona shakes her head. "Direct appeals," she says. "Direct appeals are always useless." She laughs shortly. "Ask a favor and make a foe. Wouldn't you think I'd learn that little rule?" She goes now to her bed and sits down heavily on it. She opens her purse and fumbles, Edith thinks, for a cigarette. But then there is a sudden long, choking sob, and Edith sees that Leona has her transparencies in her hands, pulling at them as if to rip them apart. "What are you doing?" Edith cries, rushing to her. "Stop it!" Clutching at Leona's hands, she tries to force them apart and for a moment or two they struggle there at the edge of the bed. "Stop this!" Edith says. "Behave yourself! Stop being hysterical!" Leona's hands fly apart and, released, the transparencies scatter across the bed. "Now stop this, Leona!" Edith repeats. "You should be ashamed of yourself!"

Leona has fallen now, sobbing, across the bed.

"Harpers are not put together with flour paste and water!" Edith says. "Behave yourself! Sit up! Tell me what's the matter!" Edith collects the transparencies, one by one. "Your beautiful pictures," she mutters. "What's to be accomplished by tearing them to pieces?"

"Oh, Granny! He's . . . he was so . . . damned . . . mean. Why are people so damned—*mean!*"

"Self-indulgence!" Edith snaps. "Who are you talking about? Your short-necked man? I told you I didn't like his looks!"

Leona says nothing for a moment. Then she sits up on one arm. She fishes in her purse again, this time for a handkerchief. She blows her nose noisily. "Sorry, Granny," she says. "You're right. Self-indulgence."

"Leona," Edith says, "I want to know what's the matter."

"I'm broke," she says. "That's all. I'm broke, and so I'm scared."

"What are you talking about!"

"Broke. Flat broke. I have thirty-two hundred dollars in the savings bank. When that's gone, there'll be nothing left. I'm scared."

"Thirty-two hundred dollars! Come now!"

"That's all. I figure it might last me six months in New York—maybe a little longer." She pauses, twisting the handkerchief around her index finger. "Well," she says in a flat voice. "Now you know. That's it."

"That isn't possible. What about—" But suddenly Edith does not know: What about what? She can't remember, all at once, what it is Leona has. She has always had something, an income. How can she be broke when she has an income from—oh, yes, of course, the things she got from Edith's mother's estate. Leona was left a nice share of Mama's things—didn't someone tell her Leona would have at least ten thousand a year? And besides, there is Diana—who got such a giant share of Papa's money, more than Edith herself. No, it is not possible.

"You're simply being dramatic," Edith says. "You're indulging in histrionics. What makes you think you have no money?"

"I don't think. I *know*, Granny."

"But what about the things you got from Mama? Mama's—"

"Gone. Sold."

"Mama's Du Pont?"

"Sold."

Her Du Pont stock was one of the things that supported

Mama all those years after Papa died and left his money to Harold, Arthur, and Diana.

"I don't believe it."

"I sold it. All of it."

Edith's reaction now is simple fury. "Who gave you permission to do this?" she demands. "What right have you got to sell—"

"I owned it, and I sold it! I didn't have to get *permission* from anybody, Granny!"

Edith looks hard at her. "Edouardo?" she says softly.

Leona nods.

"The Spaniards," she breathes. "Dear God, I thought it was only the earrings." And then, angry again, "How could you let them *do* such a thing? *Are* you flour paste? Did you just lie there like a lump and let them *rob* you?"

"I guess—at the time—I thought it was worth it, worth anything, to get out of it."

"Dear God. Dear God in heaven. That terrible man."

Leona buries her head, once more, in the coverlet. "Now please, Granny . . . go away and leave me alone. I feel awful enough."

But Edith sits there—too stunned, actually, to move at this point. "Does your mother know about this?"

"Of course," she says into the coverlet. "And what was her answer? It's fun at the Ritz. Direct appeals—always useless."

"Ssh!" Edith says. "I'm trying to think. Obviously, we've got to do something. Three thousand in a bank—you can't live on that."

Leona says nothing.

"I suppose that's why you were thinking of an art gallery," she says. "But starting a gallery would cost money, I suppose."

"I asked Mother for fifty thousand dollars—just as a loan! For the gallery. I promised to pay her interest—everything."

"Well, I'd have known better than to do that," Edith says. "Your mother only understands money when it's going into her pocket, not out of it. Why didn't you ask me, Leona?"

Leona looks up at her again. "Granny, don't you know I was ashamed of how I'd messed things up? I didn't want you do know—ever."

"Well, now I know."

"I'm such a flop at everything."

"Stop feeling sorry for yourself! After all, you are my heir. When I'm dead practically everything I have will go to you—you know that. So all this is, really, is a temporary crisis."

"Please don't talk that way—"

"Hush, I'm trying to think. Obviously, I'm going to take care of you. If Diana won't, I will. So you're not going to starve. I could put you on an allowance, or—why not? I could advance you the money for your gallery. I could even do that, I suppose..."

"Granny—"

"I don't keep that kind of money lying around the house, naturally. It will take a little time. Or wait a minute—I've just thought of something. Why couldn't I give you a share of your inheritance right now? My father did that—once—for me. My lawyer has been suggesting it himself—saying I should begin distributing things, little by little, so that everything my heirs inherit won't be gobbled up by taxes..."

"You're only—entitled to one kind thing!" Now Leona is crying again. "This will make two—I can't take two—"

"I don't know what you're talking about. Anyway, I see no reason why we couldn't work out something. I'll contact Harold—"

"If he knows it's for me, he'll never let you have anything."

"Now wait a minute, Leona. Harold does not control *everything* of mine. My trust from Papa, yes. But not the Harper stock I got from Mama. That's mine, free and clear. Harold merely banks it for me."

Leona sits straight up now and looks at Edith. "Granny," she says soberly, "rather than *give* me any money, please make it a loan. I want to start off on the right foot with this, you see. I want it to be businesslike. I want to pay you interest. I want—"

"Oh, well," Edith sighs, suddenly weary. "We'll talk about the details tomorrow, Leona. It really doesn't matter to me. The main thing is, we'll work it out." She stands up. "I take it you approached the short-necked man about your—financial problem," she says.

Leona lowers her eyes for a moment. Then she shrugs. "Someone told me he was rich," she says.

"Your great-grandfather may not have been a saint, Leona, but he was not flour paste, and he was not a nincompoop. He used to say, 'Where money is concerned, stay within the family.' It's good advice. Remember it. Don't go to outsiders for it, and don't," she adds with a significant look "go throwing it away to outsiders, either, without finding out who they are and what they want it for. Now get some sleep." She turns to go.

But Leona reaches out quickly and catches Edith's arm. "Granny," she says urgently, "just tell me one thing! Tell me you *believe* in my gallery! That's terribly important for me to know! Not just that you're going to help me with it." And suddenly Leona's voice quavers. "Because sometimes I'm not sure I believe in it myself! Say you believe in it, Granny!"

Edith hesitates, looking down at her. "Why—why, of course I believe in it," she says, but her tone is doubtful. "Of course—"

Leona smiles. "Thank you, Granny." She releases her arm.

"Now, good night." Edith goes toward the door.

"Granny!" Leona calls. "I love you! I love you so!"

Her hand on the door, Edith says, "And I love you too, Leona."

But all the way down the hall to her bedroom, Edith cannot rid her mind of the Spaniard—the painted Spaniard—of all people! Of all the people in the world to have gotten Leona's money away from her—Mama's Du Pont, Mama's other things—this is the last, the least, the most despicable, the most horrible person who could have got it. And yet he got it, apparently, just like that! In the cold hall, Edith shivers, shudders with disgust. And the next thought is, of course, inevitable. After she dies, it is terrible to think it, but Edith can see it: all her own money being randomly distributed, little by little or large by large, to a long succession of Spaniards down the corridor of years.

Eleven

Two days have passed. It is Saturday afternoon, and Leona is off at the beach.

Sibbie Sanderson's new picture, which Sibbie thinks is not her *Arbeit,* has just arrived at Edith Blakewell's house. *Arbeit* or not, it is certainly very large, and Edith has no idea where she is going to put it. "Just put it there, against the stairs," she says to the native boy who has delivered it. "Goodness, it's immense!"

After he goes, she studies the picture. It is mostly green trees, with stretches of blue water between, but in the lower left-hand corner is a rather graceful reclining female nude. The nude is the best thing in the picture, Edith thinks, and she considers snipping that corner of the canvas out and framing it, throwing away the rest. She could do that but, of course, Sibbie would have umpteen fits.

Edith returns to her desk where, for the last day and a half, she has been hard at work organizing things. Since dispatching her telegram to Harold with instructions to sell two thousand shares of her Harper stock, she has been determined to make her own base of operations, the desk, shipshape; if there is going to be a change in the order of things, there must first be order. The big desk contains packages of old letters bearing ancient, faded two-cent stamps commemorating such events as the Hudson-Fulton Celebration and the opening of the Panama Canal (Valuable stamps? she wonders; better save them, just in case); bank statements back as far as 1909; yellowed newspaper clippings; old theatre programs; dress patterns; hints, scissored from the pages of a woman's magazine, on how to install a Turkish corner in one's living room; an advertisement for orthopedic corsets; a cigar box full of old buttons; and much, much more. Astonishing, what a detritus of *stuff* descends upon one during one's life. Edith becomes momentarily sidetracked by the discovery of an old photograph album in one of the drawers, and there they all are as they once were, in their ferrotype poses: herself, in a studio portrait, her hair in the style of a Harrison Fisher girl, sniffing a rose; and there are Arthur and Harold, Papa and Mama—Mama looking chic but haggard, standing stiffly in front of the Daimler, squinting at the camera, very much as she must have looked that afternoon they set off for tea together. Odd, she thinks, the way something seems to go out of a photograph of a person after the person has died; she is sure that a stranger could tell, looking at these pages, the living from the dead. There is even a photograph of Charles' mother. . . .

She is so absorbed in the photograph album that she does not hear Leona come in, and she is a little startled to hear Leona's voice asking, behind her, "Were there any calls for me, Granny?"

She turns. "Calls?" Leona's face is bright from the beach. "No, no calls."

"Eddie . . . Winslow didn't call, did he?"

"No. What was the expression we used here during the war? Telephone silence, there has been telephone silence today. Were you—"

Leona has turned toward the hall. "My God," she says, pointing. "What's *that?*"

"What? Oh, it's Sibbie's new painting. She's given it to me. I—I rather like it, don't you?"

"Lord! She can't even *draw!*"

Edith hesitates. "I thought the figure, the nude in the corner, was rather nice . . ."

Leona laughs. "Well, I suppose it's all right—if you're a raging lesbian like the woman who painted it! Well, I've got to rush, Granny."

"Now just a minute, Leona!" Edith says sharply. "Sibbie is a very old and dear friend of mine. I won't have you speaking like that about her. Sibbie's just a little mannish, that's all. Now come in here a minute and sit down. There's something I want to discuss with you—an idea I have."

"Will it wait, Granny?" Leona says. "Please? I really want to go out now and start combing the town for Eddie Winslow. I'm worried. I haven't heard from him. His hotel room doesn't answer."

"What do you need to see him for? I thought that was all over."

Leona frowns. "It isn't like him to leave without even calling me to say good-by. I'd just like to find him, to say good-by."

"And end it on a pleasant note? Well, all right."

"I won't be late, Granny. But it may be after dinner. We'll talk then."

"All right," Edith says.

Leona pauses in the doorway. "You haven't—changed your mind about the gallery, have you, Granny?"

"No," Edith says carefully. "No, it isn't that."

"Well, I'll see you later, then." She blows Edith a kiss, and is gone.

Edith returns to the album pages.

"When Edith was a very little girl," Edith remembers her mother saying as she held a shell-thin teacup, "I tried to explain to her why it was necessary for us to move to St. Thomas. How old were you then, dear? Seven or eight?" They sat in the drawing room of Mrs. Blakewell's house, a brownstone on the corner of Fifth Avenue and 36th Street. It was not a large room, but it was elegantly furnished, all in pale cream and gold. Ailanthus leaves from the trees on the street outside dappled the windows and created a green shade.

With her teacup poised, Dolly Harper mused. "Let's see, my husband acquired his West Indian sugar interests in ninety-five, and it was a few months after that—yes, Edith would have been about seven, and I tried to explain to her why we had to go, and Edith kept saying, 'But Mama, why do we have to move? Why do we have to go and live with the Indians?' Indians! Imagine! And I said to her, 'But Edith dear, your Papa has made a little money in rum, and so we must go to the West Indies to help him make his rum.' And little Edith looked up at me and said—" Dolly Harper made a long face in imitation of the way Edith had looked at her "—and said, 'Mama, what is rum?' Oh, my! Isn't that a funny story? 'Mama, what is rum?'" Dolly Harper laughed gaily, and sipped her tea.

Mrs. Thomas Blakewell smiled at Edith. "Poor little waif," she said in her throaty voice, "you must not have known what to make of it." Then, turning to Edith's mother, she said, "Edith is your eldest child, Mrs. Harper?"

"Yes. The two boys were born—later." She laughed again. "By that time, you knew what rum was, didn't you dear?"

Her mother went on. "Now to be sure," she said, "Edith absolutely hated St. Thomas at first. It was so much unlike what she'd been used to, you see. But now, of course, she absolutely adores it, don't you, Edith?" Without waiting for an answer, she continued, "Your dear son really must visit us down there, Mrs. Blakewell. Honestly, I cannot tell you what a pleasure it was to have that nice young man as our houseguest last weekend in Morristown. Edith and he got on so well together, and my husband and I enjoyed him too. I do hope he'll be able to visit us again—so we can get to know him even better. But Charles and Edith had so much fun together, didn't you, dear? They rode, they walked. Of course we keep horses in St. Thomas too. Do you think, Mrs. Blakewell, that your son would like to visit us this winter at Sans Souci?"

Mrs. Blakewell had a rattling laugh. "Well, Mrs. Harper, that would be entirely up to him," she said. "He's very much his own man. I wouldn't dream of predicting what he'd like to do."

"Oh, but I'm thinking, Mrs. Blakewell, of how you must need him here. Especially now, these days, since your dear husband passed on."

"I refuse to tie my son down," she said. "He is to have his own life, and not be saddled with me."

The woman was handsome, Edith thought, in a curious and

perhaps not so formidable way. There was much of her in her son's face. She looks, Edith thought, the way she talks: cynical, bitterly witty, mocking, self-assured, dry.

"The only thing I cannot adjust to in St. Thomas is black servants," her mother was saying. "I simply cannot get used to being waited upon by black faces. They look so fierce. And there is an element among them that is really quite dangerous, you know, and they cause my husband no end of trouble in the canefields. One tries to weed out the bad element when selecting people for the house. But of course they all steal, and they're lazy. But," and she laughed, "what can one do?"

"Yes," Mrs. Blakewell said.

"That's why I'm personally glad my husband has so many other business interests, and that the sugar and the spirits part of it have become relatively minor. Still, we must all have sugar, mustn't we? Why, I imagine there may be a bit of our sugar right there in that exceptionally handsome sugar bowl of yours."

"I shouldn't be at all surprised."

"Well," Dolly Harper said, putting down her cup, "we really must be going, Edith. And I can't tell you, Mrs. Blakewell, what an enormous pleasure it has been to meet you, after meeting your charming son. And I shall certainly issue him an invitation to come to Sans Souci this winter, and hope that he'll be able to accept. And perhaps, in the meantime, I shall be able to persuade you to visit me in Morristown?"

"I should enjoy that, Mrs. Harper," Mrs. Blakewell said.

While the maid was helping them into their wraps, Mrs. Blakewell stepped over to Edith and smiled. "You've kept admirably mum while we two old ladies chattered," she said. "I congratulate you."

"Thank you. I've enjoyed—just listening."

Mrs. Blakewell put her face close of Edith's and tilted her chin up at her. "Tell me," she said in her hoarse whisper, and Edith could feel the warm, dry breath against her cheek, "do you like my son?"

"Yes."

"He's a nice man, don't you think? A good person?"

"Oh . . . yes. Yes, I do think so."

Mrs. Blakewell laughed. "You are a little waif," she said. "But I like you."

"I can't thank you enough again, Mrs. Blakewell," Edith's mother was saying. "You were too nice to have us."

And Edith heard Mrs. Thomas Blakewell say, "Please call me Nancy, dear."

In the car, going home, her mother said thoughtfully, "They say that when she travels she goes by private railway car—someone else's car. She takes a house in Newport for the season. A borrowed house. She doesn't have a fraction of the money I have, but she's one of the great social leaders of New York. Royalty beats a path to her door. She doesn't do it with money. She does it with something else—a *je ne sais quoi*. . . ."

The following weekend Charles arrived in Morristown again. Edith was standing on the back lawn, with her golf clubs, practicing her chip shots, and she saw him come out into the terrace. Seeing her, he leaped over the azalea hedge and came running down the lawn to her—running with that particular, unemphatic grace he always had right up until the end. "There's a conspiracy against us," he said when he reached her. "They're marshaling their forces—the older generation."

"What do they want us to do?"

"We're being put together. If we're not careful, before we know it we'll bc man and wife."

"Oh," she said casually. "Do you really think so?"

"Come on, let's walk." They started slowly across the grass. Glancing at her briefly out of the corner of his eye, he took her hand. "You charmed the pins off my mother. Did you know that?"

"I think you simply told her to be nice to us."

He winked at her. "You think too much," he said. "The point is, she liked you. She wouldn't say so if she didn't."

They walked in silence for a while. "Well, what about it?" he asked. "This conspiracy."

"I don't know."

"Your mother asked me to St. Thomas this winter."

She nodded.

"I could refuse the invitation. Do you want me to refuse it, Edith?"

She hesitated. "No," she said. "I don't want you to refuse it."

"Do you want me to accept it, then?"

"Yes."

He pointed. "Let's go this way." He led her behind a huge copper beech with spreading branches. "Nobody can see us here," he whispered, taking her shoulders, and turning her to face him.

She touched his sleeve. "Why should you want to get involved with me? Meredith Harper's daughter."

"I've thought about you all week long," he said. "Have you thought about me?"

She looked up at him anxiously. "Yes."

"Well, then?" He drew her closer.

But something, some movement in the distance, caught her eye, and she turned. "Oh," she said, pulling away from him.

His look followed hers. "Who—him? He can't see us, can he? Who is that fellow, anyway?"

"Just—just a man who works for my father. A Frenchman."

"You're shivering."

"Let's walk back this way," she said. They turned and walked back slowly toward the house.

And then, when their return to St. Thomas was just a week away, Mrs. Thomas Blakewell came to tea in Morristown, and Charles came with her to spend the weekend. Edith's father joined them, and the five sat on stiff little gilt chairs in her mother's drawing room while her mother, in a silk brocade from Molyneux, poured.

There was a boyish exuberance about Charles that seemed more and more striking to her, the better she got to know him. It had nothing to do with silliness, but was a way his strong-jawed face had of going quickly from repose to animation, a quickness of response. He seemed to take small, spontaneous joys from the reactions of other people. Clearly, he was enjoying the tea. He had a way of holding up his hand, leaning forward eagerly to interrupt the conversation when he wanted to make a point; he interrupted, that is, without really interrupting—by sitting forward with that hand raised until he was given a chance to speak. Edith, watching him make a gesture like that, found that it took her breath away and made her a little dizzy, and she decided it was easier not to watch him. She listened as he laughed, very heartily, at the end of her mother's Mama-what-is-rum story, and, when she sensed that his eyes had turned to look at her, her eyes were on her teacup.

After tea, her father said, "You ladies can amuse yourselves for a while, I imagine. Mr. Blakewell and I would like a talk." Charles looked up, startled, and then nodded. The two men went into the library and the doors were closed. Edith's mother continued talking animatedly to Mrs. Blakewell, and Edith excused herself and went out into the garden.

She sat on the edge of the unplumbed fountain, where the three bronze nymphs played in nonexistent splashes. The days were growing shorter now. The sun was already low in the sky.

Charles came out of the house, about half an hour later, and found her there. His face was grave. He sat down beside her without speaking.

"What did you and Papa talk about?" she asked him.

"I probably shouldn't ask you this—but I'll ask it anyway," he said. "Your father. Is he—sane?"

"Why, I don't know!"

"The business about all the money he's made. I've never heard anybody talk about money that way. I'll say this for your father—he doesn't believe in hiding his light under a bushel."

Edith had laughed. "No," she said. "But I think he's sane. He's just—Meredith Harper."

In a different voice, he said, "There'll be no objection if we marry."

She said nothing.

"Queer. The queerest position I've ever been in. Having him offer you to me before I'd even asked you. I did plan to ask you, you see."

She continued to sit very still in the growing darkness, her hands in her lap.

"Will you marry me, Edith? I love you."

"But I'm not sure I love you," she said.

And it was true. She wanted to add, now, "I'm afraid it's only passion." But the words sounded so foolish, so pompous, as they formed in her head that she couldn't utter them. Mademoiselle Laric, in her day, had talked to Edith a good deal about passion, explaining its difference from "love." The two things, she had said, were incompatible forces; one was misleading the other true. And Edith had begun to think that her feeling for Charles must be passion, the false one, and she wished ardently that someone like Mademoiselle could be there to help her decide. She had thought a great deal, in the past weeks, about her feelings for Charles, and surely there was something rather unseemly, a little primitive, about the way she had begun to think of him. She had had a thoroughly primitive dream about him, and certainly this was a sign. The books were all there, she had found them in her father's library, and she had searched through all of them for a clue. But Doctor Sigmund Freud, whom everyone had begun saying had answers to everything, had hardly a word to say on the subject of passion. And though Doctor Freud had a number of things to say on a number of matters, she might have wished he would be a bit more specific about certain things. She had thought, again and again, of speaking to her mother, or to Mary Miles. But, too timorous and squeamish, she had not done so. "Is there such a thing as a woman having too much passion?" she wanted to ask someone. But she had asked no one anything at all.

"Well," Charles said quietly beside her, "you go back to St. Thomas next week. Will you think about it? And perhaps, when I come—"

"I'll think about it, Charles."

"If you still want me to come."

"I do want you to come. Very much."

"Good," he said. He stood up and looked down at her.

"Charles," she said quickly, "I just want to tell you that if you hadn't come here that first weekend when you did, I don't know what I would have done. Because just a few days before you came, a terrible, awful thing happened—one of the worst things that's ever happened to me. If you hadn't come when you did, I don't know if I'd even be alive. Because I thought of killing myself. It was something I did that was all my fault. That's all I want to say now. It's made me—not sure."

Bending, he kissed her. He started off quickly through the dark garden.

Leaning forward, she called, "Charles?"

He stopped and turned. "Yes?"

He was coming toward her again, and so she had to say it; she couldn't see his face clearly in the gloom, which made saying it easier. "Charles," she whispered, "your room is—just down the hall from mine. No one sleeps in the bedrooms between."

He stood very still beside her.

"Perhaps . . . I mean—perhaps, later on, when the house is quiet . . ."

"Yes," he said.

"My door won't be locked. I—I won't be asleep—"

"Yes," he repeated.

"Unless—"

"Unless what?"

"Unless you think it's wrong. Unless you think it's wrong for me to—feel the way I do. Then, in that case—no. No, because I think it is wrong. No. We'd better not."

"No," he said in a husky voice. "I don't think it's wrong."

There were tears in her eyes and she was lucky to have the darkness. She tried to speak, and couldn't. "Then—" she began at last, trying to make her voice sound gay and offhand, as casual as possible, "then—"

"Then I'll be there," he said. He touched her shoulder briefly and was gone, and she sat there, bunched, huddled, on the fountain's lip, feeling that if she didn't hug herself tightly her whole being would fly apart.

Thc bar is called The Stick of Dynamite, and it is the fourth such place Leona has visited in her search for Eddie. Its interior is redly dark, illuminated with rushlights on the small, crowded tables, and she stands at the door, peering into the smoky, noisy room. In one corner, a Negro is playing slow, almost inaudible blue piano. A waiter approaches her, but she shakes her head. "I'm looking for a friend," she says. Then she sees him, or rather the familiar shape of his back. He is sitting alone, at the far end of the long bar. She pushes her way between the tables. A group of the gay boys looks up at her and giggles coyly, and then, as she murmurs, "Excuse me . . . excuse me . . ." between the backs of chairs, a man reaches out and touches her arm. "Hi, buddy," he says.

"Oh, hello, Arch." He is with a large party of men and women, who turn their heads and look up at her with tanned, disinterested faces.

"Sit down a minute. Meet my friends."

"I can't, Arch."

"Looking for your friend Winslow? He's at the bar. Drowning his sorrows."

"Yes."

"Look," he says, standing up and separating himself from the others, "about the other night. I'm a blunt guy. I say what's on my mind. I believe in the direct approach, in calling a spade a spade. When I want to go to bed with a girl, I say let's go to bed. Don't hold it against me. Don't blame me for being the kind of guy I am."

"No," she says, "I don't blame you, Arch."

"I don't hold it against you for running off on me. That's the way you are. This is the way I am."

"Yes."

"Then are we still buddies?"

"I guess so," she smiles.

He nods in the direction of the table behind him. "This bunch of swingers wants me to take off in their boat for Montego tomorrow. But I'm not going. I'm going to stick around here for a few more days. So maybe we can get together again. Give it some thought."

"Yes. Well, good night, Arch."

Grinning, he shakes her hand. "'Night, buddy. See? I still like you."

She continues toward the bar. She sits down in the empty stool next to Eddie and says gently, "Hey. . . . Hey, remember me?"

He swivels on the stool, his drink cupped in his hands, and gives her a cloudy look. "Oh," he says, "it's you. How are you this lovely night?"

"Why haven't you called me, Eddie? I've left all sorts of messages at your hotel."

"Yeah. I got some messages. All sorts of messages. Buy you a drink?"

"All right."

He lifts his glass and drains it. Then he slides his empty glass across the bar and says, "Two more. Two Scotches. A pair." Then, turning to her, he says, "Scotch okay for you?"

"Sure," she says with a little smile. "Scotch is fine." And then, "What have you been doing, Eddie? I've been worried."

"Doing? Me?" He gives her another dim look. "Well, I've been drinking. Drinking, and—oh, yes—thinking."

"What about?"

"About this kid. This little kid I used to know, back in the town I grew up in. In Massachusetts. A kid I went to grammar school with. A little mouse-faced kid. He had a—a face like a mouse's. Mice. Micey eyes too. Nobody liked him, but he had a function. A function, you see. Thanks," he says as a fresh drink is set down in front of him. He picks it up and takes a swallow of it. "Where was I? Oh, this kid. Henry Nichols. That was his name, Henry Nichols. But we used to call him Henry Quarters. Get it? His function was—when anybody did something, like throw a rock through a window of the girls' can, or put a tack on the teacher's chair—" He pauses, thoughtfully, stirring the ice in his glass with his finger. "But I don't think anybody ever did that, come to think of it. But I remember the rock—through the window of the girls' can." He laughs loudly. "*I* did that. But anyway, my point is this. That any time anybody did something like that, and the principal of the school would be mad as hell and trying to find out who did it, Henry Nichols—or Henry Quarters—would come up to the kid who did it, and say, 'If you'll give me a quarter, I'll say I did it.'" He takes another swallow of his drink. "Anything bad anybody did you could pay Henry Nichols a quarter and he'd say he did it. Of course if you didn't give him the quarter, if you didn't play Henry's game, he'd just tell on you. Isn't that something?"

"Yes," she says, "it certainly is."

"And so I've been sitting here wondering what ever happened to old Henry Quarters. I have a feeling he's gone—far." He scowls darkly at his glass. "How's your drink?" he asks. And then, "I love you."

"I know," she says quietly. "You told me that."

He leans back, away from the bar, hooking his feet in the legs of the stool. "Christ, I must be out of my mind," he says.

Leona says nothing.

"Give me another Scotch!" he calls to he bartender.

"Don't have another drink, Eddie," she says. "Let's go somewhere else. I hate this dreary place."

"Nope. Want another drink," he says thickly. "This place is fascinating. Full of fruits and nuts. You should see the people that have been coming in and out of this place. They're either queers or whores. You wouldn't think that the queers and the whores would hang out in the same place, would you? Fascinating. It's a fascinating—sociological study."

Leona sighs.

"Now where was I?" he says. "Oh, yes. You asked me what I've been doing. Well, aside from drinking, and wondering about Henry Quarters, I've been working. Yessir. Working. Phone rings in the room when I'm working, I don't answer it. Get lots of messages that way. Damm editors keep calling me up from New York to see how I'm coming with it." He gives her a sideways look. "With the Harper story."

"I see," she says.

He accepts his new drink and leans forward again, one hand curled around the glass, his elbows on the bar. "Yeah," he says.

"And how *are* you coming with it, Eddie?" she asks him.

He stares at her for a moment, then says, "It's all done. Want to read it?" He reaches in his pocket and pulls out a folded sheaf of yellow foolscap and hands it to her. "Here," he says. "Read it."

"Read it and weep?" she asks with a bitter laugh. Carefully, she lights a cigarette. Then she unfolds the typewritten pages. "Dear me," she says, riffing the pages, "it's awfully *long*, isn't it?" She begins to read.

She asks him only one question during the reading of it. "What does 'possible suspension of trading' mean?"

"Maybe take the damn stock off the market."

She nods, and continues reading. When she has finished it, she holds the manuscript pages in her hands and looks at him.

"You thinking of tearing it up? Go ahead. Tear it up." He gives her a crooked smile. "I've got a carbon copy in my room."

"You can't print this, Eddie. It will ruin us. If any of this is true."

He says nothing. The piano has switched to "Twelfth Street Rag."

"I'll say this for you, Eddie," she says. "You've got guts. You realize that if this story appears Uncle Harold will sue you, *and* your magazine, for every cent you've got."

"Let him sue."

"You've bitten off more than you can chew, Eddie. You don't know Uncle Harold. I do."

"Listen," he says, "there's no law against printing the truth. I've spent three months working on this. These are facts. I deal in facts." He taps his forehead. "Facts."

Leona bites her lip. She looks down at the pages again. "And it seems—it seems as though you've gone out of your way to say everything in just as *nasty* a way as you possibly can. Is this just to hurt me, Eddie?"

He shakes his head. "No. It's not just to hurt you."

"You can't do it!"

He is silent for a moment, and then says, "Look. What difference does it make to you? He's only your great-uncle. It doesn't affect you."

"It affects me very much! My gallery!"

"Gallery?" He begins to hum, tapping out the rhythm of the song with his finger on the bar. "'It seems to me I've heard that song before.... It's from an old fa-mil-iar—'"

"Stop it! Granny's offered to give me the money for the gallery! If you ruin Uncle Harold you ruin Granny, and if you ruin Granny you ruin me!"

"I get it. A chain reaction. Boom, boom, boom."

"Stop it! Stop treating this as though it were all a great big joke! You can't do this to me, Eddie!"

He turns slowly on the stool and faces her. "If I don't send in this story, will you marry me?"

"What a dirty thing to say! I think your—your friend was named Eddie Winslow, not Henry Quarters!"

"I'm sorry," he says, lowering his eyes. "I didn't mean that. I meant it—no kidding—I meant it in a different way, Leona." He sips his drink. "What I meant is," he says slowly, "that I have a choice. A choice."

"What sort of choice?"

"I showed you that story for a reason. Let me give you a little bit of the background, okay? Background. I'm way out on a limb with this one. Way out. About three months ago, I went to him, my boss in New York, and said I think there's a story in the Harper empire. 'Think so?' he said. 'Well I don't.' So I argued. Finally I won, I sold him. So he said, 'Okay, go ahead. Take some time. If it's as hot as you think it is, maybe we'll give it a cover.' Now it's three months later, I've got my story, and I can either send it in and be pretty sure of a nice fat raise. Or"—he pauses, giving her a hard look—"or I can *not* send in the story. Tell them, sorry, but there isn't any story. Three months' work, but I couldn't find out anything. Sorry, pal, but Eddie struck out. And I'd probably get fired. Now *you* tell me. Which should I do?"

"You certainly know what I want you to do."

"Tell me. Just tell me. Which should I do? It's not just a moral decision for me. It's a financial one too. So tell me, Leona."

"Tell them there isn't any story."

He says nothing. Then he nods. "Yeah. That *would* be what you'd say to do."

"You asked me!"

He looks at her for a moment through narrowed eyes. "Aw," he says, and then, scooping up his drink in one hand, he turns his back to her. "Rich kid," he says. "Lousy rich kid. Yeah, why should *you* care? Why should a rich kid care if some poor jerk loses his job. Jesus! Why did I have to fall in love with a lousy rich kid? Aw, you rich kids are all alike."

Leona jumps to her feet. She stands for a moment staring at his back. Then she crumples up the pages of his manuscript into a ball and tosses it on the bar beside him. "Here!" she says. "Use your carbon copy!" She turns and, looking neither to the right nor left, she walks quickly out of The Stick of Dynamite.

Edith is still at her desk when Leona comes into the house. "Ah," she says. "Here you are. Now come. Sit down. Let me tell you about my little notion."

But Leona does not sit down. She stands with one arm resting on the side of the door, and says in a tired voice, "What is it, Granny?"

"I'm going to let you have the money, and I'll turn it over to you as soon as I get the check from Harold. But I'm going to give it to you on one very small condition."

"Condition—"

"Yes. I'm going to ask you to let me write that letter to Gordon—asking him to come down. Maybe nothing at all will come of it when he gets here, but at least I will have tried and you will have tried. You see, dear, I'm not getting any younger, and I think you'll agree that you've been a little—rash—with your money in the past. Just a *tiny* bit rash. That's why I want, if I possibly can, to see you settled—with someone substantial, someone suitable, someone who will take care of you. Someone who has a business head, like Gordon, who can help you. So you may have your gallery money, but with that one little proviso."

Leona stands very still. "A deal, Granny?"

"Well, if you want to put it that way, yes. A deal."

"A deal. Everybody wants to make a stinking deal!" She runs her fingers upward through her hair. "Oh, God!" she cries. "Oh, God!"

"Now Leona. It isn't much I ask."

"You scratch my back, I'll scratch yours! Oh!" She turns, pulling the yellow cardigan from her shoulders and swinging it in her hand. She starts across the hall. "No!" she cries. "No deal, Granny! I don't want the money—keep it! I don't want the gallery! I don't want anything!"

Edith rises from her chair and follows her. "Now steady down, Leona! Steady down. After all, I think that I'm entitled—"

"Entitled! Oh, no! No—go away!" She starts up the stairs, Edith behind her. "Everybody," she sobs, trailing the yellow sweater behind her on the stairs, "everybody go away!"

"Now see here—"

"Shut up! Go away!"

"Don't you speak to me that way, Leona!"

They are in the upstairs hall now, and Leona is almost running—a little knock-kneed run in her slim yellow skirt—toward her bedroom door.

"I have a few rights with you, Leona. If I'm going to give you fifty thousand dollars I'm entitled to see to it that you don't spend it on another gigolo. I have a few—"

Leona slams the door.

Edith approaches the door. "Don't you slam doors on me, young lady! Open that door!" She hears the key turn in the lock. "Open it!" She raps her knuckles sharply on the panel of the door. "I have a few things to say to you, young lady. I'd like to know exactly who you think you are! You're not to tell *me* to shut up, young lady! I've heard a little bit about your activities lately. Stories travel pretty quickly here, and Alan Osborn's told me a little bit about you—sitting up half the night, night after night, with your men friends—one man after another! Just *who* do you think you are? What kind of reputation are you trying to get? You seem to forget—" She raps hard on the door again. "Open this door!"

Edith pauses, listening. The only answer is the rapid click of high heels across the floor of the room beyond.

"This is my house, Leona," Edith says. "This is my hospitality you've been enjoying—a fact which you seem to have forgotten. Now do as I say! Unlock this door."

Faintly, from beyond the door, she hears again: "Go away."

Leaning against the door, Edith says, "If anybody tells anybody to go away around here, it will be *I* who tells *you*. Do you hear me? I can very easily tell you to pack up your traps and get out of my house, young lady! Do you hear? If you aren't willing to behave like a guest in my house, you can pack up your traps and get out!"

The answer now, from the room beyond, is only silence.

Edith stands outside the locked door for several minutes, waiting. Then, pressing her cheek against the panel, she says, more gently, "Leona—I didn't mean any of that. Please open the door."

But there is still no answer.

Twelve

MONEY. It towered over all their lives. It governs the present just as it controlled the past. Everything that has ever happened to any of them, Edith sometimes thinks, has been shaped by the heavy weight of Meredith Harper's fortune, and everywhere they have ever gone they have simply been guided along the money's tortuous path.

"We won't let the money get hold of us, will we?" Charles had asked her once. "There's such a godawful lot of it. Sometimes money seems to have a life of its own."

She had assured him that the money would not get hold of them. But of course it had. There was more of it then than there is now, but its grip is every bit as strong.

Charles had come to St. Thomas that winter on the old Quebec Line steamer from New York. The island fascinated him. He loved the brown, hard angularity of the hills, the jagged profile of West Mountain, dry and bereft of trees, and the soft green contrast of the valleys and the yellow shore. He loved the violence of the surf off William Head. Hardness, toughness, sharpness—those were the qualities that appealed to him about St. Thomas. He used to say that it astonished him to see how humanity had been able to carve any sort of an existence out of it. There was a love of adventure in Charles, the future soldier taking root within him, and of all the places he had ever seen St. Thomas seemed to him to contain the most possibilities for adventure. He wore old clothes. They walked and they rode. (And yes, she remembers tenderly, they slept together, on certain furtive nights . . . the door opening, then quickly closing, the quiet footsteps approaching across the dark room.) He had asked her again to marry him, and this time she had said yes. She no longer worried whether her feeling for him was love or desire. It didn't seem to matter any more; she wanted him too much.

She told him about Andreas. "He ran away," she said. "I suppose he was too weak to stand up to Papa" (for this was how she had begun to think of Andreas then).

"Was that the awful thing that happened to you before I came to Morristown?"

"No."

"Then there was another man. Between Andreas and me."

She nodded. He didn't ask her more. It was another of the things, at the time, that didn't seem to matter.

"Your father and your mother think I'm marrying you for your money," he said once.

"Did they say that?"

"They don't have to say it."

"I'll tell them it isn't true!"

He laughed at her. "It doesn't matter what they think. Let them dream on. You and I have our secret . . ."

Once, on one of their walks, they stopped to watch as the silhouette of a mountain suddenly eclipsed the setting sun, the sun leaving only a bright aurora around the mountain's cone. "You know," he said thoughtfully, "your father *goes* with this place. He doesn't belong in a place like Morristown. He belongs here. This island suits him. I wonder if he realizes it?"

Edith said nothing. She had begun to wonder whether her father really approved of Charles. Though outwardly cordial, her father had begun referring to Charles as "your New York aristocrat." "Your New York aristocrat seems to be enjoying himself," he would say to her.

There was a party, late that month, to announce the engagement. Dolly Harper was never happier, and St. Thomas society turned out for it. Afterward, Charles sailed for New York, but he was to return to St. Thomas in April, for they had agreed to be married then. One day after Charles left, shopping with her mother in Charlotte Amalie, they encountered Louis Bertin. "Congratulations, Edith," he said.

"Thank you," both women replied. Edith was surprised to find how easy a thing it was to speak to him, and congratulated herself.

"Crust," her mother said as they walked on. "Calling you Edith. That man is *no* gentleman."

It was in April, when Charles returned, that Edith first learned that her father had offered Charles a job as manager of one of the sugar plantations. And she also learned that a sum of money was changing hands—a gift to Mrs. Thomas Blakewell.

"Compensation," she said to Charles. "For the comedown of having her son marry me!"

He laughed at her for that remark too. "No," he said, "it has nothing to do with that."

"What is it then?"

"You have to understand my mother," he said. "She's a woman who's always had to be taken care of. If it wasn't by my father, then it was by my Uncle Julius—or someone else. She's a woman who has to be cruised on yachts, and entertained in ballrooms, in big houses. When she can't provide those things herself, someone else provides them. Your father is just doing the sort of thing for her that people have always done. It's the world she lives in." Then, smiling, he said, "And thank God it's not my world. It has nothing to do with you or me."

"The thing you said about money getting hold of us," she said. "Isn't that what's beginning to happen?"

"No," he insisted, "of course not."

"But what about the job?"

He frowned. "I don't know. I haven't decided about that yet."

And then, late one night, just two weeks before they were to be married, he had come to her room again in the old house at Sans Souci. He had risen from her bed, wrapped himself in his robe, and crossed the room to the window where he stood looking out at the dark tropic night. From the bed she watched his dark shadow against the open window. "Living in New York," he said in a soft voice, "would mean having a house in town. I'd put on a stiff collar every morning and go downtown to practice law with all my father's old partners. You would invite the partners' wives to tea—"

She lay there, her eyes on the still shape of him framed by the curtains that stirred in the warm breeze.

"Do you know what this place is like for me?" he said. "When I was eighteen, the summer I finished school, I took a trip to Maine with two other boys. We climbed Mount Katahdin. It was one of the best times I ever had. We weren't experienced hikers, but we had plenty of provisions, and we shot small game along the way, and we took it slowly. At night we slept out, with a fire going. One night bears came into the camp. Another time we were sure we were lost. But by the time I got to the top of Mount Katahdin I knew there was something else for me besides reading law in my father's office. I guess that's why I didn't want to go on to college, because whatever it was I knew I wouldn't find it there. Do you see? That's what this place is like for me. Like Mount Katahdin."

"Remember that there are people who hate him here," Edith whispered. "You'd be working for him."

He laughed. "I can handle him," he said. "I can handle his daughter, can't I?" He turned toward her across the dark room.

"Oh, Charles," she said, holding up her arms, "am I a very bad woman to be letting you make love to me like this—before we're—"

"Yes," he whispered, settling himself beside her and nuzzling her throat. "A very bad woman . . . very bad for me."

Later he said drowsily, "Look at the moon. Diana—off on her hunt."

The next morning Edith's mother said to her, "I think it would *look* better if Charles moved to the Grand Hotel until the wedding. For appearances' sake, you know. I realize the Grand Hotel is not at all grand, but it's the only hotel we have. And your father keeps some rooms there, you know, for business purposes."

The suite of rooms her father rented at the Grand Hotel was customarily at the disposal of Monique Bertin. It struck Edith as odd, and even in a perverse way amusing, to think of her future husband occupying quarters that had been temporarily vacated by her father's mistress. But naturally she did not mention this to Charles.

They were married, that April of 1908, in the Anglican Church of All Saints in Charlotte Amalie. As they left the church, native girls threw flowers in the street in front of them, a touch her father had provided. Edith remembers that. And then there was the drive up Government Hill with Papa, who wanted to show them the thing that was to be his surprise.

They stopped in front of the house and got out of the carriage. "I had it built for you and Charles," he said, and handed her the key. "Your wedding present from me."

As they walked through the empty rooms of the house, her father stopped her once with his hand. Smiling at her he said softly, "Are the ceilings high enough, princess?" Then he said, "Furniture is part of the present too, but I wanted you to choose your own." And a peculiar remark that may have meant nothing at all: "Perhaps you'd prefer furniture in the French style?"

After he left them alone in the house, Charles was silent, and so was she. They walked slowly through the rooms again.

"This house echoes," he said.

"A new house always echoes. When we've lived in it a while, the echo will go."

They went out into the wide, empty veranda and looked at the yard, which was nothing but heaps of tossed earth and rocks and wheelbarrow trails and scraps from the builders. Charles went down the steps and picked up a handful of dry dirt in his hand, and crumbled it. "We could build a garden," he said. "We may not have been able to build our own house, but we could build a garden."

It was several months after they had moved into the house that it dawned on Edith Harper Blakewell that what her father had said about having the house built for her and Charles was a lie. It had to be a lie, because work on the house had been started the preceding spring, before she and Charles had even met. Perhaps—since she had never known on which of their Paris summers Monique had come into her father's life—the house had been built for Monique; perhaps for some other purpose or person. It may also have occurred to Charles, at some point, that the house could not have been built for them. It must have occurred to him. But in the seven years they lived there together he did not mention it to her, nor did Edith ever mention it to him. They had accepted the house on the terms Meredith Harper set. It was too late to ask questions.

Morning comes tentatively to tropical places. It pricks out the hilltops with a certain hesitancy, and seems uncertain about invading the deeply shadowed valleys. Leona, up early, and without having said a word to anyone, is descending the streets of Government Hill in a taxi through this cautious mixture of light and shadow. "I'll walk from here," she tells the driver finally. She pays him, and gets out of the taxi.

Very well. Walk where? She is at the foot of the hill, in the center of the town. Across the street is Fort Christian and, ahead of her, Kings Wharf and the Harbor. Already, though it is barely six o'clock and a Sunday morning, the streets are alive and busy; there is a shrill air of hurry and importance everywhere. Bicycles scoot by with bells jangling, and native women, in their long skirts, move nodding and talking up and down the street with their baskets balanced miraculously on their kerchiefed heads—baskets of wash, baskets of bread, baskets of coal. The baskets nod and sway as necks turn and faces smile at her. In front of the town pump a queue of women—carrying heavy jugs and pails, pitchers roped together at the handles—is forming, lining up for the day's water. (If I could paint, I would paint this, Leona thinks.) And, as does everyone who rediscovers what the glitter of very early morning is like, Leona wonders why she doesn't do this oftener: get up early and watch the beginning of day. She walks slowly toward Kings Wharf.

Self-preservation—that is the phrase that has been hammering in her head for the past few hours. Having burned a number of her bridges behind her, it is now time—high time—to start erecting new ones. Perhaps she was wrong to have turned to the old bridges, to have tried to recross them; bridges like Granny, like Eddie. Perhaps that is why they failed her. Or did she fail them? The sun in her hair is warm, but there is a cool breeze blowing off the Harbor, and the air is full of smells—the smell of coffee brewing, the smell of fruit from the little streetside stalls just opening their shuttered fronts, and the smell of the sea. Flags flutter in the wind from their masts above the towers of the old Fort. Leona tries to feel like a flag herself—bright and buffeted and whipped by the wind; confident, self-preserving.

And her marriages were bridges too—brief ones. But why *three?* Why three divorces? Is there something in you that compels you to kill kindness, or love, whenever you encounter it? she asks herself. Walking toward the long pier, the dreary headings of all those divorce papers file in front of her: Breed *vs.* Breed, Paine *vs.* Paine, Para-Diaz *vs.* Para-Diaz. Now it seems to be a case of the People *vs.* Leona Ware Breed Paine Para-Diaz. And, indeed, the People seem to have quite a case against her.

Walking slowly out along the pier, she begins to feel that a new beginning, whatever it is, will be offered to her here, and soon. This is what the urgency of the morning seems to be saying, that the idea will come soon, the inspiration. Swinging her hands deep in the pockets of her cotton skirt, she passes an ancient, white-haired Negro who squats on his haunches on the pier, whittling a piece of bamboo. Bright yellow shards of wood scatter across his knees and at his feet. He nods and grins at her. "Good morning, Miss Leona Harper. You up early."

Queer, how all the natives know her, but call her by her great-grandfather's name. She smiles at the old man. "Isn't it a splendid day?"

At the end of the pier she stands looking out—at the lobster boats rocking gently in the harbor, at the profile of Hassel Island serrated like the back of a green sea-serpent with hills, and at the short, stout tower of Cowell Battery Light. Oh yes, this is a new day, a day for starting over. One thing does not *have* to lead to another; life would be unlivable if that were true. She makes a promise to the morning. ("Leona Ware pressed on regardless with her plan.") Suppose she went back, right now, and told Granny that she is sorry. She even thinks of a little joke. When she gets back to the house, and her grandmother asks her what she wants for breakfast, she will say, "Granny, dear, do you have any humble pie?"

But perhaps that isn't a very funny joke. And besides, that seems more like a retreat than a moving forward. New beginnings should be tougher than that.

They see her standing there, and word spreads—the native boys, singly and in pairs, come running in their swim suits.

They run down the pier toward her. "Dive for coins, Miss? Dive for coins?" They cluster, laughing, around her.

Laughing too, she looks at them as they gather. "Oh, but there are so many of you," she says. "Well, let's see—" She opens her purse.

And how beautiful they are, these little boys, ranging from eight or nine to perhaps sixteen—beautiful, with the sun glinting on the cords of muscle under their black, almost purpleblack skins, wiry—even the little bunched businesses in their tight suits are beautiful—and she and the boys laugh together as, from Leona's awkward underhand, the first coin flies straight up and practically lands on top of her head. She retrieves it. "Don't you think I'm as good as Sandy Koufax?" she says.

The second toss is better. As the coin spins and flashes in the air, the boys spring like seals into the water after it. Leona steps to the edge of the pier and looks down to watch them as, arms and legs scissoring, they pursue the silver through the water. Then, with a shout, one of them surfaces, holds up the coin to show her, and pops it deftly inside his trunks. The others wave and shout for more, and she tosses another coin, and then another.

Tossing coins, she practices her aim, trying to spread the bounty among them. One boy has become her favorite—the smallest of the lot and, by now, there must be twenty of them splashing there. The little one is always being outdistanced by the bigger boys. His waving arm is frantic, and his cry is plaintive.

"Here!" she calls. "For you!" And she tries to aim a quarter directly at him but, once more, another boy is faster.

"Hey!" she cries. "No fair!" And she tries to reach the little one again. "Swim in closer!" she calls to him. He obeys, and she drops a fifty-cent piece directly in front of him in the water. He seizes it, looks up gratefully at her, and she says, "Bravo!"

Now they are all swimming in closer to the pier, and she tosses a coin far out—and, after a good deal of diving, no one gets it.

At last she is out of silver, and she gives them a wide, open-armed gesture. "Sorry," she calls. "That's all I have."

Once more, they swim closer, calling, "More! More!"

She shows them her empty change purse, turns it inside out. "See?"

The boys clamber up the pier toward her.

"Miss Leona Harper, you got more!"

"Honestly, I don't," she says, and starts to turn.

"Miss Leona Harper! You got more!" Moving toward her, one of the older boys begins clapping his hands to the rhythm of the words. "More! More! Miss Leona Harper! You got more!"

She starts quickly away from them, back along the pier. Following her, stamping their feet, clapping their hands, they shout, "Miss Leona Harper! You got more!" They slap the laden fronts of their bathing trunks where the coins jingle. "You got more! You got more!"

The old man, sitting on the piling with his whittled stick, grins up at her again as she approaches, and she gives him a helpless look. "Stop them," she says. "Tell them I haven't got any more."

Still smiling at her, he hunches forward and says softly, "Hey, Miss Leona Harper—you pretty petticoat is hanging down."

"Oh, please," she says, turning away from him in dismay, "please . . ." As she turns, the heel of her shoe wedges between the planks of the pier and she almost falls.

And the boys, hearing the new taunt, approach her in a wide half-circle, clapping their hands, pounding their bare feet against the hollow planking of the pier, shouting catcalls, whistling, chanting, "Hey, Miss Leona Harper! You pretty petticoat is hanging down!" And in all of them she sees only jeering, black and hostile faces, mouths spread open showing white teeth, pink tongues, shouting at her. Like beaters, they come closer as she struggles to extract the jammed heel of her shoe.

One boy springs to a crouch by her feet and looks up her dress. "Hey, Miss Leona Harper! You pretty petticoat is *pretty!*"

"Oh, stop!" she screams. "Leave me alone!" She kicks off the shoe, reaches down, and pulls it loose. Then she turns, while the boys shout and laugh after her, and runs stumblingly, one shoe on and the other in her hand, down the pier. The shouts and the clapping pursue her. A pebble flies through the air and strikes the pier in front of her. Another glances stingingly against her arm. She runs from the pier into the street in front of flying pebbles and there, on the corner of the square, she sees the sanctuary of an outdoor telephone booth and runs to it, squeezes herself inside it, and slams the door with her foot braced hard against it. She lifts the receiver, and a final barrage of pebbles strikes the wall of the booth as she fishes in her purse for change and realizes, of course, that she has none. And who is there to call now anyway? Leaning against the mouthpiece, she sobs into the dead telephone.

It is eleven o'clock. Breakfast for Edith is long since over, and she sits on her veranda with the Sunday newspaper, hearing the sound of church bells from the town below. Leona has not come down; this is the latest Leona has ever been for breakfast and, Edith thinks, it is now simply too late. She does not run a hotel; her guests cannot be fed at whatever odd hour they choose. If Leona comes down now and says she wants to eat, she will simply have to wait for lunch. After the scene last night, Edith has no intention of going up and rousing Leona. She is probably, Edith thinks, simply sulking up there. Very well. Let her sulk. A good sulk, coupled with hunger, may be therapeutic. She picks up the newspaper again.

Then, a little later, she puts the newspaper down. There is something about a house that is missing one of its regular occupants. It is not a silence because it is more like an added presence. Sitting on her veranda Edith has been feeling its gathering approaches; now it is fully in her consciousness. She knows, now, without having looked into Leona's room at all, that Leona is not sulking there, but is no longer physically in the house and, furthermore, that she has been out of the house for some time. She sits very still. Then she rings for Nellie.

"What time did Miss Leona go out this morning?" she asked casually.

"Oh, she left real early, Miss Edith. Five or five-thirty. Right after I got up, I saw her go."

"I just wondered if she was up in time to meet the person who was calling for her."

"Nobody called for her, Miss Edith. She left in a taxi."

"That's what I meant, Nellie. A *taxi* was calling for her."

"Will she be here for dinner tonight, ma'am?"

"I don't know," Edith says, and to allay any further suspicion she adds, "I rather doubt it. Unless there's change of plans. She's visiting friends. You know how indefinite these young people are."

"Yes, Miss Edith."

Somewhat later, when Nellie is busy in the kitchen, Edith goes quietly upstairs to Leona's room. The door is unlocked. Inside, the shape of Leona's absence is even more pronounced. Not that there is anything out of order in the room. In fact, that may be why the absence is so striking. Everything in the room is too much *in* order. The bedspread is smooth, the curtains are still. Leona's dresses hang evenly in the closet and below them on the floor in a neat row are her shoes. Such tidiness is not like Leona, and Edith doubts that Nellie is responsible for it either. High on the closet shelf are Leona's suitcases, stacked. Edith quickly counts them and finds, with a certain amount of relief, that they are all there. Cosmetics are arranged on the bathroom shelf. A half-filled pack of Leona's cigarettes is on the candle stand by the bed. Yet, despite all this evidence of Leona, it is absolutely clear from the appearance, the waiting look, of that room, that Leona is gone and will not immediately be back. Edith studies the room. It is now after one o'clock. Edith wonders what is to be done, if anything. And, if something is to be done, what?

On the terrace of the Virgin Isle Hotel the early lunchers are leaving and, from the table where Leona and Arch sit, which is at the outer perimeter of the terrace, the sunlight on the harbor below is so brilliant and refracted that it gives an illusion of spray in the air. Pelicans plunge into the blue water, emerge, seconds later, wings flapping, struggling upward with their catch. All life, Leona thinks, is feeding, voracious. She puts down her wineglass. Arch is scribbling on a corner of the tablecloth with a gold pencil. "Okay," he says. "We've got the rent, light, and heat figured out. What about telephone? What do you figure for telephone?"

"Oh—the minimum."

"What is the minimum?"

"Oh, I'd say twenty-five dollars a month? Thirty dollars?"

Glancing at her, he says, "Well, let's put down fifty dollars a month. How about your furniture? Were you planning to buy that or rent it?"

"Buy it, of course."

"Sometimes it works out better to rent those things, buddy. Same thing with typewriters, adding machines..."

"A friend of Daddy's is in the office-supply business. I could get things like that from him at a discount."

"How much of a discount?"

"Well, I don't know—exactly. I haven't approached him yet."

"I see. Now what about printing? You're going to need brochures, folders. . . ."

"A friend of mine, an art director, has offered to help me design some brochures. He knows a printer who—"

"How'll the printing be done? Offset?"

"What's offset?"

He shakes his head. "Never mind. Now what about advertising? Are you planning to advertise?"

"Oh, yes."

"Look, let's make it simple. Suppose you run a hundred lines in *The New York Times* once a week. What does a hundred lines in *The Times* cost?"

"I haven't checked on—rates."

"Well, maybe you'd better—don't you think?" he says, looking at her. "If you're planning to advertise?"

She nods. Then she says, "Arch, all these little technical things—"

"All these little technical things have got to be figured in your overhead, buddy. They're what's going to determine whether you make any profit or not. In fact, as far as I can see—"

"As far as you can see I'm *not!*" she says. "Is that what you mean?"

"No," he says easily, "that's not what I mean at all." He continues with his pencil-work on the cloth. "So let's put question marks on some of these items you're not sure about. Now what about insurance? I should think you'd need insurance."

"Yes. I wondered about that," Leona says.

"Sure. If a picture got stolen or damaged while it was in your possession, I guess you'd be in a hell of a mess. Well," he says, "let's put another question mark next to the cost of your insurance. Okay. Now taxes—"

"I'll have an accountant handle all that."

"Okay. Then there's your New York City tax."

"What's that?"

"Mayor Wagner gets a share of your profits, you know."

"Really?"

Grinning, he says, "Yeah—really." He writes on the table: "Taxes, question mark."

"Arch—all these details—"

"They aren't even details yet, buddy," he says. "They're just question marks." Looking at the tablecloth, he says, "Boy, we've got an awful lot of them too. There seems to be a lot about running an art gallery that you just don't know."

"Now look here, Arch. Of course—there are a lot of things I'm going to have to learn. But once I get into it, once I get things going—"

"Oh, sure. You'll learn. But there's just one other thing I'd like to know. Let's suppose you're all set. You've got your two painters, and you've got a couple of dozen pictures hanging on your walls, and you're all set to open your doors—for your first two-man show."

"Yes, I plan to do it with a cocktail party—you know, for the press, the critics, and the—"

"Okay, your show is open, it runs for three or four weeks, and nobody—not a soul—buys any of your pictures. What do you do then?"

"Arch, why are you so *negative?* Why can't you—"

"I'm trying," he says, "to be positive—to get down a few positive facts and figures."

"You're trying to confuse me and discourage me!"

He drums his fingertips for a moment on the tabletop. He puts down the pencil. "No," he says. "I'm not."

"Then what are you trying to do? Besides give me a hard time!"

He leans back in his chair and slowly rubs his chest with the flat of his hand. "You really want to know?" Facing her, his wide wraparound sunglasses contain a double reflection of her and nothing more—just as, she supposes, her sunglasses contain only a reflection of him. His mouth is expressionless. Then quickly he leans toward her across the table. "I'm just trying to get you to look at yourself," he says. "Have you ever looked at yourself, little girl? I don't think once in that little life of yours you ever have. But *I've* looked at you, and I see a beautiful smokescreen of little excuses and pieces of make-believe. You don't know yourself what's real and what's fake any more, and maybe you've even stopped caring. All this stuff about the people who've done you wrong. Your mother who's such a cold-blooded bitch, your father who's such a sweet slob that he let your mother walk all over you both, your grandmother who doesn't *understand* you. Aw, hell, nobody's ever understood you, right? The men in your life—the Tom, Dick, and Harry you married. You were so *young*. So abused. So disillusioned. Ah, little girl, little girl—listen to me. Cut the act, drop the smokescreen, you've been doing it with mirrors too long—and it's such a familiar act. You can't do it with mirrors when you go into business. You can't sell pictures with your girlish charm or all your hard-luck stories. Nobody's going to give a damn *then*. Look at yourself. You called me a miserable bastard the other night because I said I wanted to sleep with you. You put on your righteous-indignation act—walking off in a huff with your I'm-a-nice-girl act. Hell, you know men—don't kid me. You've been doing the dance of the seven veils for me for the past week without even dropping the first veil, and I'll bet that's exactly what you've done with every one of your husbands! There's only one reason you've had three of them. You like men. You liked number one, number two, and number three—so what? You *took* them, that's all. You're not a bruised flower, or a torn little lace handkerchief, or a woman in distress—so take off the masks. Don't be poor little lost, lonely, mistreated, misunderstood Leona with *me*. For God's sake, there's a *woman* hiding under all your veils—or there'd better be!" He pauses now, looking at her levelly. "Okay," he says, "if you need an excuse to run away from me now, there it is. I've behaved like a brute. So run away now, if you want to."

During the whole time he has spoken to her, her eyes have been fixed steadily on him. Now she lowers her eyes, twirling the stem of her wineglass. "No," she says quietly, "I'm not going to run away."

"Well, good," he says. He smiles at her and raises his glass, touching it lightly against her own. "Here's to your gallery."

In the room, his voice is quieter, gentler. He stands at the wall, fiddling with the thermostat. "All the comforts of home," he says. "Except one. The darn air-conditioning hasn't worked since I've been here." He goes to the window and opens it, but there is no breeze this hot afternoon. He turns and smiles at her. "Sorry. This is the best I can do, buddy."

From where she lies, on the bed, fully dressed, Leona holds out her empty glass. "Fix this for me, will you, Arch?"

He takes the glass and carries it to the dresser.

He has stripped—doing so quickly and casually—to his underpants. Moving about the room on bare, well-formed feet, there is an animal lack of modesty about him. Standing at the dresser he yawns and stretches. "It's not the company, it's the hour," he says, grinning at her. "It was pretty early when you got me out of bed this morning." He splashes whisky in the glass, and returns, carrying the drink to her.

"Thanks," she says.

The room is indeed warm and airless. As he stands in front of her she sees trickles of sweat down the front of his chest, across his stomach. He is well-furred, this animal—hairy of chest, of shoulders, even of back. Leona looks away from him and sips her drink. He sits down on the bed beside her. "Sorry I can't get it cool for you," he says again. "I'd like it cool, for a cool girl." He circles her waist with his arm.

Leona closes her eyes. The room pounds with silence.

After a minute or so, he says, "I like you, and maybe I'm going to like you even better. That's all I need to say for now, isn't it? That I like you, and that maybe I'm going to like you even better?" Then, close to her ear, "Ah, buddy, buddy, buddy, buddy. . . ."

"Give me another drink first," she says. "And while you're up, Arch, close the curtains and the blinds. Do you mind—?" And she adds, her eyes still closed—"darling."

He takes her empty glass and places it on the table by the bed. "No more drinks for you," he says. And he whispers an intense command to her and pulls her to him.

Time passes, the hours go by, and the days. The sun rises and sets, and the hard little wheels of the days pass over us as we lie, poor boards of flesh, in a long circle, waiting for the little wheels to make another tour across us.

Thirteen

IN the old photograph albums there are many pictures of Diana when she was a little girl. In most of them, she is on horseback, in riding costume. In the horseback photographs she grows, as one turns the cracked pages of the album, from a pretty child of six to a smooth young woman of sixteen. The riding costumes and the horses change, but not Diana's pose: turned slightly in her seat, the reins held in one hand with classical precision, her other hand at her side, she faces the camera with the trace of a smile. At age sixteen, she departs from the album—away at school in New York. Indeed, the departure is virtually final; except for studio wedding photographs, she never appears again. This is because, in the years between the last horseback picture and the wedding pictures, Meredith Harper died and left her a fourth of his estate. Suddenly rich, richer than her mother, at the age of eighteen she could afford to go wherever in the world she wanted. And did.

Sometimes Edith thinks that the year Diana was born is part of the trouble. Diana was born in the autumn of 1914. Edith and Charles had been married nearly five years before the coming of Diana announced itself, and they had begun to wonder whether they would ever have children. In the tropic evenings, and on weekends, they worked together on the garden, laying out walks and beds, planting sea grape and bougainvillea and hibiscus, and the heaven tree, surprised, together, to see how rapidly everything grew. When Edith knew that she was going to have a baby, they were both very happy. (Edith's father was even more excited with the news. He presented Edith a large check. Looking at it, Charles said dryly, "It seems we're having this baby just for him.") Helping to deliver Diana was one of Mary Miles' last duties in the Harper household. She went home, two months later, to England and to the war, "to do my bit." ("Your mother is cured, Edith," her father had said. "Miles has cured her." To Mary Miles went one hundred dollars and a one-way ticket to Southampton.) But, being born in the autumn of 1914 put Diana queerly out of key with the decades and with history. She was too young to sit up all night in speakeasies or dance the Charleston or fall in love with the elder Douglas Fairbanks. By the time she was old enough to enjoy such things, the world was tired of them. By the time she was ready for parties, the world had had enough of parties. By the time she was rich enough to swing her own rope of pearls, the world was poor.

And Edith sometimes wonders, too, if horses are to blame for Diana. If this is true, then Edith herself must share the blame, for it was she who introduced Diana to the strange climate of horsedom, to the smell of satlery and the strong dark of stalls and stables. What is it about people and horses? It is altogether curious, and sad, the things that those dumb, beautiful animals seem capable of doing to human beings—making them hard where they should be soft, soft where they should be hard, determined where they should be hesitant, resilient where they should be strong. Edith has never met a horsy person she has liked. In a group of people, she can spot a horsewoman immediately. Talking to one, she can feel the horsewoman mentally digging her heels into her sides, to make her canter. . . .

Studying the old photographs, turning the pages, with the stack of old albums beside her on the chaise, Edith Blakewell searches for an answer. But Diana remains a puzzle. Once,

Diana's first husband, Jack Ware, had said to her, "Mrs. Blakewell, can you explain something to me about Diana?" It was in the days when Leona was only four or five years old, and Jack and Diana had begun sending Leona to her for long periods while they tried to solve their difficulties. Jack had come to St. Thomas to take Leona back with them for a while. Trying to cover his embarrassment by kneading the fingers of his big hands together until the knuckles showed white, he looked at the patch of floor between his feet and said, "She doesn't like me. I love her, but she doesn't even like me. And it isn't even *me* she doesn't like. It's—well, it's sex. Do you know that she's refused to sleep with me since Leona was born? *Refused.* 'I did my duty to you by having the baby,' she said to me. 'Now my duty's done.' You know—you've read, it's been in all the columns—about this fellow Perry Gardiner who's been squiring her around? All our friends are convinced that Diana's sleeping with Perry Gardiner, and they laugh at me behind my back. But I happen to know that Diana *isn't* sleeping with Perry Gardiner. She isn't sleeping with anybody. I came right out and asked her why the devil she didn't sleep with Gardiner. If she's getting the name, she might as well have the game. And Diana said, 'Listen here, I *like* Perry. And the reason I like him is because he leaves me *alone.*' Can you explain it, Mrs. Blakewell? What's wrong?"

"Well, Jack," she says to the invisible Jack Ware now, "what do *you* think? Do you think it's *me?* But how could it be me?"

From Southport, Connecticut, where Jack Ware lives now with his second wife and four young children, there is no immediate reply.

Turning the pages of the albums, her eyes alight on a figure who has no business being there among the past and present members of the Harper family. Her presence there is ironic. It is Monique Bertin. Under the photograph, in white ink in her mother's wispy hand is written, "Europe sailing—1912. Bon voyage!" And there they are, all the members of that Europe sailing someone had photographed on the pier. The members are each identified, in the same handwriting: M. D. H. (Edith's father); D. B. H. (her mother); Mary (Mary Miles); Schiller (Schiller the governess, who has one firm hand on the eleven-year-old Harry and the other on the nine-year-old Boots, a long-ago nickname of Arthur's). And, standing slightly to one side of the others in the group are Bertin and Mme. Bertin. The photograph is so blurred and faded, and was taken from such a distance, that it is really not possible to make out the features of either of the Bertin's faces. The words *Mme. Bertin* are written with the same emphasis as the other names. Clearly Edith's mother, in the year 1912, had no inkling whatever that Monique occupied the position she did. Edith resists a sudden impulse to tear that picture off the page and to deprive Monique Bertin of the immortality of old albums. But no, she belongs there. Let her stay. "Bon voyage!"

Edith tries to remember now when it was, exactly, that she began her personal campaign to get rid of Monique Bertin, and why it was, precisely, that she had decided that the business between her father and Monique had to be broken up. Why had she taken out her old anger at Louis on Monique who, after all, was doing only what she was paid to do? After all these years, it is hard to remember what all her motives were for doing what she did. But, considering what she did do, it is easy to understand why Monique did what she did in return. Yes, that was a turning point . . . a great deal pivoted around that. Puzzling over the picture, with the album opened in her lap, Edith dozes. In their old-fashioned photographed poses, the picture people enter and populate her half-waking dream. Their voices murmur inaudibly, then rise.

She had been lying on the sofa in the drawing room, a few weeks after Diana was born, and Charles and her father were arguing behind the closed doors of the library. The drawing room was filled with fresh flowers from the garden. She heard Charles say "Murderer . . ."

"Murderer? You call me a murderer?"

"I've never seen a man shot before, Mr. Harper."

"I let his black blood put out the fire."

Then there was silence.

"Savages," she heard Charles saying. "Treat them like savages, or worse . . . like animals. The man had a wife and four children."

"I hired you to help me run my fields, Blakewell—not to tell me how to run them. Just do what you were hired to do, my aristocratic friend."

Then she heard her father say, "Meanwhile, get busy in bed again. The Harper women, you may have noticed, tend to produce female children. It's the effect of my wife's thin blood. Get busy in bed. I want a grandson."

If her father noticed her lying there when he walked out of the library, he did not acknowledge it. After a moment she got up and went into the library where Charles was sitting at his desk. His face was pale and strained. He had grown thinner those past few years, and had become a restless sleeper, and that afternoon he looked particularly tired. She put her hands on his shoulders and said, "Don't mind what Papa says."

"He shot a man."

"It's customary—if the man is caught starting a fire."

He gave her an odd look, and sat hunched forward at the desk.

"Charles," she said, "was it a mistake to go to work for Papa?"

When he said nothing, she said, "Let's go out and sit in our garden, and I'll have the girl fix us some nice iced tea..."

Some nice iced tea—was that the best she had ever had to offer him? Hadn't she ever offered more than that?

Then, a few days later, one of her mother's servants had come to Edith's house to tell her that she was needed at Sans Souci. When she arrived she found her mother on the terrace, wandering between the iron urns, her silk dress unbuttoned all the way down the back. As she walked, her shy little maids followed her, holding out soft, restraining hands.

"Come into the house, Mama," Edith said.

"No. The Governor's Ball. I've got to hurry, I've got to dress..."

"The Governor's Ball isn't for another month, Mama. Come into the house."

"No, the ball is starting. Where is he?" and suddenly seizing Edith's arms she screamed, "Meredith! Meredith! Where is he? Where is my husband? Hasn't anybody seen him?"

That night Edith had said to Charles, "We've got to do something about my mother."

He sighed. "What can you do—except try to find another nurse like Mary Miles?"

"It isn't nurses she needs. It's Papa. He's never there. She's all alone most of the time."

She was following Charles through the house, talking to him. He moved slowly, absently, pausing to pick up small objects as he went, examining them, putting them down again. It was the end of day; his collar was unbuttoned, his shirtsleeves rolled up about the elbows. He picked up a pair of grape shears and balanced them between his long-fingered hands. "It's the war," he said. "She misses her trips to Paris."

"It isn't that, Charles," she said. "Do you know about Papa and—the Frenchman's wife?"

He nodded. "Yes."

"You never mentioned it to me—that you knew about it."

Smiling at the grape shears, he said, "There wasn't any need to."

"You think there's nothing wrong with it, then?"

"He's not the first man in the world to take a mistress. He won't be the last."

Mary Miles had reacted with the same lack of interest. She had given Edith a straight look and said, "I told you I could guess what that woman was doing in her spare time. To me it's no more surprising than that cats have kittens." But Charles' remark disturbed her.

"It must be a great source of private pleasure to you, Charles—seeing what really awful people the Harpers are."

He moved away from her. "Don't be foolish."

"But she's the whole trouble, Charles—Monique Bertin. Everything was wonderful before she came." This wasn't true, of course. But it made it simpler, somehow, to believe it was. "And her husband, too," Edith said. "What kind of man knowingly lets his wife sleep with other men? And he must be a terrible coward. His country's at war with Germany, and he stays here—playing tennis."

He shrugged. "What makes you think he lets her—knowingly? Keep out of it, Edith. It's your father's affair."

"I want you to help me get rid of them, Charles. Get them off this island."

"You must be joking," he said.

"I'm *not* joking! I want you to help me do it—for my mother's sake."

"Your mother's problem isn't Monique Bertin. Your mother's problem is drinking. It's her problem, and also her solution." He gave her a vague and thoughtful look. "We all have to find our own solutions, I suppose. Hers is drinking." Edith followed him into the drawing room across the echoing front hall. In the center of the room he stopped, looked around, and said softly, "His furniture . . ."

"It's not his furniture. It's ours. Listen to me, Charles. I want you to help me get rid of that woman!"

"Well, I'm not going to help you do a thing like that."

"I'm telling you I want you to."

Smiling at her, he said, "Now you're sounding like your father, Edith."

This angered her even more, because it was true. "You *approve* of what Papa's doing, don't you?" she said. "You endorse adultery. You—"

"Stop this, Edith."

"Oh, there's something very wrong with your thinking, Charles. Yes—I keep wondering: What about you? Why won't you go to Papa and tell him he's behaving like a fool and destroying Mama in the bargain? Are you afraid? Are you as much a coward as the Frenchman?"

An hour later they were still arguing. "The woman is an insult to my mother," she said, "and the man is an insult to me."

He looked at her sharply. "To you? Why?"

"He—he gives me sly looks whenever I pass him on the street," she said quickly. "He knows I know about them."

"Then look the other way. Don't you know how to handle 'sly looks'?" Then, in a weary voice, he said, "Haven't I got enough to worry about? You, me, our baby, my job—"

"Your job! What kind of job is it? Five years of being another of Papa's lackeys—that's your job! What ever happened to Mount Katahdin?"

He stared at her for a moment. Then he turned on his heel and walked quickly into the library, closing the door behind him.

"Charles, please," she whispered, her face pressed against the door. "I didn't mean that, Charles. It was seeing Mama this morning that upset me so. Forgive me, darling. Please open the door."

And when there was no answer she cried, "All right, stay in there! I don't care. I can get rid of the Bertins myself."

* * *

Remembering this, Edith's eyes fly open. She stands up stiffly from the chair where she had been dozing and walks slowly through the quiet rooms of the house. It is growing dark. All day long she has tried not to think about Leona, but now she cannot help asking herself again: *Where is she?*

In the bar at the Virgin Isle Hotel, Leona says, "Did you notice the couple that just walked in, Arch? Their name is Rafferty. They recognized me. I'm sure they're saying, 'There's Leona Ware. She looks as though she's just moved in with that man.'"

Arch laughs. "Well, in a sense they're right, aren't they?" he says. "But look—would you rather go somewhere else?"

"No," she says, "I guess it doesn't matter. There's only one person here I don't want to see."

"Ed Winslow?"

She nods. "He's staying here too, you know. Or was."

"I saw some messages in his box," Arch says. "So I guess he's still here." He is grinning at her. "If we see him, we'll just hide under the table." Then he says, "Now, seriously—don't you think you'd better call your grandmother?"

She shakes her head. "No. I can't quite—face that yet."

"Suppose she calls the police?"

"She won't do that."

"I'd offer to call her myself—and tell her you're okay. But something tells me she wouldn't exactly appreciate hearing from me."

She makes a little face at him. "You're absolutely right."

"Well," he says easily, "you know, don't you, buddy, that the longer you put off telling her where you are, the tougher it's going to be to do it."

With an effort, she smiles at him.

His ruddy, heavy-featured face has no expression. For a moment he says nothing. He lifts his drink and looks at her over the rim of the glass. "What about tonight?" he asks her. "You want to stay with me a little longer?"

"Arch—I just don't know. I don't quite know what I should do."

"You're welcome to stay, if you'd like."

"Would you—like me to?"

His gaze at her is steady. "It's up to you," he says. "It's

all been up to you, you know. All along."

"Well—" And what difference does it make, she wonders? One night, more or less, what does it matter? All caring has gone out of her now, and practically all feeling. A hundred years from now, or even next week, who in the whole starry universe will care what she did tonight? What will it matter, now that the initial commitment has been made? Yes, it has been up to her all along, he is right, and now her involvement with him—under its own terms, within its own limitations—is as total as it will ever be. It is impossible to be partially involved with a man this way, she supposes, just as it is impossible to be partially in love. "There's a slight problem of clothes," she says finally. "I didn't bring anything but what I've got on my back."

"Spend the night here, and tomorrow I'll go out and buy you a whole flock of new clothes."

"That would really make me a kept woman, wouldn't it?"

"Actually," he says, "I get a kick out of buying clothes for women. I used to do it a lot—for Marie, my ex-wife."

"Oh, Arch!" she laughs. "You're a funny man—you really are. But no—I'm not going to let you buy me clothes."

He leans across the table toward her. "You know something?" he says. "You're changing already. Up to tonight you were all kind of nervous. Nervous, jumpy, drinking like a fish—but tonight you're calmer. You know that?"

"Calmer? Really?"

"Calmer. All cool and collected and nice. You've dropped one of your little veils. But you've got six more to go."

She reaches for a cigarette, and he lights it for her. "And you know something else? I'll bet I'm the guy who's making you change like this."

"And do *you* know something?" she says in the calmest voice she can muster, concentrating on her cigarette, "I do believe you're right."

He glances around the room. "Look," he says, "this place is getting too damn crowded. They've got a great little invention in this hotel. It's called Room Service."

Standing alone on her veranda, looking out into the warm night, Edith is still thinking of all the locked doors of her life. The lights of Charlotte Amalie are coming on below her, just as she has watched them do for so many years. "Your father's island," Sibbie Sanderson had said. But even the island has always been, to some extent, locked to her.

That was the beginning of Charles' destruction, that evening she had shouted those terrible things to him. After taking his pride away, what was left for her to take away from him but his life? They had never discussed Monique Bertin again. They had gone on, but, after that, it had never been quite the same; he had begun to lock her out. He continued to work hard in the sugar fields, but some of the spirit had gone out of him.

"Charles," she had called to him from the veranda, "it's getting dark. Don't you think you'd better come in now?"

"As soon as I finish planting this rose bush, Edith."

Going down the steps to him, she put her arms around him. "Charles, I love you so. Do you love me?"

"Yes."

"The Governor's wife was here for tea. She said that she thought ours was the prettiest garden in St. Thomas. Isn't that nice?"

"That's very nice."

"I told her, 'It's all my husband's doing. He did it all.'"

"Thank you, Edith."

"Charles," she whispered. "Come to bed now." And then, "Do you remember those nights in Morristown, and then at Sans Souci, when you used to come into my room at night? Let's pretend it's like that again. It's been so long." And when he said nothing, she said, "Don't shut me out like this! You keep shutting me out."

Then, because he still said nothing, she had shivered in the chilly night air and said, "Charles—what are you thinking about?"

"About the war. America's bound to get into it sooner or later. It's bound to happen."

Behind Edith now, from the doorway, Nellie's voice is speaking. "Dinner is served, Miss Edith."

"Think you, Nellie." She turns toward the house.

It is after midnight now. Moonlight, and light from the bright street lamps that line the long curving avenue leading up to the hotel come through the upturned blinds and mottle the darkness of the fourth-floor room. Light shifts and stirs in the dark room like the shapes of fish seen moving through deep water. Leona hears his quiet footsteps returning from the bathroom where he has been running the tap.

"Look," he says, "come on. Look, I brought you a drink of water. Snap out of it, buddy."

His weight joins hers on the bed. "Come on," he says, "drink this."

With one hand he strokes her back, between her shoulder blades. "Look," he says gently, "you're just having an old-fashioned crying jag. Try old Doc Purdy's cure. Have a drink of water. Have a cigarette, buddy. Okay? Okay?" And then, stroking her shoulder, "Ah, buddy, what's wrong?"

"I don't know," she sobs into the hollow of her arm. "All at once I don't know what's going to happen to me, Arch. I don't know where I'm going to go, or what I'm going to do."

"You've got a long way to go, buddy. Plenty of things to do."

"I used to be a nice girl, Arch. Honestly I did. Oh, please . . . oh, please. . . . Oh, can't somebody help me?"

Sitting beside her, his hand on her shoulder is motionless now. "Yeah," he says softly, "I know. You need help from somebody. But I'm not sure it's me, buddy. No, I'm not sure it's me."

Fourteen

IF it were possible to go back, Leona is thinking, where would she go back to? Last night, when Granny said that she wanted to ask Gordon to come, Leona might (could, should) have said, "All right—if we ask Jimmy to come too." Because he had as much right to be here certainly as Gordon . . . or Edouardo . . . if that was the point of inviting someone: to try to reexamine things, to reconstruct things. What's more, she thinks, Jimmy would probably have come. Gordon would have been suspicious. He would have telephoned first, full of solemn, throat clearing questions. ("Is Leona in some kind of trouble?" "Is it anything I can handle from New York?") Jimmy would stuff a clean shirt in his suitcase and hop on a plane . . . probably.

Whenever Leona thinks of Jimmy Breed she sees him standing at the foot of a staircase in that house on Long Island—at that party, the night they ran away together. It is as though she had taken a photograph of him standing there, on the bottom step of the stairs, his head above the other heads, in his dinner clothes, a drink in one hand, his other hand twisting his black bow tie. That tie, always set at a slight tilt, had been one of Jimmy's trademarks. ("Don't want to look like every other jerk," he used to say to her with a wink.) The tie and its angle gave the healthy-looking face above it an expectant, bemused look, which had nothing to do with the man behind the face. (Or boy. Because, at the time this mental snapshot was made, Jimmy Breed had not reached the years of man's estate; he was only twenty.) That tie went with him—like his habit of wearing red suspenders under his dinner jacket, or hitching up his tuxedo trousers to reveal a pair of the flashy Argyle socks that the Princeton boys were all wearing that season. It was as much a part of him as the way he had of raising his eyebrows as high as they would go and looking at you with a wide-eyed, open-mouthed stare of surprise when he saw you—as though you were the last person in the world he expected to find at the same party. Or the engaging habit he had of smoothing the top of his head when he spoke to you . . . bending his head toward you, listening, stroking his shaggy dark hair. He was tall and thick-set—too big, really, for the little red car he drove, the car they ran off in that night, heading for the Triboro Bridge, getting lost trying to find the New Jersey Turnpike. Leona has other private pictures of Jimmy, of course. But this one, this composite, composed of these attitudes, is her favorite.

"He proposed to me on the dance floor . . ." This is the way Leona now tells the story of that night. Actually, it was a little different. They danced together, yes, but he didn't ask her to marry him then. He only asked if he could take her home.

Later—perhaps two hours later—there was an impromptu parade through the house. Jimmy and a group of his friends had gone into the cloakroom, put the girls' fur wraps over their shoulders and, carrying lighted candelabra from the dining room, had marched solemnly through the rooms, in and out among the dancers on the floor—Jimmy at the lead, wearing a leopard jacket, brandishing a silver candlestick high above his head. The procession moved out through the French doors, down across the wide lawns, and went around and around the lighted swimming pool while everyone from the party gathered on the terrace to watch and applaud.

Leona's mother had been at the party too. "I understand Jimmy Breed has asked to take you home," Diana Gardiner said.

Leona nodded. "Yes."

"He's intoxicated," her mother said. "I don't want you going home with him."

"Don't worry, Mother. I'll take care of it."

"Do you understand, Leona? Find someone else to take you home. If necessary, Perry and I will drive you."

"Excuse me, Mother," she had said. "I see somebody I know—"

"Leona?" Her mother called after her, but Leona had separated herself from her, and lost herself in the crowd. She found Jimmy. "Take me home," she whispered. "Now."

In the front seat of the car he put his arms around her and kissed her heavily, smelling of whisky. That was when he asked her to marry him.

"Where . . . when . . . ?" she asked him breathlessly.

She heard him mumble "Baltimore," and the little red car headed off into the night toward the bridges and the parkways.

It used to seem to her as though Jimmy were really two distinct and different people. He fascinated her, and confused her. It had to do with the way he had of being alternately self-assured and self-indulgent, a mixture of opposing personalities. She was never sure of her ground with him, of which Jimmy she was with, and this was how he dominated her. He would be silly one minute, strong the next. Just when she had decided that he was the most responsible man in the world, he would do something gay and wild and irresponsible. He could be affectionate and tender. He could also be scathing and bitter and hard. Two natures were at war within him, and when the reliable, formal, polite side of him would give way to the reckless, anarchic side, she would try to seize him, hold him, shape him into some single, recognizable character. But it was like trying to keep a sand castle erect against the tide. His changeableness dismayed her, and his energy and vitality left her out of breath. From Baltimore, the little car headed west, for they were runaways now—running away, they both agreed, from all that crazy life before, from colleges, from parties, from parents. They were saying good-by to all that forever, and wherever the future lay it had to lie as far from all that as it was possible to go—in the West. The pattern of their days began to be one of rise and fall, a tidal pattern. They would go from stormy, tearful quarrels—over such trivial matters as which fork to take on the highway—to passionate reconciliations, in lovemaking, in the dark little rooms of motels where traffic moaned outside their window all night long like the sound of distant vacuum cleaners. They had one thing in their favor: they would never have money worries. They each had an income then; they had that in common. They figured it out very quickly once on the back of a menu: Together they had an income of twenty-five thousand a year.

But they had already, even in the first few days, begun to talk of "If this doesn't work out . . . if it turns out we've made a mistake. . . ." If it didn't work out, they could always get a divorce. Divorce was easy when you both had an income. It would be a friendly divorce, of course, a mature divorce, with no misgivings or recriminations. And yet, after some of their most violent quarrels, Leona would wake in the morning and look at his sleeping face on the pillow beside her, at his bare arm flung across her stomach, and think that no man in the world would ever be able to make her as happy as this man. And, in a way, she had been right.

They crossed the Mojave Desert in the blinding autumn heat. The sun was so brilliant, so intense, that it sent a shimmer into the air—diffuse, streaked light, rising like sheeted waves in front of them as they drove. It was like driving through gauzy mirrors. The light and the heat had a texture and a substance, spreading and pouring around the red car, seeming to pull it through a tunnel of heat. And the light distorted the shapes of everything, the cactus and century plant on the roadside. Even the mountain ranges in the distance were blurred, half-dissolved, their outlines smudged and muddied in the heat. They drove with the windows closed, for the warmth generated by the two people in the small closed sports car seemed less oppressive than the sizzle of the air outside. They stopped the car once, to change drivers—to let Leona drive while Jimmy napped—opening and shutting the doors quickly as they switched places. The road was straight and flat and empty, and she drove fast through those shifting, distorting bands of light while Jimmy, knees up, wedged in the seat beside her, slept. But it is the cheating light she remembers best, and the straightness and flatness and emptiness of the road, and the speed.

She had turned the radio on. The song it was playing—queer, the details which stand out—was . . .

"Does
your moth-
er know
You're out,
Ce-seel-ya . . . ?"

She was humming the tune the radio played under her breath to keep her mind off the heat. She had unbuttoned all the buttons of her blouse to try to be a little cooler, pulled the tails of the blouse out of her skirt, pulled her skirt up almost to her waist, but still every inch of her was damp. Dampness clung to her, trickled between her breasts, pricked the roots of her hair, and she had to keep wiping the damp corners of her eyes with the tip of her finger to clear her vision as she drove; in that hideous, unending glare; humming that tune.

"Why
should
we
two
go on wastin' time . . ."

And then, it was so sudden, out of nowhere ("Out of nowhere," she used to whisper to Jimmy later, "Out of nowhere, he just materialized!")—the little boy, a dark-skinned boy. A Mexican boy, perhaps, or perhaps a young Indian (from the reservation?). What he could have been doing there, at the side of the road in the middle of the desert, in that treacherous light, like part of a mirage himself, she could never imagine. He seemed (she remembers) to raise his arm as if to signal the oncoming car, and then to step toward it. She jerked the wheel sharply, and he seemed to step in front of the car—or perhaps, in that terrible moment, she jerked the wheel the wrong way, it is so hard to remember it clearly, it was over so swiftly. The impact on the fender of the car was so slight, so glancing—just a touch, really—that the moment it was over it was hard not to believe that she had imagined the whole thing. The whole time her foot was on the brake, pulling the car to a bumpy stop, half on the shoulder, half on the road, she made herself believe that she had imagined it, while huge, blind, shapeless prayers were delivered upward into the glittering sky. But when she looked back through the rear-view mirror there was the dark crumpled figure lying far behind her in the road. She sat very still in the stopped car in that blazing heat. She had forgotten that Jimmy was even with her. When she remembered, and turned to look at him, he was not asleep any longer, but had turned and was looking back at the road. "Oh, God," he whispered. "Oh, my God. . . ."

His hand was on the handle of the door.

"No!" she cried, starting the car. "No!"

"Stop," he said under his breath. And then, grabbing for the wheel of the car, "Stop—you've got to stop!"

She fought his hands from the wheel as he car gathered speed again. "No!" she sobbed. "No, it wasn't anything!" She pressed her foot hard on the accelerator, trying to see the road that seemed to appear and disappear ahead of her now through her tears.

"My God, Leona! Stop. You've got to stop!"

"How can we stop?" she screamed at him as the speedometer needle climbed across the white face of the dial. "We've run away from home! We're under age! If they find us—if we've hurt him—they'll take us back, they'll arrest us! We'll ruin the rest of our lives."

He leaned forward against the dash, and she had only a glimpse of his moist, pale face. "My God . . . my God . . . you've got to stop . . ." he breathed.

But she didn't stop. They drove on, out of Arizona, into California, then north, into Nevada—the runaways.

Stopping at a filling station for gas, he looked at her while the attendant filled the little red car. He looked at her, his face still ashen and stricken, and said nothing. She did not look at him.

Early the next morning they entered Idaho. They were discovered there that day, recognized checking into the Sun Valley Inn. They were made to pose, arm in arm, smiling, for the photographers. Then there were the headlines: ELOPING HEIRESS FOUND. . . .

There was never anything that she could find, in any of the papers (and the Sun Valley papers carried other Western news), about a young boy—a dark-skinned boy, perhaps an Indian from the reservation, perhaps a Mexican—found on an Arizona road. She has used this argument—that she could find nothing in the papers about the accident—to convince herself, from time to time, that the boy was only slightly hurt. But she has always known, secretly, that he was killed instantly.

How could much "work out" for the two of them after that? They had tried, perhaps, by rubbing the picture from their minds. Sometimes, from the bed where she lay, watching him examine his morning face in the mirror, she would try to draw them back to one of the old places. But they had escaped from these places too thoroughly. They returned to New York, where they took a small hotel apartment on the East Side. Jimmy began coming home seldom then, and when he did appear it was usually with the smell of cocktails on his breath. This was when Gordon Paine began his furtive courtship.

Yes, *furtive* is the word. He would telephone her, saying "Just checking in," and—just in case she was concerned, he said—he would keep her abreast of Jimmy's whereabouts, and what he was doing. "I saw Breed at the Algonquin bar today," he would say. Or, "Your husband turned up at the Tysons' dinner last night. He was in pretty bad shape." Or, "He's been drinking at the Princeton Club all morning, and he seems in *pretty* fair shape—in case you're concerned. He's talking about going back to college for the spring term. Did you know that?"

"No," she would say to Gordon. "No, I didn't know that."

Then he would ask her if there was anything he could do, if there was anything she needed. Or he would take her to dinner and a play.

When Leona started to miscarry the baby no one knew she was pregnant with, she went to the hospital by herself. When she came out, four days later, no one knew she had gone. Then, one night when Jimmy appeared at the apartment—oh, a little drunk, probably—she had said to him, "Gordon Paine wants me to marry him. He's been terribly kind to me—helpful and thoughtful and generous."

He had stood looking at her for a moment or two, a small, dry smile on his lips, and she had thought he was going to say something cutting and offensive to her. But he said, "You're looking for a state of grace, I suppose. Well, so am I, Leona."

Then he put his face in his hands and began to cry.

That was nine years ago. As Leona lies in Arch Purdy's hotel room now, dry-eyed, remembering those other tears, while the first gray light of another tropical morning filters in through the up-slanted Venetian blinds, she has the first glimmerings of that wild and implausible idea—to call the two of them, Jimmy and Gordon, to ask them to come here, to meet with her. It will be like that meeting she dreamed about, but with a different Leona as its focus.

It is Monday, and two quite unwelcome chores have presented themselves to Edith Harper Blakewell. The first, quite obviously, is to get off a reply to a singular letter which has arrived from her brother Harold in the morning mail. She had opened the letter expecting a check to tumble out, and found, instead, a lot of evasive nonsense dictated by Harold and signed by his secretary. Whether Leona is to have her gallery money or not, Edith is certainly not going to be put off by Harold like this. She carries the letter to her desk, sits down, seizes a pen and a sheet of her stationery and writes furiously:

Dear Harold:
I find your response to my telegram completely preposterous and totally intolerable. To begin with, what business is it of yours *what I want the money for? You say you "guess" it is for Leona. Well, guess away!*

She pauses, pleased with the force of her prose, then continues:

You are not my keeper, though you clearly think you are. And it is my *Harper stock which I wish sold, not yours. I know a few facts about the business which might surprise you, e.g., I know the difference between what you hold in* trust *for me and the Harper stock which Papa gave me years ago, and which I own outright, no strings attached. You are, to be sure, "custodian" of the latter—but only because I let you be. And this letter will serve as my notice to you that your custodianship has just ended, Harold. Please mail the certificates to me via registered Air Mail at once, and I shall take up all business matters with my friends at the West Indies National Bank.*

She starts to add, "Love to Barbara and the children," but decides against it. She signs the letter, "Sincerely, Edith."

Then she adds a postscript:

P.S. What do you mean *by saying "Your Harper stock is not available at the moment for the purposes you have in mind?" It had better damn well be available. Pronto!*

"I'm within my rights here," she mutters to herself. "My legal rights." The amusing thought occurs to her of having the great Harold B. Harper arrested, if he still refuses to deliver her stock to her—arrested for stealing, which is what it would amount to. She smiles at the vision of Harold in a prison uniform, behind bars, begging her for mercy.

Like all letters written at white heat, this one must be quickly folded, sealed in an envelope, stamped and posted. She does these things, slamming the stamp on the envelope with a bang of her fist, and rings for one of her maids to take the letter to the post office immediately.

The second chore cannot be handled with as much dispatch. Leona has been gone now, without word, for something over thirty hours, and certainly the time has come for serious action. The usual horrible possibilities have all passed through her mind: rape, kidnaping, murder. In a way, on those scores, no news is good news. Still, some strange things have been known to happen in St. Thomas. A woman was found, six days later, strangled and adrift in a chartered fishing boat, naked of the thirty thousand dollars' worth of emeralds she had been last seen wearing. (Deserves it, Edith had thought at the time, for going fishing in emeralds.) But for Leona's sake Edith hesitates to notify the police, not even her friends on the force. After all, one of the first problems to be faced, in any action Edith takes, will be Leona's anger at being sent out after and fetched back—assuming, that is, that she is alive and safe. If she is with the short-necked man, that is no help to Edith because, to her the man is nameless. It will do no good sending a private detective around St. Thomas looking for a short-necked man. She has, in fact, only one remotely feasible idea. This involves telephoning Mr. Winslow at the Virgin Isle Hotel.

To be sure he may not be there any more. And of course,

if he is there, she cannot launch right in with, "Where is my granddaughter?" No, her inquiry must be discreet, indirect. Bring up Leona's name, and see whether he mentions having run into her in the last day and a half. But there is the problem of finding an excuse for calling Mr. Winslow.

Then she thinks: Of course. She will call him just to thank him, personally, for his kindness in having agreed not to write about the Harpers, and to apologize for having wasted his time the other afternoon. It would be a graceful gesture. She will tell him that she is sure he understands, and say how much she appreciates Leona having spoken to him, et cetera, et cetera, which will steer the conversation, gracefully, to Leona. She goes to the telephone.

Mr. Winslow picks up the telephone in the middle of the first ring, and begins shouting at her, and it is several seconds before she realizes what he is shouting about. "Listen, will you guys get the hell off my back!" he yells. "I told you I'd have the Harper story as soon as it's ready, so for Christ's sake stop phoning me! How the hell do you expect me to write the f---ing thing with you calling me up every five minutes? I'm onto something hot down here, and you'll get it when it's ready!" He slams down the phone in her ear.

Considerably shaken, she replaces the telephone in its cradle. She sits very still while the meaning of what he has said sinks in. So, she thinks, there is going to be a Harper story after all. This means that Leona never spoke to him at all or, if she did, did not tell Edith the truth about what Mr. Winslow did, or did not, agree to do. An explanation of Leona's curious behavior is becoming clearer as, bit by bit, pieces of the puzzle begin falling unpleasantly into place. But it is a while before Edith can think of what to do next. Then she picks up the telephone again and asks for Alan Osborn's office.

"Don't tell me what you're calling about," he says in his professional voice. "You're calling to say you can't keep your appointment this afternoon for the pictures. Well, what's the excuse . . ."

"Oh, I'd forgotten about that, Alan," she says. "But I can't make it. Alan, Leona's missing. She's been gone since early yesterday morning. I've got to find her right away."

"I see," he says.

"We had a row. She left. But she didn't pack—all her things

are still here. I think she's with a man, but I don't know his name. If it's the man I'm thinking of, he has a short neck—that's all I know!" She feels her voice rising with a touch of hysteria, and she struggles to control it. "Yes, and he drives a white automobile—a *coupé,* the kind with a collapsible roof. Can you help me, Alan?"

"Well," he says quietly, "I'll see what I can do."

"Thank you, Alan."

He is silent for a moment at the other end of the wire. "It seems to be a Harper trait, doesn't it?" he says finally. "Running away."

"What are you talking about? I've never run away!"

"I was thinking of your husband," he says. He clicks off.

Then, for a while, Edith roams distractedly through the house, waiting for the telephone to ring. Suddenly she remembers the letter to Harold. She cannot send him a letter like that now—not until this other business is settled. This is the wrong time to get Harold angry at her—legal rights or no legal rights. That letter will have to wait, and Leona's money will have to wait. She hurries to the kitchen to find the girl she gave the letter to. The girl is there, helping fix lunch; the letter has been mailed. She goes to the telephone once again and calls the post office. "This is Edith Blakewell," she says to the voice that answers, "and one of my maids dropped by this morning with a letter—"

"Yes, Mrs. Blakewell," the voice says. "It's on the eleven-forty plane."

She hangs up the phone. Grimly, she thinks: Before there were airplanes, letters were easier to intercept on this island.

Meredith Harper studied the letter his daughter had given him. He read it carefully, his face expressionless. Remembering that face, Edith thinks it is remarkable how little he had aged. He was still the same tall, stern, blank man. Perhaps it was because he had become so obsessive about his health and diet, devoting himself to physical exercise with increasing fury. The years managed to be kind to him right up until very near the end. Putting down the letter finally, he said, "This is very interesting, Edith. How did you get it?"

She told him how. For a number of weeks she had been

observing, or trying to observe, the pattern of Monique Bertin's life. From the hill behind the house it was possible, with the German binoculars, to see the Grand Hotel, and to watch Monique's comings and goings. Once a week the mail boat called at the island, and mail-boat days were particularly interesting days. That morning Edith had watched Monique leave the hotel with letters in her hand. Monique had hurried down the street to the Customs House, where the post office was.

Mr. Olafsen, the Danish postmaster, smiled at Edith when she entered, and Edith said pleasantly, "My friend Mme. Bertin was in here a few minutes ago and mailed some letters. There was something she forgot to enclose in one of them, and she asked me if I'd fetch the letters for her."

Mr. Olafsen handed her three letters. Smiling, he said, "Mme. Bertin is lucky to have a friend like you, Mrs. Blakewell, who will always get her letters back for her."

Edith gave Mr. Olafsen twenty *kroner*. Two of the letters, she could see from the envelopes, were of no consequence, and these she handed back. The third was addressed to a man in Dijon and, leaving the post office, she carefully unsealed it. She had translated no more than the first few sentences when she saw that, at last, she had the weapon she wanted.

Mon cher Etien—

I write to you at last because at last I know what I must do. It has not been easy for me, these years, but at last my head is clear.

The man I thought I loved, and I thought he loved me. Now I see that neither is true. I must come home for life here could only be tolerated by a person completely without feeling. So now I turn to you for help. It is a very rich man, it is true, but very greedy and cruel, a pig [cochon]. *He has no sympathy for me and will not give me the money. Now there is only you to ask.*

It was different when there could be trips to New York and to my beloved France, but now with this miserable war I am abandoned on this island. I hear of the troubles, so grave, in my country and I long to return. If you see my mother and father you may tell them of this letter and that I beg their forgiveness. When my heart ruled me I was a fool. Now my head rules me. Send me the money for passage. I will repay it.

A très bientôt,
Niki

Edith's father refolded the letter. "Extraordinary," he said. "I didn't know you had it in you, Edith." He stood up. "Would you like a glass of whisky?"

He had never offered her a drink before, but she said, "All right."

He filled two glasses from the crystal decanter. "They say whisky is a man's spirit," he said, "but I have always felt that a little drink of whisky was something a woman could enjoy as well. This is from a rather special vat which I had shipped from Kentucky." Handing her her glass, he said, "To our good fortune, Edith." They touched glasses.

"Now you see what the woman thinks of you, Papa. Get rid of her."

He looked at her over the rim of his glass. "I'm a lonely man, Edith. I've been lonely all my life. Your mother hasn't been a great help to me. There are two sides to this."

"I understand. But Mama needs you now."

"Do you mind if I smoke, Edith?" He opened the humidor and removed a cigar. He was smiling now. "Do you ever wear the pearls I gave you, Edith?"

"Yes, I wear them."

"I want you always to have nice things." He was lighting the cigar, and then he lifted the pages of Monique's letter and held the match to them. The letter flamed brightly in his hand for a moment and then he dropped the fire into a bowl. The letter curled and twisted into ash. Watching the dying flames, Edith said, "Then you will get rid of her. Thank you."

"I'll take care of Monique," he said. "And I'm grateful for your—interest in your mother. And in me. But—" He stared at her. "What about *you,* Edith? Are you happy? You're a curious person. This is a very curious thing you've just done. What is it they say about a wise child who knows his father? I think it's a wise father who knows his child."

"I did it for Mama's sake!"

"And Charles—is he happy?"

"Yes, I think so."

"I wonder. I'll be frank with you, Edith—I'm not happy with your young aristocrat. He isn't working out the way I hoped he would. I hired a manager, not a troublemaker. And troublemakers," he said, glancing at her, "are nuisances. He has not kept up his end of the bargain. After all, he married you because he wanted to get into the sugar business—"

"That's not true, Papa!"

He raised his eyebrows. "Well, it was certainly part of his price."

"He had no price!"

He paused thoughtfully. "He was a rich man's son, you see, who discovered suddenly that he was poor. He needed money and he needed a job. He got both those things by marrying you."

"You didn't give him any money! Only to his mother—"

"Really?" He stared at her fixedly. "Well, perhaps he's forgotten taking it, though it was a reasonably large amount. But the point is that he has not kept up his end of things. If things continue this way, I shall have to consider making a change." He smiled at her. "Will you have another whisky, Edith?"

She stood up. "No thank you," she said. "I've got to get home."

"Is it true?" she screamed at Charles that evening. "Papa says it is!"

"He gave me ten thousand dollars," he said calmly. "He said it was a wedding present. I didn't ask him for it. It's in the bank, in a trust account for Diana right now."

"Why didn't you tell me?"

He looked very tired. "I suppose it's because I knew you'd react just the way you're reacting now."

"No! You didn't tell me because you were too ashamed."

He was moving toward the library door again.

"Go ahead!" she cried. "Lock yourself up again. You never loved me. It was only the money! Where would you be, if it weren't for Papa and me? In a little law office somewhere? Or on a mountaintop eating berries?"

"A long way from here, I guess," he said.

"Oh! So that's it. Now that you've got all you can get from us, you're going to leave me."

He turned to her sharply and said, "Do you want me to?"

For some reason, the question staggered her. "Of course not."

"Then stop this!" he shouted, and he slammed his fist hard against the side of the door. "Whatever you're trying to do, stop it! Stop!"

He stepped into the library and closed the door.

The next day, Louis Bertin stood at the bottom of the veranda steps looking up at her. "What did you do?" he asked her. And when she didn't answer he repeated the question: "What did you do?"

"Go away, Louis. I don't want to talk to you."

He came up one step. "Tell me what you did. It was something you said to your father, about Monique."

"What business is it of yours what I way to my father?"

"He's beaten her very badly," he said. "It was because of something you said."

She stood very still with one hand on the veranda rail, and he came up one more step toward her.

"Whatever it was, you shouldn't have done it, Edith. Why do you interfere in things you don't understand? You should have left them alone."

"How is Monique?" she asked finally.

"She'll be all right. She's with him now."

"With him? I thought she wanted to leave him."

"You see? You make so many mistakes, Edith. You don't understand anything about the two of them. She'll never leave him."

"Why not?"

"Because she loves him," he said simply.

"Even when he beats her?"

"That was your fault. He has a sense of respectability, this man. He may be a millionaire, but he has the soul of a clerk. What upsets him now is knowing that his daughter knows about it."

"It's thanks to you I know about it. Oh, why didn't you both go away—long ago?"

"You made a mistake to tell him that you knew," he said. "You made a mistake to become involved with them at all. But now that you are involved, you'll have to suffer the consequences, I'm afraid."

"What sort of consequences?"

He shrugged. "I don't know. But I know your father and I know my wife. I could have taught you a lot of things, Edith, years ago, if you'd been willing to listen to me."

She stood very still for a long time. Finally she said, "But *you*. I don't understand you at all, Louis. How can you tolerate having your wife—"

"I'm not involved with them. This has been going on for a long time, and I've kept out of it—the way you should have."

"How can you go on letting her live with you?"

"She doesn't live with me. She lives with him."

"But you—permit it."

"It's not a question of permitting. I accept it," and suddenly his hooded eyes were smiling at her. "I accept it—the way you accept the pretty husband your father bought for you."

"Is that what you think?"

"Isn't it true? Your father boasts of it all the time. He says, 'This young aristocrat I bought for Edith.' He says it right in front of your husband, and your husband says nothing. He doesn't deny it."

"Charles would never let Papa say a thing like that."

"Why should I lie to you? Your father says things like that and worse in front of him. He says nothing."

She was silent, staring at the garden.

"And isn't it funny," Louis was saying, "that the only love you've ever had that wasn't bought and paid for was the love I gave you, Edith? I taught you what love was, and I did it for nothing in return. Just for you."

"Please go now, Louis."

"Don't you remember? How easy it was, how free? Has it ever been that way for you again? I could have taught you more, but you wouldn't let me. Remember the gatehouse? I'll never forget the look on your face when you saw the dirty hole I lived in. But it didn't matter, did it? We loved each other, and there was nothing demanded in return."

"You never loved me, Louis. Never."

"What is it that I remember then?"

"It was—making love. Not love."

"Ah, so many mistakes," he said. "You make so many mistakes."

The breeze stirred the fronds of ferns that hung in hanging baskets on the veranda. The roses in Charles' garden tossed their heads, and remembering that morning now it is impossible not to think that she was almost exactly Leona's present age then: twenty-seven. Old, wise, a third of her life over. And sometimes it seems as though all human emotions have an existence of their own, apart from the human beings they possess. They float at loose in the world, roll about at random like beads from a broken necklace until, almost by accident, they touch with a little click.

That sad, monkish face looked up at her and smiled. "It's love that I remember," he said.

She blinked her eyes. "Come into the house, Louis," she said.

She remembers that he said, "I've always wanted to see what the inside of this house was like," and that she had thought of how before, in Morristown, he had said she was punishing her father. She had wondered whom she was punishing now

And now it is after five o'clock. Alan's office will have closed. All afternoon she has stationed herself within earshot of the telephone, waiting for it to ring. But it has not rung. And so, when Nellie comes to her and asks, "Will Miss Leona be coming home for dinner tonight, Miss Edith?" Edith shakes her head and says, "No, not tonight."

Arch comes into the hotel room with a copy of the evening paper under his arm, and Leona, who has been sitting at the small writing table, puts down her pen.

"Writing letters?" he asks her.

"Yes," she smiles. "Letters to old friends."

"Go ahead. Don't let me interrupt you."

"That's all right. I'll finish later." She folds the unfinished letter and puts it in her purse.

He yawns and tosses the paper on the bed. "Kind of like

being married, isn't it?" he says. He comes and stands behind her, his hands on her shoulders, and together they confront their reflections in the wide mirror over the table.

"Arch," she says in a quiet voice, "this is the first affair—" She looks up into his reflected eyes, "I hate that word, don't you? But this is the first affair with a man I've ever had. So can I ask a dumb question? What happens next?"

"Not a dumb question. A good one."

"I know it has to end. But how?"

"The trouble is, I'm beginning to care about you. A lot. And that's not good."

She nods.

"The domestic life just isn't for me. Not any more."

"Then," she says carefully, "should I leave now?"

He kneads her shoulders with his fingers. "No. Not yet." Then he smiles. "Now what would you like to do tonight?" he asks.

Fifteen

THERE was an advertisement in one of Edith's magazines which recently caught her eye. It was for men's suits made out of one of those synthetic fibers, and it showed a young man sitting with his legs crossed at the knees, looking pressed and debonair. The world, the picture seemed to state, was this young man's oyster. A proper length of shirt cuff protruded from the sleeves of his jacket, his top jacket-button was buttoned, his lapels were narrow, and a white handkerchief, folded square, flourished discreetly in his breast pocket. He wore a waistcoat, and a supercilious expression was in his eyes. He held a pipe. Though this last detail could not possibly have been there (it would have been a French cigarette), everything else about the expression and appearance of that young man suggested, to Edith, Harold at sixteen years old. At sixteen, he was already a regular little tufthunter. His conversation was sprinkled with references to titled people. He had become dandyish in his dress and, because he had begun to hear people speak of him as handsome, he was very vain.

He was tall and thin, and in those days he had extraordinarily white skin, almost milky. Tiny bluish blood vessels beneath the surface made that skin seem luminous and translucent. His mouth was small and pink (later, a thin, sandy-colored mustache would form an eyebrow over that small mouth), and he had begun to affect a droop to his eyelids, which was enhanced by very long, curled, and almost colorless lashes. His hair was soft and fine, and he wore it cut long in the fashion of the day, and a light lock always hung across that wide, white forehead of his. In later life his hairline has receded, but that one silky lock, through some artistry of the comb, still manages to tumble the same way, and he lifts that forelock thoughtfully as he talks, strokes it between his long fingers, and then lets it fall back again—just as he did then. At sixteen, he was also becoming famous among his contemporaries for his sexual exploits.

"Once Papa caught old Harry in bed with one of Mama's maids," Arthur said to Edith years later. "They'd pulled the covers up over their heads, but their feet were sticking out at the bottom. Papa yanked the covers down, just to satisfy himself that it was a girl Harry was in bed with and not a boy. Papa's biggest concern in those days was whether we were both *normal* . . ."

Thinking of Harold in those days, Edith remembers the family meeting which her father called, after Charles left. "Now that Edith's husband has departed," her father began, and Harold, smoking his cigarette, had given her that sly look out of the corner of his eye, and had begun stroking that pale forelock.

And when the meeting was over, Harold had cornered her in the hall and said with a smirk, "Well, you've gone and done it for yourself good and proper this time, haven't you, old girl?" And when she had turned away from him, he said, "You know I always thought you were such a goody-goody, Edith. But now you've redeemed yourself. That's what this is—the redemption of a goody-goody. . . ."

All this of course, was after all the little wheels Edith had set into motion had spun out their inevitable courses. ("Charles," she says to him now, "you didn't have to go!" Then she adds, "No. You did, of course you did.") What might she have done differently that year—1916, when Diana was two years old? Why had she felt it necessary to go to her father again? Hadn't there been another human being in the world she could have gone to? Why hadn't she gone directly to Charles himself, and told him the whole thing? But no, she had been too frightened to go to Charles, and too uncertain of him.

By late autumn of 1916, the news of the war in Europe was eclipsed in St. Thomas by local news: The United States had offered to purchase the Danish Virgin Islands from Denmark. In December, the question went before the Danish people, and the vote was overwhelmingly in favor of giving up the colony. It was a time for parties and nostalgic songs, and the patriotic songs of both nations. St. Thomas forgave old Denmark all her sins, all King Christian's oversights, and crossed flags appeared in all the shop windows of Charlotte Amalie. The largest and most important of the parties was to be given in the colonial governor's house, under his crystal chandeliers and potted palms. Everyone was invited, or at least almost everyone. Dolly and Meredith Harper were not—despite Edith's mother's dreams, the governor and his wife had always conspicuously overlooked the Harpers. But Edith and Charles had received one of the encrusted invitations, delivered to the house by a footman in a red jacket.

Then, on the day of the governor's party, Monique Bertin came to call on Edith.

"She's in the garden, ma'am," Nellie said. "She wants to see you."

And there she was, all in yellow, walking among the flower beds, sniffing the wilted heads of roses.

Edith went quickly out into the garden. "What are you doing here?"

"Ah, Edith!" Monique said, smiling, stepping toward her. "How are you, Edith?" Her speech was more heavily accented than her husband's, and she pronounced Edith's name *Aydeet*.

"Very well, thank you," Edith had said, too shaken by the sight of her there to say much else. "What do you want?" The woman was pretty, very pretty in her yellow dress; one might even have said beautiful. She was not much older than Edith herself.

Monique Bertin laughed and cocked her head. "How nice to finally meet you, Edith," she said. "We've only seen each other from a distance."

Edith felt the warm color rise to her cheeks. "Please tell me what you want," she repeated.

"Isn't it you who wants something?" she said. "I have heard you want me to go away."

"You're quite right. I do."

Monique pouted. "Why didn't you come to me first?" she said. "Why did you go to your father? He hurt me very much."

"I'm sorry about that," Edith said. "But in a way I think you deserved it."

"Ah, Edith," she said. "I? Who have meant so much to your father for such a long time?"

"And who have also helped destroy my mother."

She sighed. "I do not know your mother. You should have come to me first. I would have listened." Then her smile faded. "I'm ready to talk now. I'm ready to go now. All I need is the money." She held out her hand. "Give me the money."

Edith considered it. "You're ready to leave for good?"

"For good."

"They say the Atlantic is full of submarines. How do you propose to go?"

"Never mind how. I'll go. If you give me the money."

"How much money?" she asked.

"From you, three thousand Danish *kroner*."

"That's quite a bit," Edith said. And it was. Though it amounted in American money only to about five hundred dollars, it was for Edith in those days a sizable amount. With that much money she could run her household for a long time.

"It's what I need."

"Where do you expect me to get that much money?"

"You're a rich girl."

"My father may be rich. I am not."

Monique shrugged. "You can get it," she said.

"Will this cover yourself and your husband?"

She smiled brightly at Edith now, but her hand was still outstretched, the palm curved upward. "Why of course! Louis and I always travel together. We're *friends!*"

"I'll have to think about this," Edith said.

"But I need it now. If I'm going to go, I need the money now."

"I don't believe you," Edith said carefully. "I don't believe you have any intention of leaving. This is just a scheme of yours to extract a little money out of me. The answer is no."

With another little sigh, Monique sat down on the stone

garden bench, the skirts of her yellow dress falling about her. "Oh, you are not nice," she said. "I thought you would be nice to me. I hate this hot place so. It's killing me, this hot place."

"I'm sorry."

A slender water pipe with a spigot at the top rises from the ground by the stone bench where Monique Bertin sat that day—the spigot to which the gardeners attach the garden hose when they water—and Monique suddenly reached for the tap, and said, "Is this fresh water? May I have a drink? I've heard about your famous well, Edith." Kneeling by the tap, she turned on the water and let it run into her mouth, drinking deeply. "Ah!" she said at last, sitting up again and turning off the water. "Cool and good! Not as sweet as the well water in France, but cool and good." With the back of her wrist she wiped her dripping chin—a peasant's gesture, Edith thought—and smiled at Edith. "I thought you would be so nice," she said. "You have that nice husband, that handsome husband. They say he is so nice."

"Please leave my husband out of this," Edith said.

Monique put her hand on the spigot again. "Forgive me—I can't resist this—" she said. And this time she lowered her whole head beneath the tap, and let the water run full across her face, her throat, turning her head and letting it soak her dark hair. "Oh, this feels so *good!* You should try this, Edith—so cooling." Her hands splashed in the water, carrying handfuls of it to her face and arms and shoulders, splashing it across her bosom, the tiny silver crucifix spinning and shining in the sun.

"The water in my cistern is very low," Edith said. "Please don't waste it like this."

But Monique ignored her. "And wouldn't it be sad to think of what your nice, handsome husband would do if he knew how close—how very close, Edith—you and Louis have been to each other? Or what your father would do? Or what everybody on the island would say?" She turned off the water and shook her dripping head. "May I borrow a hairbrush, Edith?" she said, and she held out her hand again in that same flat gesture.

"A hairbrush?"

"Yes," she laughed. "My hair."

"This is blackmail, then, isn't it?"

"Blackmail? Blackmail? I do not know what that means. All I want is three thousand Danish *kroner,* so I can leave this island. Three thousand Danish *kroner,* and a hairbrush, please."

Slowly, Edith went into the house. She took a hairbrush from her dressing table. On the dust divider, underneath one of the dresser drawers, was where, in those long-ago days, she and Charles kept the envelope of household cash. She would have to justify the money to Charles somehow if he ever discovered it was missing. Then she went downstairs again and out into the garden.

"Oh, that's a pretty brush. Silver," Monique said.

"I might have known you people would think of something like this," Edith said. "Just tell me one thing. Did you get your—information—from Louis?"

She laughed gaily. "I do not know of what you speak!" she said. Brushing her hair, sending out spatters of water like sparks from the brush, sparks that flew through the sunlight and settled on the walk—her hair was a waterfall of those bright sparks—she said, "It didn't take much thinking, really. All I want is to be able to leave this place. When you didn't give me the money freely, I had to think of something." Brushing, brushing, her golden hand holding the long silver handle of the brush like a pistol, she brushed her hair until it gleamed flat against her skull.

"Here are your three thousand *kroner,*" Edith said. "Take it and get out. Leave this island and never come back. Don't you ever, either of you, dare to come back!"

"Thank you, Edith," Monique said, taking the money.

"Call me Mrs. Blakewell."

She gave Edith a droll look. "*Mrs.* Blakewell," she said.

For a long time after Monique had gone, Edith stood at her window, absolutely still, her temples pounding, unable to move, staring out at the garden where the silver hairbrush lay on the grass by the stone bench, exactly as though Monique had thrown it there.

Looking at its gleam, the silver object assumed a queer significance. She thought: Must my whole life be trapped forever in that moment there, in the gatehouse, that August afternoon years ago? Even though, looking back, it seemed such an unimportant moment?

* * *

That night, at the Governor's Ball, Edith and Charles passed through the receiving line to the strains of Strauss. Then, after a glass of champagne, with his arm resting lightly around her waist, they joined the dancers. The Governor's wife spoke to them. "How beautiful you look together," she said. "Beautiful young people . . ." They danced on.

A little tipsy from the champagne, she held Charles tightly and told him what she had decided that afternoon. "Charles, let's leave this island," she said. "Let's sell the house and go back North. It was a mistake for us to stay here. It was a mistake for you to work for Papa. You're miserable here and so am I. It's a rotten place."

He smiled at her and started to speak, but they were interrupted by a roll of drums, and turned to face the orchestra. There was a toast to President Wilson, and to the King, and the glasses were shattered. Then, reverentially, the two anthems were played—first "The Star-Spangled Banner" and then the stately and mournful *"Der Er Et Yndigt Land"*—"There Is A Lovely Country"—the Danish hymm. Throughout the ballroom, ladies touched white handkerchiefs to their eyes, and the men stood stern and stiff as ramrods, letting their own tears fall unheeded, but Edith Blakewell, holding Charles' arm, was too excited with the simplicity of her solution to be moved by the ceremony of changing flags—under one flag or another, the island would always be the same—and she thought, yes, there is a lovely country somewhere, and we fill find it, you and I.

When the anthems were over and the dance music began again, Charles said, "Come out onto the terrace for a minute. I want to tell you something." She followed him and when they were outside, away from the music, he said, "I'm joining the Army."

"What?" she said, not comprehending it. "What did you say?"

"I'm going to the war."

"But *why?*" she gasped. "This is Europe's war! America isn't in it. This war has nothing to do with us."

"We'll be in it before long."

"You're doing this—just to get rid of me!"

He shook his head. "It has nothing to do with that. I leave in three weeks for New Orleans. Then to Fort Leavenworth, for my commission—"

"You can't leave me! You can't leave Diana!"

"I'm doing it for your own sake."

"Well you can't. *I won't let you!*"

"Edith—"

"You can't!" she screamed. "You can't! I won't let you!"

The next afternoon Monique Bertin reappeared in the garden. "It wasn't enough," she said with her little smile. "I need two thousand more Danish *kroner.*" She held out her hand.

And so who was there left for Edith to appeal to but her father? They sat in his office and, once more, they were holding little glasses of Kentucky whisky. He listened to her for a long time, saying nothing, and, while she talked, his eyes grew sadder and more remote. He interrupted her only once, when she told him about Charles and the Army. "He's wrong about that, of course," he said. "I have friends in high places in Washington, and they assure me that America will stay out of the war."

When she finished he said, "Then it's true about you and Bertin."

"Did she tell you?"

He drummed his fingers on the top of the desk. "Ah, Edith," he said, "I can see you'd never be able to run the sugar business. What in the world ever made me think you could?"

"Just help me, Papa."

"I'll see that you get your five thousand *kroner* back. That part of it is no trouble at all."

"Do you need any more proof of how destructive those people are? Will you get rid of them now, Papa?"

He shook his head. "Poor little Monique," he said. "She's a silly, headstrong child. No, your problem goes deeper than that. These stories she threatens to tell—they're becoming a little more widespread, I'm afraid, than I think you realize."

"Started by the two of them!"

He waved his hand. "That's not important. The important thing is to keep Charles from hearing them. For your sake and the baby's sake—for the family's sake. If there weren't some basis of truth in them, it wouldn't matter."

She nodded.

"Let me think about this," he said. "Give me a little time. Come back tomorrow. Meanwhile, I'll take care of Monique."

She stood up to go. His eyes were still far away. "At least I've been relatively discreet in my little affair," he said. "It's a pity you couldn't have been as discreet in yours. No, you would never have been able to run the sugar business . . ."

When she came back the next day, he said, "I have found the solution, quite a simple one. It solves both problems—the problem of Monique and the problem of Charles." He pulled open a desk drawer and pulled out a thick stack of papers. "Charles was never cut out for this business either," he said. "And so," he riffled through the papers, "I'm going to set things up for the two of you a little differently . . ."

"Charles is tired of having you set things up for us. That's part of the trouble."

"I'm setting things up so that both of you can be independent of me. For the rest of your lives you'll be free to go and do as you wish. I'm going to give you, now, the share of my estate that would normally come to you under my will when I die. Do you have any idea how much money I estimate that to be?"

"No," she said softly.

"A million dollars. That's quite a bit of money, isn't it? This is a favorable time for you to take it, too. Until the Treaty of Cession becomes final in March, we are still operating here under the laws of Denmark. You will probably be able to avoid this new United States tax on incomes if I set it up now the way I plan. And as for Charles—"

"What about Charles?"

"I gather he has been disturbed by the thought that he is living off a rich wife. So I am giving him an equal amount, free and clear."

"He won't take it."

"He's taken money before. He can't refuse this much. They won't let him refuse. His family is not that well off. Yes, this will keep him with you, Edith. You'll both have everything you want. As you said yourself, this island is no place for either of you. If Charles wants, he is welcome to any position he chooses in my New York office, but that will be up to him. He can do as he pleases." Then he said, "Aren't you going to say thank you, Edith? I've solved all your problems and made you a rich woman."

"Thank you," she said.

"Well, then."

"I just don't know what Charles will say."

"I do. You see, I've already gone over all this with him."

"And he said yes?"

"He asked me only one question—what *you* thought of it. That's all he cares about. If you agree, he agrees. And you do agree." He stood up, and his eyes clouded over. "You'll both be free," he said. "Free of me. Whom you hate so much."

"Don't say that, Papa."

"I do say it. Now run along."

Waiting for the spring rainy season to come, there is always a desperately sweet smell in the air, a smell of rain in the wind blown across ripe sugar cane, and mixed with it are the smells of tobacco-plant flowers and perhaps jasmine, and the flamboyant and grape trees in blossom, and through it all the spice of salt from the sea. They rode side by side through this warm wind, and she felt lightheaded and almost sad to be leaving St. Thomas forever, as the cottonwood trees, in green arches, flew by over their heads and sea birds in the sky kept pace and pebbles spurted out from the red earth beneath their horses' hoofs. "Let's do more of this when we get North again," she called back to him. "The way we used to do in Morristown. Remember? Let's see if we can find a house in the country, Charles, where we can keep horses."

"All right," he said. "Perhaps—someday."

"Why someday?" she asked laughing. "Why not right away—tomorrow?"

"All right—why not? Find your house, if that's what you want."

His hair was blowing across his eyes, and she was still laughing. "Isn't it what you want too?" she asked him. His lips moved, but she couldn't hear what he was saying. She slowed her horse to a walk, and called after Charles. "Wait! Come back here a minute."

He turned the chestnut gelding and trotted back to her. "What is it?" he said.

"I asked you if it wasn't what *you* wanted," she said.

They were facing each other. He patted his horse's neck. "Edith," he said carefully. "I've told you. I'm joining the Army."

"But you can't. Not now."

"Can't I?"

She hesitated, trying to translate the expression on his face. "Of course not. We've got our share of Papa's money now. It's for us—when we get to New York."

Slowly, his fingers stroked the chestnut's mane, and the animal's neck quivered at his touch, its head went up and its tail swished. "I understand all this," Charles said. "You have your money now. You can certainly buy a house with it if you like. There's enough."

"It would be your house too!"

"No. Not yet."

"Why not? There's money for you as well as for me."

"Take the money if you want to," he said. "I won't have much need for it where I'm going."

"Don't be absurd! You're not going anywhere—except to New York with me. That's what the money's *for*, for heaven's sake! And we promised Papa—"

"I promised him nothing—except once, to help him by being some sort of decoration for his little cake. This little sugar cake of his. And now that promise has ended."

She reached out her hand and touched his knee. "That's not fair," she said. "Besides, darling—I need you. Diana needs you."

"Do you?" His eyes traveled away.

They were at the corner of the road that led into the old Mandal estate, a vacant ruin used for sheep-grazing. A sheep fence ran around it and, looking at the barred gate, she said suddenly, "Let's do some jumping. Come on. We can argue about this later."

His look followed hers. "Do you think this horse can take that gate?" he said.

"Of course he can." She measured its height with her eyes. "It's not more than four and a half feet. This will be an easy one."

"I'm not sure," he said doubtfully. "I've never jumped this fellow before. Have you?"

"You've got to *make* him take it. You're the rider—you're in command. You make him take it. That's what Papa says."

"Is that what Papa says? All right, come on."

They started the horses toward the gate, urging them to a

canter. Three lengths from the fence, Edith jerked her feet from the stirrups and pressed her knees and thighs hard into her horse's sides. Leaning forward, giving him a loose rein, she whispered into his ear, "Jump!" And they took off, cleared the top rail nicely, and came down easily on the other side. But the chestnut had veered sharply and refused the jump, the horse was rearing and snorting under Charles.

"Don't let him refuse!" she called back to Charles. "Give him the crop! Give him the crop! Don't let him refuse." She cantered back, and jumped the gate again.

Charles's horse was standing quietly now.

"Come on—make him try it again."

"You want to move people, don't you, Edith? You always want to move them. Why is that?"

"What do you mean?"

"You want to move me to New York with you."

"But darling, we're rich now—we can go wherever we want. It doesn't have to be New York."

"But I'm not taking the money."

"Do you want us to starve?"

"Somehow," he said smiling, "I don't think you'll ever starve, Edith."

"Don't be difficult, darling," she said. "Come on—make him try the jump again."

"Why don't you tell me the real reason why you want to leave St. Thomas?" he said.

She laughed, the wind in her face. "I'm thinking of us. I want us to be free."

"Are you? Or is it the same reason why you wanted to get rid of Bertin and his wife? Why didn't you tell me why you wanted to get rid of Monique?"

"I don't know what you're talking about."

"Why didn't you tell me the real reason was because you were afraid of him?"

It was suddenly hard for her to hear what he was saying, and easier, safer, in the wind to dismiss his words. She let the wind blow them away. "Afraid of him?" she said. "Why should I be afraid of him?"

"Why didn't you tell me he was the one?"

She was too terrified to look at him now. "What one? Which one?"

"The one before me."

"It's a cheap, disgusting lie!"

"And you've seen him since, haven't you?"

"No!"

"Edith," he said, "is Diana my child or his?"

Tears jumped to her eyes. "I refuse to answer such a question!" she cried. "How can you ask me a thing like that?"

"I guess," he said easily, "it's because it's something I'd like to know before I join, as we say, Our Doughboys Over There."

She raised her hand.

"Are you going to give me the crop?" he said. His brown eyes were steady. "Go ahead. Give me the crop, if it helps."

"Damn you," she whispered. "Oh, damn you!" And then, pleading, she said, "Charles, please believe me."

"I can't. That's why I want to go away, and why I'm not taking any money."

"You took money when you married me, don't forget!"

He smiled. "That was different," he said. "I accepted his money then because you were included in the price."

"I still am!"

"It was different then. I loved you then."

She turned her horse away. "Come on," she said. "Make your jump."

Once more they turned their horses toward the sheep fence and broke into a canter. Turning to Charles, she cried out, "Who told you all this about me? Was it Papa? I never loved Louis, Charles—only you!" He turned his head to her and laughed. "Don't laugh at me!" she shouted. They approached the gate, and she lifted her heels from the stirrups. "Jump!" she cried to her mare. And to Charles, beside her, she said "Jump!" But she saw the chestnut's head begin to shy, about to refuse again, and she reached out and seized the other bridle. Charles seemed to turn in the saddle and to give her a sudden look of intense interest; not fearful, but questioning. Holding his bridle in her gloved hand just below the bit, she cried, "*Jump!*" and their horses rose together. There was a clatter of hoofs as the two horses touched, their bodies thrown instantly against each other, then flung apart, and then the noisier crash of hoofs and shoes striking the fence rail. Her head snapped forward, and she clung to her mare's neck, her face in the mane. Her horse struck the ground with its front feet, stumbled, and almost fell; then it leaped up, rearing and whinnying. She had dropped her crop and, while she tried to calm the horse, she realized that she held a broken bit in her hand. She looked back. The gelding stood very still, its nose down, nibbling the grass beside the fence, and Charles lay, a graceless burden, against the lower rail, his legs twisted awkwardly beneath him. One hand clutched at the air and, as Edith leaped from her horse and went running back to him, the hand moved slowly downward.

The news from the hospital, in the beginning, was confusing. At first Edith understood that both legs were broken; then it seemed that only one leg was broken, but in several places. "Compound fracture of the right lower femur, and simple fracture of the right tibia and fibula," was the final diagnosis which young Doctor Alan Osborn, who had only recently come to St. Thomas, gave her. It was several days before he would permit her to see Charles. And when at last she was allowed to go to the hospital Alan Osborn met her at the door and said, "We're quite sure he'll be able to walk again, Mrs. Blakewell." They moved slowly down the hospital corridor. "Of course it will always be with difficulty. There was severe damage to the muscle and vascular tissues. But at least we managed to save the leg." Outside the door to Charles' room, he said, "You realize that he doesn't want to see you."

She nodded, and went into the room. Inside, the room was dark. Bending over him, she said, "Charles, *what's happened to me?*"

He looked up at her, "Hello, Edith," he said. And then, "Well, you've won."

"Oh, don't say that."

"Is Diana my child or his?"

"Don't . . . don't . . ."

He turned his head away. "Please go away now," he said.

A few days later, Alan Osborn called at her house. "He thinks he could get better treatment if he were moved to a hospital in New York," he said. "And of course he's probably right. So, as soon as it's possible to move him, I think he should be moved."

"Yes."

"Will you be going with him, Mrs. Blakewell?"

"No."

"I see . . ." Alan Osborn said with a noncommittal, professional face.

Two weeks later, riding in a wheelchair, Charles boarded the Quebec Line steamer *Guiana*. A nurse accompanied him. By the time the *Guiana* reached New York, America was in the war.

Then there was that little family meeting in her father's house. It was the last time Edith was inside Sans Souci until the time, years later, when she and Harold and Arthur and their respective wives went through the place dividing up the furniture after Meredith Harper died. She had told the family at the meeting that she wanted to stay in St. Thomas. They acted quite surprised. But after all, there was really no place else for her to go.

In the summer of 1918 she had a letter from Charles, postmarked from France, which was to tell her that he was safe and well, and that he had got into the war anyway—"as a soldier of sorts," he put it—and was driving a Red Cross ambulance. That was the last she heard of him until September of that year when she was notified that a mortar had exploded beneath the ambulance, killing the driver and three civilian passengers.

His body was returned to St. Thomas for burial, and Mrs. Thomas Blakewell arrived from New York for the services—the same dry, brittle woman she had always been, only drier, brittler, ten years older. After the services she paid a brief visit to Edith at her house.

"Would you like to see your little granddaughter?" Edith asked. Diana was nearly five years old.

Mrs. Blakewell pulled on the glove which she had removed to shake hands. "I'd rather not," she said in her husky voice. "I came mostly out of curiosity—to see the place where he was buried. It's really a terribly ugly island, isn't it? I had thought it would be prettier. Still, I suppose it's where he belongs. He used to write me such enthusiastic letters about the place." Then, turning to Edith, she said, "Blood tells, doesn't it? I've always thought that the most absurd remark. But, like most absurd remarks, it turns out to have a lot of truth in it. A silk purse cannot be made out of a sow's ear. Heaven knows what made me think it might be otherwise. But more than anything else I feel sorry for you, Edith—yes, sorry. It always seemed to me you had so much. I suppose it was a case of having too much. Was it? I don't really care to know the answer. The only trouble is there won't be any punishment—none good enough for you, in any case. Maybe the punishment will come in the next world. I hope so." She turned and went out the door.

Old Nellie—young Nellie then—had come into the room and said, "Will you be having dinner alone tonight, Miss Edith?"

"What?" Edith said absently and then, suddenly, throwing her arms around the little housemaid, she cried, "Nellie! Don't ever leave me, Nellie! Promise me you'll never leave me!"

And the startled Nellie, clutched in the white woman's frightening grip, said, "No, Miss Edith. I won't leave you, Miss Edith. I promise you that."

Sixteen

VERY little of the morning has entered the hotel room—only enough to discover the worn stretch of carpet by the door, a thin film of dust on the dresser top, and the curls of smoke that float up from Leona's lighted cigarette. She sits on the bed, tailor-fashion, with the top sheet pulled up around her shoulders, watching him as he moves about the room getting dressed. Now he pulls up the Venetian blind with a noisy rattle, and sharp sunlight floods into the room.

"Oooh," she says, shielding her eyes, "did you have to do that?"

"Oh, sorry," he says, starting to lower the blind again.

"No, leave it up," she says. "It's time to rise and shine."

With his foot on the window sill he tightens the laces of one shoe. She smiles at him and says, "Good morning." And then, after a moment, she says, "Are you going out?"

He looks at her uncertainly. "I thought I might play a few holes of golf," he says. "Do you mind? It's nice day. Can't spend a nice day—"

"Of course I don't mind."

He pulls a blue cashmere sweater over his head. "Just a few holes."

"When I was a little girl," she says, "when I first began coming here, I remember it used to bother me. I'd wake up in the morning and look at the sky, and think: *another* nice day? How can it always be like this? Just one nice day after another—never any difference, never any foggy days or cold days, or snowy days, always the same."

"How about some breakfast?" he says, moving toward the phone. "What would you like?"

"Nothing, thanks," she says, carefully shaping the end of her cigarette against the rim of the already overcrowded ashtray. "And you—why don't you pick up something, on your way, Arch."

"I might pick up a bite."

"As long as you're all ready—to go."

He hesitates, looking at her. "You want to come with me? Play some golf?"

She shakes her head. "No," she says, "golf's not my sport, Arch. You said the night I met you that we had a lot of things in common, but golf isn't one of them. No, you play your golf, and I—" She looks up at him. "Well, Arch, I get the point."

His eyes evade hers. "Point? What point?"

"Signals, little signals. Not too many signals get across to people, but I've gotten all of yours. Yes, don't worry. I understand. I'll be gone when you get back."

"Well, now, look," he says. "You don't have to do that."

"Ah," she says, "please don't try to say anything gallant. I understand. I don't mind. I'm even grateful."

"You see," he says slowly, "I don't want you to care about me, either. It just isn't in the cards for us. Maybe I wish it could be. But it can't be."

"I understand."

He sits down in the chair facing her, and looks at his fingernails. "I don't want to fall in love with anybody," he says. "I don't want anybody to fall in love with me. I'm just—not up to it any more. But you'll find somebody. That is, I hope you will."

"Yes."

"Just promise me one thing," he says. "Don't start going

from bed to bed. I've seen that happen to too many other girls, but that's not for you. It's no solution. So promise me—" He looks up at her thoughtfully, then gives her a brief smile. "Hell, you don't have to make any promises to me," he says. "I just don't like to think of that happening to you, that's all." He stands up. Slowly he runs a hand through his stiff brown, crewcut hair.

By smiling fixedly at him it is somehow easier. Please, she prays, don't let him ask to kiss me good-by. If he does that, all the screams that are inside her head will come flying out into the room, and that must never happen. Because the sad little secret she has just discovered is that she dreads, yes, dreads having him leave. Does that mean that she has begun to love him a little? No, it couldn't, but perhaps she has begun to like him too much, or to count on him too much—this man she had sworn to take so dispassionately, as . . . as what? As a kind of medicine. As therapy. She cannot bear the thought of him leaving, nor can she bear the thought of him remaining for another minute in the room. Just let him go now, she begs. Let him go.

"If you do go," he says, "where will you go?"

"Oh," she says brightly, "I have plenty of places to go, Arch, plenty of places. The whole world is my—home."

"You'll go back to your grandmother's, I suppose."

"Don't worry about me."

He turns, goes to the writing table and sits down. He fishes in the drawer for something. Then he takes out a pen and begins to write. It is a moment or two before she realizes what he is doing, and then she puts her feet quickly over the side of the bed and says, "No!"

"They know me here at the West Indies Bank," he says. "They'll certify this for you, if you like." He turns in the chair and holds out the check to her. "Here," he says.

"No, Arch."

"Don't be silly—please take it."

"No," she says rapidly, "tear it up, Arch. I don't want it."

"I may be a miserable bastard, but I keep my promises," he says. "Go ahead—take it, Leona. You still want your gallery, don't you?"

"Yes, but not this way."

"Look, call it a loan if you want. You can issue me some

stock in the gallery. I'll consider it an investment—in you. So take it. I want you to have the gallery too."

"To keep me off the streets? No—"

"What about this story Winslow's writing? What if he says some of the things you told me about? What if the Harpers are wiped out? A little cash might help keep the old family ship afloat, don't you think? So take it."

"Don't worry about the Harpers. We have great staying powers—we're famous for that. We'll survive."

"Listen," he says, leaning toward her, "I give my wife this much every year, and she means nothing to me. You do mean something. So please take it."

She continues to shake her head. "No."

"Don't you understand? I know it's only money. But it's the best I can give you. In fact, it's the only thing I can ever give you. And I want to give you something. Here," and he tries to put the check into her hand, but she withdraws the hand.

"For a smart man, you're not very perceptive, Arch," she says. "I didn't sleep with you for the money, don't you know that? Don't you know why I slept with you? It was because of the things you said to me on Sunday, after lunch, at the table. That was why I came here—not for the money. What is it the hysterical girl says in a melodrama when somebody slaps her face? 'Thanks, I needed that.'" She laughs a little shrilly. "That's the way I felt when you said what you said to me, and that's the way I feel now, Arch. And I may sound a little hysterical myself, but I assure you I have never been more clearheaded. Now tear up that check."

Looking at her now his eyes are sad. "Why don't I leave this here, on the desk," he says finally. "You think about it for a while."

"'Your three dollars is on the dresser, Gertie.' No, I want you to tear it up. I'll tear it up myself if you won't, but I'd rather have you do it—so I can watch you doing it, and you can watch me watching you!"

"Please."

She shakes her head and tries to speak, but suddenly no words will come. She tries a jaunty wave of her hand. "Oh," she says, "can you ever imagine that there could be a *reason* for me being me?" Her throat tightens on the words, and she has to stop. She waves again. "Do it now!"

He stares at the check in his hand. "I think you're crazy," he says. "But I guess you've got principles. Crazy principles I don't understand." He tears the check in half and tosses the pieces in the wastebasket.

"Thank you. Now go—go play your golf."

"Look, you're welcome to stay here as long as you want. I mean, you're welcome."

"Are you just trying to make me feel rotten? Please don't. I can do that all by myself. Please just go. Before I say all sorts of things I don't want to say, and won't mean, and will just make you hate me. I can do that all by myself too, it doesn't need your help. . . ."

"You're sure there's nothing—"

"No. Good-by, Larry."

He stands up slowly. "Larry? The name's Arch, remember?"

She laughs. "Oh, but by calling you Larry, I'm making it a neat, clean break! Swift and clean. No looking back. Isn't that what men want? Out of sight, out of mind. Not even a beautiful memory. I'm making you vanish. I'm giving you a whole new name, which is the same as no name at all."

"Well," he says carefully, "I'll be here for a few more days. Maybe I'll see you around—"

"Oh, yes, yes. Undoubtedly. I'll see you around."

"Well, then. So long, buddy."

"Good-by!" she says. "So long! See you around!"

He pauses at the door, his hand on the knob. "I'm just not cut out for anything more," he says. "My divorce taught me that. I'll never marry again. That's why—"

"Oh, please—I understand!"

"But I won't forget you. Not for a long time. Because I like you, even in your veils. And maybe I've got a few veils of my own. That's all I want to say." His blunt, sunburned face is sad. "That's all."

She nods. "Good-by."

"Good luck," he says. "Take care of yourself." He opens the door, steps out, and quickly closes it. She is all alone.

Leona continues to sit on the bed for a minute or two, and then the lighted cigarette burns between her fingers and she puts it out in the ashtray among the others. She makes a burnoose of the sheet and stands up and goes into the bathroom.

For several minutes she brushes her teeth vigorously and thoroughly as though she were preparing them for an examination by the dentist, and when she rinses her mouth and spits out tooth-pasty suds into the bowl two tears fall into the swirling water of the bowl and she has a vision of her tears descending through the labyrinthine plumbing of the hotel, out into drains and sewers that will carry them at last to the sea. Then, looking up and seeing a bottle of Arch's yellow sleeping pills—along with the masculine toilet things, razor, brush, shaving lotion, deodorant, talcum powder, she is swept with a wave of self-despair that is almost nausea, remembering the other time when she had thought of sleeping pills. It was with Edouardo—but had she thought of it seriously? Or only as a way to get even with him? She cannot help but think, with an inner smile, what a considerable embarrassment she could become by being the dead woman found in Arch Purdy's hotel room. She scrubs her face with cold water and a cloth and, still wrapped in the sheet, she goes back out into the room. She picks up her purse and examines its contents: her checkbook, with its balance indicated; her return-trip ticket from St. Thomas to New York; and twelve dollars in cash. Then she finds the two unfinished letters.

Trailing the sheet, she sits down at the writing table and unfolds first one letter, and then the second. "This is known as a 'What have I got to lose?' letter. . . ." she reads. She faces these words for a while, then picks up the pen and writes a few more—slowly, pausing at the end of each. And then, for several minutes, her pen moves swiftly and she writes blindly, because she is all at once saying all the things she should have said, might have said, had wanted to say, had thought of saying, but had never said, long ago, to either of them.

Finished, she stands up and tosses the bedsheet from her shoulders. She picks up Arch's silk robe from where it lies on a chair and puts it on, wrapping it tightly around her. She goes to the window and looks out at the hills and the green Caribbean. Which way is home? When she was little, she remembers standing on Granny's big veranda, and asking Granny, "Which way is home?" Meaning which way was New York. Her grandmother had very carefully picked up Leona's hand and pointed it due north, over Lee Hill, and said, "One home is that way,

Leona." And then, turning the hand so that it pointed directly at the front door of the old house, she had said, "And another is here."

Leona returns to the bed now and sits down upon it. Pressing her knees tight together and holding her hands clenched into tight fists in her lap, she repeats, "Oh, I've got plenty of places to go. Plenty of, plenty of, plenty of places to go."

At eleven o'clock the telephone finally rings. Edith picks it up, and it is Alan at last. "Well," he says, "I've found her. Or rather located her, Edith. She's at the Virgin Isle."

"Not with Mr. Winslow!"

"No," he clears his throat. "The man's name is Arch Purdy. His neck is on the short side. They share a room. Do you want the usual rundown on him? To begin with, he's solvent."

"Oh, never mind. Oh, *Alan!* How can she do such a thing to me!"

His voice on the other end of the line is dry. "What makes you think she's doing anything to you?"

"She wouldn't treat me this way if she knew!"

"If she knew what?"

"If she knew I was dying of cancer she wouldn't treat me the way she does!" It is the first time, since that talk of hers and Alan's two years ago, that she has permitted herself to use the word *cancer*, or even permitted herself to think that word. Pushed back in the very bottom of her mind, she has kept it where it belonged, out of her life and out of the world. And the utterance of that word just now, flinging it out where it has no right to be, so dismays and disorients her that she almost drops the telephone, and the long pain comes stabbing back, and she hears her own voice demanding, "Would she? Would she?"

"Perhaps not," he says, and his voice is very cool.

"Oh, Alan—I'm sorry. Thank you for finding her, Alan. Alan—dear Alan—what would I ever do without you?"

"Don't mention it. We have a new appointment for you. Three o'clock tomorrow."

"Thank you, Alan."

"Good-by, Edith."

It does not take her long, then, to decide what to do. She rings for Nellie, and asks Nellie to have John bring around the car.

The young manager at the Virgin Isle Hotel is a man known to her, and as Edith Blakewell approaches the desk he gives her a small, abashed smile and mutters a greeting.

"I presume you know what I'm here for," she says.

He nods.

She opens her purse and takes out a carefully folded fifty-dollar bill and hands it to him. He takes it, pockets it quickly, and reaches behind him for a key. "Four-seventeen," he says.

She takes the key. "Is this a good time to go up?"

"Yes. She's alone. He went out about an hour ago with a bag of golf clubs. If he comes back, I'll detain him till you're gone, Mrs. Blakewell."

"Thank you."

She crosses the lobby to the automatic elevator.

On the second floor, the elevator stops, and a great many small children in dripping bathing suits flood in. Their wet hands reach up and press all the buttons. "This is *fun!*" one of them says. With the authority of a parent (since these children seem to be parentless), Edith reaches up and unsnaps all the buttons. The children gaze at her hatefully. On the fourth floor, she pushes her way through the wet suits and disembarks. The corridor is empty, and she goes quickly down it to number 417, then hesitates, looking at the key in her hand. Then she knocks. From within, there is a murmured response and a stir of feet. Then Leona opens the door.

"Oh!" Leona gasps. And then again, "Oh! What are you doing here?" And she starts to close the door.

"Leona," Edith says very rapidly and softly, "I didn't come here to scold you or to ask you to come back. I simply came to see whether there was anything you needed."

Then Leona opens the door again. She throws her arms around her grandmother and immediately bursts into tears. Edith steps into the room and closes the door behind her.

"Leona," Edith whispers. "Leona—this has got to stop."

"Yes," she sobs. "Yes, yes, yes. . . ."

They sit on the bed, Leona's arms around her. Leona has

on a man's raw-silk robe, and the bed is unmade. The Venetian blinds are down and the curtains are drawn, and the room is quite dark. They sit, letting Leona cry, and outside the closed window the sound of a springboard pounds from the pool.

"What's going to happen to me?" Leona asks. "What's going to happen to me?"

"Nothing at all," Edith says. "Nothing at all. Will you come home with me now?"

"Yes."

"John's outside with the car. I'll wait for you there while you dress."

"All right."

"Leona—you're all I have. Really all. Why didn't you let me know where you were?"

"I couldn't, Granny. I was afraid of what you'd say."

"Oh, Leona. Afraid of me?"

"This is the worst thing I've ever done, isn't it?" Leona says. "The worst. It's the worst thing anybody's ever done."

"Oh, Leona, I've done much, much worse things than this," Edith says. "You just don't know." Edith stands up. "Now hurry. Don't be too long. I'll be outside in the car." She leaves the room and walks to the elevator again.

A few minutes later, when Leona comes spinning through the wide glass doors and starts down the steps of the hotel, her head high in the yellow sunshine, her white skirt blowing in the breeze, her purse on her arm, she looks so radiant and young that Edith almost forgets that Leona has ever done anything to hurt her. Edith's chauffeur steps smartly out of the car, clicks his heels, tips his cap, and holds open the rear door for Leona. When they are enclosed at last in the back seat of the automobile, Edith leans forward and rolls up the glass partition between them and the driver. The car turns slowly down the long, curved drive, away from the hotel, and Edith says, "I've—learned that Mr. Winslow still plans to go ahead with his story."

"Yes."

"You weren't able to persuade him otherwise?"

"No."

"But you did try."

"I tried and it didn't work. I'm sorry, Granny."

"Well," Edith says with a sigh, "that's still no reason to run away for two days. When I heard you were here, I was afraid you were trying a more—physical approach to him. But I'm glad it wasn't that."

"No, it wasn't that."

"We shall just have to sit tight, then, and prepare ourselves for the worst—from Harold. He'll be furious with us both if a story appears, and it may delay my getting the money to you for your gallery. But you'll get it, don't worry—though it may take a little longer. I'll see that you have it." Then she adds, "And with no letters to Gordon. I'm sorry about that. It was a bad idea."

"No, it was a good idea, Granny," Leona says. "I've thought about it, and I've written to both of them."

"I beg your pardon?" Edith says. "Both who?"

"Both Gordon and Jimmy. I've asked them to come."

"Gordon and *Jimmy!* Are you out of your mind? Whatever *for?*"

"It didn't seem fair to ask one and not the other."

"Fair! You talk about fair after this—this God knows what that you've been up to with some man? You mean Gordon and Jimmy both here at the same *time?* Do you intend to use my house for this? To hold a *convention* for all your old husbands? Oh, how can you do such stupid things! It's one thing after another with you, isn't it? Not that I think there's a chance in the world they'd both ever come!"

As the large black limousine descends through the streets of Charlotte Amalie, through the heavy noontime crush of bicycles and traffic, Edith says, *"Now* why are you crying? I merely said I don't think there's a chance in the world they'd both come. Do *you* think they'd come? Oh, *please* stop crying, Leona!" Gripping the woven handstrap at the side of the door in her gloved hand, Edith says, "Oh, how much longer do we have to go on having these tempests, Leona? I'm spent from them, Leona—do you hear me? *Spent.*"

Seventeen

"And now, if you can believe it, Sibbie," Edith is saying, "they *are* both coming. Jimmy Breed telephoned last night, and there was a letter from Gordon this morning. Why in the world would they agree to such a thing?"

From the top of the stepladder where Sibbie Sanderson stands, her mouth full of picture wire, Sibbie says, "The whole thing is completely nutty, sweetie. It makes no sense at all." Four days have passed, and Sibbie has arrived to hang her new picture. She has decreed that it be hung in the small sitting room in place of the Inness, which has been taken down and now stands in a corner, its face to the wall.

Sibbie climbs down from the stepladder, and surveys her work. "You know," she says, "the more I look at it, the better I like it. Yes, if I do say so myself, sweetie, it's pretty damned good."

"You don't think it's too large for that spot?" Edith asks.

"No, it's perfect there. The only thing it needs is better light. It should be lighted from the top, with a museum light."

"There's one over Papa's portrait in the library."

"Let's switch it," Sibbie says.

"But the bulbs are burned out."

"Got any fresh ones?"

"Look in that little drawer."

Armed with fresh light bulbs and lugging the stepladder, Sibbie leads the way into the library. She places the stepladder in front of the Sargent and mounts it.

"Hello, Papa," Edith says softly. And then, looking up at the two of them—the tall, thin, intense-eyed man in evening clothes and the large woman in the ballooning dirndl and copper bracelets who lean toward each other, face to face, almost nose to nose—their combination is so bizarre that she has to laugh. They look as though they are about to dance.

"What are you laughing at?" Sibbie asks, screwing in bulbs.

"Be careful Papa doesn't come crashing down on you."

"Boy," Sibbie says, "what I wouldn't give to own this picture, sweetie."

"Would you like it, Sibbie?" Edith asks. "I could leave it to you in my will."

"When I think of the prices Sargent gets—"

"Well," Edith says tartly, "I'm certainly not going to give it to you if you plan to sell it. Anyway, it should probably stay within the family." Then, looking up at Sibbie on the ladder, she says, "The only explanation could be that they're both still in love with her."

"Well, I wouldn't even try to look for an explanation if I were you, sweetie. It's all too nutty. Besides, I don't believe in love. Not with these young people. All it is is sex. Here, hold this for me," she says, handing down a burned-out light bulb.

"But what am I going to *do* with them, Sibbie—this husband-convention I seem to be having? Where am I going to *put* them all?"

"When do they get here?"

"Jimmy arrives this afternoon, and Gordon will be here by dinnertime."

"How's she coming with her art gallery thing?"

"It's—progressing," Edith says.

"Hmm," Sibbie says. And then, "Now try the switch."

Edith flips on the switch, and the portrait lights up.

"My God," Sibbie says, standing back so abruptly that she

almost topples off the stepladder. "My God, what a man!"

"Yes."

Sibbie stares at the picture for a moment, and then says, "Run get me a screwdriver, sweetie, so I can get this bracket off."

But Edith, looking up at her father's illumined, hard-jawed face, says, "No. Let's leave him with his light. He needs his light. It's good for him . . ."

The imminent arrival of Gordon Paine and Jimmy Breed has posed, for Edith, something in the nature of a hostess' dilemma. She has, she realizes, let things slide a bit around the house in recent years—particularly in the area of mattresses and pillows, sheets and bedding. Curtains too, in some of the upstairs rooms, have disintegrated and have never been replaced, and a number of the smaller bedrooms are simply no longer habitable—certainly not in fit condition for receiving guests. And so, Edith has somewhat reluctantly concluded, the best solution is to give Gordon her own room. Naturally it is a nuisance to have to move out, but this—after saying good-by to Sibbie—is what Edith and Nellie are doing now: emptying dresser-drawers and closets, preparing the room for Gordon, and carrying Edith's things to one of the bedrooms in the back of the house. As for Jimmy, he will simply have to put up at a hotel. It will put a better appearance on things if the two are not under the same roof, and it will also reduce the chances of any friction between them. Whether either man knows that the other is coming is something Leona has neglected to mention.

One hopes that Jimmy will behave himself. Edith's most enduring picture of him was obtained in a motion-picture newsreel she happened to see a few years ago. The film showed a New Year's Eve crowd scene in Times Square, but one young man stood out from the crowd. In white tie and tails, he was seated cross-legged on the roof of a taxicab that was moving slowly down the street, and the young man—it was unmistakably James Machado Breed—was very carefully pouring a magnum of champagne over the windshield of the taxi, while the taxi's windshield-wipers beat furiously at the froth.

* * *

"Do you remember the night you poured champagne over the car?" Leona asks him. "That was how you celebrated your New Year's Eve. I celebrated mine in the hospital, miscarrying our baby."

"Ah, bitter, bitter," he says. "How can I be blamed for not being around for something I was never told was happening?"

The afternoon sun has left the beach, and most of the afternoon swimmers with it. They have the beach to themselves, the sand pocked with the indentations of hundreds of feet, and as they walk they add their own to the existing craters—craters which the tide and the trade winds will have erased by morning. Jimmy still wears the city clothes he wore when she met his plane—arriving, as she had guessed he would, with only a slim brief case for luggage—but he has left his jacket in the rented car, along with his shoes and socks, and he walks in his shirt sleeves and bare feet, his trousers rolled up above his ankles. Leona has removed her shoes too. Jimmy stops now to nudge a piece of rockweed with his big toe. "Ah, the lure of tropic islands," he says. "I might have known this was where you'd be. You always come winging back here, don't you, Lee, like a boomerang."

"I'm glad you came, Jimmy."

"Well, a letter like the one I got from you made it kind of a command performance. The age of chivalry is not dead, in spite of what you read."

They continue along the beach. "Gosh," he says wonderingly, as though bewildered and delighted by the thought, "but I did use to drink a lot, didn't I? I don't drink like that any more, though, and it's too bad. They were kind of fun, those drinking days."

"I never liked you when you drank. It changed you."

"Well, that was the point, for God's sake. I was sowing my wild oats. But you can't blame me for that either, Lee. You've sown a few yourself, I understand, since I saw you last."

"I know."

"But then one day I realized that no matter how much or how fast I drank, the distillers of America could always make the stuff faster. I saw I couldn't win. That's why I cut down. I was being outdistanced by the distillers of America. Besides, I'm not a kid any more." He bends his head to her. "See the bald spot that's the envy of all my friends? And neither are you, I might add, a kid any more, Leona."

"I know that too. That's why—"

He cuts her off. "When are you going to tell me what's up? Why the command performance?"

"I want to wait till Gordon gets here."

He stops dead, looking at her. "Gordon?" he says. "Gordon Paine, the squash player? The man you married—Gordon Paine? *He's* coming? Jesus, Lee—what is this? A double post mortem? When's the next plane out of here?"

"Please, Jimmy—it's important to me to talk to both of you. I had a dream—"

"A dream!" He snorted. "You had a dream. Oh, Leona, come *on!*"

"I'm quite serious. I thought if I could talk to both of you—"

"It *is* a double post mortem. You, me, and Gordon Paine. Jesus, Lee!"

"Please try to be nice to Gordon when he gets here. He was nice to me once—when you weren't being quite so nice."

"*Nice* to him? Why shouldn't I be nice to him? I'm crazy about Gordon. Gordon's a prince. He's like a brother. He's a damned stuffed shirt and a horse's ass and you know it. Besides," he adds, "there's no question of my being nice to him because I'm not even going to see him. I'm leaving. To hell with your fun and games." He turns and walks to the water's edge.

"Please," she says. "It isn't fun and games. It's the most serious thing I've ever done."

He stands with his back to her, looking out at the water, his hands in his pockets, and says nothing.

She crosses the sand to him and touches his sleeve. "Please, Jimmy."

"It's always the same with you, isn't it? Fun and games."

"Not this time, truly. I thought if we could meet—on neutral territory—"

"Neutral territory! This is about the most un-neutral territory you could have picked—your own private little island hideaway. Remember how you used to threaten to go to Saint Thomas?" He mimicks her. "'I'm just going to go to Saint Thomas, where people are *nice* to me.'" He kneels, still with his back to her, looking out at the sea. "You don't seem to realize how stubborn you used to be," he says, "how determined. Being married to you was like being married to an institution. Like being married to the First National City Bank."

"I'm different now. I'm broke now. The institution is on its last legs. Please don't go till I've said what I want to say to you both."

"Hell," he says quietly, trailing his fingers in the scurf of a wave, "I'm already here. I might as well stay."

"I've got you a nice room at Smith's Fancy. Granny says she doesn't have room for you both—only for Gordon. But I've got you a pretty room."

"Granny," he says, still not looking at her. "She never changes either, does she? Good old Granny." He stands up and dusts his palms on his trouser legs. "Well, let's go say hello to the old dragon." He starts back along the deserted beach to where he has left his car.

"Actually," Leona says, to fill the awkward silence that follows, once the hellos have been accomplished, "this was really all Granny's idea."

"Ah," Jimmy says, nodding gravely. "The wisdom of the elders."

"Well, I wouldn't say that, Leona," Edith says hastily. "No, it wasn't my idea at all." They stand in the small sitting room, and Edith says, "Well, sit down. Let's have a drink. What'll you have, Jimmy? What is it you young people say? Name your poison?"

Jimmy smiles, passing a hand across his mouth. "Nothing, thanks. Not right now."

"Hm," Edith says. "That's not like you, Jimmy. Well, *I'm* going to have a drink." She goes to the cellaret and splashes whisky in a glass. "No," she says. "My father was always holding little family meetings. I'm not sure they ever accomplished much." Then she says, "I'm sorry I can't ask you to stay at the house, Jimmy. But I think, under the circumstances—"

"Don't give it a second thought, Mrs. B," he says. "I'm all checked in at Smith's Fancy."

"Not to be Mrs. Grundyish, but I just don't think it would *look* quite right if both you men were staying here."

"Of course," Leona says thoughtfully, "since Jimmy's the first one to get here, he really should be the one to stay at the house, shouldn't he? Would you stay here, Jimmy, if Granny'd let you?"

"It's not a question of *letting* him, dear."

"Would you, Jimmy?"

Smiling at Edith, Jimmy asks, "Am I invited, Mrs. B?"

"Well—" Edith hesitates. She is certainly not going to give up her own room for Jimmy Breed. And yet she has already moved out of it. There are other rooms, to be sure. She starts to ask: Do you really think this is wise? Then she says, "There's a slight problem of sheets and pillowcases."

"In the Navy, I slept between the same pair of blankets for five weeks."

"Well, I suppose I can do a little better than the *Navy,*" Edith says.

"Oh, thank you, Granny," Leona says. "Nellie?" she calls. "Will you phone Smith's Fancy and tell them Mr. Breed won't be staying there? Ask them to send Mr. Breed's things over here. Oh, isn't this nice?" she says to Jimmy.

Edith looks at both of them under raised eyebrows.

Then there are things to do—to try to put another of the back bedrooms into as decent shape as possible, and get Jimmy settled there. Then it is two hours later, and quite dark, when the three of them gather in the sitting room again—Leona bathed and changed—and, since the two of them have still refused her offer of a drink, Edith has fixed another for herself which is beginning to have the desired effect: it is putting her in a better mood. The sound of another car is heard stopping outside the house, and Leona goes to the window and says quietly, "Yes—it's Gordon."

"You have your quorum," Edith says, adding a tot of whisky to her glass. "Hooray."

"Hello, Gordon," Leona says as Nellie ushers him into the room

Gordon is shaking hands with Leona now, but he is looking at Jimmy Breed. Gordon is a very erect young man, not as tall as Jimmy and more compactly put together. He stands very straight, and his tailor does well by him in emphasizing the straightness of his spine. Edith has never seen the two men together before, and it is interesting to see how Gordon's chiseled neatness contrasts with Jimmy, who is big and loose-limbed and whose general attitude is sloped and lounging. Well, Edith admits, at least Leona has always chosen good-looking men for her husbands. They are both that. The two men face each other now. "Bit of a surprise to find you here, Breed," Gordon says.

"Life," Jimmy drawls, "is full of surprises."

"May I ask what you're doing here?"

"I could ask you the same question," Jimmy says. "And get the same answer. She asked me to come."

There is a long silence then. Leona stands very still.

Then, nodding in Leona's direction, Gordon says, "Our friend here looks well, doesn't she?"

"Yes, she does indeed."

Wishing, briefly, that Gordon would not refer to her as "Our friend here," Leona says, "You've both got to be very nice to each other. It's one of the rules."

"Oh, we have rules for this?" Gordon says.

"Have a drink, Gordon!" Edith says, in a voice that is louder than she intended.

He shakes his head. "No thank you." To Leona he says, "I only meant that from the tone of your letter I expected to find you at death's door."

"Well, *I'll* have another," Edith says, and starts toward the cellaret which, for some reason, seems a little nearer to her than she thought it would be. She bumps into it, rattling all the bottles and decanters. But fortunately no one seems to notice.

"It's good to see you, Edith," Gordon says, the only one of Leona's husbands permitted to call her by her first name.

"And it's nice to see you, Gordon."

Gordon sits down carefully in one of the straight chairs. Looking around the room, he says, "Now all we need is the Spanish count."

"Oh, we certainly don't need him!" Edith says.

Jimmy taps out a cigarette from his silver case—a case which, Leona suddenly remembers, she gave him long ago. Standing in the center of the room, she says, "Actually we probably should have Edouardo here. I thought of it. But he's in Alcalá and he seemed difficult to import."

"Oh, Leona! Not that dreadful man!" To Gordon, Edith

says, "His mother stole her diamond earrings!"

"I heard he gave you quite a run," Gordon says.

"Oh, *quite* a run," Leona says. "The quickest, fastest run I've ever taken in my life. I've still got a stitch in my side from it."

"Not to sound smug, but I warned you, Leona," Gordon says.

"Of course you did," Edith says.

"Poor Leona."

"No. Don't say 'Poor Leona.' None of you really knows anything about Edouardo. Oh, dear, he was—"

"Don't let's talk about him," Edith says.

Slowly moving across the room, Leona says, "Why not? I don't mind. On the beach at Torrevieja, we had a quarrel. And, to get even, Edouardo took his little speedboat and, right in front of everybody, picked up Alfonso, the little fairy beach boy, and ran off with him. They were gone till the next morning. It was a strange way for him to get even with me."

"Disgusting," Edith says.

"And the quarrel was strange too. It started because a little boy came galloping along the beach on a horse, and the horse kicked one of Edouardo's water skis that was lying there, and nicked it. Edouardo was furious. He went chasing down the beach after the boy. He yanked the boy off the horse and began cuffing him. He dragged the boy back—just a little boy, no older than eight or nine—and Edouardo insisted on calling the police. 'Don't be silly,' I said. 'Just over a nicked water ski. What difference does it make?' But the water skis were a new pair—"

"Purchased by you, I'm sure," Edith interjects.

"—and the paint was chipped, and Edouardo called the police. The police came and took the little boy away—the police in Spain are such terrible-looking creatures, I could have wept. *'Soy el Conde de Para-Diaz,'* Edouardo kept saying. 'I am Count Para-Diaz. . . '"

Gordon shakes his head. "A bad actor from the start," he says. "I knew it the minute I laid eyes on him."

"But he was beautiful. Beautiful to look at."

"The pretty-boy type," Edith says to Gordon. She moves cautiously to the cellaret again, adds a little whisky to her drink, surveys its level critically, then adds a little more.

"There was a cruel streak in Edouardo that was very puzzling," Leona says. "Once he said to me, 'Let's go out and gaff some turtles.' So we went out in the boat to a place near the mouth of a stream where we'd seen some sea turtles swimming, and sure enough, there they were—their heads above the water, very handsome Roman-looking heads. I drove the boat and Edouardo stood in the stern with the gaff, and he'd shout to me, 'There's one!' And I'd try to head for it, and he'd try to get the gaff into it. 'What are you going to do with the poor thing if you catch one?' I asked him. He shrugged. The point was to catch one. But fortunately the turtles were quicker than Edouardo, and every time out boat came racing at a turtle, he'd just sink, like a big green grand piano under the water, and Edouardo would stand there, cursing and screaming. Cruel—"

"The dirty Spik," Gordon says.

Leona looks quickly at him. "Don't use that word."

"I'm sorry, Leona. But—"

"I don't care. I don't like that word. Don't use it again, please. He was my husband. I married him. It wasn't his fault he had a cruel streak. He was descended from cruelty on both sides."

"You're well rid of him," Edith says.

Leona's eyes are gauzed, meditative. "He was a member of the human race," she says.

From the chair where she has seated herself, Edith says, "Oh, brother!"

Suddenly everyone is looking at her. "Why, Edith," Gordon says, "I don't believe I've ever seen you smoking."

"I hardly," Edith says, carefully holding the lighted match to the end of the cigarette, "ever do."

Then they are all silent for a while. Jimmy, who has said almost nothing since Gordon's arrival, sits folded on the sofa—like all big men on sofas, his knees stick up—his eyes studying the ceiling. Gordon breaks the silence. "Well, when's the inquisition start?" he says. "Or whatever it is that this is supposed to be."

"It's not an inquisition," Leona says. "It's discussion. I'm taking you both out to dinner—to Bluebeard's. Come on. Let's go."

"Oh," Edith says. "I thought you could all have dinner with me tonight. A party. . . ."

"Do you mind if we don't, Granny?" Leona walks to where Edith sits, bends, and kisses Edith lightly on the cheek. "Remember," she whispers in Edith's ear, "this really *was* your idea—basically."

Watching them go out the door, Edith thinks: Well, perhaps Leona is being very modern. But what is to be accomplished by this? What has been accomplished thus far—aside from the fact that she has gotten herself a little squiffy from all the drinks with which she had tried, without much success, to bridge the gap between generations. A little hiccius-doccius, as the British say. She gets out of her chair and moves slowly through the rooms to the stairs, mounting them carefully, her hand gripping the railing. When she gets to her bedroom she stands for a moment, eyeing the murderous little Oriental runner in front of her bathroom door. The evil yellow swastikas of its design catch in the lamplight, echoing their old colors, and seem to squirm. Yes, perhaps this is why the rug has turned against her: it is old, fifty-four years old; old and crabby and tired of doing what it has always done. Too late, it has decided to rebel, just as most of us decide to rebel too late. She does not dare walk across it now, in her present condition, not even as an endurance test. She makes a wide, careful circle around it, into the bathroom. The bathroom smells of fresh flowers. Then she remembers that, for the time being, it is not her bathroom. It is Gordon's.

The three of them sit at a candlelit corner table in the restaurant at Bluebeard's Castle. *Purified*, Leona is thinking, having glimpsed, when they came through the bar, Arch Purdy at a table with another girl. It was an act of purification that she performed with him. Why is it possible to walk through mud and come out feeling cleaner on the other side? Yes, she is almost tempted to go over to Arch's table and tell him that she is happy—happy he has found a warm, compliant girl to share his tender evenings with. Because he wasn't so bad—not mud at all, though she had thought it would be mud when she first stepped into that room with him. He wasn't so bad and, purified by him, she wishes him well. In retrospect, nothing was so bad. She has never felt so sure of herself before. "Now remember this is my evening," she says. "I don't want any arguing over the check when it comes." She looks around for a waiter. Smiling, she says, "I'm afraid Granny had a little too much to drink tonight."

"I thought it politer not to mention that," Gordon says.

Turning back to them, tracing the rim of her water glass with one red fingernail, she says, "Poor Granny. She tries so hard to get to know me, but I've never really let her. I don't know why." Then she says, "Now tell me—both of you—what made you come? I wasn't at all sure you would."

"I came," Gordon says, leaning toward her, "because you sounded as though you were in some kind of trouble, and needed help. And I'm sure Breed here came for the same reason."

Jimmy, slumped in his chair, shakes his head. "No," he says. "I came because I was curious. I came to see what was up. Which I still don't know."

"I was about to burn another bridge behind me," she says, "and I suddenly didn't know why. I've always been a bridge-burner, without knowing why."

"And now," Gordon says, "you're wondering if some of those bridges can be re-erected."

"No," Leona says. "It isn't that exactly. It's that I suddenly thought perhaps the two of you knew more about me than I knew myself. It's as simple as that. This afternoon, for instance, Jimmy said I was stubborn and determined—"

"*Willful* would be my word," Gordon says. "Rash. Impetuous. Rushing into things without examining them first. No self-discipline. One might even say spoiled, because there's always been someone to pull you out of your jams as soon as you've got into them."

"But I wouldn't have come," Jimmy says, "if I'd known this was going to be a group-therapy session."

"Not that there's anything wrong with group therapy, of course," Gordon says.

"I also want to know," she laughs a little helplessly, "why all my marriages went wrong. I think it must be my fault—somehow. And who can really tell me but the two of you?"

"In other words," Gordon says, "you want, before you turn over a new leaf, to examine some of the old leaves. You want to return to some point in the past and start over. It's a sensible enough idea, Leona—except for one thing. As Shakespeare said, you can't go home again."

Jimmy, who has been making some sort of pattern on the tablecloth with paper matches torn from a folder, says, "It wasn't Shakespeare. Anyway, that's a lot of nonsense. Who says you can't go home again?"

"Have you ever tried it, Breed?" Gordon asks a little sharply. "With any success?"

"But—" Leona tries to interrupt.

"Go home all the time," Jimmy says. "For weekends, Sunday dinner with the folks. It's a lot of fun. Don't you ever go home to see your mother, Gordon?" He clicks his tongue, and returns to his match design.

"Of course I go home to see my mother!" Gordon says. "I was speaking of home in a larger sense. As I'm sure Leona is not too dense to understand."

"If I were going to try to change—" Leona begins.

Gordon cuts her off again. "Another misconception," he says, and she wishes that he would not always be so flat, so pedantic. And a dark thought scurries through her head: *Was* this all a terrible mistake, as Granny said? "People never change," Gordon says.

"More damned nonsense," Jimmy says. "People change all the time. They change for the better, and they change for the worse."

"Not basically," Gordon says.

"Look at me. I've changed. I used to be a playboy, now I'm a stockbroker—whether that's for the better or for the worse I don't know. I'm not saying Lee's changed, though," he says, looking at her with a slow smile. "Or," he says quietly, "that she really needs to change much, except—"

"Except what?" she asks him.

"Except to stop looking at herself through a microscope all the time. If someone's a louse, and starts trying to find out *why* he's a louse all he ends up doing is *proving* he's a louse!"

"Are you trying to say Leona is a louse?" Gordon demands.

Looking steadily at her, Jimmy says, "What happened before—you were only eighteen. Things like that happen when you're eighteen. It's that simple. Don't try to make things complicated, Lee."

"What happened before, as I recall," Gordon says, "was that you showed signs of becoming a habitual alcoholic."

"Now just a minute—" Jimmy begins.

But Gordon turns to Leona again. "You see," he says, "you've always run away from things. You ran away from boarding school, as I recall. You ran away from Bennington with—" he nods in Jimmy's direction "—him. You ran away from me, and for a pretty silly reason. My main thought for you, Leona, if you want to understand this pattern of yours, is that you should see a psychiatrist. I went to see one, after our divorce."

"Did you, Gordon?" she says. "So did I. But it didn't help."

"It didn't?"

"No," she smiles. "I don't know why, but the whole time I went to him—it was only a couple of months—I kept feeling I had to entertain him. He used to look so bored. And the facts of my life seemed so dull and ordinary that I started making things up. Lurid dreams that I hadn't really had. But the trouble was, he never seemed to know the difference between what was true and what I was making up."

"You were blocked," Gordon says. "If you'd continued the treatment you would have unblocked."

"But he never seemed to *care* whether I was telling the truth or not. It began to seem so pointless."

"It is not his job to care whether you tell the truth."

"Well, what's the point of going to an analyst, then," Jimmy interrupts, "if it isn't to get at the truth?"

"The doctor is interested in truth in the larger sense."

"Baloney!"

Leona thinks that food might help but they have been ignored since sitting down at the table. They have not even been given menus. She looks around the room, trying to catch a waiter's eye.

"What was your doctor's name?" Gordon asks her.

"Hardman," she says. "Gordon, see if you can get us a waiter."

"I've never heard of him," Gordon says. "My man's name is Doctor Edmund Zauner—I'll give you his card. Marvelous man, and an enormous help to me. It occurred to me that the divorce thing might have been my fault. Well, as it turned out in the analysis, it wasn't. Of course, in analysis, things are never that clear-cut—there's no such thing as anything being anybody's fault. But Ed Zauner dug up some pretty interesting things about me, and I think one of them might pertain to you. It seems I had a deep-seated and unconscious fear of failing. Of inadequacy. Actually," he laughs modestly, "it turns out that the basis for it was the fact that I was never circumcised."

Jimmy, who has been busy with the torn-out matches, suddenly says, "Jesus! What a thing to have to live with! Gosh!" he says, smiting his forehead with his big square hand. "I can see it—all the other boys giggling when Gordon came into the shower room. And for twenty-five bucks you could have had it fixed! I need a drink after that one." Turning in his chair, he says, "Where are the waiters in this place?"

"Well," Gordon says quickly, ignoring Jimmy's outburst, "it turned out that I had this fear of failing and that, in compensating for this, I was unconsciously projecting myself into situations were *I had to fail*. Do you see my point? Well, in terms of yourself, Leona, this running-away business is probably an expression of the same anxiety neurosis, and—"

"Now wait a minute," Jimmy says. "Are you trying to say Lee's crazy?"

"Waiter!" Leona cries, waving forlornly to the back of a disappearing white jacket.

"Running away is a highly neurotic pattern. It indicates—"

"Please," she says. "We promised—no arguments—"

"I want to hear what this uncircumcised nut has got to say! Go on with your story, Mr. Paine, and with what it's got to do with Lee."

Gordon looks at him. "I see, Breed, that you are also something of a bully."

"Gordon—Jimmy—stop this, both of you."

There is a long pause. "Please explain," Jimmy says, "what you mean by *also* something of a bully."

"I mean that in addition to being a lush and a no-good, you are also something of a bully."

"Just a minute," Jimmy says. "*Just a minute!* Repeat that, what you said."

"I said," says Gordon smiling, "that in addition to being a lush and a no-good, you are also something of a bully. And also a noisy roughneck."

On his feet, Jimmy says, "Why, you lousy little Dartmouth stuffed-shirt prig, do you think I'm going to let you get away with that? You're also a goddamned bigot. You're an anti-Semite, you're a—"

"Stop! Just stop!"

"It's not a defenseless woman you're speaking to now, Breed."

"You're goddamned right I'm not, you dirty little wife-stealing shyster. Sniffing around my apartment and taking out my wife behind my back."

"Your back was usually planted on a barroom floor."

"Stop!"

"Would you care to step outside?"

"I damn well would!"

"Oh, please—please stop this!" Leona begs. She tries to pull both of them into their seats again, but they push her hands angrily away. She turns to the room at large. "Please—somebody stop them!" But all she sees are, now, too many waiters and a restaurant full of bored, disinterested faces turned upward from dinner plates and cocktails to observe the commotion at the corner table.

"You said let's go outside. What're you waiting for? Have you changed your mind?"

"I have *not* changed my mind!"

"Well . . ."

"Oh, come on!" Leona says. "This isn't *about* anything!"

The two men start rapidly for the glass door which leads from the dining room out onto the terrace, and Leona runs after them.

On the terrace, the two men face each other. Leona turns once more to the restaurant and calls, "Can't somebody stop this?" But now the bored and somewhat less disinterested faces have moved to the door and to the windows to watch. Leona hears:

"The big one'll flatten him. Look at the size of that bastard's shoulders . . ."

"Don't be too sure. The little one looks pretty wiry."

"What's it all about, anyway?"

"The little one's a Jew. The big one made some crack about Jews."

Gordon and Jimmy remove jackets and ties and toss them in a heap on the terrace. Gordon removes his wrist watch and Jimmy, grateful for this suggestion, removes his also. Then they face each other again, crouched this time, rocking on the balls of their feet.

"For the last time, I'm telling you to stop," Leona says.

At the first blow, both men stagger apart, stumble, and fall on their hands and knees on the terrace. For a moment, they approach each other, on all fours, panting. Then they are up again, swinging, and for several minutes the air is filled with the cracking of fists, and the grunts, and groans, and gasping breaths of the two opponents. They fight in these guttural voices, uttering no words, and shirts rip, and suddenly they are both on the ground again, rolling over and over across the terrace, pummeling each other as they go. Jimmy is certainly the heavier one, but Gordon, as that observer observed, is wiry, and keeps himself in shape with squash and handball. It is so ludicrous, seeing them tumbling about on the terrace and punching each other like schoolboys, that Leona almost laughs. If they were even fighting over her she would laugh. But instead she begins to cry. "Oh, you damn fools!" she says. "Damn fools!" She turns and runs back into the restaurant.

To reach the front door, she must pass through the bar again. As she pushes through the crowd, a man's hand reaches out to detain her. "Hey," he says, "is that ruckus out there over you?"

"Arch," she says, "will you help me break it up?"

"Are you kidding? I don't want to get mixed up in it. I've got something for you," he says, reaching in his pocket. "From this morning's paper." He hands her a small clipping.

"What?"

"Thought you might be interested," he says. "Well, see you around."

"Yes," she says.

Standing under the orange light by the front door, she reads:

> Rumor has it that one of the nation's top business weeklies will explode this week with a story on the wheeler dealings of that enigmatic Wall Streeter, Harold B. Harper. Details are still unknown, but sources say the story will make the fur fly at Harper Industries, Inc. H. B. Harper is the son of West Indian sugar baron Meredith Harper and uncle of socialite Diana Gardiner. His grandniece is ex-deb Leona Harper Ware, popular and much-married Jet-Setter, presently the Countess Edouardo Para-Diaz. . . .

"Are you all right, Miss Harper?" the doorman asks her.

"Please get me a taxi."

Eighteen

FIVE years ago, in the winter of 1959, Nellie came to Edith to tell her that a Miss Mary Miles was here to see her. It was a minute or two before Edith connected the name. She went downstairs, and there she was—a little old lady, much wrinkled, wearing a beige suit, beige shoes, and a little beige hat. "Did they ever get a decent girl for your mother?" was practically the first question she asked.

"It took some finding, after you left. Mama had her ups and downs."

She clicked her tongue. "Exactly as I feared," she said.

"She had a series of little strokes. They were what finally made her stop. Those strokes scared her just the way you used to scare her, Mary."

"When did she pass on?"

"In nineteen fifty-one."

"Well, that was a nice long life, wasn't it—considering? And your father? Gone too, of course . . ."

They went into the sitting room for tea. Mary Miles still

worked as a nurse, she said, but she was on holiday. She had taken herself on a Cunard winter cruise, and the cruise had a free day in St. Thomas.

"And your baby?" Mary said. "Grown and away, I suppose."

"Grown and away. Here's a picture of her I ran across in a magazine."

"Gracious!" said Mary Miles, looking at the picture. "Isn't she elegant? Hard to think I was the first person to take her in my arms."

"I follow her career in these magazines. And I have a grown granddaughter now." She got Leona's picture from the table where it stood. "This is Leona."

Mary studied the picture. "Very pretty," she said, and handed it back. "My. How times does fly." Then she said, "And your husband? Is he still living?"

"Charles died years ago."

"Ah. Well, we women do seem to live longer than the men. Persistent creatures, aren't we? And rather mean of us—to hang around so long after the men are gone." And then, with that sudden forthrightness that is so particularly English, she said to Edith, "By the way, whatever happened to the girl your father was having the affair with? What was her name?"

"Monique."

"Ah, yes. French. Did that little fling ever run its course?"

"Until he died. Then they wandered off."

"Found some other meal ticket, I suppose. *Sycophants* was the word for them. And I've never understood it, Edith, why your father let that woman say things about you that she did. She used to say you were an immoral woman. She cornered me once and tried to tell me that you misbehaved with every man in sight—even tried to convince me that you had misbehaved with her husband! Your father could have stopped her, but it was almost as though he didn't want to. You know, I really think he loved you very much, and then suddenly began to hate you for some reason. Was it when you broke those pearls? Well, he was a very queer fellow, your father."

"Yes, queer."

"And to think that your mother had to put up with that woman all those years. Poor little lady. She was a lady, you know—for all her airs."

* * *

Edith had only one other meeting with her father. It occurred several months after Charles was buried, when her father arrived unannounced one evening at her house. This was at the beginning of his long decline, and the decline had begun to age him. The United States' purchase of the islands, which all the planters had taken as a signal of better days to come, had turned out to be the opposite. Almost as soon as the purchase had been accomplished, the United States government stuck a knife in the planters' backs with the passage of the treacherous Volstead Act. The rum market collapsed, and cane sugar did not fare much better. Many of the planters left, but Meredith Harper stayed on, struggling to establish new markets in Canada and elsewhere, losing money at a steady rate. She noticed that he had begun to stoop and that the climb up her front steps had made him short of breath. "I have some papers for you to sign," he said. She took him into the library, where they sat down. He handed her a sheaf of legal documents.

"What is this all about?" she said at last.

"This is your consent to make me Diana's legal guardian. She can continue to live with you, but as my ward. We have decided that this is best."

"I'm not going to sign any such agreement. Take these papers back."

"I'm sorry, but I'm afraid you must."

"Must I indeed? Well, I won't. You're not going to take Diana from me."

He sat forward in his chair. "I'm afraid you can't refuse, under the circumstances. There is some question as to whose child Diana is."

"There is no question. Now get out of here. I'm sick to death of you."

"Not until you sign this agreement."

She ripped the agreement down the middle and threw the pieces on the floor. "There. Now go."

He looked at her with expressionless eyes. "Then you force me to take other measures," he said. "I shall take it to court and start adoption proceedings. She'll be taken away from you altogether on the grounds that you are an unfit mother. My own daughter is a common hunker, a slut, a whore."

"Oh, Papa. Go away."

"You don't think I'm serious?"

"All right," she said, "take it to court. If you do, I'll fight it. I know a few things about you, and I'll shout them from the rooftops! We'll see what your precious name and reputation look like when I get through—and which of us looks the more *unfit* to take care of a little child."

"You wouldn't dare." He was struggling out of his chair, and suddenly his hand went to his chest. "I'm sick," he gasped. "My heart . . ."

"Get out of this house and don't ever come back."

"I'm dying . . ."

"Oh, I wish you would die, Papa."

She watched him struggling and gasping in the chair for several minutes, wondering if he actually *was* dying. Finally she went out of the library and out of the house to the street where his chauffeur sat, dozing over the steering wheel of the car. "Mr. Harper's sick," she said, prodding the man's shoulder, "you'd better come in the house and get him."

Of course he was not dying. It would take more than a few strong words from her to kill him. It would takc more of the heart attacks, real or feigned, which she heard about. His death was speeded by an increasing accumulation of business problems. Prohibition, which he never lived to see repealed, undoubtedly helped. So did the collapse of investments in Germany, and the worthlessness of his accounts in prewar Deutschemarks. When he died it was peacefully, in his sleep, in his house at Sans Souci and, though the fortune he left was a far cry from what it had been, he was too widely diversified to have died poor. He died worth roughly twelve million dollars, and the marvelous simplicity of his last will and testament was in all the newspapers. In dying, Meredith Harper succeeded in taking Diana Blakewell away from her mother in perhaps the most effective of all the ways at his command. He left her three of his millions.

"My beloved daughter Edith," his will stated, "will understand why she is not to partake of my Estate, since she has already been separately provided with her rightful share. I do, however, bequeath to her my gold signet ring embossed with the Harper family crest, which I instruct her not to dispose of. The remainder of my Estate I will to divide in four equal portions, thusly: To my devoted wife, Dolly Elizabeth Bruce

Harper, one fourth; to my sons, Harold Bruce Harper and Arthur Meredith Harper, one fourth each; and to my granddaughter, Diana Harper Blakewell, one fourth. My elder son, Harold, who upon my death shall become head of the Harper family, I appoint as trustee of all funds and properties accruing to my other heirs." Not a penny to any of his servants. Not a penny to Monique Bertin. Not a penny to charity.

"This is a great deal of money you will be receiving, my dear," Edith had written to Diana, at school in Westchester at the time the details of her grandfather's will were published. "I trust you will not let it go to your head. . . ." But that much money, in all likelihood, had already gone to Diana's head, and it stayed there.

After her husband's death, Dolly Harper, also wealthy, decided to move to Paris. She was tired of the tropics, she said, and after all she was not old—sixty-seven was not really "old," was it? She didn't feel that old, and she didn't think she looked that old, did she? She begged Edith to go with her, and Edith remembers her mother on the day she left, wearing a traveling suit of dark blue wool, a blue hat and gloves. She was still a handsome woman, still thin, and she had taken to wearing the cosmetics that were by then the vogue—red lipstick, rouge, and nail lacquer. But her handsomeness had acquired a certain angular, haggard quality, and she stood there, gold bracelets jangling, tapping the pointed toe of one blue patent pump on the floor, and said, "*Please*. Come over and join me, Edith—for a little while, at least. We'll have fun. We'll do the couturiers, and the modistes—the opera, the theatre, the ballet. We'll entertain . . ."

And then they heard, along the grillwork of the garden gate—*click, click-click-click-click*, and the children's voices, "Edie, Edie, fat and greedy . . ."

In a rush of perfume and dark blue wool, her mother came toward her. "Listen to that! Oh, Edith—have sense! Have some sense. Don't stay here another minute. Think of Paris. Haven't you had enough of this wretched island? Can't we go back to people who are our equals, away from this riffraff? Don't give yourself up to the Hottentots! Aren't you sick of islands? Every dreadful place I've ever lived has been an *island*—from Staten Island to this dunghill. I'm ready for continents now, aren't you?"

She shook her head. "No, Mama."

"You're giving yourself up to this terrible island, to a life too hideous to think about. You'll end up like everybody else here. Nigger men and women sitting, dreaming in doorways, waiting for something to happen that never does happen, that never will happen—"

"But this is my home," Edith said, not meaning it to sound melodramatic. After all, she reflected, it was high time she discovered what a home was.

After Dolly Harper left, Edith Blakewell stood in the garden for a while, looking out at the hills and the town below, at the harbor, sickle-shaped, with Hassel Island trapped in the blade's path. Though she could not see any of the others, she could feel them there—the satellite islands circling and guarding the craggy quarry of St. Thomas. Buck Island, Little St. James, Great St. James, Mingo Cay, Thatch Cay, Hans Lollik and Little Hans Lolik, Outer Brass Cay, Inner Brass, Cricket, Cockroach, Savana, Saba, Water Island, Hassel—the queer little names which she knows by heart reminding her that this is home. With Hassel Island, the circle completes itself, begins again with Buck Island, Little St. James. . . . And, after a while, she began to feel that she was not giving herself up to the island at all, but that the island was being offered at last to her, and she stood admiring the amplitude and wonder of the gift.

From that day, it was seven years before she saw her mother again—when failing health and the threat of another war in Europe drove Dolly Harper back to the island again.

Now, from the small back bedroom where she has temporarily put herself, she hears footsteps in the hall outside. Leona's meeting, apparently, is over, and Edith cannot help thinking that it did not last long. She considers getting out of bed and going to Leona's room for a report on the evening's proceedings, but decides against it. Questions of chaperonage and supervision of this quaint gathering of people also occur to her, considering Leona's own somewhat . . . lax attitudes. Oh, to the devil with it, she thinks. Let them both sleep with her, together or in relays, all night long if that's what Leona wants! Edith lies back on her pillow and closes her eyes. She has developed a splitting headache and, a few minutes ago, giving in to it, she reached for the bottle with Alan's prescription—ONE CAPSULE, AS NEEDED, FOR PAIN—and took a pill.

* * *

At Bluebeard's Castle, the fight has continued for perhaps twenty minutes, and the two opponents have long since rolled off the terrace and down the slope of dry grass where they grapple and pound at each other now, under the sea-grape bushes by the wall. They have taken brief, mutually agreed-upon rest periods, then thrown themselves at each other again, and most of the spectators, bored with the fight and by the non-appearance of any decisive victor, have gone back to their dinners or their drinks.

In the panting darkness under the bushes, Jimmy Breed suddenly goes rigid and says, "Jesus! What's that?" Both men lie still.

"Huh?" Gordon says, looking up. "Oh. One of those damn lizards."

Five inches of gray chameleon are stretched on a twig above them. The creature stares down at them with wicked eyes.

"They're harmless," Gordon says.

"Yeah. But Christ, they always give me the creeps."

Jimmy pushes himself to his feet and begins brushing himself off. He spits out a bloody wad of saliva, and wipes his mouth. Gordon starts to rise, and Jimmy gives him a hand and pulls him to his feet, and then the two men totter, and lean heavily against each other like ancient lovers parting. "You all right?"

"Yeah, I guess I'm all right. Are you all right?"

"I guess so. Come on inside, I'll buy you a drink."

"No, I'll buy you a drink."

Jimmy's shirt has lost a sleeve, and the back of it is ripped out from the collar, and Gordon's shirt is also torn and bloody, and one leg of his sharkskin trousers is torn from the bottom of the side pocket down to the cuff.

"Can't go in this place looking like this," Gordon says.

"You're right. Got to get cleaned up."

"Where'll we go? Can't go back to Mrs. Blakewell's looking like this. Granny'd . . ."

"Granny . . ."

Suddenly they have both fallen against each other again, this time roaring with wild, almost giggled laughter, repeating, "Granny . . . Granny!" Just the mention of the word *Granny* is enough to set them off again. Staggering back, hugging his sides, Jimmy says, "Did you see her when she . . . practically . . . fell over the bar?" They both collapse again, doubled up, choking and gasping with laughter. Then there is silence.

"Where's Leona?" Gordon asks. "Probably in the laides' room, I guess."

"No," Jimmy says almost absently. "Not if I know her. She's left. Leaving is a specialty of hers."

Somehow, this seems funny too. "Yeah," Gordon says. "Well, we've got to get cleaned up somewhere . . ."

Gordon has lost a shoe. Groping about on their hands and knees in the darkness under the bushes, looking for the lost shoe, Gordon says, "I'd say the hell with it, but it's one of a pair I had made in England . . ."

Crawling about beneath the bushes, patting the earth, their heads crack together.

Sitting back on their heels, they rub their heads. "No harm done," Jimmy grins.

"No, no harm done."

"Granny . . ."

Giggling softly, they resume the search for the English shoe.

Leona has been lying for a long time in her dark bedroom, still in her clothes, on top of the coverlet. She has tried to light a cigarette, but her shaking hands cannot control the match, and she has had to give up. Now she lies very still in the darkness. Escape. Just escape. Run just as fast and as far as you can, farther and faster than you've ever run before, faster than you ran from Edouardo, farther than the moon. "I'm sorry, Madame, there are no night planes out of St. Thomas." "But I must get on a plane. It's urgent. It's a matter of—" "I'm sorry, Madame." Frightened, she thinks; yes, frightened. For the first time in your life you are really frightened, and it is almost a relief to know that this is what being frightened is like, and that there is absolutely nothing left to do. She hears hushed male voices in the hall beyond, murmured good nights. She lies very still. Then she hears her doorknob turn, and a tall figure stands silhouetted in the doorway. "Leona." The door closes. "Turn on the light."

She snaps on the light. "Jimmy . . . you're hurt."

"Never mind about that." He moves toward her, and then stops abruptly as he sees her airplane ticket lying on the dressing table where she has left it. He picks it ip. "Yes," he says softly. "That's what you'd do, isn't it? Hop a plane out of here—leave old Gordon and me with your grandmother. What the hell? Gordon and Jimmy are big boys now, they can find their own damn way home. Little Leona's in a bigger hurry. Has a man ever beaten you up, baby? Because somebody's going to one of these days—really smash that beautiful jaw of yours and knock you halfway across the room. If I had the energy I'd do it myself, right now." He puts the ticket down.

"Jimmy—I didn't want this to happen!"

"Shut up. Who cares if you wanted it to happen or not? You haven't *wanted* a lot of things to happen, but they've happened, and they've happened because you've made them happen. What did you *expect* would happen, for Christ's sake—from this crummy trick you've pulled, dragging us down here just to flatter your poor little hurt ego."

"It wasn't that!"

"Shut up. This is the cheapest, ugliest idea you've ever had, and you've had a few. What did you expect it to be? A ladies' tea party? Are you just *stupid?"*

"All right! I admit it was a mistake! I admit it!"

"Sure—I should think you might. Now. And what do you do whenever you find out you've made a mistake? You hop a fast boat out of wherever you are. A plane is even faster! You've been hopping planes out of situations you've created all your life, baby, and do you know why? Gordon thinks you need your head examined, but I don't think your problem's as fancy as that. You're just selfish—selfish and lazy. A selfish, lazy slob!"

"I admit it!" she cries. "I admit it! I know."

"A slob who's managed to get away with murder just because you happen to have a pretty face. Well, I'll tell you something about that face, baby, the years are beginning to show. I give that face about five more years, and then what'll you have? You'll be a tough little middle-aged woman, exactly like your mother. You've lost one thing after another—peace, grace, love, in that order. Your looks will be next. And what do you do each time you lose one of those rather important qualities? You run."

"I think if I keep running I might get there! Somewhere!"

"Somewhere. That's a lot of bull because you don't run

anywhere at all, except in great big circles. You land up in the same places time after time, all ready to make another big mess for yourself."

"I know all this! That's why I can't bear myself."

Looking at her, his eyes glitter. "You know what you are?" he says. "You're pathetic. Not tragic. Just pathetic. You're too pathetic even to beat up." He sits down heavily on the corner of the bed, his back to her, and puts his head in his hands. "Jesus!" he says. "And it's like talking to a bank. Like bawling out the First National City Bank."

"No," she whispers, "because I know everything you say is true."

A thin trickle of blood descends from the corner of his mouth, and he wipes it away with the back of his hand.

"Jimmy . . . you're hurt."

"You've hurt a lot of people, haven't you? You're going to run out of people to hurt one of these days. Then you'll have only yourself to hurt."

"Do you think you need a doctor, Jimmy? Your lip . . ."

"To hell with my lip. Your little meeting has accomplished one thing, Lee. It's taught me not to underestimate Gordon Paine. And that I could use a few sessions at the gym when I get home." His head hangs between his shoulders and he runs one hand through his thinning hair. "Peace, grace, love," he mutters. "In that order."

"But don't you see? I want those things back, Jimmy. So badly!"

"I used to be something of a slob myself, you know," he says. "But all these years I've worked, trying to make myself into some kind of a human being. Not you. You're still the same as you were that day you killed—that little boy. The same."

"Oh, but couldn't I try, Jimmy? Couldn't I go on trying?"

"Run . . . hide. All these years. You ought to be ditched, you know. Dumped. But why can't I ever dump you? I've tried, though. All these years. Tried to shake you out of me, but I can't. Isn't it funny? You're stuck in me some funny way, and you won't shake loose. But Christ, I've tried."

"Jimmy!"

"So what could I do when you called," he asks in a whisper, "but come?" His body sags back across the foot of the bed. "Got to go now . . . too tired . . ."

She rises to her knees on the bed and puts her arms around him, holding him almost desperately. "Jimmy, Jimmy," she says to that beaten face, "couldn't we go back to the beginning and try to begin again? Not the same beginning, a different one—and try? Oh, couldn't I have another chance? Just one more chance? I'd try! Jimmy, I promise you I'd try! I'd try so hard!"

Nineteen

"WHO is that funny-looking old lady?"

"Why, don't you *know?* That's Edith Harper Blakewell—yes, the old despot's daughter. Still lives here. She's pretty much taken for granted now, but in her salad days, around the first world war, she was the talk of the island. They say she had lovers by the score . . . there was a French one who was the husband of her father's mistress—how's *that* for planning? Sexy old harridan—her husband finally walked out on her. They say she took up with a new man at the age of fifty-five! Oh, she's odd as Dick's hatband now—a bug about water conservation. But she's done a few things for the island, gave a wing to the hospital, built the marine museum. . . ."

Talk like this has drifted through her window, or over her garden wall, or across the square as she sits in the back seat of her big, Detroity car, pretending to doze while John waits for the policeman under the umbrella to raise his white-gloved hand and signal them to proceed.

It would certainly not be true of a woman like Edith Blakewell to say that there were no more men in her life after her husband died, and after her mother and her daughter moved away. There were several. Two of them treated her well. One of them cost her money. None of them meant anything to her, perhaps because at that point she no longer wanted a man to mean anything to her, or to offer her anything more than consolation, like candy; Edith doesn't really know. All she knows is that she has managed to forget their names over the years; they have blurred into one. All, that is, except Wallace Townsend—the one the gossips refer to as "the new one at age fifty-five"—who, ironically, was never a lover at all. (Poor Wallace would blush crimson if he knew he had assumed the position of lover in peoples' minds.)

The gossip at the time seemed to center on the fact that Wallace was several years younger than she—the old lady, it seemed, was turning to young men to try to recapture the luster and innocence of her youth. Nothing could have been farther from the truth. It was not the youth of Wallace Townsend that appealed to her; rather it was his quietness and gentleness, his industry and scholarship. There was no romance between them, though she had, once, asked him to kiss her—a mistake, the suggestion distressed him so. Romance with a woman, Edith has since decided, would not have been a possibility for Wallace. Not that he was a feminine man, but his manliness was more an abstraction of that quality. Once, on one of their walks, Wallace slipped and fell on a bit of crumpled wall and hurt himself in a sensitive place. His horror at Edith's witnessing the accident was not, it seemed to her, a result of the physical pain but more because the area of the pain drew her attention to his sex. Edith loved him for his company, and grieved for the disappointments of his life. At college in the Middle West, he had been a promising young scientist. If he had continued in his field Edith is certain he would have become one of the great archeologists of his day. But his father had died, and he had had to discontinue his studies to support a quarrelsome mother at a job he hated. He had finally come, after his mother's death, to St. Thomas with his savings. He had heard of the Indian kitchen middens that are still occasionally unearthed on the island. Edith often gave him meals and, in that sense, helped support him. She also gave him a room in her house for his books and papers. By day, they walked, explored, and dug.

Edith helped him sift the ashes and humus and sea-sand of the buried middens, helped him catalogue the sea-shell implements, bones, artifacts, and fragments of broken Indian pottery that they found. She remembers their joint excitement whenever they discovered a piece of pottery whole, and she still has a small, simple mortuary vessel he gave her, and which he explained had doubtless been filled with foodstuffs, fruits, cassava bread, perhaps even human flesh, which were to serve the departed on his journey into the beyond. It was curiously appropriate, she thinks now, that she should have been left with the past, and a quiet companion to help her probe deeper into it, back into Indian prehistory, before any white man knew these islands existed, pulling aside all the diluvia of time. They walked the middens until the day he died.

Now it is morning again, another day. What went on last night is quite beyond her. Coming down this morning and finding the three of them at the breakfast table, Edith had merely stared at them. "We had a little disagreement last night, Granny," Leona said. "But we're all friends again." From the looks of the men's swollen, bruised faces and bandaged hands, the disagreement must have been considerable. Today, at least, they seem subdued. But Edith has really stopped trying to understand what is going on. Sibbie, she has decided, was right; it is past trying to understand. It is too nutty. After breakfast, taking a picnic basket, the three friends departed for the beach.

On the dresser in Leona's room, Edith has come upon the unused half of Leona's airplane ticket, written out to that same unlikely name: "Mrs. L. Diaz." The date for the return trip is still a blank, but Edith knows Leona must be thinking of going or she would not have taken out the ticket. However, Edith reminds herself, Leona cannot leave until she gets her gallery money. She will have to wait for that. This reminds her that Harold must have received her letter, and she wonders how long it will be before she hears from him. "Get a wiggle on, Harold!" she whispers aloud. Yes, she realizes with a pang, it's true. She would like the money to arrive immediately, now; she would like them to be gone—Leona, all of them; she is ready for the old, complacent, Edith-centered peace to return to her house. She stands there, holding Leona's ticket in her hand. Beside her, the telephone rings.

"Mother?" she hears someone say. "Mother—is that you?"

"Diana!" she says in surprise. "Where are you, dear?"

"In the West Palm Beach airport. Mother, what's going on down there?"

Edith laughs. "Well, I don't really understand it myself," she says. "It was Leona's idea. How did you hear about it?"

"*Hear* about it! It's going to be in all the evening papers!"

"Oh, Diana—you're not serious."

"The hell I'm not. *What is going on down there,* Mother?"

"Don't shriek so! She simply wanted to invite them both. And did."

"What? What are you talking about?"

"Leona—Jimmy and Gordon."

"*What?* Oh, Mother, for God's sake! I'm talking about this magazine story and all the things you've been saying about us and this whole business about the Luxitron Corporation and Uncle Harold's maneuverings, and—"

"Wait! Don't talk so fast, Diana. I can't understand. What is it?"

"This magazine story I'm holding in my hands."

Edith holds the phone very close to her ear. "What does it say?"

"Well, besides making Grandfather sound like a monster and a maniac—practically whipping slaves and making old men jump over tennis nets, according to *you*—in addition to that—"

"Yes . . . what else . . ."

"What they're saying about Uncle *Harold*. And Luxitron!"

"What is this Luxitron?"

"You're going to hear of nothing else until this thing is settled. Where is Uncle Harold?"

"I don't know. Isn't he—"

"His office said he's in St. Thomas."

"But why should he be here?"

Diana's voice becomes a wail. "He *must* be! Mother, our Harper stock has dropped twenty points since the market opened!"

"Stocks go up and down, it doesn't affect—"

"Oh, Mother, how can you be so stupid! Don't you see—this story calls Uncle Harold a crook."

Edith hesitates. "Well," she says defiantly, "he always was a crook!"

"Oh, wonderful! Why didn't you tell *that* to the reporters?"

"Well, I'm sure that if there's anything in that story that isn't true, Harold will sue."

"What good will that do? Our stock is dropping! Mother, I'm getting on a plane now and flying down there. Don't do a thing till I get there; don't talk to anybody. We've got to figure out something, and find Uncle Harold."

"You're coming—here?"

"I'll be there in an hour and forty minutes."

"Is Perry with you?"

"I've left Perry, but that's another story. No, I just have Poo and Mrs. McCutcheon."

"Oh, dear! You've left Perry?"

"We don't have to talk about *that* now, do we, Mother? Oh, they're calling the plane. I'll be there at one twenty-five. Have your car meet me."

Dazed, Edith sits on the edge of the bed for several minutes. There is really only one person in the world who can give her a straight answer on this, and that, of course, is her brother Arthur. And why, she thinks, didn't she go to Arthur right in the beginning, the minute there was any doubt about Mr. Winslow, instead of entrusting it all to Leona? Why does she always think of things too late? She picks up the phone and gives the operator Arthur's number in New York. After a delay the operator reports, "I'm sorry, there is a long list of calls stacked up for Mr. Arthur Harper. Your call will have to wait its turn. I will call you."

"Thank you," Edith says, and hangs up the phone.

She has been clutching Leona's ticket in one hand, and has crumpled it considerably. She goes to the dresser and flattens and smooths the ticket as best she can. She goes out of Leona's room toward her own. At the door, she stops. "Your Harper stock is not available at the moment for the purposes you have in mind," she remembers. She stands quite still, her hand on the doorknob, leaning against it. She had told Leona that they would have to prepare for the worst. But, she thinks, now that the worst—whatever it is—seems about to happen, we have made no preparations for it at all.

She steps into the bedroom and rings for John.

"Take the car and find Miss Leona at the beach."

His cap in his hand, John says, "Which beach, Miss Edith?"

"How do I know which beach?" Edith cries. "Try all the beaches! Just find her and bring her home right away."

"Oh, dear God," she whispers when he has gone. "Dear God. . . ."

But Edith cannot lie down with a cold cloth over her head and worry—not with Diana on her way. There is the problem, now, of where to put Diana. And Poo, and Poo's nurse. Diana is so particular. Diana must have a nice room, with plenty of closet space and of course its own bath, and here in the islands Edith knows that Diana likes cross-ventilation when she sleeps. Then she remembers the room Wallace Townsend used for his papers and specimens. The walls are lined with bookcases and cupboards, and she is sure the room needs a thorough dusting, but there are two largish windows—one with a sliver of a view of the sea—and it is on the side of the house, over the library, which means it is shaded and cool and away from the noise of the street. Diana has always been such a light sleeper (sleeping with a black domino over her eyes and plugs in her ears), and that room of Wallace's is one of the quietest in the house. It has a bathroom (which, she suddenly remembers, is missing a toilet seat, but someone can run into town for one of those or, if necessary, borrow one from one of the other bathrooms). A bed will have to be moved in and, yes, a dresser, and surely there are some pictures around the house that could be hung on the walls to brighten things up (the Inness, of course, which Sibbie's picture made homeless), and she will tell her girls to pick some flowers, and isn't it nice to have so many things to do to keep one's mind from worrying?

A rosebud in a bud vase beside Diana's bed. And a bowl of cigarettes, and an ashtray. The windows themselves could probably stand a washing, if there's time. Diana notices everything that's out of place. If only Jimmy and Gordon weren't here, it would all be so simple. It will be Wallace's room, and the result may be a little makeshift but perhaps, just possibly, Diana will understand. Edith thinks isn't it odd that this big house, which was built for so much large-scale entertaining, will never have had such a large crowd under its roof before? Edith sits at her desk making furious lists of things to be done. Then she rings for Nellie to summon her staff into emergency session. In the middle of everything, she remembers that Diana asked to be met at the airport. But John has been dispatched with the car to look for Leona, and now there is no one to meet Diana!

Less than two hours later, Diana's Vuitton trunks and suitcases and hatboxes form a small pyramid in the front hall. "Why wasn't I met?" were her first words. "I had to take a taxi."

Now Diana, still in the suit and gloves and hat she arrived in, is on the hall telephone, talking to the Long Distance operator. "I don't care how many calls he has stacked up!" she says. "This is urgent. This is his niece, Diana Gardiner, and I must speak to Mr. Arthur Harper immediately. . . . Yes, it's an emergency!"

Diana neglected to mention that, in addition to her son Poo, and Poo's Scotch nanny, Mrs. McCutcheon, she was also arriving with her two white standard poodles. The excited dogs leap and bound about the hall, bejeweled with rhinestone-crusted collars, dash into the drawing room, and come careening out again, barking, and the even more excited Poo runs after them, screaming with mad glee, while Mrs. McCutcheon in her gray uniform runs after Poo, saying, "Now, sonny. . . . Now, sonny. . . ." Edith stands in the center of the hall, trying to read the magazine article that Diana has flung into her hand.

"No! I tell you this call *must* have priority," Diana says. "Put him on at *once*. Operator, tell them that this is his niece calling, Diana Gardiner. If he knows it's *me* he'll talk to me, you idiot woman! Yes it *is* essential. . . . No, I can't wait!" Covering the telephone mouthpiece with her gloved hand, she says, "Poo, sweet, can't you see that Mummy's on the phone?" And then, "What? What did you say, Operator?"

"Now, sonny . . ." says Mrs. McCutcheon in pursuit of Poo.

"In his efforts to gain stock control of the juicy Luxitron Corp.," Edith reads, *"the senior Harper brother began, some six months ago, a carefully devised campaign . . ."*

The dogs return from another whirling tour of her house, with Poo and Mrs. McCutcheon behind them, and Diana is saying, "Give me the Chief Operator. . . . Give me the Supervisor . . ."

". . . Instead of staging a proxy battle, Mr. Harold Harper chose . . ."

Poo comes running into his grandmother's knees and nearly overturns her, and the two white dogs dance around them in a circle. Then one of the dogs stops, stands still, and then begins to sit in such a fashion that it is quite apparent what is going to happen next.

Diana, seeing it, points and screams, "Oh—look, look!" too late. "Oh, Marcel, you naughty boy!"

"Mrs. McCutcheon, please get these animals out of here!" Edith says. "Take the dogs, and Poo, out into the garden."

"Is this the Chief Operator?" Diana says. "I must get through to Mr. Harper. It *is* an emergency. . . . yes . . . I'll hold on . . ."

". . . Availing himself of every scrap of Harper Industries stock he could lay his hands upon" (Including mine, Edith thinks. Including mine) *"Harper went to the banks, the big boys. To the money men of Wall Street, it came as a surprise . . ."*

"I'm holding, Operator. I'm holding. . . ."

"Meanwhile, the SEC, long suspicious of illegal 'insider' activity in connection with the rapidly rising Harper stock, moved quietly in to investigate. Was Harper himself forcing the price of his stock upward? Why? To increase its borrowing power so that he could wrest control of giant Luxitron? To the Street at large" (Oh why do journalists have to write like this? Edith thinks) *"it looked as if Harry Harper was a genius, he had the Midas touch. The SEC was not so sure."*

"Operator, can't you just cut in on whoever it is he's talking to? . . . Why not? Why can't you just . . ."

"When Luxitron officials first got wind of Harper's scheme is not yet known, but simultaneously they learned of the SEC's peculiar interest in him. One thing was clear immediately: Luxitron wished no part of Harry Harper. As the Market rose, with heavy trading in both Luxitron and Harper . . ."

"Why can't you just unplug one of those little plugs and plug *me* in . . . ?"

". . . and with 24% of Harper Industries stock still family-owned, and personally controlled by Harry Harper" (But you don't control mine, Harold—not mine!) *"and, with considerable charm and what appears to have been a good amount of plain old-fashioned gall, wangling smaller shareholders into letting him be 'custodian' of their shares . . . with promises of fat gains, supplemented by an organized whisper-campaign that Harper was 'hot' . . ."*

"Operator? Operator? I've been disconnected! Operator. . . ."

Diana Jiggles the bar on the telephone rapidly up and down.

"Borrowing furiously . . . forcing the price of his stock upward, and then borrowing more . . ."

"Oh, what the hell's the matter now? Operator? Hello?"

"Meanwhile, in St. Thomas, V.I., where the original Harper fortune was amassed (Harper-West Indies Sugar Products, Ltd.), the only member of the Harper family willing to discuss brother Harry's curious juggling act is his older sister, plumpish, peckish Mrs. Edith Harper Blakewell, also an important Harper stockholder. If her stock has played a role in Harry's adventure, Edith Blakewell seems unaware of it. Concerning her brother's activities, she has only this to say: 'As long as my checks come once a month, I don't ask questions.' When informed that Harper stock had doubled in the last six months, Edith Blakewell replied, 'Gracious! Is that good or bad?' The answer to her question will come from the Securities and Exchange Commission. . . ." (This is all your fault, Leona, Edith thinks. You made me see that Mr. Winslow.) *"At this point, a glimpse at the family's business history is more than a little revealing. . . ."* Turned, twisted, her words to him that afternoon about her father fly back at her like knives.

"'Where you find sugar, you will also find flies. . . .'"

"Uncle Arthur? Uncle Arthur, it's Diana—" Edith hears, and puts down the magazine.

"Yes . . . yes . . . but where *is* he? Obviously the first thing to do is find where he is. Yes . . . but what do they mean 'illegal'? Is borrowing illegal? Couldn't we just say—listen to me, Uncle Arthur, I know a little bit about money, don't forget. I'm not *Mother*. Is my stock involved in this?" She puts her head in her free hand, and her voice becomes soft and small. "Yes. Oh, good God! How much? Good God. But look, couldn't we say we knew about it, we approved—? Oh, good God. . . . No, no I'm here at Mother's. . . . Yes, she's here. Just a minute." With her face absolutely blank, Diana holds out the telephone to her mother. "He wants to talk to you," she says.

Edith takes the phone from Diana who sits, huddled and still, in the chair beside her.

"Edie," his distant voice says, "Edie, this is terrible . . . it's godawful, Edie."

"Tell me what happened."

"The banks are calling for more collateral. I don't know

where I'm going to get it. We're trying—"

"Where is my stock?"

"The banks have it all."

"He stole it . . ."

"There are more people involved in this than just us. I'm just beginning to find out. It looks as if—Jesus, it looks as if he's been borrowing on thousands of shares that were never his. I had no idea what he was up to—honestly I didn't. If I'd known—"

"Of course . . . of course."

"The extent of it. . . . We're just beginning to find out. There are company funds we suddenly can't locate, Edie. Do you understand?"

"Where is Harold?"

"He left at noon yesterday, and we can't locate him. There's nobody at the house. We can't locate Barbara. It looks as if—"

"He's run away."

Beside her, Diana stiffens in her chair. "Run away. Oh, the dirty, yellow, chicken-livered coward! Of course he's run away."

"All because of what this magazine says, Arthur?"

"The magazine just brought it before the public. Apparently there was a letter from you, asking for your certificates. I think that's what scared him, Edie, because he didn't have them. By noon yesterday, the stock was off two points. He must have known then that the jig was up. And today, when this story hit—Edie, you can't imagine what it's been like. You'll be getting calls, I'm sure, from reporters. But none of us is talking to the papers at the moment, do you understand? If I were you, I'd take my phone off the hook and leave it there for the next three days. And don't see anybody who comes to the house. We don't want to make any announcements till we know exactly where we stand."

"I understand."

"And frankly, Edie, where we stand looks pretty bad. It looks godawful."

"Oh, Arthur . . . oh, Boots . . ."

"And don't blame yourself about the magazine story, Edie. It was bound to come out sooner or later. The SEC's had its eye on him for months, as it turns out. If this story hadn't come out this morning, the SEC would have published its findings next week. So don't blame yourself."

"Yes."

He chuckles softly. "But I must admit you had some colorful things to say about Papa," he says.

"Arthur, believe me, I had no idea—"

"But they were all true, weren't they? All true. Well, good-by, Edie. I'll be in touch as soon as I know more."

Edith hangs up the telephone. Diana is on her feet now, and has lighted a cigarette. She moves slowly and absently about the hall, the cigarette trailing from one hand, and for several minutes the only sound is the clicking of her thin heels on the polished floor.

"I still don't understand it," Edith says at last.

"Don't you?" Diana says in a dead voice. "It's simple. He's broken every SEC regulation in the book that's all. Borrowed money on stock he didn't own. Taken company money without authorization. We could say we gave him our permission to mortgage our share, but they'd just charge us with complicity. It's against the law, you see, to try to force the price of your own stock upward. He could go to jail for this—and may. And now our stock is dropping, and Luxitron is dropping because of his connection with it, the banks are calling for collateral—and where's Uncle Harold? He's—just—run away. Robbed us and run away!"

"At least Arthur's doing his best—"

"Arthur! He's such a sad sack!" All at once she turns to Edith and cries, "Mother! This is all your fault! *You* did this!"

"I did not do it. Harold did it. I broke no laws. Harold broke laws."

"So what? If you'd kept your trap shut, he might have gotten away with it, and we'd have all been rich. Now we're paupers! Paupers! Oh!" And leaping over what the dog has done in the center of the floor, Diana Gardiner comes running at her mother, her gloved hands upraised, as though to tear her mother limb from limb.

Edith is saved from Diana's flying hands only by sudden, terrible shrieks from the direction of the garden, shrieks that seem to come from several people at once, and that are accompanied by the sound of running footsteps. Edith and Diana stop, then run to the front door. On the veranda they are met by Mrs. McCutcheon, dripping wet, her straw-colored hair down across her face, her gray uniform clinging to her adhesively. She has a wailing and equally dripping Poo in her arms.

Mrs. McCutcheon glares at Edith accusingly. "He fell in your pool!"

"Oh, Poo—Poo! How did it happen?" Diana cries, accepting the damp, sobbing burden of her child.

"He was running and he ran right in! I had to jump in after him, and I'm no swimmer, either!" Mrs. McCutcheon says, continuing to look at Edith as though it, too, were all her fault.

"Well, I can see that neither of you is drowned," Edith says, as Poo coughs and spits and sobs.

"Really, Mother! You should be more careful of that place with tiny children around! It's not safe! That pool should be fenced! And Poo hates salt water!"

Edith is about to make a retort to this, but changes her mind. She would say to Diana that if Diana spent less time trotting Poo around with her to Paris dress collections, and more time teaching him how to be a little boy, and how to swim . . . but she doesn't say any of these things. She goes to the wet and howling grandson in her daughter's arms. "Poor little Poo!" she says.

But Poo takes one terrified look at Edith and screams, "Mum*ma-a!*" and throws his arms around Diana's neck and buries his face against her shoulder, and the destruction of the afternoon seems complete.

But Diana says, "Oh, Poo—don't you remember your own dear Granny? It's your own dear darling Granny, Poo. . . ." There are tears in Diana's eyes now, and then both women are weeping over the weeping child. And Mrs. McCutcheon, sensing that a family crisis has arisen which excludes her from its significance, withdraws.

The little Negro chauffeur, in his dark green uniform and polished boots, walks slowly along the crowded beach, the sun flashing on his bright brass buttons. He nods, smiling, at old friends, for he is a well-known figure on the island, and he stops to make occasional polite inquiries. Then he continues, peering at groups of reclining bodies, scanning the swimmers in the sea. Curious faces turn upward and follow his zigzagging progress.

Leona, Gordon, and Jimmy are discussing the newspaper clipping she has shown them. Gordon, the lawyer, and Jimmy, the broker, have different opinions.

"This is simply from a gossip column," Gordon says. "I wouldn't make too much of it if I were you. Besides, these so-called exposés are never quite as startling as the magazines make them sound as though they're going to be. There are such things as libel laws."

"Still, there's been an awful lot of talk along the Street," Jimmy says.

Leona is the first to see the approaching John. She jumps up from the sand and says, "Oh, dear. Something's happened."

Twenty

"You!" Diana Gardiner is screaming at Leona. *"You* did this! This man was a friend of yours, it seems! You let him come here, let him talk to Mother!"

Leona sits huddled in a velvet chair, a cigarette between her shaking fingers.

"Now wait a minute, Diana," Edith says, "Leona honestly didn't know—not in the beginning—that this was the kind of story he was going to write. Be fair. It was a mistake on Leona's part, but it was an honest one."

"Read it!" Diana says, waving the magazinc at Leona. "Just read what he says!"

"I've already read it," Leona says quietly. "He showed it to me."

"You see?" Diana cries to Edith. "She *knew!* She knew it all along! He showed it to hcr. And she did nothing! Just sat here like a silly goose, going to the beach! Didn't you *comprehend* what he had written? Did you just sit, doing nothing at all while he went right ahead ruining us?"

"I tried," she says. "I tried to stop him."

"How? In what way? By saying *please?* Uh!" she snorts and hurls the magazine, pages fluttering, to the floor. "Did it even *occur* to you that the *only* sensible thing to do would have been to call Uncle Harold *immediately* and tell him what this man was planning to say about him? It seems to me that any halfway intelligent human being, with an ounce of family loyalty, would at *least* have thought of that. But no. You didn't do anything. With a little advance warning, Harold might have been able to stop it. Now it's too late. Because you sat on your fanny in the sun."

Gordon Paine, a few minutes earlier, mumbling something about getting dressed for dinner, has managed to escape the scene and the women's voices. But Jimmy Breed has remained. He sits in the corner of the room, saying nothing, his face grave, his eyes intently on Leona.

Diana picks up her highball glass and rattles the ice cubes. She extends the glass in Jimmy's direction. "Fix this for me, darling, Scotch and water," she says, not looking at him. He stands up slowly and takes Diana's glass.

"Oh, I'm through with you, Leona!" Diana says. "I don't think I ever want to see you again. How I ever could have produced a child like you I'll never know!"

"Now Diana," Edith says. "Harold *was* up to some kind of monkey business! He had no right to borrow money on my stock."

"Mother, if Harold had had the *teensiest* warning that this was in the wind, he would have done something—at least have been ready with a rebuttal. But this caught him off his guard. No, Mother," she says, shaking her head. "You see? She's Jack Ware's daughter. That's all she is—Jack Ware's daughter." She touches her eyelids, brushing tears away.

"Don't say that to me, Mother!" Leona says.

"Why not? It's true! I never should have married him, and I never should have had you. You were both bad—bad news, right from the start. I married a stupid, disgusting man, and had a stupid, disgusting daughter."

Leona jumps up from the velvet chair. "What about this news of you and Perry? *That's* pretty disgusting, if you ask me!"

"My personal life is none of your affair. But if you want

to talk about personal lives, take a look at your own. What are you? Just a little tramp."

"Oh!" Leona says, and starts for the door.

From the bar where he is stirring Diana's drink, Jimmy turns and looks steadily at Leona. "Taking off?" he asks her in a quiet voice.

Leona stands very still in the center of the room.

Then there is a long silence. Jimmy returns with Diana's drink, and offers it to her. But Diana, weeping silently in her handkerchief now, does not see his outstretched hand, and so he places the glass on the table beside her chair. Edith sits looking at a space of floor between her feet. Leona continues to stand addressing Jimmy with her eyes. Suddenly Diana's head comes up, and she sniffs. "I smell smoke!"

"What? Oh, good heavens!" Edith cries.

And now they are all on their feet, for a cloud of very dark smoke is rising from the cushion of the velvet chair where Leona had been sitting.

"It's her cigarette!" Edith cries. And then, "Oh! Help! Help! Nellie!" she shouts. "Help! *Fire! Fire!*"

Nellie, rushing in, apprises the situation quickly, and is the only one with presence of mind enough to seize Diana's highball from the table and empty it on the fire. There is a noisy hiss from the interior of the chair, and then a penetrating, acrid smell in the air.

"Now, on top of everything else, I'm an arsonist," Leona says to no one in particular.

At this point, Edith thinks, the best suggestion would be that they all repair to their rooms to change for dinner. The four mount the stairs together, in silence, and move in their separate directions down the upstairs halls.

When she opens the door to her bedroom, Edith stops abruptly. A man—Gordon Paine, no less!—is standing, stark naked, in front of her pier glass, examining his body for cuts and bruises.

"Hey!" he cries a little wildly, seeing her, and he makes that curiously girlish gesture of trying to cover his private parts with his hands. Then he grabs for the bedspread and pulls it off the bed, wrapping it around him. "Hey!" he says again.

"Oh, for heaven's *sake!*" Edith says, recovered from the confusion of finding him there. "I simply forgot you were using this room." Then she says, "Don't worry. I've seen lots better than *that.*" And she slams the door on him.

Outside in the hall she thinks: Isn't it funny. Terrible as this day has been, the sight of Gordon trying to hide himself has somehow redeemed a bit of it. Yes, she thinks, life has its little rewards.

"To the beach?" Edith asks in a drowsy voice. "Oh, Leona, I'm not a beach person—not any more." It is morning again, and Leona stands beside Edith's bed.

"Please, Granny. There's so much I want to talk to you about."

"Why to the beach? Why can't we talk right here?"

Leona nods in the direction of the hall outside, and lowers her voice to a whisper. "I don't want to talk here, Granny."

"Don't be hard on your mother. She's taken all this very badly."

"It isn't that. It's something I want to tell you. Come."

"I hope it's good news," Edith says. "I've had enough bad news for a while."

"Come to the beach and find out. Please."

"Well—" Edith is thinking of such things as beach attire, and of how people her age *sit* on the beach these days, and of sand in the shoes and the underthings. Will there be a folding chair? An umbrella? As though she can hear her grandmother's thoughts, Leona says, "I'll get the things together. All you need to do is get in the car and come. And let's hurry, Granny—before everyone else gets up."

"But what about—" What about people, she thinks? The news is out, it was in the papers, full of words like *swindle* and *manipulator*. Last night the telephone began to ring; it rang until she did as Arthur suggested, removed the receiver from its hook. Surely, on the beach, people will recognize her and say, "There's old Edith Blakewell—I wonder how *she* feels today? Did you read about her brother. . . . Have they found him yet? Do you suppose she's completely wiped out?" This makes up Edith's mind; she would like to know what people are saying. "Very well," she says briskly. "It would do me good to get out. Run along and get things ready, and I'll get dressed."

* * *

When Edith gets downstairs, Leona is nowhere in sight, but she finds Gordon Paine sitting on the veranda, dressed, with his suitcase. Seeing Edith, he jumps up.

"You're up bright and early, Gordon."

He laughs nervously. "Yes, I've got to go, Edith. Things at the office. I—I've got to get back."

"Of course," she says. "Well, it's been nice seeing you, Gordon."

"This whole thing—this business about your brother—is completely incomprehensible, and I'm sure none of it is true. But anyway—"

"I'm afraid it is true, Gordon."

"Anyway, I want to thank you for your hospitality."

"What hospitality? I haven't given you much of that."

Shifting his weight from one foot to the other, he says, "I'm awfully sorry about what's happened. And of course—not that it's apt to come up, but in case it does—you won't mention to anybody that I've been here, will you? To the newspapers, or anything? I mean it sounds like a pretty nasty business, and by the fact that I've been here it might look as though I were connected with it in some way. As though I, or my firm, had been advising you or something. Mostly for your sake and Leona's—it wouldn't look right if my name were involved."

"I understand, Gordon."

"And as for Leona—"

"Yes?"

"She understands that it wouldn't be wise if she and I were seen together for a while. But perhaps, when this thing blows over—"

"Yes."

"I always thought it would be nice if we could patch things up, but—"

"Such things will have to wait a while. I understand."

"Well—" He stands awkwardly, looking embarrassed, his eyes averted. It is as though he thinks she is still picturing him with all his clothes off—which, of course, she is. An auto horn sounds outside the gate. "My taxi," he says, picking up his suitcase. "Good-by, Edith. Say good-by to Leona for me. Tell her I'll be in touch with her—later on."

He walks rapidly along the veranda and down the front steps, carrying his bag.

A few minutes later Leona comes out with her striped canvas beach bag. "Ready, Granny?"

"Yes, I'm ready." They go down the steps to where John waits with the car.

Seated in the back seat beside Leona, Edith says, "You know, I'm almost beginning to *enjoy* this! Isn't that the damnedest thing? It's getting to be fun, in a way—seeing how various people react to what's happened."

Leona touches her grandmother's knee. "When I was little you used to tell me, 'Saying you're sorry doesn't help.' I know it doesn't help. But anyway, Granny, I want you to know I am—terribly sorry."

"Let's not talk about it any more."

Behind John's uniformed shoulders and cap, they descend the hill in the air-conditioned car and then, at the intersection of Garden Street, they are forced to pause to let a short funeral cortege pass by in front of them; it moves slowly, the headlights of its cars blazing, and Leona says, "Hold your breath, Granny."

"Whatever for?"

"For good luck. Whenever you pass a cemetery or a funeral procession, hold your breath. Don't you know that rule?"

The dark little cars crawl by.

Edith taps the window glass that separates them from John, and he lowers the glass. "Who is it, John?" she asks. "Do you know?"

John turns and smiles, showing them the trove of gold in his mouth and speaks in his soft Cruzan patois. "Andreas Larsen. But he was an old man, Miss." (But surely that was not the name John murmured; not him, not today, it couldn't be, because isn't he already dead? Didn't she hear, once, that he had died? No, this is her imagination working; she is dreaming, and this is a dream.)

"Why, Granny—what's the matter? Are you feeling sick?"

"Nothing, nothing." She grips Leona's hand tightly. The cortege passes, and they drive on.

"Did you know the man, Granny?"

"I think so. I'm not sure."

"Ah, Granny. I'm sorry."

Beaches bring everything into such bright focus. Perhaps it

is the dazzle of sun on sand, the sun on the tinfoil surface of the water that intensifies every object, counteracting any gauziness in the air . . . it intensifies the people, the lounging ones, the sleeping ones, the love-making ones, the running and splashing ones. Clad in what goes for beachwear these days—clothes not designed to conceal those few, poor, typically human glands, but rather to emphasize them—the atmosphere of sex is thick and soft as butter in the air; you could slice it with the handle of a spoon. Beaches intensify and focus without clarifying anything. It is astonishing to see, even at this early-morning hour, how many and how much the old beach contains—dried kelp and rockweed, ice-cream sticks, peanut shells, coconut husks, sticky glasses covered with sand and aswirl with the warm remnants of soft drinks, and the rubber balls and the floating toys of children; and the children's screams, and the scolding of mothers, the shouts, the hellos, the dashes into water, the splashes and the squeals and the dunkings and the shrill lifeguard whistles. Leona is off at one of the little shops at the edge of the beach—open, palm-thatched shops that sell everything from popcorn to comic hats—to rent beach chairs for the two of them, and now there is an unpleasant-looking boy of fifteen or so, with a gritty voice and wearing an elasticized figleaf, who comes prancing across the sand with a small barracuda he had netted. Everyone throngs around him to admire this remarkable catch.

"Throw it back!" Edith demands.

"Look, lady," he says, "a barracuda is a dangerous, man-eating fish. You want me to throw him back so he can eat somebody? You must be nuts." And very vigorously and thoroughly he beats it to death by swatting its head an excessive number of times against the armrest of a beach chair. All muscle and openmouthed cruelty, he wields the tiny fish as though it were a billy club, until its head hangs as humbly as a darning egg inside a sock. Gratified, he turns and gives Edith a glum look.

"How are you so sure that it was a male?" Edith asks. "Just because you obviously are? There are thousands more spet like that one in the sea. Destroying one will hardly do any good."

A dream . . .

"How I dislike beaches," Edith says to Leona when she returns with the chairs, unfolding them and setting them up.

"Why, Granny?"

"Because I can't swim in the raw any more!"

They sit down.

"You can't believe how this beach has changed since I was here last," Edith says.

Leona is looking at Edith curiously. "Are you sure you feel all right, Granny?" she asks.

Edith laughs. "No—I'm not sure I am at all! I think I've had too much excitement in the last few weeks."

"And I've brought a lot of it on, haven't I? Well, Granny, one of the things I have to tell you is that I'm going back to New York."

"Oh," Edith says.

"Coming here was—it was a mistake, this time. I'll come back for visits, but they won't be visits like this one. But first I've got to straighten out—oh, so many things."

Edith nods.

"And maybe you'll come to New York and visit me."

"I'm too old for New York. I wouldn't know what to do."

"It's really not that far away. It's not the moon."

"But what about your gallery?" Edith asks. "Of course we'll have to get this other business settled first. This business that's happened with—with whatsisname—with—" (Has she suddenly forgotten her brother's name? "Who are you?" she asks that pale, downy, bored young face. "Harold," he answers.) "With Harold."

"Granny, are you sure—" Leona begins. "Are you sure you feel all right? Are you ill?" What is it, Leona wonders? Is it perhaps only seeing her grandmother in such strong sunlight that makes the old woman's skin look so extraordinarily pale, oily-white, and the bones beneath the skin so fragile? And the white skin hatched with lines, and the mortality of the veined hand she touches . . . is that it? The cruel light?

And Edith is thinking that of course if Leona goes this time, she will not come back, not for visits, not for anything. If she leaves now, they will never see each other again. She sits very still.

"Would you like to borrow my sun hat, Granny?"

Edith shakes her head.

"We might be able to work it out so that you could start your gallery on a smaller scale," Edith says. "In New York—or even here in St. Thomas."

"No, Granny."

"Don't tell me you've changed your mind about the gallery."

"It's just that other things are more important now. Granny, last night I couldn't sleep, thinking of all the things you've done and wanted to do for me. The gallery—everything. You've always been so good to me, and I've hardly ever thanked you—once. But my life was running on such a crazy track. I never seemed to be able to think. Or see. Anything."

"Leona," Edith says quickly, "you don't have to go yet, do you? Can't you stay here with me just a little longer?"

"No," she says, shaking her head slowly. "No, it's time to go." She smiles a small, faint half-smile that seems more like a smile at herself than at Edith. "I'm a city kid, Granny. A jungle cat. It's time for me to go back to my jungle."

"But that's the point. Leave the jungle. Escape now. Escape. Stay here where it's safe and warm."

Her smile fades, but she continues to look at Edith. "The way you did, Granny?" she asks finally.

"Yes, the way I did." Then, all in a rush, Edith says, "Listen to me. No one has ever belonged to me. I've killed or crippled every person I ever loved. Someone has got to belong to me, Leona. Won't you belong to me? Leona, I'm seventy-five years old. Stay here."

At the end of the long silence that follows, Leona stands up slowly, pulling the striped beach towel around her shoulders. She looks away across the sand. "My enemy lives in that jungle, Granny. I've got to find him and track him down." Then, almost as an afterthought, as though it didn't matter, she says, "And there's another thing. I'm not going alone. I'm going with someone." But the look in her eyes says that of course it does matter, and that the words were experimental, spoken to test their permanence and substance upon the ear.

"With a man?" Edith says. "Do you mean you're going to get married again? Is that what you're trying to say?"

"No. He hasn't asked me to marry him, and I don't want him to ask me—not yet. We're not ready for that, either of us. But he is willing to let me go with him, and so I'm going to go with him."

"What?" Edith cries. "You mean you're going to be some man's *mistress?* Who? Short-neck?"

"Oh, look," Leona says, pointing. "There he is—looking for us!"

"What? Where? Leona, listen to me—"

"See?" She waves her hand. "He doesn't see us. Let me get him. Wait here." With the towel over her shoulders she runs off across the beach.

"Leona!" Edith calls.

Edith Blakewell stands up. Her sunglasses are steamed from the salt spray in the air, and she removes them and cleans them with her handkerchief. Standing there in the blazing sun, she is not conscious of the beach any more, and is thinking only: No, I cannot have this; *I will not have this!* Then, like running specks, she sees them coming from the far end of the beach. Hand in hand, darting between umbrellas and around sunbathers, they come—their hands breaking briefly apart, then joining again, as they run. From a distance they wave to her, and a strange thing happens. Edith's eyes blur and she sees, in the young man running, Andreas. He stops to scoop up a handful of sand, and he tosses it, scattering in their path. An indolent woman sunbather turns on one elbow to look at them, and it seems impossible to behold any longer this vision of her own happiness; a surf of years rolls over her, turning her in it, transposing Leona and herself. Then, with an effort, she pulls herself back. Her cobwebbed eyes clear, and she sees that it is not Andreas but only Jimmy Breed.

"Don't look so unhappy, Granny."

The folly of everything she has ever dreamed or planned for Leona overwhelms her. It doesn't matter. He is terrible. They are all terrible—all Leona's men. They have always been; they will always be.

"Granny?"

"Unhappy!" Edith cries. "Oh, I will not *have* this, Leona!" And she turns and runs herself, awkwardly and heavily, away from them, across the beach.

Twenty-One

ONCE more it is Wednesday afternoon, and Alan Osborn is with her. The examination is over, and they are having their brandy in her room.

"So now they've gone," he says.

"They left for the airport half an hour ago. And good riddance."

"Poor Edith."

"Don't say 'Poor Edith.' I said good riddance, and I meant it. One thing's certain. She goes out of my will entirely. I'm not going to help support her in her little flings. My mind's made up. Everything I have goes to your hospital, Alan."

He is smiling at her with one of his white-rabbit smiles.

"Of course there won't be as much money now. But there's this house, some leases on the old Sans Souci property, and I have a few good paintings, and some good pieces of jewelry. Despite what Diana keeps saying, we are not all going to be paupers as a result of this—though there'll be some tough sledding for a while."

"Have they located your brother Harold yet?"

Edith laughs. "One report has him in South America and another has him in Switzerland. Last night I had a dream that he was here, in St. Thomas, and that he came stalking me through the garden with a gun to get even with me for the things I said. But I'm sure I shall have no such luck as that."

He continues to smile at her.

"Have you been following this thing in the papers, Alan, the way I have? Have you noticed how wonderfully Arthur has been emerging through all of this? To me, that's the best thing that's come out of it. Suddenly everyone can see how much of a man Arthur is."

"Yes."

"Well," she says, "I've just told you I was leaving everything to your hospital, and you haven't even said thank you. Isn't this what you want? What do you think?"

He twirls the brandy in his glass. "I think," he says, "that you are your father's daughter."

"Well!" she says. "That was a reasonably unpleasant crack, wasn't it?" She sips her brandy. "You don't seem to understand, Alan, there were a lot of things I could have told her, but she would never listen to me. I could have told her things that would have helped her—things about the past—"

"The past can be a pretty chilly gift, if nothing else goes with it."

"Nothing *else!* I was going to leave her all my money!"

"Ah," he says, "you *were*, but now you're not. When there was a lot of it, you were going to give her all of it. Now that there's not so much of it, you're not going to give her anything. Poor Edith. You're stymied, aren't you? Without any money, what have you got left to fight with? Yes, there is going to be some tough sledding—some very tough sledding for a while."

"Well," she says after a moment. "I asked for this, didn't I? I asked you what you thought. Now you've told me."

"At least Leona won't be all alone."

"You mean she's luckier than I am. She has someone. I have no one. Well, perhaps you're right." Then she says, "Very well. What shall I do?"

"Do about what?"

"Should I leave everything to Leona—or not?"

With a wink, he says, "I thought you said your mind was made up."

"Money never did a damned thing for me, I'll say that. It never gave me anything but misery. But in her case—"

"Perhaps she should be allowed the chance to try it on her own," he says. "It may not do anything for her either, but it might be worth it to her to have the chance."

"Yes. That's what I meant," she says. "So suppose I keep my will just as it is, leaving everything to her—except the car, which is for Sibbie—and add a codicil—just a little note. Asking her, if she doesn't want the house, or any of the other things, to consider giving them to your hospital, or selling them to you for a nominal figure."

He smiles a particularly male smile, the smile men give you which means that their thoughts have been running several yards ahead of your own. "Whatever you think, my dear," he says.

A breeze stirs the heavy curtains of her big old room, and there is a chill in the air. "February," she says, almost absently. And then, "Well, I'll think about this."

"February—yes, and more tourists coming to get away from winter."

"I'll be alone here for a while," she says. "Now that Leona's gone. Let's see more of each other, Alan. I want to plan a series of little dinner parties, Alan, for people like you and Sibbie Sanderson, the old friends. We'll pass the time. We'll have fun. Let's be kind to one another, Alan, as long as we're all there is."

"Yes, dear."

She comes toward him and his pale eyes are sparkling behind his spectacles. "Drink to that," Edith says.

They touch glasses.

"And—who knows?—someday we may become lovers after all," she says.

"It's a great temptation." He goes to the window. "Look, Edith—there's your daughter," Alan says.

"Daughter . . .?"

Half understanding, forgetting really that Diana has not left yet, and thinking that he must have meant to say granddaughter, Edith steps to the window and looks out, and there is Diana, seated on the stone bench in the garden. The twin poodles, Marcel and Marceau, sit at her feet, their powderpuff tails wagging in the dust, their tongues hanging out happily as Diana scratches them, tenderly and absently, behind the ears, her fingers deep in the tops of their tufted heads.

Looking out at Diana from the window, why is she suddenly reminded of another scene, one that she had all but forgotten? It is Dolly Harper sitting on the stone bench, Dolly Harper over twenty years ago. It was after Edith's mother came home from Paris, returned to St. Thomas, just before the second war. She had bought herself a small house on Signal Hill and sometimes, in the afternoons, she would come to visit Edith. They would sit in the garden and talk of the old days, when St. Thomas was still a Danish colony. They would talk of the gay balls that used to be held in the colonial governor's house and, though Dolly Harper had never been invited to any of them, they would pretend that she had been to every one. They would talk of the champagne, and what the women wore. The series of little strokes had affected Dolly Harper's speech, and she spoke with halting pauses, her lips puckering and working, and her fingers tugging at that laboring mouth as though to pull the words out. "Let's . . . sit with our backs to the sun," she said one day. "I've always . . . hated the sun in my eyes. Sunburns are so . . . unbecoming, and I do believe they cause wrinkles." They sat on the stone bench under the heaven tree.

"I've always loved this . . . time of day best in the islands," she said. Her hands roamed anxiously about, patting her silk skirts, pressing the soft spots of her knees, and then one hand covered Edith's left hand, kneading Edith's knuckles with her strong fingers. "Yes," she said, "this is the best . . . time. Your father used to say it too. We'd sit in the garden of the old house at Sans Souci, and . . . wait for the sun to go behind the wall. Then the stones of the terrace held their heat, and one's . . . feet were warm, though the breeze was . . . cool. Yes. Oh, we must see a great deal of each . . . other, Edith, while I'm here. We'll play cards. Do you . . . remember the card games we used to play? Piquet . . . Rubicon Piquet! I imagine I've forgotten how to play . . . Rubicon Piquet now, but as soon as I . . . play it I suppose it will come back. Oh, so much time has gone by, so many years. Sometimes I wonder what it all meant."

"What it all meant, Mama?"

"Yes. Was it . . . necessary? Oh, I suppose it was. I suppose it had to be the way it . . . turned out. If only there were some way of knowing ahead of time how things will turn out. But of course there never is. It's like a . . . war, isn't it? No one ever knows how a war will turn out . . . all you can do is guess and hope. I thought it was going to be so . . . simple, but it got . . . complicated." She laughed, and her eyes were clear and cool. "You and Charles . . . and I thought he really liked you. I never knew he'd . . . go away like that, never dreamed."

"I've had a good many years to think about it, Mama. And I think he loved me—for a while."

"But then he went . . . away! Who'd have thought it? *I* never did. I never dreamed that would be the . . . result of all my plans. Remember, dear, that it was *I* who got Mrs. Blakewell to ask us to tea at her . . . house. I and nobody else. I did that and you said it could never . . . be done. But I won the wager! I won the dollar!" And she laughed again.

It seemed queer to be sitting there and talking, so dispassionately and almost gaily, about the dead, and the things the dead had done, and the plans that had been spun out for their future.

"I never dreamt he'd . . . act that way," Dolly Harper said.

"Act what way? I don't quite know what you're talking about, Mama."

"Act the way he did, so . . . violently . . . and then running off when he was still not well after I told him about the threat of Bertin."

Edith sat very still. "You told him?" she said.

"Yes. You see, Bertin was a . . . threat, I knew it. It was dangerous to have him in the same town with you, much less coming . . . to call on you again! After all, your affair with Bertin was of . . . long standing. It had begun back in Morristown before you and Charles were even . . . married, and it was continuing here."

"And you told all this to Charles," Edith said.

"Oh, yes. I wanted him to take you . . . away, to New York. I wanted him to keep a closer . . . watch on you, away from the unhealthy influences. Love is like a . . . disease, you know. If you . . . catch the wrong kind it can kill you and ruin everything and everything around you."

"A disease—"

"It was I who suggested to your . . . father that he turn over the money to you, that he set you up . . . independently, so you and Charles could afford to go anywhere you wanted. If you and Charles had . . . money of your own, you wouldn't have to depend on Papa and . . . me. You'd be free and independent and able to go away."

"You told Papa all this too."

"It was my . . . plan! I worked it out so carefully. I didn't know Charles would act so . . . outraged. He'd accepted our money once, when we made the marriage agreement, when we'd struck our original . . . bargain with him. He was not supposed to kick up a fuss! I couldn't believe he wouldn't accept money . . . again, after all we'd done for him, taking care of him and his . . . mother, especially when the second time the money was so much . . . more."

"Oh, Mama. Mama."

"But there . . . must have been a stubborn streak in Charles, a stubborn streak I never knew about or . . . bargained on. Or else—"

"Or else what?"

"Or else he . . . cared about you more than I thought he did."

"Which seems odd to you, doesn't it?" she said.

"Well, a . . . little. After the . . . negotiations there, when you became engaged. After all, Edith, you were never . . . I don't want to sound unkind . . . you were never what one would call a *pretty* girl. It seemed . . . hard to believe—"

"That anyone would ever love me? Yes, I guess it did." Suddenly Edith laughed. "You know, this is fantastic! All these years I've blamed Papa for telling Charles about Louis Bertin. I never thought about blaming you."

"Blame? Why should I be blamed for anything? My . . . job was to try to keep there from being any scandal that would . . . hurt the family. And I wanted you to have a . . . happy life. It was you who'd made the initial mistake. You had that . . . tendency. It was in the blood. It was Harper . . . blood in you. It had to be . . . controlled."

"And so you controlled it! Just tell me one thing, Mama. What was Charles' first reaction when you told him what a naughty woman I was?"

"Oh . . . horrified. Furious with . . . me. Said it wasn't . . . true. He accused me of . . . telling a lie, or being drunk. He didn't know you as I did. And when I told him how in Morristown you had spent day after day with Bertin, how I used to . . . watch you, the two of you. I said to Charles, 'Why she . . . admitted the whole thing to her father . . . everything.' And then I said,

'If you . . . don't believe me, Charles, just ask her . . . ask her who's taken to . . . calling on her again while you're out of the house,' and I said . . ."

"You told him! Just the way you told Papa about Andreas!"

Dolly Harper paused, her lips working. "Andreas?" she repeated. "Who?—Oh, do you . . . mean the boy . . . that boy who was half . . . nigger, or something? Oh . . . that had to be stopped. You . . . know that. I mean he wasn't white. I used to watch you with him from my . . . window. I knew that had to be stopped. The thing with the Frenchman was . . . similar."

"Mama," Edith said, "tell me one more thing. Did you ever know about Papa and Monique?"

Her eyes closed briefly, her mouth trembling. One nervous hand still clutched at Edith's own in relentless little attentions that seemed intended to reassure Edith of her mother's love for her, and the other hand pinched at the fighting mouth. "Oh . . . yes," she said at last. "I . . . knew about that. But you see your father was . . . the kind of man who needed a thing like that because he was . . . a man who had strong . . . appetites. She could give him something I couldn't. But then I knew that I . . . could give him things that she could not. Things . . . like purity and honesty and . . . decency and devotion. And . . . children. I had . . . treasures for him that she could never have, and he knew it because he said that to me . . . once. I was his . . . wife, you see." Her eyes flashed at Edith. "But if you're trying to . . . say that your father did the same sort of things you did, and that if it was a . . . mistake for you then it must have been a mistake for him too, that . . . argument means nothing at all to me. Promiscuity or . . . unfaithfulness in a woman is unthinkable, Edith. Unfaithfulness in a man is . . . thinkable. The standard is not the same. And a man like your father deserved special . . . rules, anyway. You . . . did not know this man. He was a man bigger . . . than life. Magnificent. People called him . . . cruel, and a slave-driver, and . . . lots of things, but they didn't know him! Not as . . . I did! I *knew* him. Magnificent . . . and splendid . . . beyond comparing with any other human being. You never knew your father, Edith. But he was the . . . sun and the moon to me."

Edith sat quietly beside her mother. There was a wind in the branches of the heaven tree, rustling its spiky leaves, and the sun at their backs was warm.

"But what's the . . . use of talking about it?" Dolly Harper said. "Talking . . . doesn't change anything, I suppose. Though . . . remembering is pleasant."

"Yes," Edith said. "Remembering is pleasant, and talking doesn't change a single thing."

"But I've never . . . understood why Charles turned his back on all that money," her mother said. "The . . . Blakewells, were a distinguished family, but they were never that . . . well off." She paused, shaking her head back and forth, puzzling the unfathomable quirks of human nature. "Let's . . . play some Rubicon Piquet," she said. "I've forgotten how to play, but I'm . . . sure I'll remember, once the cards are in my hands."

Edith sighed. "Yes," she said finally. "The rules are fairly simple. I'll get the cards."

And so she had gone into the house for the cards, she remembers now, not angry at her mother, not angry at anybody, but filled with him. She moved, Charles-filled, through every room of her life, not as though he had been taken from her but driven into her, like a long bright nail.

She turns away from her window now and back into the room, and she discovers that Alan Osborn has picked up his bag and quietly departed.

"I am going to have that pool fenced," Edith says, coming down the steps. "It isn't safe. You were quite right. I'll call Mr. Barbus in the morning and have him take care of it."

Diana looks up and smiles at her briefly, and the white poodles look up and wag their tails. Poo is running about in his blue-and-white Breton sailor suit, playing hide-and-seek with himself under the trees.

Edith sits down on one end of the stone bench. "I thought she looked very pretty when they left."

Diana nods, scratching the dogs' ears. "Yes."

"She seemed happy."

"Yes." Diana runs her slim white hands under the dogs' jeweled collars. "My bad boys," she says. "Do you know what I found my two bad boys doing? Digging in your rose beds, Mother."

"I only wish it could have been someone else—anybody else but him. And not on these—terms."

"I don't," Diana says quietly. "He'll do. So will the terms."

"But Diana, don't you see—"

"Most people don't understand loneliness," she says. "It can make people do some curious things."

"I've had plenty of loneliness," Edith says. "Don't forget that."

Diana looks at her mother thoughtfully, then her eyes move away. "You've *experienced* loneliness, Mother. But it's possible to experience it without understanding it. Just as it's possible to experience love, and not understand it. I was just thinking of how, when I was a little girl, in this house, and you were never there, I got to know loneliness very well. We became dear friends." She smiles absently. "We trusted each other, loneliness and I."

Edith hesitates. "What do you mean—when I was never here?"

She looks at Edith again, her eyes wide. "*Were* you? Were you ever *here*, Mother? It always seemed to me that you were so busy hating Grandfather, or missing Daddy—whatever it was, there wasn't much of you left over for me."

"Diana—was that it?"

"And this thing with Perry, for example. When he told me he'd fallen in love with this other girl, I didn't like it much, but I understood. She's younger than I, and prettier. Loneliness. And in Leona's case—well, one solution is to try to go back to where you started."

They sit very still, on opposite ends of the stone bench, Diana's hands hooked in the dogs' collars, and Edith's hands in her lap.

"But I'm tired, Mother," she says. "*Tired*. This fall I'll be fifty years old; think of that. I guess it's time for me to be tired. I'm too tired to go anywhere, not even back to the beginning."

There is something now that Edith wants terribly to say to her, and she knows she must say it. But she is afraid to say it, afraid Diana will give her an answer she doesn't want to hear. Then she says it. "You could stay here with me, Diana—for a while."

Diana stands up, and slides her arm through the dogs' tandem leashes. "Oh, Mother."

The dogs interpret Diana's rising as a sign that a walk, or

some other adventure, is about to begin, and they leap about her, struggling and pulling at her arm.

"What does that mean?" Edith asks. "'Oh, Mother.' Like that."

"It would never work. We'd be at each other's throats in two days. You know how we are."

"I'd try," Edith says. "And it only needs to be . . . for a little while."

"Is there. . . ."

"Is there what?"

"Is there anything I could *do* here, Mother? This garden—"

"Oh, this garden needs so much work done to it!"

"When I was little, I used to talk to the flowers. I gave them all names. I'll bet you didn't know it, Mother, but I have a green thumb."

"We could work on it together!"

But Diana shakes her head. "No, it's impossible, Mother. Poo would drive you crazy, and so would I. It would be mad."

"But you could at least stay a few weeks. Couldn't you? I'd like it. Wouldn't you like it?"

Sitting there, Edith tries to think of some inducement, some lure. Entreaties float to her head, then burst, like bubbles, their words lost. If only I could promise her something, Edith thinks. What can I promise her? If only Charles could miraculously join them, move with his old urgency down the steps and across the terrace to where Diana stands, a few feet away; with his purpose, he could persuade her. But no such accessory is provided. Edith demands wings, with which to fly across the intervening space to her daughter, but these are not offered either, and she sits very still on the stone bench watching Diana, and the dogs who sniff and paw the ground at her feet.

Diana rubs the fingers of her free hand up and down across her thigh and smiles at the dogs. "Still, it would be nice to get out of my stockings and girdle for a few days, and just lie in the sun, and bake. That would be nice," she says to the dogs, "wouldn't it, boys?"

"Then stay. Just for a little while. Please."

"Well, perhaps . . ."

In the changeful pattern of sunlight that falls through the garden trees, Edith leans forward, one hand gripping the corner of the stone bench. This bench, this territory, becomes the only thing of substance which she has to offer. It is the monument to everything she has, and must keep, and must gather around her. Diana must come to her on this ground. "Come sit by me," she says.

But the dogs are straining at their leashes. Even the poodles seem to be urging Diana to be gone.

Edith holds out her hand. "Come . . ."

The Customs House clock strikes the hour, as usual a little off. Distracting them, its stroke seems to pull the world away from them, away from the stone bench, away from the garden, away from the house, away from the hill and over the town to the sky where a plane circles above the island, cutting an invisible path in the air.

Diana looks at her watch, then looks up. "That must be their plane," she says. "Why couldn't you at least have gone to the airport, Mother, to see them off? It would have been nice."

"I could ask you the same question," Edith says. "Why couldn't you? She's your daughter."

"Oh, I know. And all you did was bring her up."

From the sky, the island is shaped like a fish in flight, with Picara Point forming the long dorsal fin, and the cluster of satellite islands seeming to pilot St. Thomas on its escape through the blue water.

"It looks as though it's flying away from us, doesn't it?" Leona says, her face pressed against the glass. "Instead of us flying away from it." And then, "Running away. Am I just running away again?"

"That will depend."

"Will we ever find what we want? Will we?"

The plane departs the sky, abandons the island to the sun which shines impartially on half the earth, even though it seems so personal; to the sun which doesn't care whether two women ever sit on a stone bench in a garden, or whether their hands ever touch, or whether, having touched even once, even tentatively, they will ever touch again.